W9-CYU-030

9 780812 522839

50699>

Edited by

FRED SABERHAGEN

AN ARMORY
OF
SWORDS

... Whichever Sword he held had somehow killed at least one animal without making physical contact.

The bats had not been routed for more than a minute or so when the demon arrived—drawn up out of the rocks, perhaps, by a sense of the proximity of helpless human prey, or simply by the disturbance man and bats were making.

Even sightless as he was, Keyes could tell that a demon was near him, and coming nearer. He knew it by the feeling of sickness, a gut-deep wretchedness, that preceded the monster's physical presence. Again the man experienced overwhelming fear, panic that made him cry out and tremble. Better to be torn to bits by flesh-devouring bats than to wind up in a demon's gut, where flesh was the last component of humanity to be destroyed.

And then he heard the creature's hideous voice, a tone of dry bones breaking, dead leaves rattling, reverberating more in the man's mind than in his ears. It sounds as if it were standing almost within arm's length of Keyes...

"The *Swords* notion is an arresting, supple, and durable one, with plenty of mileage left in the various permutations."
—*Kirkus Reviews*

Tor Books by Fred Saberhagen

THE BERSERKER SERIES
The Berserker Wars
Berserker Base (with Poul Anderson, Ed Bryant, Stephen Donaldson, Larry Niven, Connie Willis, and Roger Zelazny)
Berserker: Blue Death
The Berserker Throne
Berserker's Planet
Berserker Kill

THE DRACULA SERIES
The Dracula Tapes
The Holmes-Dracula Files
An Old Friend of the Family
Thorn
Dominion
A Matter of Taste
A Question of Time
Séance for a Vampire

THE SWORDS SERIES
An Armory of Swords
The First Book of Swords
The Second Book of Swords
The Third Book of Swords
The First Book of Lost Swords: Woundhealer's Story
The Second Book of Lost Swords: Sightblinder's Story
The Third Book of Lost Swords: Stonecutter's Story
The Fourth Book of Lost Swords: Farslayer's Story
The Fifth Book of Lost Swords: Coinspinner's Story
The Sixth Book of Lost Swords: Mindsword's Story
The Seventh Book of Lost Swords: Wayfinder's Story
The Last Book of Swords: Shieldbreaker's Story

OTHER BOOKS
A Century of Progress
Coils (with Roger Zelazny)
Earth Descended
The Frankenstein Papers
The Mask of the Sun
Merlin's Bones
The Veils of Azlaroc
The Water of Thought

AN ARMORY OF SWORDS

Edited by
FRED SABERHAGEN

A TOM DOHERTY ASSOCIATES BOOK
NEW YORK

AN ARMORY OF SWORDS

A Tor Book
Published by Tom Doherty Associates, Inc.
175 Fifth Avenue
New York, NY 10010

Tor Books on the World Wide Web:
http://www.tor.com

Tor® is a registered trademark of Tom Doherty Associates, Inc.

ISBN: 0-812-52283-4
Library of Congress Card Catalog Number: 95-4275

First edition: June 1995
First mass market edition: May 1996

Printed in the United States of America

0 9 8 7 6 5 4 3 2 1

Copyright Acknowledgments

Contents

AN ARMORY
OF
SWORDS

Blind Man's Blade

Fred Saberhagen

The gods' great Game of Swords, and with it the whole later history of planet Earth, might have followed a very different course had the behavior of one or two divine beings—or the conduct of only one man—been different at the start. Even a slight change at the beginning of the Game produced drastic variation in the results. And Apollo has been heard to say that there have been several such beginnings.

One of those divergent commencements—which, in the great book of fate, may be accounted as leading to an alternate universe, or perhaps simply as a false start—saw all of the gods' affairs thrown into turmoil at a remarkably early stage, even before the first move had been made in the Game. It happened on the day when the Swords, all new and virginally fresh, all actually still warm from Vulcan's forge, were being brought to the Council to be put into the hands of those players who had been awarded them by lot.

The sun had just cleared the jagged horizon when Vulcan arrived at the open council-space, there to join the wide circle of deities already assembled in anticipation of his coming.

They were his colleagues, all of them standing much taller than humans, their well-proportioned bodies casting long shadows in the lingering mists, but still dwarfed by the surrounding rim of icy mountains. There were moments when they all looked lost under the breadth of the cold morning sky.

The Smith brought with him a whiff of forge-smoke, a tang of melted meteoric iron. His cloak of many furs was wind-blown around his shoulders, and his huge left hand cradled carefully its priceless cargo of steel and magic, eleven weighty packages held in a neat bundle. And, despite the fact that a small but vocal minority of the Council still argued that no binding agreement on the rules of the Game had yet been reached, the Swords—almost every one of the Twelve Swords—were soon being portioned out among the chosen members of the meeting.

Among those gods and goddesses who received a Sword in the distribution, no two reactions were exactly the same. Most were pleased, but not all. For example, there was the goddess Demeter, who stood looking thoughtfully at the object limping Vulcan had just pressed into her strong, pale hands. She gazed at the black sheath covering a meter's length of god-forged steel, at the black hilt marked by a single symbol of pure white.

Demeter said pensively, in her high, clear voice: "I am not at all sure that I care to play this Game."

Mars, who happened to be standing near her, commented: "Well, many of us *do* want to play, including some who have been awarded no Sword at all. Hand yours over to someone else if you don't want it." Mars had already been promised a Sword of his own, or his protest would doubtless have been more violent. Actually he thought he could do quite well in the Game without benefit of any such trick hardware; but he would not have submitted quietly to being left off the list.

"I said I was not sure," Demeter responded. A male deity would probably have tossed the sheathed weapon thoughtfully in his hand while trying to decide. Demeter only looked at it. And she was still holding her Sword, down at her side, the dark sheath all but invisible in one of her large hands, when her tall figure turned and strode away into a cloud of mist.

Another of her colleagues called after her to know where she was going; and as an afterthought added the question: "Which Sword do you have?"

"I have other business," Demeter called back, avoiding a direct answer to either question. And then she went on. For all that anyone could tell, she was only seeking other amusement, displaying independence as gods and goddesses were wont to do.

Meanwhile the distribution of Swords was still going on, a slow process frequently interrupted by arguments. Some of the recipients were trying to keep the names and powers of their Swords secret, while others did not seem to care who knew about them.

The council meeting dragged along, its proceedings every bit as disorderly as those of such affairs were wont to be, and not made any easier to follow by the setting—a high mountain wasteland of snow and ice and rock and howling wind, an environment to which the self-convinced rulers of the earth were proud to display their indifference.

Hera was complaining that the original plan of allowing only gods to possess Swords, which she believed to be the only good and proper and reasonable scheme, had been spoiled before it could be put into effect: "That scoundrel Vulcan, that damned clubfoot, enlisted a human smith to help him make the Swords. And then chose to reward the man!"

Zeus stroked his beard. "Well? And if it amuses Vulcan to hand out a gift or two to mortals? Surely that's not unheard of?"

"I mean he rewarded the human with the gift of Town-saver! That's unheard of! So now we have only eleven Swords to share among us, instead of twelve. Am I wrong, or is it we gods, and not humanity, who are supposed to be playing the Swordgame?"

The speaker had meant the question to be rhetorical; but not even on this point could any general agreement be established. Many at the meeting expected their human worshipers to play a large part in the Game—though of course not in direct competition with gods.

Debate on various questions concerning the distribution of Swords, and the conduct and rules of the Game, moved along by fits and starts, until Vulcan himself came forward, leaning sideways on his shorter leg, to demand the floor. As soon as the Smith thought he had the attention of a majority, he haughtily informed his accusers that he had decided to give away the Blade called Townsaver, because the gods themselves had no towns or cities, no settled or occupied places in the human sense, and thus none of them would be able to derive any direct benefit from that particular weapon.

"Would you have chosen that one for yourself?" he demanded, looking from one deity to another nearby. "Hah, I thought not!"

As the council meeting wrangled on, perpetually on the brink of dissolving in disputes about procedure, at least one other member of the divine company—Zeus himself—complained that the great Game was already threatened by human interference. How many of his colleagues, he wanted to know, how many of them realized that there was one man who by means of certain impertinent magic had already gained extensive theoretical knowledge of the Twelve Swords?

Diana demanded: "How could a mere human manage that? I insist that the chairman answer me! How could a man do that, without the help of one or more of us?"

Chairman Zeus, always ready for another speech, began pontificating. Few listened to him. Meanwhile, Vulcan sulked: "Who pays any attention to human magic tricks? Who cares what they find out? No one said anything to me about maintaining secrecy."

In another of the rude, arguing knots of deities, the discussion went like this: "If putting Swords in the hands of humans hasn't been declared officially against the rules, it ought to be! It's bound to have a bad result."

"Still, it might be fun to see what the vile little beasts would do with such weapons."

Mars drew himself up proudly. "Why not? I hope no one's suggesting that *they* could do *us* serious damage with any weapon at all?"

"Well . . ."

Someone else butted in, raising a concern over the chance of demons getting their hands on Swords. But few in the assembly were particularly worried about that, any more than they were about humans.

A dark-faced, turbaned god raised his voice. "Cease your quarreling! No doubt we'll have the chance to learn the answers to these interesting questions. If we are to use Vulcan's new toys in a Game, of course they'll be scattered promiscuously about the world. Sooner or later at least one of them is bound to fall into human hands. And, mark my words, some demon will have another."

* * *

Meanwhile, in a small cave at the foot of a low cliff of dark rock about two hundred meters distant from the nearest argument, a mere man named Keyes, and another called Lo-Yang, both weather-vulnerable human beings, shivering with cold and excitement though wrapped in many furs, were sitting almost motionless, watching and listening intently as they peered from behind a rock. Keyes, the leader of the pair, had chosen this place as one from which he and his apprentice could best observe the goings-on among the gods and goddesses, while still enjoying a reasonable hope that they would not be seen in turn.

A dark and wiry man, Keyes, of indeterminate age. His companion was dark as well, but heavier, and obviously young. They had come to this place in the high, uninhabited mountains searching for treasure, wealth in the form of knowledge—Keyes, an accomplished magician, was willing to risk everything in the pursuit.

Lo-Yang was at least as numb with fear as with cold, and at the moment willing to risk everything for a good chance to run away. He might even have defied his human master and done so, at any time during the past half hour, except that he feared to draw the attention of the mighty gods by sudden movement.

Keyes was in most matters no braver than his associate and apprentice, but certainly he was more obsessed with the search for knowledge and power. He cursed the fact that though some of the gods' stentorian voices carried clearly to where he crouched trying to eavesdrop, he could understand nothing that he heard. Despite his best efforts at magical interpretation, the language the gods most commonly used among themselves was still beyond him.

Keyes, exchanging whispers now and then with his companion, whose teeth were chattering, considered an attempt to work his way even nearer the place of council. But he rejected the idea; it would hardly be possible to do better than this well-placed but shallow little cave, inconspicuous among a number of similar holes in the nearby rock.

He was in the middle of a whispered conversational exchange with his apprentice Lo-Yang, when without warning a great roaring fury swirled around him, and Keyes realized that he had been caught—that the enormous fingers of some god's hand had closed around him. Hopelessly the man tried to summon some defensive magic. Physically he struggled to get free.

He might as well have endeavored to uproot a mountain or two and hurl them at the moon.

Mars, who had captured Keyes, was not really concerned with the obvious fact that the man had been spying. Who cared what human beings might overhear, or think? The god was focused on another problem: he was due to receive a Sword, though Vulcan had not yet put it in his hands. Mars wanted a human for experimental purposes, so that he could learn a thing or two, in practical terms, about the powers of whatever Sword he was given before he used it in the Game. Mars considered himself fortunate to have been able to grab up a human so promptly; the creatures were not common in these parts. Keyes had happened to be the nearer of the two specimens Mars saw when it occurred to him to look for one.

The captured man, knowing nothing of his captor's purpose, certain that his last moment had come, could feel the cold mist on his face, and thought he could hear the echo of his own frightened breath.

The god-hand which had scooped Keyes up did not immediately crush him into pulp, or dash him on the rocks. The sweeping breeze of god-breath, redolent of ice and spice and smoke, told Keyes that an enormous face loomed over him.

But his captor was not even looking at him. Only when the man saw that did he fully realize how far he was, for all his impertinence, beneath the gods' real anger. Nothing he might do would be of any real consequence to them—or so most of them thought. Some mice were doubtless nearby too, scampering among the rocks, but none of the debaters paid any heed to them at all.

The god who had captured Keyes considered how best to keep him fresh and ready. Physically crippling the subject might affect the results of the experiment; and anyway some measure less drastic should suffice to do the job. A simple deprivation of eyesight, along with a smothering of the man's ability to do magic, ought to make him stay where he was put . . . so one god-finger wiped Keyes's face . . .

Now. Where best to put him, for safe-keeping, until Mars should come into possession of the Sword he wished to test?

The captor, still holding casually in one hand the wriggling, moaning, newly blinded human form, looked about. Presently the terrible gaze of Mars fastened on the handiest hiding place immediately available. A moment later, treading windy space in the easy, heedless way of deities, he was descending into a house-sized limestone cave, by means of the wide, nearly vertical shaft which seemed to form the cavern's only entrance and exit.

At the bottom he set his helpless captive down, not ungently, on the stone floor. Keyes was still mewing like a hurt kitten.

"Here you will stay," Mars boomed in Keyes's human language. "Until I get back. That won't be long—there's something I want to try out on you. As you can see . . . well, as you

probably noticed when you could see . . . the only way out of
this cave is a vertical climb up a steep shaft with slick sides
and only a few scattered handholds."

The god started to ascend that way himself, but disdaining
handholds, simply walking in air. Halfway up he paused in
midair, looking back down over his shoulder, to warn the
once-ambitious wizard about the deep pits in the floor. "Better not fall into one of them. I don't want to find you dead
and useless when I return." The tone seemed to imply that
Keyes would be punished if he was impertinent enough to kill
himself. And then the god was gone.

The newly blinded man was seized by an instinctive need to
try to hide, some vague idea of groping his way voluntarily
even farther down into the earth. Maybe the god who'd
caught him would forget about him—maybe he wouldn't
even notice if Keyes disappeared—

But soon enough the man in the cave ceased his gasping
and whimpering, his pointless attempt to burrow into the
stone floor, and regained enough self-possession to reassure
himself that although his vision was effectively gone, at least
his eyeballs had not been ripped out. As far as he could tell
his lids were simply closed, and he could not open them.
There was no pain as long as he did not try. Attempts to force
his eyes open with his fingers hurt horribly, but produced not
even a pinhole's worth of vision.

Physically his body seemed to be undamaged. But he felt
that even more important components of his being, directly
accessible to the divine intervention, had been violated . . .

Presently, his mind having begun to work again at least in-
termittently, he went on groping his way around the cave, in
search of some way out, or at least of better knowledge of his
prison. He had barely glimpsed even the entrance to the cave

before his sight was taken from him. It was warmer down here out of the wind, so much so that he shed some of his furs. In some locations, as he moved about, he was able to feel the warmth of the sun, which was now beginning to be high enough to penetrate the cave. There was tantalizing hope in the red glow of the direct sun through his sealed eyelids.

In a conscious effort to force himself to think logically, Keyes took an inventory of his assets. He had the clothes he was wearing, a small dagger sheathed at his side, and a small pack on his back, which his captor had allowed him to retain. The pack contained a little food, and very little else.

Lo-Yang, Keyes's assistant on his dangerous quest for knowledge, had been ignored by the deity who had grabbed Keyes up. And moments later the stout apprentice, unpursued, had scrambled successfully away, running for his life in the direction of the distant camp where he and Keyes had left their riding-beasts.

After sprinting only a short distance, Lo-Yang, out of shape and also unable to endure the suspense, had felt compelled to look back. Then he had paused, panting. The god who had caught Keyes was in the act of disappearing underground, his prisoner in hand. All the other gods were considerably more distant, and none of them were paying the least attention to Lo-Yang.

Fatalistically, the apprentice dared to crouch behind a rock and wait, catching his breath. Paradoxically his fear had become more manageable, now that the worst, or almost the worst, had come to pass.

Presently the great god who had taken Keyes—Lo-Yang was able to identify Mars, by the helmet the god was wearing, and by his general aspect—Mars came up out of the ground again, but without his prisoner, and went striding away to rejoin his colleagues.

Time passed, and the sun rose higher. The frightened apprentice remained behind his rock. Eventually, gradually, the council of the gods broke up, though not entirely. The remnants, still wrangling, moved even farther off.

When it seemed to Lo-Yang that all the gods were safely out of the way, he crept out from behind his rock, and dared to come back to the upper rim of the cave, looking for Keyes. With a surge of relief he saw that his master was at least still alive.

But Keyes took no notice when his apprentice waved. Lo-Yang called down to him cautiously.

At the sound the man below raised his head, turning it to and fro, in a feverish motion that spoke of near-despair and sudden hope. "Lo-Yang? I'm blind, I . . ."

"Oh."

"Lo-Yang, is that you? Where are the gods?"

"Yes sir, I am here." The apprentice raised his head, squinting into the sunlight, then looked down again. "They're all moving away, at the moment. Slowly. Still bickering among themselves. No one's paying any attention to us. Master, if Mars has blinded you, what are we going to do?"

"Your voice seems to come from a long way above me."

"I'd say twelve meters, master, or maybe a little more. I saw him carry you down there, and I thought . . ."

"Lo-Yang, get me out of here, somehow."

The young man surveyed the entrance to the cave below, and shook his head. It pained him to see his proud master reduced to such a state of helplessness, to hear an unfamiliar quaver in the voice usually so proud. "We need a long rope, master. Looking at these rock walls, I wouldn't dare to try to climb down without one. I'd only fall in there with you, and . . ."

"Yes. Of course. And you have no magic that will get me out."

"Unhappily, master, you have as yet taught me nothing that would be useful in this situation."

"Yes. Quite true. And I also find that my own magic has been taken from me, along with my sight." Keyes paused. When he spoke again, his voice had lost its urgency, had become slow and resigned. His shoulders slumped. "Hurry back to our camp, then, and get the rope. We have a coil in the large pack."

"Yes, master." A pause. "It might take me a couple of hours, or even longer, to get there and back. Even if I bring our riding-beasts back with me. Should I bring them back here, master?"

"Yes. No! I don't know, I leave the details to you. Go!"

"Yes, master." And Keyes could hear the first few footsteps, hurrying away. Then silence.

He was alone.

Fiercely Keyes commanded himself to be active, more to keep himself from dwelling on his fate than out of any real hope. Slowly the approximate dimensions and contours of the flatter portions of the cave's floor revealed themselves to the blind man's probing. With his hands he explored as much of the walls as he could reach. Seemingly the god had not lied. The cave consisted of a deep shaft, down which Keyes had been carried, and an adjoining room or alcove whose bottom remained in shade. The whole space accessible to the prisoner's cautious crawling was no larger than the floor of a small house, and it was basically one big room. Here and there around the perimeter were certain crevices which might, for all Keyes could tell, lead to other exits. But the crevices were too narrow for him to force his body into them. He was going to have to wait until Lo-Yang got back, with the rope.

If Lo-Yang came back in time.

If the assistant ever came back at all. If he had any intention of doing so. Mentally the newly helpless magician reviewed the times in the past when he had treated his apprentice unjustly. He had hardly ever beaten him. Surely, on the whole, he had been a fair master, and even kind. . . .

Mindful of the divine warning about pits, Keyes continued his exploration for the most part on all fours, and, when he did stand up, walked very carefully. By this means he located several perilous gaps in the floor, holes into which tossed pebbles dropped for a long count before clicking on bottom. Presently in his groping about the cave he came upon some bones. After he had found a skull or two, he became convinced that the bulk of the bones were human, evidence that other human victims had died in this cave before him. Sacrifices, perhaps? Or simply unlucky hunters, blinded by night or by driving snow, who had fallen in by accident.

Lo-Yang had said that the god was Mars—and Mars had said that he was coming back, and soon. Mars had spoken of using Keyes in some kind of an experiment. . . . Once more quivering with horror and fear, the trapped man persevered in his compulsive search for something, anything, that might offer him some chance of escape.

And so it was that at last, behind some loose rocks in the corner farthest from the entrance, the blind man's trembling, groping fingers fell upon something that was round, and smooth, and narrow, and was not rock. When he pulled on the object, it came toward him.

When he stood up again, he was holding in both hands the padded, meter-long weight of a sheathed Sword.

Even with his sense of magic almost numbed by Mars, Keyes could tell this was no ordinary weapon. He had no real doubt of what he had discovered, though he had never seen or touched one of Vulcan's Swords before, and had not expected to ever have the chance to touch one—at least not for a long, long time.

Thanks to his magical investigations at a distance, the difficult, painstaking studies he'd carried out even before the forging of the Blades had been completed, he knew the Twelve Swords well in theory—understood them better, no doubt, than all but a few of the gods yet did. But how one of the Twelve Blades had come to be tucked away in the remotest corner of an obscure cave was more than the human magician could understand. Certainly it had not been placed there for him to find; only his fanatical thoroughness in searching, his determination to keep busy, had led him to the discovery.

Slowly one possible explanation took shape in the man's mind: One of the divine gang might have stolen another's Sword, as a prank or as a ploy in their great mysterious Game, and had found a handy, nearby hiding place at the very bottom of this cave.

Impulse urged Keyes to draw the unknown Sword at once, to end, if possible, the suspense of waiting in ignorance, and to endow himself immediately with whatever powers his find might confer upon him—but there was one ominous contingency which made him hesitate. Fate, or some cruel trickster of a god, might have given him Soulcutter.

He was aware that in recent months his ambition had, perhaps more than once, irritated certain of the gods. Until now, by good fortune, none of them had become more than half-aware of him, as humans might be vaguely cognizant of some troublesome insect in the air nearby—but his magic, practiced as subtly as possible on Vulcan's human assistant, had been clever and strong enough to bring him extensive theoretical knowledge of the Twelve Swords and their unique powers.

It was utterly frustrating that he had no way to determine which Sword lay in his hands. He knew that all but one of the Twelve Blades were marked with distinguishing white symbols on their black hilts—a target shape for Farslayer, a human eye for Sightblinder, and so on. But sightless Keyes had no way to perceive the sign, if any, on the Sword he held. Holding his breath, he tried with all his will and care to find and read the symbol with his fingertips—but for all he was able to discern by touch, there was no sign there to read.

Ah, if only Lo-Yang with his two good eyes had stayed with him a little longer!

Suppose it was only the black hilt, unrelieved—that would mean that he was holding Soulcutter. Keyes shuddered. But he could not be sure. The odds seemed to be against it. For all he knew, there might very well be a symbol right under his hand, dead flush with the rest of the hilt, undistinguishable by touch.

Everything depended upon his finding out. An enemy more powerful than any demon had stuffed him into this hole, and was coming back, perhaps at any moment now, to use him in an experiment. It was vitally important to identify the Sword, before he made any plan to use it.

Which one did he have?

Well, there was one sure way by which Soulcutter, at least, could be ruled out. Hesitantly Keyes began to draw the weapon, starting it first one centimeter out of its sheath, then two. Meanwhile he held his breath, hoping that if the hilt in his hand was indeed Soulcutter's, he could retain enough sense of purpose to muzzle that deadliest of all Blades again before its growing power overwhelmed him with hopelessness, before all possible actions, and even life itself, were robbed of meaning.

If this experiment should demonstrate that he was holding the Sword of Despair, Keyes decided that he was desperate enough to use it, by threatening to draw it against the returning god.

His cautious tugging was exposing more and more of the Blade, but still no black cloud of despair rose up to engulf Keyes. He felt no more miserable with the Sword half-drawn. With a sigh of relief he concluded that his prize had to be one of the other eleven.

He pulled hard on the unseen hilt, and with a faint, singing sigh, the long steel came completely free.

Keyes soon disposed of any lingering doubt in his own mind that the weapon he held was genuinely one of the Twelve Swords. Proof lay in the facts of its unbreakableness, and that the extreme keenness of the edges—he tested them on the tough leather of his dagger's sheath—could not be dulled by repeated bashing on rock.

Several of the Swords, his earlier investigations had informed him, ought to produce distinguishing noises when they went into action. But the only sound so far generated by this one was the bright clang, purely mechanical, of thin steel on tough rock.

The blind man uttered a prayer to Ardneh that the hilt he was gripping belonged to Woundhealer, and that that Sword's power would let him see again. Feverish with hope, maneuvering the long Blade awkwardly, he nicked first his eyebrow, finally the bridge of his nose and very eyelids, with the keen edge. All he achieved were stinging pains and a blood-smeared face. His fevered hope that he might be holding the Sword of Healing, that its steel would pass painlessly, bloodlessly, into his flesh on its mission of restoration—that hope was lost in a few drops of blood.

Hope was lost briefly but not killed. Actually his situation would be better if this was one of the other Swords, carrying some power that could free him completely from his enemy.

Under the stress of his predicament, the attributes and powers, even the names of all the Swords seemed to have fled his memory. Might this be Wayfinder, then, or Coinspinner?

Keyes whispered a short string of urgent requests to the magic Blade he held. He asked it to show him how he might get out of the cave, and where he might find help. When nothing happened, he repeated his demands more loudly, but as far as he could tell, he was granted no response of any kind. In this situation, either Coinspinner or Wayfinder ought to be pulling his gripping hands around, bending his wrists in a particular direction, showing him the way he ought to move. And Coinspinner, whether it indicated any particular direction or not, would bring him great good luck, in fact whatever extreme of luck he needed. If necessary the Sword of Chance could call up an earthquake on behalf of its client, to shatter the rocky cage around him and let him walk or climb away unharmed.

But nothing of the sort was happening. Two more possibilities, it seemed, eliminated.

When it occurred to Keyes to make the effort, testing for Stonecutter was simple enough. One thing he had in ample supply down here was rock. And Stonecutter in fact could be just what a man in his situation needed, the very tool with which to carve his way out, creating a tunnel or a stair, slicing hard stone as easily as packed snow.

But the cave's walls did not yield effortlessly to this Sword

when he swung it against them, then tried it as a saw. Now he
realized that his first attempts to test the durability of the
blade ought to have been enough to convince him of this fact.
Hard, noisy hacking produced only dust in the air, small
chips and fragments which stung the man's blind face. A
steady pressure, indestructible edge against limestone, did no
better.

Well, then, quite possibly he was holding Farslayer. But
Keyes could think of no way to distinguish that Sword from
its fellows, short of naming a victim and throwing it with intent to kill. The stony walls that closed him in would pose no
obstacle to the Sword of Vengeance, which would pass
through granite as through so much air, if that were necessary to reach its prey. Farslayer would kill at any distance—
but would not come back peacefully to its user. To employ
that weapon at a distance was to lose it, and even should
Keyes succeed in slaying the god who had trapped him here,
he would still be trapped.

His musings were interrupted by the onslaught of a swarm of
large, furry, carnivorous bats. No doubt disturbed by the
racket he'd been making, the creatures came fluttering out of
some of the high, dim recesses of the deep cave. Indifferent to
sunlight, they erupted from their holes by tens or dozens to
threaten Keyes, who at the sound of their approach got his
back against a wall and raised his Sword.

He could hear the bats piping, crying out blurred words in
their thin little voices, uttering incoherent threats and slaver-
ings of blood-hunger. They were flapping their wings violently—they got close enough to let him feel the breeze of
their wings, and he cringed from the expected pain of their
needle-like teeth and claws—but that did not follow. In blind
desperation he waved the naked Sword at his attackers, and

he remained untouched. Once the blade clanged accidentally on rock, but he had no sensation of it striking anything fleshy in midair. Still, one after another, the little bat-cries became shrieks of anguish, and then died away.

Panting, gripping the hilt of his still-unknown weapon with both hands, Keyes stood waiting, straining his ears in silence. Not a bat had touched him yet, nor had he touched them, but when he cautiously changed his position by a step or two, his foot came down on a dead one. Gingerly he felt the furry little thing with his free hand, making sure of what it was, then kicked it away from him.

Not Farslayer, then. Whichever Sword he held had somehow killed at least one animal without making physical contact.

The bats had not been routed for more than a minute or so when the demon arrived—drawn up out of the rocks, perhaps, by a sense of the proximity of helpless human prey, or simply by the disturbance man and bats were making.

Even sightless as he was, Keyes could tell that a demon was near him, and coming nearer. He knew it by the feeling of sickness, a gut-deep wretchedness, that preceded the monster's physical presence. Again the man experienced overwhelming fear, panic that made him cry out and tremble. Better to be torn to bits by flesh-devouring bats than to wind up in a demon's gut, where flesh was the last component of humanity to be destroyed.

And then he heard the creature's hideous voice, a tone of dry bones breaking, dead leaves rattling, reverberating more in the man's mind than in his ears. It sounded as if it were standing almost within arm's length of Keyes.

With stately formality the demon announced its name. "I am Korku. Will you introduce yourself?"

"My name is Keyes."

"Unhappy man named Keyes! Here you are down in this deep hole with no way to get out. And newly blind! Is it possible that you have angered a god? If so, that was unwise."

"He's coming back, the god who put me here. He'll be angry if anything happens to me."

"Oh, will he? But he is not here now."

Keyes was silent. His lungs kept wanting to pant for air, for extra breath with which to scream, and he struggled to control the urge.

The demon said: "It is too bad that you are unable to appreciate my beauty visually. If only you could see me, I am confident that you would be—overwhelmed. Most humans are."

"Go away."

"Not likely." The dry bones crackled, the sound formed itself into words. "Not until you have handed over to me that ridiculous splinter of metal you now clutch so tightly. Then I will leave you in peace to wait for your dear god."

"Go away!" Keyes tightened his grip upon the unknown hilt.

In response came a voiceless snarl that made his hair stand up, and then the voice again: "Hand it over, I say! Or I will cut you into a thousand pieces with your own weapon, and swallow you a piece at a time—and put you back together in my gut, where you will dwell for a million years in torment."

"Not likely!" Keyes replied in turn. He thought it quite possible that this demon had as yet learned nothing about the Twelve Swords and their god-given powers. Or maybe the damned thing had learned just enough, or guessed enough, to make it determined to have this Sword for itself. But demons were notoriously cowardly; and so far it was being cautious.

This was not the man's first contact with a demon—no magician adept enough to acquire deep skill was able to avoid all encounters with that evil race. But only magicians who had turned their faces against humanity entered willingly into commerce with such monsters, and Keyes still found pride in being human. In his present desperate situation, he might well have tried to bargain with a demon to lend him its perception, as other more powerful and unscrupulous wizards had been known to do—but he had nothing with which to bargain.

Except his unknown Sword; and that was all he had. He continued to brandish the mysterious weapon at his latest enemy, instead of handing it over as Korku had commanded.

The demon tried a few more arguments. It shouted at Keyes more loudly. But presently, when it saw that it was getting nowhere with mere words, it lost patience and reached out for the man with its half-material talons.

Keyes saw nothing of his enemy's extended limbs. Nothing at all happened to the blind man waiting. But he heard Korku's screaming threats break off abruptly in a muffled, bubbling sound. Then came a soft thump, as of a heavy mass of wet pulp falling some distance upon rock, followed by a slithering, which gradually receded.

Then silence.

Straining to hear more, unable to interpret what he had heard, the man uttered a small moan, compounded mostly of relief with a strong component of tormented puzzlement. Again his Sword, whichever Sword he held, had saved him somehow!

Yes, the demon must have been defeated. But perhaps not slain, not annihilated. Keyes probed about on the cave floor with the point of his Sword, and his imagination shuddered at the image of himself stepping blindly into a demon's body.

For several minutes he discovered nothing more helpful than a few more dead or dying bats. But eventually, when the blind man bent, listening intently over the brink of a certain deep but narrow pit, he heard Korku again. A tiny, screaming, threatening voice, muffled almost below the threshold of hearing, rose from the distant bottom of the pit.

After listening for a little while, the man dared to call down: "Korku? What has happened to you?"

The faint sounds coming back included nothing he could interpret as an answer—and, in any case, a human would be foolish to trust anything a demon said.

Logical thinking was still required—was more essential now than ever, since time was passing, and Mars would be coming back to subject his prisoner to some unknown horror. But logic was still difficult to sustain. By eliminating possibilities Keyes had made a beginning in the task of identifying his weapon. But the task was not accomplished. Which possibilities had he not yet considered?

There was Dragonslicer. There was Townsaver. There was Doomgiver, of course. Ah, in that last name might lie some real hope of survival! If only Keyes could be certain that he had the Sword of Justice in his hands, then he would dare to brazenly defy the gods. Even gods would risk bringing disaster on their own heads if they tried to harm him further. For example, if they poured in fire or water on him, he might make his way out to find them all burned or drowned.

Unless . . .

Unless, of course, one of the gods confronting him happened to be armed with Shieldbreaker. If Keyes's extensive research was correct, and so far he had no reason to doubt its accuracy, no other weapon in the world, not even another Sword, could ever stand against the Sword of Force.

The thought of Shieldbreaker gave him pause. Suppose that he, Keyes, was now holding that one? Shieldbreaker's invincible presence in his hand would have easily disposed of the demon, and the bats. But wait—here in the presence of enemies and danger, the Sword of Force ought to be audibly beating its drum-note of power.

Of course the drawback to relying upon Shieldbreaker was that any unarmed god, unarmed man, or unarmed child for that matter, could easily take that Sword away from whoever held it, regardless of the holder's normal strength.

Keyes, probing gently with one finger at the slight self-inflicted cuts around his face, decided that the bleeding had already stopped. He tried desperately to recall whether wounds made by one Sword or another ought to heal quickly or slowly. But that information, if he had ever possessed it, escaped his memory.

Touch, smell, taste, none of them of any use in his predicament—but hearing! In that sense might lie his way to the answer!

Thinking, keeping track by counting on his fingers, Keyes decided that seven of the Swords, if all he had found out about them was correct, generated some kind of sound when they went into action. The other five exerted their individual powers in silence.

The man's thoughts were interrupted by a pair of deep booming voices up above, outside the cave. The conversation of the gods was still somewhat muffled with distance, but coming closer at a pace no walking mortals could have matched. They were speaking to each other in the god-language that Keyes did not understand.

Mars, the god who had put Keyes in the cave, was coming back, holding like a toothpick between two fingers the sheathed metal of the weapon he had just been given by Vulcan, and now wanted to test. Hermes, a fellow-player in the Game, came with him, and the two deities discussed the matter as they walked.

The Wargod's plan was to drop Soulcutter into the cave for Keyes to find, and let the man draw it, just to see what effect the Tyrant's Blade really had on humans. Vulcan had promised the Council that Soulcutter—and indeed all the Swords—would have tremendous, overwhelming impact upon all lesser beings.

Mars commented: "I expect our respective worshipers will be using the Swords a great deal on each other, you know, when the Game really gets going."

"What if he doesn't draw it?" his companion asked.

"My man down in the hole? I think he will. Oh, not intending to use it on us!" Mars laughed. "I doubt he'll be that arrogant. But there are some vermin down there, bats and such, that are probably bothering him already. He'll want the best tool he can get to fight them off."

Hermes shook his head. "Those flesh-eating bats? They may have finished him by now."

Mars frowned. "You think so? He was carrying a little dagger of his own."

"But getting back to this Sword, Soulcutter—what about the effect on us? We'll be nearby, won't we, when your subject draws the weapon?"

"Bah, nothing we can't overcome, I'm sure. And I understand that Soulcutter's effect on humans, whatever it may be precisely, spreads comparatively slowly."

Keyes continued to listen intently when the two voices stopped, not far above him. He was startled, and immediately suspicious, when a moment later he heard some object, obviously dropped by one of the beings above, come providentially bouncing and sliding down into the cave, landing with a thump practically at his feet.

Without loosening his grip on the hilt already in his possession, he groped his way forward to where he could put his free hand on the fallen object, and identify it as another sheathed Sword.

Only now, it seemed, did the pair of gods above really take notice of the man who was trapped below, and of the sprinkling of dead and mortally wounded bats around him. Only now did they observe that their subject was already holding a drawn Sword.

Mars's companion pointed down, in outrage. "Look at that! Where in the world did he get *that*?"

And Mars himself, gone red-faced, bellowed: "You down there! Drop that Sword at once! It doesn't belong to you, you have no business using it!"

Keyes needed all his resolution to keep from yielding to that shouted command. But instead of dropping his Sword, he raised its point in the general direction of his enemies, as if saluting them, and turned his blind face up to them at the same time—let them do their damnedest. He had naught to lose.

He called out, in a voice that quavered only once: "You have just given me another Sword—why?"

"Impudent monkey!" the Wargod shouted back. "Draw it, and find out!"

They have given me Soulcutter now—it is the only Blade one would give to an enemy.

But trapped as he was, his life already forfeit, Keyes saw no other course than to accept the gamble. Silently he bent again, swiftly he pulled the second Sword out of its sheath. Doubly armed, he straightened to confront his tormentors.

The sun was shining fully on the man's face, and in an

amazing moment he was once again able to see the sun. Whatever magic spell had blinded him was abruptly broken, and his lids came open easily. His eyes were streaming now with pent-up tears, but through the tears he could see the two gods on the high rim of the cave.

He could see the two tall, powerful figures quite clearly enough to tell that they were gods—and also that they were stricken, paralyzed with Soulcutter's poisonous despair, turned back on them by Doomgiver. The strands of their own magic had come undone. Keyes could recognize Mars, who'd captured him, and now Mars abruptly sat down on the rim of the pit, for all the world like a human who suddenly felt faint. The Wargod slumped in that position, legs dangling, for a long moment staring at nothing. Then he buried his face in his hands.

The other god—Keyes, seeing the winged sandals, now knew Hermes—took no notice of this odd behavior, but slowly turned his back on the cave and his companion, and went stumbling off across a rocky hillside. Now and then Hermes put out one hand to grope before him, like a blind man in the sun. In a moment his mighty figure had vanished from Keyes's field of view.

Doomgiver had prevailed! The Sword of Justice had turned Soulcutter's dark power back upon the one who would have used it against Keyes, while immunizing the mere man who had been the intended target. Both gods on the rim of the pit had been caught in the dark force, as must everyone else in range of its slow spread.

Keyes almost cried out in triumph, but the hard truth restrained him. He was still a prisoner. His own eyes, searching the smooth cave walls, now confirmed that neither Lo-Yang nor Mars had lied about the hopelessness of his trying to climb out.

He was beginning to feel dizzy, and ill-at-ease, a normal reaction in one holding any two naked Swords simultaneously. Now he could easily see the symbol, a hollow white circle, on Doomgiver's hilt. To keep himself from collapsing he had no choice but to put away the other Blade, the unmarked one. He slid the Sword of Despair back into its sheath, and his rising dizziness immediately abated.

In this case, at least, Doomgiver's power had been dominant over that of another Sword. There was at least a chance that some of the other Swords might also prove inferior to Doomgiver. That anyone hurling Farslayer would be himself skewered by the Sword of Vengeance. That Sightblinder's user would see a terrifying apparition, but would himself remain vulnerably visible. That the wielder of the Mindsword would be condemned to worship his would-be victim. And Coinspinner's master would suffer excruciatingly bad luck.

But of Shieldbreaker's overall dominance there could be no doubt. And the unanswered question still gnawed at Keyes: Which god had Shieldbreaker? Or might that Sword have somehow come into the hands of another human?

After Soulcutter was muzzled again, a minute or two passed before Mars, who was still sitting on the rim of the cave, took his hands down from his face. The Wargod's expression was blank, and he appeared to be sweating heavily. His great body swayed, and Keyes thought for a moment that the god was going to topple into the pit. But instead Mars, taking no notice of the man below, shifted his weight and turned. Quietly, on all fours, he crawled away from the cave's mouth and out of sight.

Keyes knew that Soulcutter's effects ought to linger for several days, at least, in humans. Probably the stunned gods would recover somewhat more quickly, but how soon they might come back to deal with him, Keyes did not know. When they did, he would have to risk drawing the Sword of Despair again—even though Doomgiver might not protect him next time. This time Soulcutter, though in his own hands, had really been a weapon directed against him by another.

What now?

Pacing nervously about in the confined space, trying desperately to imagine what he might do next, Keyes paused to look down into the hole from whence the demon's muffled groans still rose. Far below, almost lost in shadow, something moved. Something as big as a milk-beast, but truly hideous to look at, like a mass of diseased entrails. In a moment Keyes realized that Korku on attacking him had suffered Doomgiver's justice—the demon had promptly found himself folded painfully into his own gut, in effect turned inside out. When that had happened, the self-bound and helpless thing, still almost immortal, had gone rolling away to plunge into the deeper pit.

Now the creature in the pit, perhaps sensing that the man was near, was turning its muffled, barely audible threats to equally faint pleas and extravagant bargainings for help. Keyes made no answer. Probably he could not have done anything, if he had wanted to, to relieve the demon's doom.

Some minutes later, Mars, who was still in the process of gradually regaining his wits, and his sense of divine purpose, was having speech again with Hermes. They were standing fifty meters or so from the cave.

"What happened?" demanded Hermes, who seemed to be recovering somewhat more rapidly.

Mars stood blinking at him. Then he proclaimed defiantly:

"To me? Nothing. A little test of the Sword called Soulcutter. As you see, there was no great harm done."

His companion stared at him in disbelief. "No great harm? We both of us were stupefied! You should say that nothing happened to your human in the cave—except that his sight was restored, when your magic came undone. Oh, and he still has his Sword—no, now he has two of them!"

The Wargod remained determined to put a good face on the whole situation. "But he was forced to put away the one that annoyed us." As usual, his tone was bellicose.

"Annoyed!"

Hermes went on to insist that dropping Soulcutter into the pit had been a serious mistake, in fact a debacle had resulted. Other gods must have been at least somewhat affected. They were going to be angry about having been put at risk.

Mars, still struggling against the lingering effects of Soulcutter, refused to tolerate such an attitude. The very idea, that a *god* could be endangered, not simply inconvenienced, by Sword-powers!

Mars darted away, but soon came back. He had argued or bargained or bullied another of his colleagues into loaning him another Sword, which happened to be Stonecutter.

Again Hermes protested. "Your man in the cave now has two Swords—are you going to give him a third?"

Mars considered this mere sarcasm, unworthy of an answer. Muleheadedly determined to do what he had set out to do, conduct tests on his specimen, he announced that he was going back to the cave again, with a new plan in mind.

"I think we had better first consult the Council?" Hermes paused. "Unless you are worried about what they might say," he added slyly.

"What? I? Worried?"

* * *

Keyes, pacing his open-air cell on weary legs, kept shooting frowning glances at the Sword of Despair where it lay on the cave floor. He was trying feverishly to think of some way he might trade the sheathed Soulcutter for his freedom. Suppose another god, or goddess, were to appear on the upper rim of the cave, and he suggested some kind of trade? But no, he doubted they would be in any mood for bargaining. And he was still unable to climb out of the pit unaided. His magical capabilities, which might have got him free, were stirring, but he could tell that their restoration was going to take much longer than that of his eyesight.

Again he was being threatened by a sense of hopelessness.

He had now been in the cave for hours, and straining to study the gods for long hours before Mars caught him. As the afternoon wore on, Keyes sat down to rest, and in a few moments fell helplessly into an exhausted, stuporous sleep—with Doomgiver still gripped in his right hand.

A number of the gods, including Mars and Hermes, had hastily reconvened in Council. They were enough, or so they said, to form a quorum. And they were much concerned with Shieldbreaker too. None of those present would admit to being in possession of that weapon, or to knowing where it was. Who had received it in the lottery? Regrettably Vulcan was absent, and could not be asked. Maybe he would not have revealed the secret anyway.

Around midafternoon, the Council passed a resolution stating it as their intention that all Swords should be reclaimed from human possession.

Mars the warrior, still stubbornly determined to establish himself as above Sword-power, volunteered to enforce the order.

Zeus told him to go ahead. Others, enough, it seemed, for a

majority, were in agreement. "If there is any real problem, you seem to have caused it. Therefore you should find a remedy!"

Still, Hermes once again tried to argue Mars out of taking too direct an approach. "Doomgiver has now overcome you twice—wait, let me finish! I tell you, we must either arrange to borrow Shieldbreaker from whoever has it, or else get that other Sword out of the man's hand by guile."

"Guile, is it? I have other ideas about that. And I wasn't overcome. I was only taken unawares, and—and *distracted* for a moment. Who said that I was overcome?" Mars glowered fiercely.

Hermes heaved a sigh of divine proportions. "Have it your own way, then."

. . . and then Lo-Yang, like some figure out of a dream, was bending over Keyes, shaking him awake. The magician's body convulsed in a nervous start, bringing him up into a sitting position. He comprehended with amazement that his apprentice had returned after all. He saw the long, thin rope, its upper end secured somehow, hanging down into the cave.

"Master! Thank Ardneh, you can see again! What's happened? Your face is all dried blood. And what are these two swords?"

"Never mind my face. Pick up that Sword on the floor, and bring it with us, but as you value your life, do not even imagine yourself drawing it. Let us go!"

They scrambled toward the rope. But before either of the men could start to climb, Mars appeared, his face set in a mask of stubborn anger, and put out one finger to snap the long rope from its fastening at its upper end.

Keyes could feel all hope die with the falling coil.

Mars said nothing, but he was smiling, ominously. And he had another Sword in hand. It was soon plain which Sword this was, for the god wielding it began carving out a block of stone, part of the solid cave-roof. It was a huge slab, and when it fell the men trapped in the cave would have to be very alert and lucky to dodge it and escape quick death.

Lo-Yang collapsed on his knees, forehead to the ground.

Mars's companion, he of the winged sandals, was standing back a little watching, with the attitude of one who has serious misgivings but is afraid or at least reluctant to interfere.

Maybe, thought Keyes suddenly, all hope is not dead after all. A moment later, he could see the sudden opening to the sky as the block of stone came loose. Aiming Doomgiver at it like a spear, he saw the slab twist in the air, and then fall up instead of down, looping through the precise curve necessary to bring it into violent contact with the Wargod's own head.

Mars reeled, and his helmet, grossly dented, flew aside. Only a god could have survived such an impact. The Wargod did not even lose consciousness, but in his shock let Stonecutter fall from his hand into the cave, the bare Blade clanging on rock.

"Now you know as well as I do, what I have here." At first Keyes whispered the words. Then he shouted them at the top of his voice. "Doomgiver! Doomgiver! *I hold the blessed Sword of Justice!*"

Mars, battered, lacking his helmet but refusing to admit that he was even slightly dazed, still pigheadedly confident of his own prowess, came down into the cave with some dignity, treading thin air as before. Mars was coming to take the Sword back, hand-to-hand, from Keyes. Well, Shieldbreaker could be captured that way, couldn't it? And it the strongest Sword of all?

While the two men cowered back, the god first grabbed up the sheathed Soulcutter, and tossed it carelessly up and out of the cave, well out of the humans' reach. Any god who thought he needed a Sword's help could pick it up!

Then Mars turned his attention to Doomgiver, and confronted the stubborn man who held it. Keyes noted with some amazement that his great opponent, bruised as he was, appeared less angry now than he had at the start of the adventure; in fact the Wargod was gazing at Keyes with a kind of grudging appreciation.

"You seem a brave man, with the fiber I like to see among my followers. I would be willing to accept your worship. And for all I care personally, you might keep Vulcan's bit of steel and magic. Humans might retain them all; we who possess the strength of gods have no need of such—such tricks. But the Council has decided otherwise. Therefore, on behalf of the Council, I—"

And Mars reached out confidently, to reclaim Doomgiver from Keyes's unsteady grip—but somehow the Sword in the man's hand eluded the god's grasp. Mars tried again, and failed again—and then his effort was interrupted.

A roaring polyphonic outcry reached the cave, a wave of divine anger coming from the place a hundred meters distant where the Council had so recently passed its resolution.

"My Sword is gone!" one of the distant voices bellowed, expressing utter outrage.

"And mine!" another answered, yelling anguish.

The protest swelled into a chorus, each with the same complaint. Keyes could not interpret the wind-blown, shouted words. But he needed only a moment to deduce their meaning. Mars acting in the Council's name and with its authority had assaulted a man who held Doomgiver, by trying to deprive the man of his Sword, and intending to fling that Sword away—and Doomgiver had exacted its condign retaliation. The Council of Divinities had lost all of *their* Swords instead. The great majority of Vulcan's armory had been flung magically to the four winds, and lay scattered now across the world.

The uproar mounted, as more deities realized the truth. A number of gods at no great distance were violently cursing the name of Mars, and the Wargod was not one to let them get away with that. He listened for a moment, then rose in his divine wrath and mounted swiftly from the cave.

His mind was now wholly occupied with a matter of over-riding importance—the names the others called him. So he had forgotten Stonecutter, which still lay where he had dropped it.

Several more hours had passed, and the westering sun was low and red, before Demeter returned to the cave in which she had hidden the Sword of Justice. She had wanted to get it out of the way for a time, so that her colleagues should not nag her with questions when they saw her carrying a Sword.

Demeter had spent most of the day thinking the matter over and had come to a decision. The Game still did not greatly appeal to her, and it would be best if she gave Doomgiver to someone else.

On her approach to the cave, Demeter observed the tracks of a pair of riding-beasts, both coming and going, and when she looked in over the edge of the deep hole, she beheld a set of crude steps, more like a ladder than a stair, freshly and cleanly hewn out of one solid wall. Human beings! No other creatures would carve steps.

Rising wind whined through the surrounding rock formations. The only living things now in the cave were a helplessly immortal demon, strangely trapped in a lower pit, and a few mortally wounded bats.

No need to look in the place where she had hidden her Sword, to know that it was gone. Well, why not? Let it go. Perhaps the humans needed Justice more than any of Demeter's divine colleagues did.

Perpetually at odds with each other as they were, the members of the Council needed some time to realize that their terrible Blades had been scattered across a continent, perhaps across the whole earth, among the swarms of contemptible humans. As that realization gradually took hold, the gods met the crisis in their usual fashion, by convening to enjoy one of their great, wrangling, all-but-useless arguments.

The only fact upon which all could agree was that their Swords had all been swept away from them. All the Swords, that is, except for Shieldbreaker, which remained, as far as could be determined, immune to the power of any other Sword, and thus would not have been affected by Doomgiver's blow.

But whichever divinity still possessed the Sword of Force was obviously refusing to reveal the fact, doubtless for fear it would be taken away by some unarmed opponent.

For good or ill, the Great Game was off to a roaring start.

Woundhealer

Walter Jon Williams

The horn echoed down the long valley, three bright rising notes, and it seemed to Derina—frozen like an animal in the bustle of the court—as if the universe halted for a long moment of dread. A cold hard fist clenched in her stomach.

Her father was home.

She went up the stone stair by the old gatehouse and watched as her father and his little army, back from the Princes' Wars, wound up the mountain spur toward her. The cold canyon wind howled along the old flint walls, tangled Derina's red-gold hair in its fingers. The knuckles on her small fists were white as she searched the distant column for sign of her father and brothers.

Derina's mother and sister joined her above the gatehouse. Edlyn carried her child, the two of them wrapped in a coarse wool shawl against the wind.

"Pray they have all come home safe," said Derina's mother, Kendra.

Derina, considering this, thought she didn't know what to pray for, if anything, but Edlyn looked scorn at her mother, eyes hard in her expressionless face.

When Lord Landry rode beneath the gate he looked up at

them, cold blue eyes gazing up out of the weatherbeaten
moon face with its bristle of red hair and wide, fierce nostrils.
As her father's eyes met hers, the knot in Derina's stomach
tightened. Her gaze shifted uneasily to her brothers, Norward the eldest, gangly, myopic eyes blinking weakly, riding
uneasily in the saddle as if he would rather be anywhere else;
and Reeve, a miniature version of his father, red-haired and
round-shouldered, looking up at the women above the gate
as if sizing up the enemy.

Derina's mother and sister bustled down the lichen-scarred
stair to make the welcome official. Derina stayed, watching
the column of soldiers as it trudged up to the old flint-walled
house, watched until she saw her father's woman, Nellda,
riding with the other women in the wagons. Little dark-
haired Nelly was sporting a black eye.

Mean amusement twisted Derina's mouth into a smile. She
ran down the stair to join her family.

Nelly was halfway down the long banquet table and her eyes
never left her plate. Before the campaign started she'd sat at
Landry's arm, above his family.

Good, Derina thought. Let her go back to the mean little
mountain cottage where Lord Landry had found her.

The loot had been shared out earlier, the common soldiers
paid off. Now Landry hosted a dinner for his lieutenants, the
veterans of his many descents onto the plains below, and the
serjeants of his own household.

The choicest bit of booty was Lord Landry's new sword,
won in the battle, a long magnificent patterned blade,
straight and beautiful. Norward had found the thing, apparently, but his father had taken it for his own.

"In the hospital!" Landry called. His voice boomed out
above the din in the long hall. "He found the sword in the
hospital, when we were cutting our way through their camp!

It must have belonged to one of their sick—well," bellowing a laugh, "we helped their shirkers and malingerers on to judgment, so we did!"

Derina gazed at her untouched meal and let her father's loud triumph roll past unheeded. This war sounded like all the others, a loud recitation of cunning and twisting diplomacy and the slaughter of helpless men. Landry did not find glory in battle, but rather in plunder: he would show up late to the battlefield, after giving both sides assurances of his allegiance, and then be the first to sack the camp of the loser. Sometimes he would loot the camp without waiting for the battle to be decided.

"What does Norward need with a blade such as this?" he demanded. "His third campaign, and as yet unblooded."

"M-my beast fell," Norward stammered. He turned red and fought his disobedient tongue. "T-tripped among the, the tent lines."

"Ta-ta-tripped in the ta-ta-tents!" Landry mocked. "Your riding's as defective as your speech. As your blasted weak eyes. Can't kill a man?—I'll leave my land to a son who can." He gave a savage grin. *"I* was a younger son—but did it stop me?"

Reeve smirked into his cup. Lord Landry had been loud in the praise of his younger son's willingness to run down and slay the helpless boys and old men who'd guarded the enemy camp.

Reeve was strong, Derina thought, and Norward weak. What had her own feelings to do with it?

Landry put the sword in its sheath, then hung it behind his chair, above the great fireplace, in place of his old blade. He turned and looked over his shoulder at his family. "None of you touch it, now!"

As if anyone would dare.

* * *

The banquet was over, Lord Landry's soldiers dozing in their chairs or stumbling off into dark corners to sleep on pallets. Only the lord's family remained—they and Nellda—all frozen in their chairs by his glacier-blue eyes, eyes that darted suspiciously from one to the next—weighing, judging, finding everyone wanting.

Derina looked only at her plate.

Landry took a long drink of plundered brandy. He had been drinking all night but the effects were slight: a shining of the forehead, a slow deliberation of speech. "Where is the son I need?" he said.

Reeve looked up in surprise from his own cup—he had thought he was the favored one tonight. He swallowed, tried to think how to respond, decided to speak, and said the wrong thing.

Anything, Derina knew, would have been the wrong thing.

"I'll be the son you want, Father."

Landry swung toward his younger son, every bristle on his head erect. Slowly his tongue formed words to the song,

> *"See the little simpleton*
> *He doesn't give a damn.*
> *I wish I were a simpleton—*
> *By God, perhaps I am!"*

Reeve's face flushed; his lower lip stuck out like a child's. Landry went on: "Perhaps I *am* such a fool, begetting a child like you. *You?* D'you think killing a few camp followers makes you a man? D'you think you have the craft and cunning to hold on to anything I give you? Nay—you'll piss it away in a week, on drink and gambling and girls from the Red Temple."

Reeve turned away, face blood-red. Landry's eyes roved

the table, settled on his older son. "And you—what have you to say?"

Nothing, Derina knew. But the old man had him trapped, obliged him to speak.

"What d-d'you wish me to say?" Norward said.

Landry laughed. "Such an obedient boy! Bad eyes, bad tongue, no backbone. Other than that—" He laughed again. "The perfect heir!"

"Perhaps—" Kendra said, and made as if to rise.

Landry looked sidelong at his wife and feigned surprise. "Oh—are you still alive?" Laughing at his joke. "Damned if I can see why. I'd kill myself if I were as useless as you."

"Perhaps it's time to go to bed," Kendra said primly.

"With you?" Landry's eyes opened wide. "God save us. God save us from getting another son such as those you gave me."

"It isn't my fault," Kendra said.

She had been pregnant with a dozen children, Derina knew, miscarried five, and of the rest all but four had died young.

"Whose fault is it, then?" Landry demanded. The red bristle on his head stood erect. "Blame my seed, do you?" He beat his looted silver flagon on the table. "I am strong," he insisted, "as were my sires! If my children are milksops, it's because my blood is commingled with yours! You had your chance—" He gestured down the table, to where Nellda, unnoticed, had begun quietly weeping. "And so did yon Nelly! She could have given me a son, but she miscarried—damnation to her!" He shouted, half-rising from his seat, the powerful muscles in his neck standing out like cable. "Damnation to all women! They're all betrayers."

Edlyn's little girl, startled out of her slumbers by Landry's shout, began to wail in Edlyn's lap. Landry sneered at the two.

"Betrayers," he said. "At least your worthless husband won't be siring any more girls, to eat out my substance and shame me with their snivelling." Edlyn, cradling her child, said nothing. Her face, as always, was a mask.

Landry lurched out of his chair, tripped over a sleeping dog, then staggered down the table toward Derina. Her heart cried out at his approach. "You haven't betrayed me yet," he mumbled. "You'll give me boys, will you not?" His powerful hands clutched at her breasts and groin. She closed her eyes at the painful violation, her head swimming with the odor of brandy fumes. "Ay," he confirmed, "you're grown enough—and you bleed regular, ay? We'll find you a husband this winter. One who won't betray me."

He swung away from her, back toward his brandy cup. Derina could feel her face burning. Landry seized the cup, drained it, looked defiantly down the table at his family—frozen like deer in the light of a bull's-eye lantern—looked at Nelly weeping, at his soldiers who, no doubt roused by his shouting, were dutifully feigning slumber.

"The night is young," he muttered, "are all feeble save myself?" Edlyn's child shrieked. Landry sneered, poured himself more brandy, and lurched away, toward the stair and his private chambers.

Kendra turned to Reeve. "I wish you hadn't provoked him," she said. Reeve turned away mumbling, pushed back his chair, and stumbled for the door to the courtyard.

"What was that you said?" Kendra called. Her voice was shrill.

Reeve, still muttering, boomed out into the fresh air. Derina hadn't heard but knew well enough what her brother said. "No one provoked Father," she said. "It doesn't matter what we do. Not when he's in these moods."

"We should try to make his time here easy," Kendra insisted. "If we're all good to him—"

Derina could still feel the imprint of her father's fingers on her breasts. She rose from the table.

"I'm going to bed," she said.

Her sister Edlyn rose as well. Her little girl's screams were beginning to fade. "Daryl should sleep," she said.

Edlyn and Derina made their way up the stairs to their quarters. They could smell Landry's brandy fumes and followed cautiously, but he was well gone, off to drink in his suite at the top of the stair.

Edlyn paused before Derina's door. Edlyn looked at her, eyes flat and emotionless. "Your turn now," she said. "To be his favorite."

Your turn, Derina knew, to be married off unknowing to some coarse stranger—to learn, perhaps, to love him, as Edlyn had—then to have his child, to have him die in one of Landry's wars and be left, scorned, at her father's house with an unwanted babe in her arms.

Derina, a lump in her throat, could only shrug.

"*Good*," Edlyn said, malice in her eyes. She turned and went to her own door.

You bleed regular, ay?

Numbly, Derina fumbled for the latch, entered her room, and locked the door behind.

The courting had already begun, and Landry home only three days. Any number of Landry's peers, soldiers, and retainers were happening by, all with oafish, sullen sons in tow.

Few of them bothered to acknowledge Derina. They knew who made the decisions.

Derina fled the sight of them, went for a long ride to the high uplands, the meadows where the summer pasture was, the close-cropped grass already turned autumn-brown.

She did not expect to find her brother there. But there he was, gangling body in saddle as he rode along the low drystone walls that separated one pasture from another. Nearsighted, Norward didn't see her until she hailed him.

"Inspecting the walls," he said.

"No point in doing that till spring."

"I wanted t-to get away."

"So did I."

He shrugged, pulled his cap down against the autumn highland wind. "Then r-ride the walls with me."

They rode along in cold silence. Derina looked at the splashes of lichen coloring the stone walls and wondered if Norward, with his poor vision, could see them at all.

"I'm caught," Norward said finally. He pulled his beast to a halt. "Reeve pushing from below, and F-father pushing from above. What can I d-do?"

She had no answer for him. Norward was weak, and that was that. It wasn't his fault, and it was sad that Landry despised him, but any sympathy on Derina's part was wasted effort.

Her father had taught her that only power mattered. Norward had none, and Derina could lend him none of her own. And so she left his question unanswered, just rode on, and Norward could do nothing but follow.

His lips twisted, a knowing, self-hating smile. "Have you looked c-closely at f—at our parent's new sword?" he asked.

"I'm not engrossed by swords," Derina said.

"Ah. Well. This one is interesting. I f-found it, you know—and got a look at it before Father took it away."

"What's so interesting about it?" Derina demanded.

That smile came again. "Perhaps nothing."

Derina rode on, Norward lagging behind, and wished she were alone.

* * *

The next morning Derina looked at the sword hanging above the mantel in the great hall, and wondered what it was that had attracted Norward's interest. The hilt was fine work, that was clear enough, possessing a handsome scalloped black pommel with the badge of a white hand on it. But there was little special about it, no exquisite workmanship, no gilt or jewels.

She did not dare defy her father by touching the sword, drawing it to look at the blade.

"Please, miss."

The voice startled her, and she jumped. Derina turned and saw Nellda, and a bolt of hatred lodged in her heart.

"Please, miss." Nellda pushed a packet into Derina's hands. "Give this to your father."

Derina looked at the packet, badly wrapped and tied with a bit of green ribbon. "Why should I?" she said.

There were tears in Nelly's eyes. "He won't see me! You can get to him, can't you?"

Derina fingered the ribbon. "What is it? Love tokens?"

"And a letter. I can write, you know! I'm not just a foolish girl."

"So you say." Coldly. Derina thought a moment, then shook her head. "Go home, Nellda. Go back to whatever little sty it was he found you in."

"I can't! He turned my father out! We had a bad year and—" Her voice broke. "He said he'd take care of me!"

For a moment a little spark of sympathy rose in Derina's heart, but with an act of will she stamped it out. Power was all that mattered, and Derina's, such as it was, was only to hurt. "Go away," she said, and held out the packet.

Nellda, weeping, fled without taking it.

Derina turned and—she hesitated, and for some reason

she glanced up at the great sword—she threw the packet into the fire.

Burning up, it scarcely made a flame.

So there was her future husband, pimples and round shoulders and hoggish eyes. His name was Burley, and his father was a gentleman of no great land or distinction who lived farther up the valley, a man of thin beard and cringing deference.

"His arm will be of use to you, sir," said the father, Edson, whose own arm was of little use at all.

"It's not his arm that's in question," Landry muttered. Derina caught Reeve's smirk out of the corner of her eye and wanted to claw it off his face.

Derina looked at her family. Kendra looked as if she were trying to make the best of it. Norward was gazing at his feet and frowning. Edlyn was quietly triumphant, eyes glittering with malice.

I won't make your mistake, Derina thought fiercely; but she knew that Edlyn's mistakes hadn't been Edlyn's to make—and her own mistakes wouldn't be hers, either.

"We'll send to the temple for a priest to draw up the contract proper," Landry said. He looked at Derina, grinned at her.

"Kiss your future husband, girl."

All eyes were on Derina and she hated it. She stepped forward obediently, rose on tiptoe—Burley was taller than his posture made him—and kissed his cheek.

His breath smelt of mutton. His cheek was red with embarrassment. He didn't seem to be enjoying this any more than she was—which was, she supposed, a point in his favor.

She would never dare to love him, she knew. Most likely he wouldn't live long.

* * *

The wedding took place a few weeks later, in order to give all
the poor relations a chance to swarm in from the countryside
to get their free meal. The ceremony was at noon, the priest
already drunk and thick-tongued, and the rest of the company was drunk soon after.

Nellda was seen, at the food of the long table, wolfing
down food and drink. One of the servants, sensitive with long
practice to Lord Landry's moods, pushed her away, and she
was seen no more.

Derina looked down at her dowry, a small chest of coins
and a modicum of old loot, silver cups and candlesticks polished brightly to make them seem more valuable than they
were—the guard, standing by with his pike, seemed almost
unnecessary. Described in the marriage agreement, signed
and sealed with red ribbon, was another part of the dowry: a
lease on some high pastureland.

"Nice to know what you're worth, eh?" Reeve said.

"More than you," Derina said.

Reeve sneered. "You don't think father favors me? You
don't think I'll have all this in the end?" He gestured largely,
swayed a bit, and leaned harder on the milkmaid under his
arm.

He followed his father in this as in all things.

"If you live, perhaps," said Norward's mild voice. He had
ghosted up without Reeve's noticing.

Reeve swung round. His compact, powerful body seemed
to puff like a bullfrog's before his brother's gangling form.
"And who'll kill me?" he demanded. "A blind man like you?"

Mildly Norward placed a hand on Reeve's chest. "Yourself," he said, "most like," and gave Reeve a gentle push.
Reeve went down hard, the milkmaid on top of him in a

flurry of skirts. The dowry's guard, stepping back with a grin, put out a hand to still a rocking candlestick. Reeve, sprawled on the flags, pushed the girl away and clapped a hand to his belt for a knife that wasn't there; and then he glanced for a moment at Landry's sword, hanging just a few feet away—but Norward just stood over him, looking down, and after a long, burning moment Reeve got to his feet and stalked away, the milkmaid fluttering after.

Some people laughed. Norward himself seemed faintly puzzled. He looked at his hand and flexed it.

"I must not know my own strength," he said.

"He was drunk, and off balance."

"That must be it," Norward agreed. He looked at the dowry on its table, then at Derina. "I like your Burley," he said.

"He's not my Burley," Derina said, "he's Father's Burley."

Norward nodded, looked at his hand again. "Have you noticed?" he said. "My stammer's getting better."

The wedding bed, surrounded by curtains and screens, was set before the fire in the great hall and wrapped with symbols of fertility—ivy and pinecones and orange and yellow squash, the best that could be done in autumn.

The newlyweds would have the big bed in the main hall for a week, then move to Derina's room. They wouldn't be leaving Landry's halls till Yule, when their new rooms at Edson's house would be ready.

Derina endured the public "consummation," sitting upright in bed with Burley while the guests cheered, filled their cups with wine, and made ribald jokes. Landry loomed over her, patted her, placed a wet kiss on her cheek. "You're my treasure," he said. "My truest daughter."

Something—wretched love, perhaps—churned in Derina's heart.

Edlyn watched with cold, hidden eyes—less than two years ago, she'd been put through the same business, received the same caresses and praise.

Next came the closing of the curtains and Landry's loud orders ending the festivities. Lights were doused. The dowry was packed and carried to Landry's strongroom—"just for the night," he said.

In the corners of the big room, drunken relations snored and mumbled.

Derina looked at Burley, profiled in the firelight. His wedding garments—black velvet jacket slashed with yellow, jaunty bonnet with feather—had shown him to advantage, far more presentable than in his country clothes the day they'd met. Now, in his shirt, he looked from Derina to his wine cup and back.

Derina felt the warmth of the big fire warming her shoulders. She tilted her head back and drank her wine, hoping it would bring oblivion. She put the cup away and lay on the bed and closed her eyes.

She hoped he would get it over with quickly.

She tasted wine on his breath as he kissed her. Derina lay still, not moving. His hands moved over her body. There was nowhere for them to go where her father hadn't already been.

Burley's hands stopped moving. There was a loud crack from the fireplace as a log threw up sparks.

"We don't have to do this," he said, "if you're not in the humor."

Faint surprise opened her eyes.

Burley rolled himself onto his stomach, propped himself on his elbows. Firelight reflected in his dark eyes. "Perhaps you had no mind to be married," he said.

She shrugged. Wine swam in her head. "I knew it would happen."

"But not to me."

Another shrug. "As well as another."

Burley gnawed a knuckle and stared at the fire. Derina propped herself up on her elbow and regarded him. Wine and relief made her giddy.

"I think my father was afraid to say no to this," Burley said. "I think it was Lord Landry's idea, not his."

Derina was not surprised. People in the dales treaded warily where Landry was concerned.

"My father says that the connection will be of advantage," Burley said. "And we need the grazing on the upland pastures."

"I hope you'll get it."

Burley gave her a sharp look. "What d'you mean?"

The wine made her laugh. "Edlyn's dowry gave the mowing on forty hectares of river pasture, but there wasn't much hay made there, for my father's beeves grazed the land all summer."

Burley nodded slowly. "I see."

"And Edlyn's dowry never left my father's strongboxes." The wine made her laugh again. "It was an autumn wedding, like ours, and father always had an excuse. Bad autumn weather, then winter snows, then muddy spring roads. And by summer, Barton was dead, and his father with him, and the beeves already in the pasture."

"And the little girl—"

"Daryl."

"Daryl. She's the heir to her father's estate, and Barton the eldest son."

"And my father has use of the estate through her minority, which will last forever. And that is why Edlyn will never be allowed to marry again, for fear that Daryl would have another protector."

And that is why Edlyn hates me. Derina left the concluding thought unspoken.

Burley frowned for a long moment, then spoke with hesitation. "How did Barton and his father die?"

Derina's head spun. Probably the wine.

"In battle," she said.

"And who killed them?"

For a moment Derina was aware of her father's looted sword, bright and powerful, hanging over the fireplace.

"I don't know," she said.

Burley didn't reply. Derina watched him frowning into the fire, eyes alight with thought, until wine and main weariness dragged her into sleep.

When she woke in the morning, her father-in-law had gone, and all his folk with him.

The conventions forced Edlyn to be sisterly, which included helping Derina make the bed. "No blood on the sheets," she observed. Her flat face regarded Derina. "Was he incapable? Or you no virgin?"

Derina felt color rise to her face. For all they never talked of it, Edlyn knew perfectly well who'd had Derina's virginity, two years before when Edlyn married and moved out of the room they shared.

At least it hadn't lasted long. Landry had found a girl he'd liked better—another of his fleeting favorites.

"Whatever version you like best," Derina said. "When you talk to the old gossips in the kitchen hall, you'll say whatever you like anyway."

Edlyn's expressionless face turned back to her work.

Derina fluffed a pillow. "Perhaps," said Derina, "he was merely gentle."

Edlyn's tone was scornful. "So much the worse for him."

There was a lump in Derina's throat. She put the pillow down. "Can we not be friends?" she asked.

Edlyn only gazed at her suspiciously.

"It's not my fault," Derina said. "I didn't ask to marry any more than you. It's not my fault that Barton died."

"But you profit by it."

"Where's my profit?" Derina demanded.

Edlyn didn't answer.

"Father's favor changes with the wind," Derina said. "He does it to divide us."

"And what good would combining do?" Scornfully. "D'you think we could beat him?"

"Probably not. But it would ease our hearts."

Stony, Edlyn looked at her.

Lord Landry's voice rose in the court. *"Gone?"* The doors boomed inward, and Landry stalked in, rage darkening his face. He swung accusingly to Derina. "D'you know what that brother of yours has done?"

"I l-looked for you." Norward's voice. He came tumbling down the stair, having heard his father's bellow from his quarters. "Y-you weren't there."

"You gave away the dowry, damn you!" Landry rampaged up to his son, seemed to tower over him even though Norward was taller. "Edson's gone, with all his folk!"

"It—" Norward struggled for words through the stammer that had suddenly returned, bad as ever. "It was his. Edson's. He asked for it."

"You should have delayed! Sent for me!"

"I—I did. But Edson's relatives were all there—I couldn't refuse 'em all. But you weren't in your room, and hadn't slept there."

"Who are you to tell me where to sleep?" Landry roared.

"I didn't."

"Liar! Liar and thief!" Landry seized his son by the neck, began wrenching him back and forth at the end of his power-ful arms. Norward turned red and clutched hopelessly at his father's thick wrists. Derina desperately searched her mind for something she could do.

"Is it a matter of the dowry, then?"

Burley's voice cut over the sound of Landry's shouts. He had followed Norward down the stair, was watching nar-rowly as father and son staggered back and forth.

Landry froze, breath coming hard through wide nostrils. Then he released his son and forced a smile. "Not at all, lad," he said. "But Norward let your father leave without telling me of his going. I would have said my farewells." He glared at Norward, who clutched his throat and gasped for air. "Reeve would not have so forgotten."

"My father bade me thank your lordship for all your kind-ness," Burley said. "But he and our folk wanted to get an early start lest a storm break."

A storm, Derina thought. Apt enough analogy.

"I would have said goodbye," Landry mumbled, and turned to slouch away.

Derina, seeing Norward and Burley exchange cautious looks, knew then that this had been carefully arranged. For a moment anxiety churned in her belly, fear that Landry would discover she had talked too freely to Burley the night before.

There was a touch on Derina's shoulder, and she jumped. Edlyn clasped her arm, squeezed once, looked in her face, and then silently returned to her work.

Truce, Derina read in her look. If not quite peace, at least an end to war.

* * *

A real storm, snow and wind, coiled about the house the next two days, glazing windows with sleet, shrieking around the walls' flinty corners, banking up shoals of sooty white in the courtyard. Landry's relations and dependents, unable to leave for their own homes, ate up his provender and patience at an equal rate. The huge fire in the great hall blazed night and day and almost cooked Derina and Burley in their bed.

The storm died down the third night after the wedding. Burley and Derina, next morning, hadn't yet risen when Norward brought in Nellda, who'd fallen in the storm the night before while trying to leave the house.

Nelly's flesh was turquoise blue and cold, and her breath was faint. There was snow and ice in her tangled hair. Norward put her in Derina's wedding bed, and called for a warming pan.

"I was at the north corner," Norward said, "checking the roof for storm damage. And there she was, past the Stone Eagle, halfway to the valley and lying in a drift."

"Who saw her?" Derina asked.

"I did."

Derina looked at him in surprise. "But your eyes—how could you see her?"

Norward shrugged. "My eyes seem to be better."

With warmth and warm broth brought by a servant, Nellda was brought around. Her eyes traveled from one member of the family to another.

"Where is he?" she asked faintly.

"He isn't here," Norward said.

Nellda's eyes trembled, then closed. "He's with Medora," she said. "You should have left me in the snow."

Burley frowned and took Derina aside. "Who is this person?" he asked. "Does she have a place here?"

"She's my father's whore," Derina said. "And apparently now my father has a new whore, this Medora."

"And who's *she?*"

"I don't know. Probably some crofter girl. That's the sort he likes."

Burley narrowed his eyes in thought. "Can't we find her a place here? We can't let her die in the snow."

Derina's spine turned rigid. "In our house?" She shook her head. "My mother lives here. I won't insult her by having Nelly around. Not when Father doesn't want her anymore."

Burley sighed. "I will try to think of something."

Derina caught at his sleeve as he turned. "It's not your task. This isn't your family."

His odd little smile stopped her. "But it *is* my family now," he said.

Burley returned to the bed, leaving Derina standing stiff with surprise.

He had his work cut out, she thought, if he thought himself a part of *this* family.

And, she reminded herself, he probably wouldn't survive it.

Nelly was hidden away in the servants' loft, and Norward ordered one of the older maidservants to nurse her. When her strength returned she'd have a job in the stables, where Kendra wouldn't encounter her.

Landry gave Reeve a ruby ring and a pair of silver spurs—"for his loyalty." Reeve preened as he strutted about wearing them, the spurs clanking on the flags or catching on the carpet. At dinner Landry sent his wife down the table, and sat with Reeve on one side and the girl Medora on the other. Landry had given her a gold chain belt. She was a frail little blonde thing, giggly when drunk. Derina didn't think she'd last. She didn't have brains enough to follow Landry's moods.

Kendra chatted away at dinner and pretended nothing was

wrong, but next day, while Derina was helping her mother at carding wool, Kendra began to weep. Derina searched through her mother's basket for a strand of wool, pretending that she didn't see the fat tears rolling down Kendra's cheeks.

Sometimes, when Kendra was weak, Derina hated her.

"If only I'd given him the sons he wanted," Kendra moaned. "Then everything would be all right."

"You gave him sons," Derina said.

"Not the sons he wished for," Kendra said. "I should have given him more."

"It wouldn't have made any difference," Derina said. "He'd have despised them, too. Unless they were stronger, and then he would have hated and feared them."

Kendra's eyes opened wide in anger. "How dare you say that about your father!"

Derina shrugged. Kendra's mouth closed in a firm line. "Is it Burley putting these notions in your head?"

Derina wanted to laugh. "I've lived here all my life," she said. "Do you expect me not to know how things are?"

"I expect you to show your father respect, and not to go tattling to Burley or his kin."

Derina threw down the wool. "They have eyes, Mother. They can see as well as anyone."

"Be careful." A touch of fear entered Kendra's face as Derina stood and moved toward the door. "Don't tell!"

Don't tell what? Derina wondered.

Everything. That's what Kendra meant.

"I'll say what I like," Derina said, and left the room.

But doubted if she'd ever say a word.

Derina and Burley had slept in the huge marriage bed for almost a week. After tonight the bed would be taken down, and Derina and Burley moved into her small room in the family quarters. The huge canopied feather bed was much too large for the room, and Derina and Burley would share Derina's old narrow bed, their breath frosting in the cold that the smoky fire never seemed to relieve.

Before sleep he turned to her. The dying firelight glinted in his pupils. "Derina," he said. "I hope you like marriage a little better than when we met."

"I never disliked it."

"But you didn't know me. Perhaps you know me a little better now."

"I hope so." Marriage, she considered, seemed to suit Burley at any rate. He stood straighter now, and seemed better-formed; his skin had cleared, his breath carried the scent of spiced wine. His warmth in the narrow bed would be welcome.

Burley fumbled under the covers, took her hand. "What I meant to say," he began, "is that I hope you like me a little. Because it will be powerful hard to lie here next to you in that narrow bed, night after night, and not want to touch you."

Derina's heart lurched, and she felt the blood rush to her face. "I never said you couldn't touch me," she said.

He hesitated for a moment, then began to kiss her. Pleasantly enough, she decided. After a while of this she felt some action on her part was necessary, and she put her arms around him.

What followed was not bad, she thought later, for all they both needed practice.

A few nights later Derina forgot the leather jack of wine she'd put by the fire to warm, and so she left Burley in their bed, put on a heavy wool cloak, and went down the main stair to fetch it. She heard angry voices booming up, and moved cautiously from stair to stair.

"Who has the spurs?" Reeve's voice. "Who has Father's eye?"

Norward's answer was cutting. "Medora, it would seem."

"Ha! She won't have the land and house when he dies! And neither will you, you useless gawk."

Derina slid silently down the stairs on bare feet, saw Norward moving close to Reeve in front of the fire. Norward seemed so much more impressive than he'd been, his once-lanky form filled with power. Reeve looked uneasy, took a step back.

"Are you planning on Father dying soon?" Norward asked. "I wouldn't wager that way, were I you."

"If he lives to a hundred, he won't favor you!" Reeve shouted "Never in life, blind man!"

"My eyes have improved," Norward said. "A pity yours have not."

"Fool! Go to the priesthood, and spend your days in prayer!" Reeve swung a fist, hitting Norward a surprise blow under the eye, and then Norward thrust out a longer arm and struck Reeve on the breast, just as he had at Derina's wedding, and Reeve lurched backward. One silver spur caught on a crack in the flags and he tumbled down. Norward gave a brief laugh. When Reeve rose, his neck had reddened and murder glowed in his eyes.

"I'll kill you!" he shouted, and leaped toward the fireplace, his hands reaching for Lord Landry's sword. Norward tried to seize him and hold him still, but Reeve was too fast—the long straight blade sang from the scabbard and Reeve hacked two-handed at Norward's head. Norward leaped back, the sword-point whirring scant inches from his face.

Derina cried in alarm and started to run back up the stair, hoping she could somehow fetch Burley and bring an end to it—but one of her feet slipped on the flags and she fell on the stair with a stunning jolt.

Norward leaped to the woodpile to seize a piece of wood to use for a shield, and Reeve screamed and swung the sword again. There was the sound of a sigh, or sob, and Derina wanted to shriek, afraid it was Norward's last. Dazed on the stair, she couldn't be certain what happened—but somehow Norward must have dodged the blow, though to Derina's dazzled eyes it looked, impossibly enough, as if the sword passed clean through his body without doing any hurt. But then Norward lunged forward and smashed Reeve in the face with his log—Reeve shouted, dropped the sword, staggered back. Norward grabbed him by the collar, wrenched him off his feet, and ran him head-first into the fireplace.

Derina screamed and came running down the stairs. Norward was grinding the side of Reeve's head against the fire's dying embers. "Take my place, puppy?" he snarled. "Draw sword against me? Have a taste of the hell that awaits kinslayers, Reeve of the Silver Spurs!"

"Stop!" Derina cried, and seized Norward's arms. The scent of burning hair and flesh filled her nostrils. The strength of the knotted muscle in Norward's arms astonished her—she couldn't budge him. Reeve screamed in terror. "Don't kill him!" Derina begged.

Norward flung Reeve up and away from the fire, then down to the flags. Reeve wept and screamed as Norward took the long patterned blade and hacked off his spurs, then kicked him toward the stair. Reeve rose to his feet, his hands clutching his burns, and fled. Derina stared in amazement at the transformed Norward, the tall young man, half a stranger, standing in the hall with drawn blade . . . Tears unexpectedly filled her eyes and she sat down sobbing.

Norward put the sword away and was suddenly her brother again, his eyes mild, his expression a little embarrassed. He reached out a hand and helped her to her feet.

"Come now," he said, "it was a lesson Reeve had to learn."

She clung to him. "I don't understand," she said.

"Truthfully," her brother said, "I am a bit puzzled myself."

Next day Reeve kept to his room. At dinner, Lord Landry looked at the bruise on Norward's cheek and said nothing, but there was a pitiless, amused glint in his eye, as if he'd just watched a pleasing dogfight; and he sat Norward down at his left hand, where he'd had Reeve before.

Six weeks later, after Yule, Burley and Derina left for Burley's home, where a new wing had been built for them. To Derina, the three small rooms and their whitewashed stone walls seemed more space than she'd had ever in life. It was not until spring that she and Burley journeyed back to the great flint-walled house perched above the switchback mountain road, and then it was not on a mission that concerned pleasantries.

Derina rode the whole way with her insides tying themselves in knots. Burley marched a captive before them, a man bound with leather thongs, and Derina was terrified that the captive—or the news she herself bore—would mean Burley's death.

But Burley's family had decided this course between them, and brushed her objections aside. If they had known her father as well as she, they would have been much more afraid.

When she arrived the old flint-walled house seemed different, though she could see nothing overtly changed. But the people moved cheerily, not with the half-furtive look they'd had before; and there was an atmosphere of gaiety unlike anything she remembered.

But Burley was not cheered: grim in his buff coat, he

marched his captive into the hall and asked for Lord Landry. The servants caught Burley's mood, and edged warily about the room.

Landry, when he came, was half-drunk; and Norward was at his elbow, a tall man, deep-chested and powerful, that Derina barely recognized.

"Daughter!" Landry said, one of his cold smiles on his lips, and then he saw Burley's captive, the shivering shepherd, and he stopped dead, looking from the shepherd to Burley and back again. "What's this?" he growled. The shepherd fell to his knees.

"First," Burley said, "I bring proper and respectful greetings from my father and my family to Lord Landry. This other matter is secondary—we found this fool grazing his flock on the upland meadow that was ours by marriage contract, and he had the temerity to say he was there on your order, so we had him whipped and now we bring him to you, to punish as you will for this misuse of your name."

Landry turned red, his neck swelling; his hand half-drew the dagger at his belt. Norward put a restraining hand on Landry's arm. "Now's not the time to make new enemies," Norward said, and Landry forced down his rage, snicked the dagger back in its sheath, then strode briskly to where the captive cowered on his knees and kicked the shepherd savagely in the ribs. "That's for you, witless!" he said.

"My lord—" the shepherd gasped.

"Silence!" Landry shouted, before the man could say something all might regret. He looked up at Burley, staring blue eyes masking his calculation. "You've handled this matter well," he admitted grudgingly. "I thank you."

"I bring other news that will please you, I think," Burley said. He took Derina's hand. "Derina is with child, we believe, these two months."

For a moment Derina was petrified—with a child on the way, what more use was the father? But then an unfeigned smile wreathed Landry's features. He embraced Derina and kissed her cheek. "There, my pet," he said, "have I not always said you were my favorite?"

Even though she knew perfectly well it was Landry's style to play one family member off against another, still Derina's nerves twisted into a kind of sick happiness, the assurance of her father's favor.

"You'll give me the boy I need," Landry said. "These others—" He looked at Norward. "—they league and conspire against me, but I have the mastery of 'em."

He turned to the shepherd, drew his knife again, and sliced the captive's bonds. "In celebration, we'll give this simpleton his freedom."

The shepherd rose, bowed, and fled.

Nicely done, Derina thought. Not a single regrettable word spilled.

Norward advanced to clasp Burley's hand. "Welcome to our house," he said. "Your advice, and that of your family, will be valued in the days to come."

Burley smiled, but his eyes glanced to Derina, who looked back in purest misery. There was something happening here, and it was nothing good.

Dinner found Landry at the head of the table, with his wife on one side and Norward at the other. The big sword still hung in its sheath behind her father's head. Reeve—burlier than ever, and full of smiling good humor despite the burn-scars on the side of his head, sat beside his brother, and Edlyn played happily with her daughter at his elbow. There was no sign of Medora or any other plaything.

Derina watched it all in silent, wide-eyed surprise. Her fa-

ther was smiling and complimentary, and praised her in front
of the others. She found herself casting looks at Edlyn to see
how her older sister reacted; but Edlyn's attention was all on
her daughter, and the anticipated looks of hatred never
came.

They all looked so *well*. Happy, strong, their skins glowing
with health. Derina felt like a shambling dwarf by comparison.

Then, offhand, Landry changed the subject. "There's an
army marching in the lowlands," he said, "one of the Princes.
He's got three thousand men, and his proclaimed ambition is
to invade the highlands and tame our mountain folk." He
barked a laugh. "If so, he'll find us a hard piece of flint to
break his teeth on."

"There is not enough wealth in the highlands to pay a
Prince's army," Norward said. "If he comes, he will find the
pickings poor indeed."

"Likely he intends somewhere else, and the story is a mere
diversion," Landry said, "but there's no reason in taking it
lightly. I'm bringing in supplies, and preparing the place for a
siege. They can't drag any engines up the mountains big
enough to hurt our walls." His eyes flicked to Burley. "I'll
trust your kin to support us, and raise up their strength
against any invaders."

"We have no love for lowland princes," Burley said.

Landry laughed. "Let 'em lie outside our walls till the cold
eats their bones!"

Landry snatched up a cup and offered a toast to the defeat
of the Prince—and his sons and Burley drank with him. They
were mountain men pledging against their ancestral enemies
of the lowlands, and in a matter as fundamental as this their
views were united.

Derina felt cold as ice as she saw Burley pledge himself to

Landry's war, and remembered Edlyn's husband doing likewise, three years ago.

The Prince's messenger came the next day with a small party and blew his trumpet from the path below the gatehouse. Lord Landry knew of their presence—he'd had scouts out, which showed he took the threat of invasion seriously. Perhaps he'd even known they were coming before he'd brought up the matter, so casually, at dinner. When the trumpet was blown Landry was ready, standing above the gatehouse with his family—all but Reeve, who had particular business elsewhere.

Derina wrapped herself in a cloak to hide her trembling. She had seen the preparations Landry made, and knew what he intended.

"His Highness bids you return that which you took last summer, when you attacked his camp," the messenger said. "If not, there will be war between you that will not end until your hold is burnt up, your valleys laid waste, and your children scattered over the hills with stones their only playthings. His Highness offers you this, if you heed not our command— or, if you choose wisely, he offers his hand in friendship."

A vast grin broke across Landry's face at the sound of the messenger's words—but Derina, who knew the smile, felt herself shudder. "What's mine is mine!" Landry called. "If this Prince wants what is his, let him look for it in a place closer to home."

"The Prince's friendship is not so lightly to be brushed aside," the messenger said.

"When was the friendship of a lowland man ever worth a pinch of salt?" Landry asked. He plucked up a crossbow from where it sat waiting, aimed briefly, and planted the missile a foot deep in the messenger's heart. Other missiles whirred down from Landry's soldiers. Then the gates swung open to let a group of riders under Reeve sally out. The Prince's party were killed to the last man, so that none could return to their prince with any of the intelligence they'd doubtless gathered.

Burley watched the massacre from the gatehouse, fists clenched on his belt. He turned to Landry. "Let me head homeward, and tell my kinfolk to prepare," he said. "And let me take Derina to where she'll be safe."

Landry shook his head, and seeing it Derina felt a cold chill of fear. "Send a letter instead," he said.

"Sir—"

"No," Landry said. "A letter. Your father will be more likely to help us if his son and grandson—" A nod to Derina. "—are guests here with us."

Derina's head swam under Landry's cold blue gaze. She was in her father's house again, under his power, and her husband was a pawn in her father's war—a pawn set ready for sacrifice.

The burning arrow was sent from door to door along the valleys, and as men armed the great house was readied for siege. The spring lambs were killed, and their flesh salted for the cellars or dried in the pure mountain air. The herds and flocks were driven up to the highland pastures by secret ways, where an enemy would never find them unless he first knew where to look. The people of the valleys were prepared for evacuation, either to the great houses or to the high meadows with the flocks.

The Prince's army paused in the lowlands for a week or so, perhaps awaiting the messenger's return, and then began its toilsome march into the hills. Lord Landry arranged for the heads of the messenger's party to await them on stakes, one every few kilometers along the road.

Lord Landry was in his element—boasting, boozing,

swaggering among his old veterans or the country gentlefolk.
Parties of warriors arrived under their local chiefs, were
added to the defense of the great house or sent out to harry
the enemy column with ambushes and raids.

The guards Landry posted were as polite as their duties allowed, but it was clear that neither Burley nor Derina were
allowed to leave the house. Derina was almost thankful: Burley was safe as long as he remained here, held genteel hos-
tage. If Landry should send him to war, Derina knew, he
very well might not return.

But the blackmail served its purpose. Word came that Burley's father Edson had brought his men into the war, and was
already harassing enemy scouts and foragers.

"What a fool this Prince is!" Landry shouted down the
length of the dinner table. It was crowded with soldiers, and
Landry's family were packed in at the top. "Come to fight us
over booty worth less than what he's paying his men to take
it—and last year's loot already shared out among our men as
soon as we returned home! We could not return if it we
would!"

"A fool and his army," Reeve smiled, "are soon parted."

Derina caught Norward's look, a quick glance to the head
of the table—as if he would say something, but chose not to.

The meal ended in singing, boasting, and boisterous talk of
swordplay and the prospect of large ransoms. Derina, ears
ringing, withdrew early, and went to bed. A few hours later
Burley joined her, swaying slightly with wine as he un-
dressed.

"Reeve and I are to leave tomorrow," he said. "We'll set
an ambush above Honing Pass."

Fear snapped Derina awake. She sprang from the bed and
clung to him.

"Don't go!" she cried.

Burley was bemused by her vehemence. "Don't be silly. I must."

"Father—" she gulped. "Father will kill you."

Burley's look softened. He touched her hair. "Your father won't be coming."

"His soldiers will be there. And—" She hesitated. "Reeve. If Reeve has not changed."

Burley shook his head. "Landry still needs my father. I'm not without value yet."

Derina buried her head in the curve of his neck. "Your father is mortal. So are you. And the lord my father will take your land in the name of our child."

He put his arms around her, swayed gently back and forth. "I have no choice," he said.

Derina blinked back hot tears. When had they ever had a choice? she thought.

Hoping desperately, she said, "I'll speak to Reeve."

Reeve listened carefully as Derina stammered out her fears the next morning. Unconsciously he rubbed the scars on his forehead. "No, father has not asked any such service of me," he said. "Nor would he—Norward and I are strong enough to stand against him now, and Edlyn and mother support us. When we refuse to let him play us each against the other, he calls it 'conspiracy.' "

"But his other men? His old veterans?"

Reeve looked thoughtful. "Perhaps. I'll speak to them myself, let them know that I look to them to keep Burley safe."

Derina kissed her brother on both cheeks. "Bless you, Reeve!"

Reeve smiled and hugged her with bearlike arms. "I'll look to him. Don't worry yourself—it's an ambush we'll be setting, not a pitched battle. All the danger's to the other side."

Reeve and Burley made a brave sight the next day, riding out in buff coats and polished armor, their troopers following. Derina, standing above the gatehouse, waved and forced the brightest smile she could, all to balance her sinking heart.

In a driving rain, five days later, the remnants of the party returned. The tale was of the ambushers ambushed, the Prince's spearmen on the ridge above, advancing under cover of arrows. Reeve wounded to the point of death, run through with a lance, and Burley taken.

"His beast threw Master Burley, miss," said an old serjeant, himself wounded in the jaw and barely able to speak. With dull eyes, Derina listened to the serjeant's tale as she saw Reeve carried into the house on his litter. "The enemy ran him down. He surrendered at the last—and they didn't kill him then, I saw them taking him away. He survived the surrender—that's the most dangerous moment. So he'll be held for ransom, most like, and you'll see him ere autumn."

And then Lord Landry came howling among the survivors, Norward following white-faced behind. Landry lashed at the nearest with a riding whip, calling them fools and cowards for letting his son fall victim. Then, snarling, hands trembling with the violence of his passion, he stood for a moment in the cold rain that poured in streams off his big shoulders, and then he turned on his heel and marched back to the main house. Derina ran after, feet sliding in the mud of the court.

"Burley was captured!" she said. "We must send his ransom!"

Landry turned to her as he walked, face twisting in a snarl. "Ransom? That's his father's business."

"His father's poor!" Derina cried.

Landry laughed bitterly. "And *I'm* rich? I've given away enough sustenance with your dowry. Don't expect me to deliver your fool of a husband, not when you're carrying his fortune in your belly."

Derina seized his sleeve, but he shook her off savagely, and she slipped in the mud and fell. Strong arms helped her rise. She looked up at Norward's grim face.

"I'll speak with him," Norward said, "and do what I can."

When Norward and Derina caught him, Landry had barged into the house and stood shouting in the great hall.

"Arm!" he bellowed. "A sally! When this rain ends, I'll have revenge for my son!"

Servants and soldiers bustled to their work. Norward spoke cautiously amid the melee. "You need your every son in this," he said. "Burley's your son now, and could be a good one to you."

Landry swung around, derision contorting his features. "That country clod! Whip my servant, will he? Steal my valuables? Is *that* a son of mine?" He shook his whip in Norward's face. "Let him rot in chains!"

Tears dimmed Derina's eyes and her head whirled. She heard Norward's protest, Landry's dismissal, then Norward's raised voice. Suddenly there was a violent whirl of action, and Derina looked up to see Landry holding Norward by the throat, his dagger out and pricking Norward beneath the ear.

"Think to replace Reeve, whey-face?" Landry demanded. "You'll never be a true son to me!" Derina cried out as the dagger drew a line of red along Norward's neck; and then Landry dropped his son to the floor and strode off, calling for his armor. Derina rushed to Norward's side, held her shawl to the wound. Norward pushed it aside.

"A scratch," he said. His face was grim and pale as death. He stood, then helped Derina to a chair. "Wait here—I know how to get Burley back. But promise me you'll say nothing—trust me in this."

He walked to the fireplace. He stood looking for a moment at Landry's long battle sword, then took it from its place and walked toward the stairs.

Derina was terrified to follow but more terrified to stay, alone and not knowing. She followed.

"Out!" Norward cried. "Out!" He was driving Edlyn and Kendra from Reeve's room. The two left in a bewildered flutter; but Derina, grimly biting her lip, pushed past them and into the room.

Norward had his back to her. He stared grimly down at Reeve, who lay unconscious, pale as death, his midsection bulky with bandages.

Derina could not say if she screamed as, in one easy gesture, Norward drew the blade from its scabbard and plunged it into Reeve's belly.

Landry had come down to the great hall, wearing his breastplate and chain skirts. He scowled as he saw Norward with his sword.

"Father," Norward said. "I suspect I know why the enemy have invaded." He held out the sword. "The Prince wants this back. It's one of the Swords of Power."

No! Derina thought. *Don't tell him!*

Then was a silence in which Derina heard only the beating of blood in her ears. Landry stood stock-still, then came forward. He took the sword from Norward and looked at it carefully. Then a savage smile crossed his features, and he drew the blade from the scabbard and whirled it over his head. "Maybe you're a son to me after all!" he said. "A Sword of Power—ay, that makes sense! But which one?"

To stifle any cry of surprise, Derina put her hand to her throat at Norward's answer.

"Farslayer would kill the Prince for you," Norward said. "And you wouldn't have to leave the room."

"And I'd have it right back again, through my heart!" Landry scorned. He stopped, looked at the sword. Then, deliberately, he spoke the words, the simple rhyme, known to all children, that would unleash Farslayer, and named as its target one of his own men, the wounded serjeant who had brought the news of the ambush to him.

A target so near would make the job of retrieval easy enough.

As Derina knew it would, nothing happened. Her creeping astonishment was turning to knowledge.

She knew what Norward was trying to do, and she wondered if she dared—if she wanted to—put a stop to it.

Landry looked at the hilt. "The white hand," he said. "Which sword is that?"

Norward shrugged. "The white hand of death, most like. What does it matter? What matters is that the war is won the moment you use the blade."

A grin crossed Landry's features. "The men are all to mount," he said. "We'll empty the place. You'll ride with me, and have pick of the Prince's loot!"

Derina, wide-eyed, stood and said nothing. *Decided* to say nothing.

A few hours later, as the last raindrops fell, Lord Landry and his army rode from his flint-walled house on his mission to crush the Prince and his army with their own weapon.

A few moments later Derina watched her mother's astonishment as she saw Reeve strolling casually down the stair, a crooked grin on his face. Even his burn scars had vanished.

"I seem to have improved," he said.

Four days later Norward was back with the body of Lord Landry, who had been killed leading a reckless charge on the enemy army. "The Prince has his sword back," he said. "The war is over."

Derina, standing in the courtyard, looked numbly at the body of her father, lying cold on his litter hacked by a dozen armor-crushing blows. Her brother Reeve put an arm around her.

She looked at her mother Kendra, who stared at Landry as if she didn't believe her eyes, and at Edlyn, who looked as if she were just beginning to dare to hope.

"Burley?" she asked.

"Alive," Norward said, "and his ransom well within our means. We'll pay his release as soon as the Prince's army reaches the lowlands again, and then you'll have your husband back."

Derina cried out in joy and threw her arms around him. He—Lord Norward now—stood stiffly for a moment, then gently took her arms and released himself from her embrace.

"Our father always wanted me to kill someone," he said. "Who'd have thought he would himself have been the victim?"

Landry would never have understood, Derina thought, a man such as the Prince, who would fight a war for a talisman not of destruction, but of healing.

"You didn't strike the blow yourself," Derina said.

"I misled him. I knew what would happen."

She took his hand. "So did I."

He looked at Landry and tears shimmered in his eyes. "Woundhealer would not kill, not even for our father," he said. "I wish I could have thought of another way, but there are some so maimed they are beyond the help even of a Sword of Power."

Fealty

Gene Bostwick

Templar Jarmon's eyes strained in the dim light to pick out Lord March's body. The debris-laden cellar smelled more than a little of recent enchantment, a honey odor that hung in the dusty air. Thick, blood-red wine oozed from the seams of huge casks along the basement's far wall, and rats with oddly human faces stared from the shadows. March had dabbled in strange magics.

Wide pine planks from the deck above hung down with jagged edges, and a long oak ceiling timber, roughly hewn and broad as two men, lay splintered and broken across the stone floor. One end had crushed March's chest.

A shiver ran down Jarmon's back, not entirely due to the cold. He hunched low and worked his way forward, smudging the patterns of frost that decorated crates and stores for the coming winter. His chain mail and braced leather armor were not meant for these tight quarters, but the Delfland border was close enough to demand caution. As he neared the body, something larger than a rat stirred in the shadows, and he pulled out his dagger. The rats squealed and retreated, and the shuffling noise stopped, replaced by an eerie quiet. Jarmon had heard stories of how an exposed blade could dampen the effects of magic, but he wasn't sure what had aided him here, anti-magic, or the simple threat of the weapon.

As he reached the body, he kept his dagger ready lest some residual sorcery still animated the flesh. March had already stiffened with rigor. His eyes bulged from the shock of the impact, and blood had pooled in his mouth. The tyrant was dead.

Under a shattered scrap of beam, the Sword lay nearby, still sheathed in its scabbard. March had stretched out his left hand and clutched the hilt, but he'd died before he managed to bare the enchanted blade.

The priests at the Temple of Dawn had prayed to Aurora for divine intervention against Lord March. The goddess had obliged, striking a blow before March could react. Her immense fist had shattered the small lodge, piercing roof and floor, and pinning March where he now lay. Templar Jarmon glanced up through the jagged hole, half-expecting to see her radiant face. The first stars of twilight glinted back at him.

He turned his attention to the Sword. The scabbard was splintered and torn, and what showed of the long blade glimmered with intricate scrollwork. It retained its fine twin edges despite the mayhem recently at work around it. Jarmon brushed a shred of wood aside and studied the hilt. Half concealed by March's fingers, the only adornment was a simple banner. Mindsword. The Sword of Fealty.

An urge seized him to take it up, and his hand reached out. He stopped short of touching it. "Gods devour me," he cursed, low and angry. "The temple has sworn me against you." He glared at the Sword as if it could reply. "The world cannot stand another empire from your hand."

The urge diminished, and Jarmon gritted his teeth as he set to work. He used his dagger to cut through March's arm a the elbow, a slow, grisly process without saw or hatchet. March's death-grip on the Sword held, and Jarmon slid arm and blade aside. The unearthly quiet lifted abruptly, and sounds of evening drifted down to him, cold wind in the pine trees and the flutter of bats' wings. Up the canyon behind the ruined lodge, an owl hooted twice.

Other creatures would be prowling soon, and Jarmon hurried. Starting under the arm, he sliced March's side open with his blade. The dead man's innards were still soft, and they bubbled out as Jarmon cut through belly and intestines. When he reached March's groin, he paused, sweating from the effort, and took a measure. March had been a tall man, a hand short of two meters. With the Mindsword's point shoved through his neck and into his skull, the weapon would just fit inside his body.

Jarmon used March's hand and his own dagger to set the tip of the Sword at the body's neck. A hard shove drove it upward into the head, and a final kick of his boot buried it in the cold flesh. As March's body swallowed the weapon, Jarmon lost any remaining urge to take up the Sword. Jarmon fell back, panting. His stomach churned, and the smell clawed at his throat, but he'd completed the worst of the job. Satisfied, he felt himself relax.

In the next hour he levered the beam aside and dressed March in fresh servant's clothes from the quarters above. As cold seeped into the dead body, the smell of death ebbed. He borrowed from March's finer wardrobe to replace his own splattered garments, and cleaned his mail and leather with icy water from the kitchen cistern.

March's followers had fled with his riding-beasts, but Jarmon found a small wagon and hitched his own mount to the yoke. With a blanket and a few bales of straw to cover the body, he pointed beast and wagon northward and departed

from Lord March's once-grand abode. A half moon hun
overhead, and the clear sky promised a very cold night.

Keaf crouched among the scrub oak and watched as th
young men from the village of Palmora played a rough gam
of football. He wanted badly to join in the competition, bu
Keaf lived in the graveyard hut, and at seventeen he'd jus
inherited his stepfather's profession. Gravediggers were th
shunned people, in a class with sin-eaters and demon danc
ers.

Among the players, Lane was the biggest, and he used h
size cruelly against the others. He charged into Kaye, the vi
lage barber's youngest son, and knocked the boy over int
half-thawed mud. Kaye sprang up, fists clenched and charge
after the wool-stuffed ball.

The young men didn't like Keaf hanging around, but mos
of the time they ignored him in favor of the game. Chancin
that they would leave him alone today, he toed his own ba
around in a small circle, practicing a few moves as the gam
continued. It felt good to stretch his muscles in the cold.

He'd fashioned his ball out of leather taken from
corpse's tunic, and he'd watched Lane and the others until h
knew every play by heart. He still had aspirations that e
tended beyond the cemetery fence, and in those dreams h
was one of the team, a good player, admired by his friend
Friends. Keaf had only had one in his life, his father, an
he'd buried him six months past. Time had dulled the hur
but it hadn't reduced his need for friendship.

Kaye deflected a pass intended for Lane and sprinte
down the field before the bigger lad could catch him. Tw
teammates helped finish the play, scoring easily against Eva
The moneylender's son was too slow and too lazy to real
play, but the other boys knew, even in their teens, that he wa
destined to inherit power in Palmora.

Lane stormed up to Kaye after the goal was made and cuffed him alongside the head. "Cheater!"

Keaf watched from a dozen paces away, excited at the prospect of a fight as Kaye curled a fist. "It was a fair goal," Kaye shouted.

Lane raised himself up to tower above Kaye. "I say you cheated." He swung at Kaye again. Kaye ducked, and Lane sprawled forward into an ice-scaled puddle. It was too much for Keaf, and he burst out laughing.

Lane scooped a handful of mud and flung it. Kaye dodged and laughed, and Lane came raging up from the puddle. He lunged at Kaye, missed, and landed in the mud again. When he lifted his head, he was only a few paces away, facing Keaf. His anger shifted immediately. "Damn ghoul-lover!" He flung a stone at Keaf's head and charged.

"Leave him alone," Kaye shouted. "Let's play ball." Alone among the villager boys, he never picked on Keaf, but the others ignored him and followed Lane.

They chased Keaf into the woods with hurled stones and clots of mud. One stone hit his back, but he was quick, and he was used to the forest, and he outdistanced the rest. He wound deliberately through thick brush and over fallen logs, and the shouts dwindled behind him. Well after he'd lost the others, he kept running, caught up in being a part of the group, even if it was as the prey. His father would have laughed as his foolishness and warned him not to make a habit of enjoying it. *We're shunned,* his father had often said, *but gravediggers have dignity.*

Keaf choked back other memories and kept going. Before he knew it, he cleared the far side of the woods and burst onto the cart path where he nearly collided with a small wagon.

"Whoa, boy," the driver said as his beast skittered. "Where are you rushing to?"

"Home," Keaf stammered, puffing steam in the cold air. He backed away, wondering why a riding-beast was hitched to a cart, and bowed his head. "To the graveyard," he added. A faint but familiar smell emanated from the wagon, and he glanced sidelong at the straw in the back.

The man looked at Keaf with open surprise. "A gravedigger?" He turned to the east and made a quick sign with his right hand. "Goddess, you have guided me true."

Keaf retreated another step, but the man slid to one side of the buckboard seat and motioned for Keaf to join him. "Would you like a ride, then . . . your name, boy?"

"Keaf," he said, startled. He kept his eyes pointed down at the dirt, mindful of his proper station.

"Well, Keaf, come along."

"I can't," Keaf said. "I dig graves."

"Too good for Jarmon's company?" The words didn't challenge. "I'll admit that Templars aren't well received in some circles, but I've never been ostracized by a gravedigger."

Keaf looked up in bewilderment, and the grin that lit Jarmon's face reminded him of his father. Underneath his heavy overcoat, the fellow was dressed like a lord or noble with chain mail and leather armor. A temple banner decorated his chest, white with rainbow-fringed edges. He didn't seem to understand the custom of shunning. "No, my Lord Jarmon," Keaf said, confused. "I'm the outcast one. You can't let me ride with you."

A moment later, Lane and the other young men charged out of the woods. The day was already warming, and their panted breaths dissipated quickly. "There he is," Evar wheezed. He bent low, gasping for air as he pointed with a stubby hand. As Lane led and the others advanced, Keaf jumped behind the wagon, ready to run again. The smell was worse there, and he spied the edge of brown blanket under the straw.

When Lane was a few steps away, Jarmon stood and pulled a long bright blade from the sheath at his side. "Do you have business with me?" he asked. His voice was loud and booming deep.

"Not you," Lane said. "But that ghoul-lover is going to learn who his betters are." He pointed with a thick hand, and someone threw a stone. It hit the wagon and disappeared in the straw.

"And I think my friend Keaf and I will be going." Jarmon pointed his sword at Lane's chest.

Lane stepped back. "You can't defend him, he's shunned." His voice was close to whining. "We need to teach him a lesson."

"Ten against one," Jarmon growled. "I think you'd better reconsider." He twisted the reins of his beast around a notch in the seat and hopped to the ground in one smooth motion. His size hadn't been apparent until then, but he was a head taller than Lane and broader at the shoulders. "You had better run along home and think about whom you bully."

Lane dropped his stone, and all the boys retreated before Jarmon's glare. "We'll get you, Keaf," Lane said. He turned on his heels and led his fellows back toward the woods.

After they disappeared into the trees, Keaf came around and bowed before Jarmon. "My Lord. I can never repay you."

"Well, now," Jarmon said, "I think you can." He reached over the side of the wagon and raised the blanket enough to reveal a body. "Even with the cold nights, old Wend is growing foul. I've been traveling north these past two days looking for a good omen on where to bury him, and I have found my omen in you." He let the cover fall and brushed a handful of straw over it.

Jarmon hiked himself back onto the wagon seat. "Don't waste more time, boy." He offered a hand and plucked Keaf off his feet as he pulled him up. "Now where is this graveyard of yours?"

Keaf pointed down the road. "Not more than ten minutes' walk, and then take the lane up toward the Ludus Mountains."

The riding-beast pulled them along quickly, and Keaf was glad they traveled into the wind. As they reached the trail up to the graveyard, Palmora came into view down the valley. Dormant winter air and too many fireplaces made for a band of gray haze over the jumble of cottages and shacks, but a few larger buildings stood out.

"A crossroads?" Jarmon asked.

"A branch of the Eastern Highway comes along the foothills here. It connects a few villages." Keaf rocked nervously on the seat, unused to being close to people, and especially not someone like Jarmon. At the same time, there was something familiar about the Templar, an air of quiet trustworthiness that continued to remind Keaf of his father. "The graveyard's just up the way," he said. "I can run on ahead and start digging."

"Easy, boy," Jarmon said. His huge hand found Keaf's shoulder and squeezed. "After this long, my friend in the back isn't in that big a hurry."

"Why bring him so far?" Keaf asked. As soon as he said it, he remembered his father's admonition against questioning people. *You won't like what you learn,* his father would say.

"Wend was a faithful servant," Jarmon said. "He was born near the mountains, though he never said exactly where, and he requested that he be buried near them when his time came."

As they turned up the path, a gust of wind carried the smell of rot, and Jarmon covered his mouth and nose. Even this late in the season, flies buzzed in the straw. The clouds of the past few days had gone, and the sun was at work. "It's time to lay old Wend to rest," he said.

Keaf looked back and wondered. There were plenty of mountains in this part of the country, and one hardly had to travel for two days to reach them. But he held back any more questions.

They followed the trail up to the base of steep foothills and reached the tree-shaded graveyard. A neat split-rail fence surrounded the cemetery proper. Keaf's father had worked hard to build it, to give the place a respectable quality, and Keaf maintained it out of that respect. Every grave was neatly squared off by small stones, and an orderly pile of rocks waited to mark the new digs. Keaf had seen many a body laid to rest here, and he'd buried some five souls in the months since his father had died. The ground was a series of names and faces to him, a macabre resumé of his family's works.

"I have a good spot for him," he said. "One that looks up toward the peaks."

"Fine," Jarmon said, somber now that his task was nearly ended.

Keaf hopped down and reached for the body to haul it over to the gravesite. Wend's left arm was missing below the elbow—oddly, his sleeve was neither pinned up nor cut short—and his chest looked caved in, perhaps from long sickness. He didn't look old. Keaf had him half upright before Jarmon stopped him.

"You get to digging," Jarmon said. "I'll bring him."

Keaf looked at him and frowned. "He's too many days dead. You don't want to touch him."

Jarmon's expression agreed, but he insisted. "I'll do it. Go dig."

As Keaf let the body back down he was surprised at the stiffness in the torso. Wend's head remained straight and facing forward as if it were on a spit. All the strange things about the body added up in Keaf's head, but he ignored the mysterious total in favor of Jarmon's story. His father had taught him the importance of trust, and Keaf wanted to trust the Templar.

It took little time to dig the hole. The frosts of winter hadn't penetrated very far, and Keaf knew how to break the ground and make it yield. He squared out a hole a meter and four hands deep and extra long for Wend's height.

Jarmon sat on the rear of the wagon and watched until Keaf was ready to climb out. "Deeper," he said. "I want two full meters of good soil on him."

Warning words sounded in Keaf's head. Two meters—*twenty hands,* as his father said, *was the demon's deep.* He scrambled out of the hole and gripped his shovel like a staff. "I won't bury a devil-held soul in my cemetery."

Jarmon's expression hardened. He stood slowly and drew his sword. "Lad, I will only tell you once. No devil or demon possesses this body. I have sworn on my Templar's oath to see him buried. He will rest in that hole this day, even if I have to lay you alongside him."

Trapped between Templar sword and graveyard demon, Keaf felt the confrontation smoulder. An urge told him to run, but his father's wisdom held him fast. Trouble was like a weed. The longer you ignored it the bigger it grew. He considered Jarmon's words and tried to imagine a truth that would fit them. What could be so awful, other than a possessed soul, that it required two meters of earth to bury it?

Finally, Jarmon lowered his blade. "Please, Keaf. I give

you my word as a Templar of the Goddess of Dawn. No evil
spirit possesses this body. It's just a custom in some parts to
bury bodies deeper."

Keaf let his instinct to trust the Templar win. More than
ever, Jarmon reminded him of his father, a big man whose
soft-spoken words carried truth and wisdom. He felt the tension inside him drain away, and he let out a long breath. A
little more depth wouldn't take long.

With the last of the dirt patted into place, Keaf went to select
some stones to mark the grave. Other than carrying the body
over and laying it carefully into the hole, Jarmon had
watched from the wagon seat. Now he stood.

"No stones, boy. I don't want the grave marked."

"But how will anyone know where it is?"

Jarmon let out a long sigh and ran a hand through his
graying hair. "You're smart enough to realize that Wend
didn't die under usual circumstances," he said. "I don't want
to bring his troubles down upon your head. With luck, no
one will know he's here." Jarmon pulled a small sack from
under his tunic and shook it. Metal coins clinked. "How
much do you get for a burial?"

Keaf ran a dirty hand through his hair and used the sweat
to wipe away some of the grime. "I get five coppers usually,
but this was deeper digging." He thought of demons again,
and his shoulders bunched.

"Will three gold delvars do?" Jarmon held out the coins,
large and shiny in the afternoon sun.

Keaf's lips pursed into a reflex whistle, and he nodded. He
didn't know what delvars were, but three of them looked like
a king's treasure. He hurried over and held out his hand.

"Good," Jarmon said. He let the coins clink one at a time
into Keaf's palm, then he moved to the front of the wagon

and unhitched his mount. "And I'll throw in this cart if you'll promise to lay another grave atop that one in the spring."

Keaf understood now, and he didn't argue. Wend, one-armed and stiff as a rod from waist to neck, was no servant, and Jarmon wanted to make sure that he was never discovered. A lord, perhaps, murdered and spirited away by an usurper. Or an enemy of Jarmon's temple—that would explain the Templar's presence. "I will," he said.

"You're a good lad," Jarmon said as he saddled his riding-beast. "Don't let those bullies push you around. Take them one at a time and show them you're not afraid, and they'll respect you after that."

Keaf snorted laughter. "Lane will beat me into the ground. He's done it before."

"You're quicker than he is," Jarmon said. "Big men tire fast. Stay out of his grasp for a little while, and he'll fall like any of the others." He mounted and pulled his beast around toward the path. "Take care, boy."

Coming from the Templar, it sounded sensible, like the advice Keaf's father had always given. Keaf felt a rise in his confidence that lasted until Jarmon was halfway down the road. Then he ran to hide the coins before Lane and the others came around.

Keaf lay on his cot next to the crude stone hearth and watched orange sparks dance over the fire. Quiet on the outside, inside he fought a battle with his morals. Jarmon had been gone for two days, and still all Keaf could think about was the secret he buried with Wend. In his imagination he saw not devils now, but treasure. Treasure that could mend many wounds.

The deepest scars in Keaf's life were not those from mud and stones. Shunning cut wounds that never healed, wounds in the mind and wounds in the heart. He survived as his fa-

her had, by growing a tough hide, by callousing over his
emotions and his thoughts so that each subsequent injury
hurt a little less.

Was it fair that he had to live alone and away from everyone else? Was it his fault that he'd been left on this particular
hut's doorstep, a baby abandoned? It wasn't unusual in these
parts for unwed mothers to give their children to the shunned
folk instead of the wolves, but which was the worse fate?

More than anything in life, Keaf wanted to be a part of the
village, to have companions, to share laughter and raise a
mug. And he wanted a wife. His thoughts turned to the
blacksmith's daughter, Toya, with her long yellow braids
and slender body. If he could have her, all the world would
be perfect. If he could have her? Hah—if he were rich and
powerful, perhaps. If he had Wend's treasure.

Keaf had believed Jarmon's story, not so much in the
facts, but in the message behind it. Wend carried some important secret to his grave, a secret that the Templar had
thought it vital to hide. But was that fair to Keaf, to put the
burden on him without the reward?

The waxing moon rose above the eastern hills, and a shaft
of light cut across Keaf's straw bed. Sleep was as far away as
the moon, and he rolled to his feet, pulling his tattered wool
blanket around his shoulders. Outside, the night was quiet
with winter chill. Wood smoke hung in the air, mingling with
the scent of fresh dirt. Down in the village, families snuggled
together with friendship, closeness, love. All things that Keaf
had barely tasted.

His eyes strayed across the cemetery to the fresh grave.
The frost would be working deep into the loose soil by now,
and the worms would have found Wend to be a ready feast.
And Wend's treasure would serve no one. Keaf grabbed his
shovel.

* * *

98   *An Armory of Swords*

Wend's body had collapsed under the pressure of the dirt, and his left side oozed with the stench of rotting innards. Keaf cleared away the worst of it, rising frequently to gasp cold clear air. The longer it took, the more his determination wavered. Jarmon had trusted him. Whatever secrets this body held, they were meant to remain here. But what good was treasure to a dead man, and what harm would a little prosperity do to a gravedigger?

Keaf straddled Wend and began to search. He found nothing in the ruined clothing, not even the usual bits and scraps of a servant man, until he felt along the body and discovered the gash in the left side. Something hard protruded, a knob of metal, a dagger, perhaps. Was that how Wend had died? He sucked a deep breath and tore open the shirt.

The odor of death reached out. Worms crawled in Wend's ruined flesh, and maggots thrived in festering lumps despite the days underground. Keaf stood, his stomach sick, and waited for the revulsion to pass. After the cold air cleared his head, he went for the metal knob. As he pulled, Wend's body twisted, and a meter's length of slime-covered blade slid free. From down in the village, a brief roar rose up, as though everyone were cheering for some champion.

On impulse, Keaf held up the blade, and his head reeled with a strange feeling of triumph, like a warrior at the end of a great battle, or a traveler completing a long journey. The beauty of the sword captivated him despite the filth that masked it. It was the finest metal he'd ever seen, and its edge split the moonlight like a silken thread. As he studied the small banner emblazoned on the hilt, something moved at his feet.

Wend's remaining hand moved slowly up in a death salute. Keaf slammed back against the dirt side of the deep pit. "Demon!" he screamed. He scrambled out of the hole with the sword and stumbled over his shovel. As he fell to his knees, his heart tried to pound its way out of his chest. "Gods forgive me, I've loosed a demon!"

Dry maple leaves swirled around him, and the owls up the canyon hooted frantic calls into the night. The earth between Keaf's hands heaved and puffed a wisp of smoke. A sulphurous odor betrayed the doom that stalked him. Creatures of darkness and death would take him to their deepest hell and torture him for eternity.

A scaly arm burst from the crack in the ground. Keaf pitched to the side before it clutched him, and a body emerged, a thing more hideous than Keaf's imagination could ever invent. It was the yellow of a dead man's eyes, a deranged human shape with bent limbs and bloated belly. Sulphur stench enveloped it, and a constant moan quivered within its breast.

Keaf couldn't breathe to cry out his terror, nor could he find the strength to flee. His bladder emptied, and tears leaked from his eyes. Jarmon had warned him, but he had not listened. His father had raised him to respect the wishes of others and to live by his word, but he'd done neither of those tonight. He would die a fool's death with the taste of guilt on his tongue.

The demon floated a foot off the ground and looked down at Keaf with black holes for eyes. "You summoned a demon," it thundered. A rending sound of breaking bones accompanied each word, and its face twisted through imitations of all the people that Keaf and his father had buried. "This is my death-yard, mortal. Would you have it?"

Keaf found the barest trace of voice. "You possessed Wend's body?"

"No." An agony-twisted face appeared in the bony plate

of the demon's chest, and the moaning grew louder until it vibrated in Keaf's head. "This one I possess."

The moan became a scream, and Keaf covered his ears. "Stop!" he cried. "It hurts. Please, stop!"

"At your command," the demon said. It opened its mouth, and a long black tongue reached out to carve a rent in its chest. Red ichor sprayed outward, spattering the ground at Keaf's feet. He skittered back and held the sword across him as some meager protection. The opening in the demon's chest widened, and the body of a naked woman, raw red and hairless, spilled out. She moaned as she hit the earth and raised her head to look at Keaf with bottomless red eyes. Then she lay still.

"You can have her now," the demon said. It settled back to the ground and hunched forward until its head nearly touched the ground at Keaf's feet. "What would you have me do? Bodies broken? Enemies tortured? Command my cruelty." Its voice rasped in Keaf's ears.

Keaf shuddered at the idea of choosing his own fate. Body broken? Torture? What else would the demon do to him? He hugged the sword to his chest and wept. "I beg you, spare me," he sobbed. "Go away, and I will *never* call you again. Begone to the furthest hell and spare me."

"Done!" The demon reared up tall as an oak and sucked all the fire and stench back inside its body. "Fare you carefully, lord and master," it said.

As it sunk back into the earth, a great whirlwind surrounded the graveyard, and the edges of the sky burned with fire. Keaf curled into a ball, awaiting sure death, and prayed for the salvation of his soul.

Keaf awoke with a pain in his side, and he rolled over to find the hilt of the sword caught in his shirt. Dawn was close, and a cold mist hung in the air. He sat up and rubbed at the very real pain in his temples. Inexplicably, he was still alive.

Close by, a flock of crows had gathered on the mound of dirt beside Wend's open grave. A good sign. Crows avoided demons. Looking around, he saw the woman. She lay where she'd fallen, a tangle of arms and legs and bright pink skin with alluring curves. Pink, not red, and a head of long black hair where there had been none. A crow lifted from the grave site and fluttered over to land beside her. Its beady eye stared for a moment, and then it pecked at her arm and drew fresh blood.

Keaf pushed to his feet. "Get away, damned bird!" He lurched forward on cramped legs. The crow hopped once, eyed Keaf up and down, and flew off with the others to circle noisily overhead.

Keaf knelt beside the woman and pressed a finger on the nick in her arm. The blood was warm, but she was very cold. He scooped her up—digging had given him strong arms—and carried her to his shack as the crows returned to their decomposed feast.

Rekindled fire, fetched water, corn mush and the last of a trapped pheasant, a too-large shirt and trousers to cover her nakedness. In an hour Keaf had done the meager things he knew to do, and the woman seemed to rest comfortably on his bed. Other than a twitch or two, she hadn't moved.

He settled by the fire and nibbled at the pheasant, and he had time to wonder. Last night might have been a dream except for the person now in his bed. The demon had been almost servile in the way it dumped out the woman, and it had spared him when he begged. Lord and master, it had said. But that made no sense. Perhaps the sword had scared it away. The Sword. He dropped his bowl and dashed out the door.

It lay in the graveyard where he'd dropped it, gleaming in spite of the smudges and dirt. He picked it up carefully and wiped both sides of the blade on his sleeve, fraying the coarse cloth along the sharp edges. Patterns danced deep in the metal, swirling and looping in designs that almost looked like words. Keaf gripped the hilt, and once again he felt a power within himself, and he heard the distant roar of the crowd. His father had told him stories of magic, of mighty wizards and strange beasts, but Keaf had always taken them to be fairy tales. Might as well fancy himself a king. But this Sword cried out with magic. It had to be worth very much gold.

He glanced at the open grave, decided Wend's body could wait, and returned to sit by the fire. The woman still slumbered. He planted the blade's point between his feet and leaned his chin on the pommel in what he supposed was a very royal pose. Before he knew it, he drifted off to sleep.

"My Lord."

The words nudged Keaf awake, and he opened his eyes to find the woman kneeling at his feet. As she bowed her head, her long black hair fanned forward to touch his moccasins. Words stuck in his throat, and his mouth hung open. The woman looked up and smiled, and her face went from ordinary to beautiful.

"You saved me," she said. Gold flecks twinkled in the dark green of her eyes, there was an earthy aroma to her that was not bad. "You banished Gemlech."

"I did?" Keaf didn't remember it that way. "Are you all right?"

"After two hundred seventy-six years in a demon's chest?" She stretched her arms and scratched at the sides of her head. "I could be worse."

Keaf watched her body move and his heart galloped with a

different sort of terror. He'd never been so close to a living woman, and though he'd explored a few dead bodies, she was an exotic mystery to him. He fumbled a cup of corn mush from the pot and snatched the pheasant's carcass from near the fire. "Are you hungry?"

She looked at the grimy mush and greasy bird and nodded. "If my Lord is through."

"I'm just Keaf," he said, embarrassed by her words. "Please, take what you want."

"My name is Dellawynn." She sat back on her haunches as she took the pheasant and tore hungrily at it.

"I don't know how we survived last night," Keaf said. "But I saw you come from the demon's chest."

Dellawynn's look grew distant. "I caused a lot of mischief once. The gods wanted to punish me."

"I thought that monster was going to kill me," Keaf said. "Something must have changed its mind."

"It was you," Dellawynn answered through a mouthful of mush. "You made him give me up and banished him."

Keaf was dubious at best. And Dellawynn's reaction seemed to fit in a fairy tale. The princess is rescued by the prince, she is eternally grateful, they fall in love, and live happily ever after. This would be the middle part.

"If I may ask, my Lord," Dellawynn said, "when do we depart for your castle and keep?"

Keaf looked around his hut and felt his elation at having a woman's attention collapse. This was where she discovered he was a gravedigger, a shunned man. He pointed wordlessly at the hut's bleak walls.

Dellawynn's eyes followed his gesture. She set down the pheasant's bones and empty bowl, and a small sigh escaped her lips. "If this is your home, then I know my purpose. I will help you get a castle." She reached out and touched his knees, leaning forward so that Keaf saw the curve of her breasts. She was much more woman than Toya, the blacksmith's daughter. "I once brought the kingdom of Delfland down in fire, and I made the Prince of Borhas give up his crown," she continued. "Getting you a castle and servants and treasures shouldn't be too difficult, and I will be your queen if you will have me." She looked down, but the hint of a smile lingered on her lips.

"But this is all I have," Keaf said. "I dig graves."

"Why don't you go somewhere else then? Start over?"

Keaf had once asked his father that same question, and the answer had made him proud. *Only a decent, honest person can be a gravedigger,* his father had said. *Any lesser man would run from the responsibility and the burden.* Keaf believed that to his soul. "I am Keaf," he said. "I dig graves. I don't know how to be anyone else."

"Then I shall serve you here, if that is your wish. I am bound to you, and I cannot think but thoughts of you." Dellawynn's hands slid up his legs and found his groin. Less than gently, she tugged at him and reached for the twist of rope that held his trousers.

"Wait!" Keaf sprang to his feet and pulled his belt tight. Dellawynn's boldness scared him worse than demons. "I think I need to tend the fire. . . . I have a grave open. . . . I have to wait. . . ."

Dellawynn managed to look understanding. "I have offended you, my Lord. I will go make myself better able to serve you." She stood and bowed like a noble. "May I have your leave, my Lord?"

"Please," Keaf stammered. "Don't go on my account. I mean you . . . you can if you want, but you don't have to."

"I think it best for now," she said. She marched to the door and was gone.

* * *

Keaf was nearly done refilling Wend's grave when a stone hit him in the back. The pain made him turn, cursing, and he saw Lane, fat Evar, and three other village boys at the cemetery fence.

"Digging up your supper?" Lane sneered. He reared back and let another stone fly, sailing it high over Keaf's head. Evar's throw was better, but Keaf deflected it with his shovel.

"Is that shovel your sword?" Lane asked. He kicked at the fence and knocked loose the top rail.

Keaf dropped his shovel, ready to fight. A stone caught him in the elbow, and a sting ran like fire up his arm. He snatched up the rock and hurled it back as hard as he could. It caught Evar square in the forehead, and the boy dropped to the ground.

"Damn you!" Lane shouted, and they charged.

Keaf dashed for his hut and slammed the door behind him. As he leaned against the coarse wooden slab, he looked desperately around the room. The hut had no other exit, no windows, and only a small chimney hole in the roof. And he could never hold the door against four people. Pushed by fear, he grabbed the Sword as the door burst inward.

The boys stopped, Lane with his fist raised to throw, as Keaf held up the Sword. "I didn't mean to hurt him," Keaf pleaded. "It was an accident. I'm sorry. . . ."

Lane lowered his hand, a look of surprise plain on his face. "We should be sorry, Keaf. I mean Master Keaf. Can you ever forgive us for attacking you?"

Keaf couldn't discern any sign of a trick. The other young men dropped their stones and cowered behind Lane with their heads lowered. One of them began to recite a prayer of repentance. Keaf had never held a real sword before, and he understood suddenly why Templars and knights garnered such respect. The mere sight of the weapon could cow one's enemies. "I'll use it," he said uncertainly.

Lane turned pale and backed into the others. "We'll do anything," he said. "Just tell us."

Keaf wondered if he'd changed somehow, if the weapon in his hand made him look bigger and stronger. He took a step forward and leveled the blade. "Get out of my hut and my cemetery, and don't come back."

The group rushed to depart, knocking the door off its hinges. Keaf hurried out and called after them. "Don't forget Evar. Make sure he's all right."

One of the young men darted over to Evar's side and helped him up. Evar staggered sideways, blood flowing down his face. "Damn," he cried. "Did you see what he did to me?"

Lane rushed over, nearly choking with horror. "Quiet, Evar! Can't you see that he's a great warrior? You'd be lucky to lick his boots!"

Evar paused, holding his head, and then remarkably, he agreed. "Oh . . . I see. I didn't know. . . ." The others hurried him away, glancing backward as they went down the trail. Remorse filled their eyes, and something akin to sorrow.

It was a look that Keaf knew too well.

Keaf sat in a patch of warm sun on the hillside above the cemetery, the Sword across his lap. Confusion twisted his thoughts like wind swirling through the fir trees. If there was magic within the blade, it seemed to affect everyone but him. Or perhaps only him. Would he know if he were under an enchantment?

Learn to use it, or get rid of it as quickly as possible. Two choices, one hard decision. Krohn, Evar's father, would have the money to buy it, but Keaf didn't think it wise to approach the man just now, not after this morning's fight. Use it, then. But he was no warrior, and he had no desire to be one. If this

blade could win him friends, well, that would be one thing,
but he suspected that the sudden change in Lane and the others wouldn't last, and they would be back, angrily in search
of vengeance.

Best then to put the Sword away, somewhere safe and well
hidden, and search out a buyer. Three days east, there were
mages in Arnon City, and there was the Red Temple a week
to the north. It would be a long trip, but frozen ground
would soon idle him until spring, and he could hunt along the
road as easily as here, perhaps better.

His plans set, he started down the hill. Halfway to his hut,
he heard a whining voice and spotted two people coming up
the path from the village. If they were coming to punish him,
they were fewer than he'd expected.

He hid in the shadow of the trees until he recognized Dellawynn's long black mane. She'd found other clothes, leather
skirt and laced sandals, a sleeveless tunic of purple cloth, and
a wide belt that glinted with silver. And a sword that she held
at a man's back. It was Krohn, Evar's father, and he whined
steadily about abduction and false pretenses.

Keaf trotted down to the cemetery fence. At the bottom
end of the graveyard, Dellawynn stopped the little man's crying with a poke of her sword.

"My Lord," she called to Keaf, "I have brought you this
swine from Palmora. He's the richest man I could find in that
sty of a village, and he can help build your castle."

Krohn looked around for someone other than Keaf. "You
said he was a king. You forced me all this way to meet this
worthless gravedigger?" He turned red with anger. "I demand you release me. I am a powerful man. . . ."

Dellawynn poked him in the chest with a finger, and he
stumbled and landed on his backside. "What shall I do with
him, my Lord Keaf?"

Keaf hurried over, hoping he could make amends with

Krohn before the whole village was up in arms. The little
man scooted backward from Dellawynn and bumped into
Keaf's legs. Keaf could smell his fear like oily sweat.

As Krohn looked up, he spotted the Sword in Keaf's hand,
and his expression changed. "My dearest young man!" He
climbed to his feet and clasped Keaf by the shoulders. He was
a full head shorter, in part because of the crook in his back
that some said was from hunching over his money box too
long. "I had no idea that you wanted a castle. I think it's the
finest idea I've ever heard." He turned a rusty smile on Dellawynn. "And you! You might have told me that this fellow
was royal blood. Obviously, he's been sent out to prove himself among us common folk."

Keaf thought he'd been confused before, but this was unbelievable. "I'm sorry about Evar. I didn't mean to hurt
him. . . ."

Krohn's laugh grated like the chatter of the crows. "Forget
that lazy boy. He needs to learn manners, and he should
know better than to bother a gentleman like you."

Dellawynn prodded Krohn again. "What about that treasure?"

"Certainly. If Master Keaf would like, I can bring it up
here. It's quite a pile of gold." Krohn's face pinched in
thought. "It might be safer to keep it in my strong boxes and
simply give you the keys."

Keaf had heard of insanities and maledictions of the mind,
but he'd never seen anyone afflicted. Maybe this was Krohn's
secret to wealth. Total madness. "You're most kind," he said
as he detached himself from the small man's grip. "But
maybe you'd better go home now. Your family will be worried." He looked at Dellawynn, hoping she'd understand.
Sooner or later, Krohn would come to his senses, and
then . . .

Krohn's expression dropped, and Dellawynn stepped up to take his arm. "I will see that he gets there safely, my Lord Keaf." She licked her lips, and mischievous fire danced in her dark eyes as she unbuckled a finely tooled leather scabbard from her side. "And then I will come back to serve you." She stepped up and strapped the leather around Keaf's waist, and her hands lingered on his hips a bit longer than necessary.

Keaf swallowed hard and motioned them away. As Dellawynn and Krohn tramped back down the trail, he thought he was beginning to sort out this day's madness. Somehow the demon had changed him so that everyone saw not Keaf the gravedigger, but a great lord, maybe even a king. At his hut he grabbed the water bucket and set it between his feet. As the water settled, he bent to look at himself.

No majestic features, no special fire in his hazel green eyes. Nothing different. Just the adopted son of a gravedigger with a smudge on his left cheek and stubbly hair on his chin. He sat down hard and shook his head. Was it the Sword then? He picked up the blade and examined its mottled surface. The faint roar resounded, from a distance, and yet from within the metal. Could it affect men's minds? It seemed a stretch of imagination, but Keaf knew little of such things.

At arm's length it glimmering, beckoning. Let the crowd cheer for Keaf the gravedigger. Let them pay for shunning him and his father and all those like him. Let them see how it feels to be less than worthy, less than equal. He shook his head to clear away the ugly thoughts, and slid the Sword into the scabbard. Maybe he could learn its power, but he would have to be careful how he used it.

Keaf paused at the edge of the village as angry voices rose in a commotion from below. His self-confidence faltered as he imagined a mob preparing to come for him, but he was deter-

mined to discover what magic he held sheathed at his side. If
he was right about the Sword, no crowd could withstand it.

On the main street, he spotted the mob outside the inn.
Innkeeper Ganton was Lane's father, and he stood tall above
the others as he raised a sickle overhead. Cornered against
the wall, Dellawynn faced them defiantly while Krohn cowered behind her.   •

"You stole that sword from one of my patrons," Ganton
said. "And left him without a stitch of clothing."

"She threw stones in my mill when I would not give her
bread," old Hagga added. Welk, the thatch-cutter, accused
her of seducing his son. Dellawynn had been busy for one
day.

"Harlot!" another old woman shouted. "She's cast a glam-
our on Krohn!"

A stone flew and hit the wall near Dellawynn's head. She
slashed with her sword, but the crowd didn't back down.

"She'll have to be burned," Ganton said. Welk held up dry
bristle and thatch, ready to light.

Ignored, Keaf marched to within a dozen steps of the mob
and planted his feet. "Stop!" he shouted over the noise.
"She's with me!"

Heads turned, and mouths gaped. Someone laughed and
lobbed a stone that fell short of Keaf's feet.

"Get back to your graves," Ganton sneered. It was easy to
see where Lane had gotten his manner.

Keaf held his ground and pulled out the Sword. As he
raised it, the sound of cheering drowned out all other noise,
not with volume, but with undeniable energy. "I command
you to leave her alone," he said.

Incredulous looks turned to adoration, and those nearest
to Keaf knelt to the ground. Murmured praises rose up—my
lord, my liege, prince, and king—and Keaf knew that any of
them could be true. He only had to wish it.

"Ganton," he called out.

The big man stepped forward and pulled his cap from his head so that the balding spot showed as he bent low. "Sir?"

Keaf reached into his pocket and tossed a gold coin at the man's feet. "I'd like your best room for the night."

"Any room, my young master," Ganton said, bending for the coin. "The inn, if you desire it. I would gladly make it a gift to you."

Keaf listened for strain in Ganton's voice, some indication that he suffered for his sudden devotion, but his words were completely sincere. A consoling magic, at least for those it spelled, but it robbed Keaf of much of his feeling of vengeance. He supposed he could command them to suffer, even to inflict suffering upon each other, but that would bring no better satisfaction, and it made him feel uneasy to realize it was possible.

Dellawynn joined his side, and the crowd cheerfully escorted them into the tavern hall of the inn.

"I had no idea who you were before this," Ganton said. At the serving bar he ordered his bartender to pour his best brew.

"A king's son," Krohn declared. "He must be out to prove himself." He waved a finger at Keaf and grinned. "You can't fool us, young sir."

"Or he's on a mission," Ganton said, pulling at his ruddy beard. "Are you on a quest, Master Keaf? We can help, you know. We can do quite a lot here in Palmora."

"I only want a room and a good meal," Keaf said. Those were enough to demonstrate his newfound power.

"And so you shall have them," Ganton said.

Lane and Kaye returned with a freshly killed silver boar, and a feast was declared in Keaf's honor. He'd tasted bitter ale once or twice, but the heady stout that Ganton served made the room too warm and the laughter too easy.

Every girl of the village knelt at his feet to praise him during the course of the evening, including Toya, who seemed far too sweet to be bound by magic. Dellawynn chased them all away in between teasing the men. Keaf basked in the adoration, sure that he'd finally discovered the secret to friendship.

Late in the night, as the room began to spin, chamber servants carried him to his room and laid him to bed, and Dellawynn was there, warm and soft and faithful as he passed out.

Keaf began the morning by puking in the vicinity of the chamber pot. He staggered back to bed and fell across it before he realized that Dellawynn was still there, rolled in the covers. She shifted against him, and one hand tousled his hair while the other slid between his legs. Startled, he pulled away, but dim memories—her excited cries, her nails raking his back—told him he hadn't shied earlier in the night. He flexed his shoulders and winced.

As he sat up, a knock sounded at the door.

"Who is it?" he asked. For a moment he pictured reality breaking in, Ganton hauling him out to be whipped in the square, a line of villagers hurling insults and stones. Instead, a young chambermaid peeked inside.

"I have your bath water drawn, my Lord, and fresh clothes waiting." She opened the door a bit wider, and Keaf saw more servants with steaming pots and a large oblong tub.

The bath was a truly wonderful experience, even when the maid got a little fresh with her scrubbing. Dellawynn awoke and watched from the bed, giggling when he squawked about the soap in his eyes or the coarseness of the bristles on his tenderer parts. Breakfast was fresh berries that someone had spent the night obtaining from a city to the south, and cream that clotted on Keaf's fingers. Afterward, in fur-trimmed trousers and ermine-collared shirt, with jewels on his belt and fine leather boots with real heels and soles, Keaf found it easier to believe in his new superiority.

The villagers had been busy while he slept. Krohn's manor was no castle, but it was the biggest house in Palmora, and it included a stable with six fine riding-beasts. Krohn had moved into another abode, displacing the family that rented it from him. His staff, now at Keaf's disposal, was determined to polish every bit of the manor before their new lord arrived. An entourage of Ganton and Krohn and every other important man of the village accompanied Keaf to the front gates, and they waited patiently while he made an absurd show of inspection. He knew no more about manor houses than he did about being a king, but the people hung on his every word and leapt to fulfill his every request. No one grumbled.

Through the morning, during a lunch of rabbit, fresh bread, and red wine, and into the afternoon, Keaf was attended and administered and fussed over. The local magistrate only visited Palmora once a month, but now Keaf became the village judge. A farmer came to ask him what to do about a wolf that had been raiding his wool-beasts over the last few days, and an angry wife dragged in her husband, accusing him of dallying with another woman. Keaf suggested a hunt for the wolf—Kaye had done it before, and he volunteered—and he sent the husband to stay home with his wife for a week. Everyone marveled at his wisdom, and a scribe wrote down his every word. Dellawynn grew tired of it before noon, and begged excuse to go find whatever mischief she could. Keaf had come to understand her well enough to know that she thrived on challenges, and he made everything too easy. He also knew that she would be back.

While Krohn was presenting his riding-beasts for Keaf to select one or all, news came that an old man who'd been sick for some days had died.

Ganton interrupted Krohn with anxious words. "Master Keaf, this is a serious problem."

Keaf nodded. He was the only one in the area suited to bury the fellow. "I understand." He cracked his knuckles and flexed his shoulders. It would be good to do the digging after two big meals in one day.

As he started away, Ganton stopped him with a gentle hand on his arm. "My Lord. Your disguise is ended, and your mission is far too important. You need only tell us who is to replace you as the gravedigger. I would gladly take the job myself, but my back is not what it used to be." He reached behind and made a poorly faked grimace of pain.

Keaf stood there stunned. All adoration aside, it had never occurred to him that he would no longer be digging graves. He had assumed that he would simply be the best-treated digger in the land.

But Ganton was serious, whatever mission he thought Keaf was on, and Krohn and Lane and the others looked genuinely worried that he might actually do something besides let them serve him. "N-no," he stammered. "You shouldn't do it, Sir Ganton. Get someone younger." A malicious choice came to him, and he spoke before he considered more. "Let Lane do it."

Lane stepped forward, looking grim and huge. "I am honored," he said with total sincerity. "Thank you for thinking of me." He turned and lumbered off in the direction of the cemetery with a whistled tune on his lips.

Keaf watched him go, and he almost yearned to follow. The irony of casting Lane among the shunned had a second edge. Power took as well as gave, and it had just taken away

Keaf's purpose in life. He would have to work at finding a new one.

By evening, Keaf was growing convinced that his new occupation was to give his followers someone to follow. He was waited on and tended to with unerring devotion, and the village seemed happier than he'd ever seen it. They had purpose as never before. And they used up their small supplies of food and stores as never before.

During the supper feast, travelers arrived seeking room and board for the night. Their leader, Baron Mallorin, was a dashing figure, a young nobleman from the Western Empire. Ganton couldn't offer them his best room, but he made his second best sound even better. While he and the baron bargained at the serving bar, Dellawynn sat beside Keaf and stared.

"I should see to your new guest," she said as Mallorin glanced around the tavern hall. Even his smile gleamed. Dellawynn had discovered a silk dress that left her stomach enticingly exposed and did fine justice to the rest of her. A Gypsy dancer had left it at the inn sometime past, departing under hurried circumstances that Ganton did not speak of around his wife.

Keaf was growing impatient with Dellawynn's roving eye, or maybe there was little else to rouse him, and he let his irritation show. "Wait until the baron comes to greet us," he said. "Then we'll see who best captures his interest."

Dellawynn sat back pouting, but her eyes remained on Mallorin. As Ganton concluded his arrangements, he took the baron's arm and led him toward Keaf. The villagers had set up two fine chairs on a raised platform of rough planks, and from there Keaf held his meager court. Meager but absolute.

The hall grew quieter. Mallorin's brow wrinkled, assessing and speculating as he met Keaf's gaze. When he looked at Dellawynn, his expression turned hungry.

"Lord Keaf," Ganton said, "may I present Baron Mallorin from the Western Empire."

Mallorin bowed slightly. Keaf stood and drew his Sword. As the distant cheering rose up, the baron dropped to one knee. "My Lord," he said. "I did not know that you possessed one of the Twelve Swords. Allow me to pledge my eternal allegiance." He bowed lower and offered his glove.

"You see," Keaf said to Dellawynn, loud enough that everyone heard. "He serves me, and none of my followers would ever go behind my back to you." He took the glove and tossed it beside his chair.

Dellawynn's pout melted away as she gazed at the Sword. "It was wrong of me to ever think it," she said. "Serving you is all I ever want."

Keaf sighed as he put the Sword away. Too easy. Everything was too easy, and everyone was too doggedly obedient. Contemplating bigger challenges, he motioned Mallorin to sit. "You know this Sword?" he asked.

Mallorin nodded. "It is one of the Twelve, forged by the Gods in the mountains north of here. I held the one called Sightblinder for a short time. Anyone who looked upon me saw a different face."

"And this Sword?" Keaf patted his side but left the blade sheathed. "It seems to work a similar magic."

"No," Mallorin said. "The Sword of Obedience was made for you to wield. In another man's hand it might make him seem great, but that would be delusion. In your hand it only confirms what my heart tells me. Once you throw off this cloak of meager birth, you will be the ultimate ruler, a god among us."

A shiver ran down Keaf's back. To hold such power in a

single blade? He'd seen practically nothing of the world in his short life, but now it was his for the taking. That was irony beyond measure, that a gravedigger could rule the Earth.

"Thank you, Baron," he said. "You may attend to your dinner and your duties. We will talk more in the morning."

"I await your call." As Mallorin steered himself back to the serving bar, Dellawynn sat quietly, her hand light on Keaf's arm.

The evening wore into night, and Keaf drank more stout and more wine. Mallorin had put visions in his head, visions that went far and promised much. Visions that made Keaf's desire for simple friendship seem ridiculously small. As he staggered off to bed, there was a knot in his stomach and a cloud in his head.

"Please, my Lord Keaf, I beg you, wake up."

Keaf wasn't sure how many times he heard the whispered words before he understood. He raised his head and lowered it again as drink-inflicted pain thrummed through his skull.

A servant girl stood at the foot of the bed and begged him to rise. "It's urgent business, the man says." She pointed to the door. "Your welfare is at stake, he says, and he must see you tonight."

Keaf reached out to tell Dellawynn that he'd be back, but she wasn't there. He rubbed at his forehead and felt the ache at his temples. "Get me a drink of water," he rasped.

The girl slipped out and returned a minute later with a mug. The water was cool and sweet, and it reduced the fire in Keaf's belly. He sat on the edge of the bed, holding his head while she worked him into pants and shirt, tied on his boots, and draped a cloak over his shoulders. "Please, my Lord." She urged him up, guided him down the corridor, and they slipped out the door into the night.

As the cold hit him, Keaf's head cleared enough to realize

his oversight. He'd left the Sword behind, and all of his loyal followers were asleep. He grabbed the girl by the arm. "Damn, girl! Fetch me my Sword!"

She darted away.

"You shouldn't have dug it up," a deep voice said from the dark.

Keaf turned to see Jarmon step from shadow into moonlight. "Templar?"

"You've been busy," Jarmon said. "News of a great new lord has traveled as far as the Temple of Dawn." His sword rang as he drew it from its sheath.

"I-I'm sorry," Keaf stammered. He stepped back as the servant girl returned with the Sword still in its scabbard. She knelt at Keaf's feet and stood the blade against him.

"Begone, girl," Jarmon said.

She looked at Keaf, and he nodded her away. After she'd gone back inside, he reached for the Sword's hilt.

"Don't," Jarmon said. His voice was tight with warning, and a stone-hard look glinted in his eyes.

Keaf pulled his hand back. "I didn't know it was magic. Truly, I only thought to sell it for a few gold pieces."

"I doubt you'd get that for it," Jarmon said. "A kingdom, an empire, maybe the whole world, but not a few gold pieces."

"I'm sorry," Keaf said, and he'd never felt any emotion stronger in his life. "I only wanted to make them like me."

Jarmon stepped forward and wrapped a mailed fist around the Sword's scabbard as he touched the point of his weapon against Keaf's chest. "And I paid you to do a job. I trusted you."

The words cut twice, like the twin edges of the Sword. Jarmon had expected trust, but he hadn't shown it himself. And Keaf had broken the trust that he'd accepted. He believed in trust and integrity, things that his father had taught him to value, and he'd looked upon Jarmon as a noble man. The truth was, they'd both failed. "You didn't trust me at all," he said, letting his shame translate into anger at the Templar. "Otherwise, you would have told me about the Sword. You tricked me into burying it."

Jarmon drew back his sword, and the look in his eyes softened. Before he could answer, an arrow whizzed past Keaf's head and pierced the heavy leather padding at the Templar's shoulder. The impact knocked Jarmon back, and the Sword fell at his feet. Keaf turned to look for the bowman, and Kaye charged out of the darkness with another arrow nocked.

"Get back, Keaf," he shouted. "I'll defend you."

Jarmon reached to tear the arrow free and growled deep in his throat with the pain. Keaf sprang for the Sword, but Jarmon's boot caught him in the chest and sent him sprawling to the side. Kaye's next arrow shot past Jarmon's head and hit the wall of the inn with a dull thump.

The Templar didn't wait for a third arrow. He wrapped both hands around his own sword and advanced to attack. Kaye pulled out his hunting knife and planted his feet, apparently willing to die for Keaf.

Keaf's chest ached from the kick, but he managed to roll to his feet. "Stop!" he shouted, but only one man there was bound to him.

Kaye froze, torn between defending Keaf and obeying him, and Jarmon struck. His sword slashed across Kaye's left hand and knocked the knife away with a trailing spray of blood. Kaye fell back clutching his wounded hand as Jarmon stepped over the Sword to deliver another blow. Keaf had only an instant to react, and he lunged.

He hit the Templar in the knees and knocked him off-balance. Jarmon stumbled a half step sideways and his blow missed Kaye's head by the barest margin. Keaf grabbed for the Sword. Before he could unsheathe it, Jarmon twisted, off-balance, and swung his blade. The blow tore the scabbard from Keaf's hands and sent it cartwheeling upward. The Mindsword slipped from its sheath. Moonlight caught the spinning blade, and it seemed to hang in the air for an eternity.

The sound of the roaring crowd echoed off the black outline of the mountains. At the edge of the darkness, Dellawynn appeared with a gash in her leg and her small sword badly notched. Dripping blood, Kaye reached for his knife, and Jarmon's mailed hand reached for Keaf's neck.

As the Sword reached the top of its arc and began to fall, Keaf saw the fight that would ensue, saw that it would end in death. And he saw the Sword gleaming with its strange designs written for gods and not for men. Not for men.

He pushed away from Jarmon and sprang toward the Sword. The Templar snagged him by the foot to stop him, but Keaf's right hand reached far enough. Far enough for the tip of the blade to slice through flesh and bone and pin his palm to the hard ground.

He shrieked with pain and curled around his skewered hand as Jarmon and Kaye regained their feet. Jarmon took a step toward Keaf, but he stopped as Dellawynn raised her weapon.

"Leave him alone," she warned.

"He's hurt!" Jarmon snapped as he backed away. "That cursed blade."

"It's that blade that you were going to kill him over," Kaye said. He held his wounded hand inside his belt and circled to trap Jarmon between himself and Dellawynn. His eyes strayed to Keaf, but as much as he wanted to help, he had first to defend his master.

Keaf struggled to his knees, each movement an agony as his impaled hand flexed, and he curled his fingers around the hilt of the Sword.

"I must help him," Jarmon said. As he dropped his guard, Dellawynn moved to strike.

"No!" Keaf cried as he yanked upward. His shout froze Dellawynn and Kaye, but not Jarmon. The Templar threw his weapon down and rushed to Keaf's side as the Sword came free. Keaf started to collapse, but Jarmon's strong arm caught him.

"My liege!" Jarmon cried as he pulled off his glove and tore out the cloth lining. "I have been a fool!" He reached for Keaf's wounded hand and pressed the cloth against the flow of blood. Another wave of pain made Keaf nearly faint.

Kaye and Dellawynn recovered from their shock and leapt to help. Kaye stripped off his woolen vest to drape over Keaf's shoulders, and Dellawynn added her scarf to the temporary bandage.

"I'll get help," Dellawynn said. She started toward the inn, but Kaye stopped her.

"This way," he said, motioning down the main street. "Lara is the village midwife. She knows medicines."

As they hurried off, Jarmon slipped out of his heavy coat, exposing the bloodstain at his shoulder. He draped the wrap over Keaf, and its lingering warmth eased a little of Keaf's misery. Tears welled in his eyes, and he turned away from the Templar.

Nothing had turned out right with the Sword of Fealty. Three people were hurt, and Keaf felt more alone than ever before. If he kept the Sword, he wouldn't be able to trust anyone not under its power, and he could never afford friendship. His one dream would remain forever out of reach.

He turned to face Jarmon. "Why did you do this to me?"

Jarmon bowed his head in shame. "I was blind to your greatness, Master Keaf. I hope you can forgive me."

"But this," Keaf said, lifting the Sword with his good hand. "What about this?"

"In my heart," Jarmon said as he tapped his fist on his chest, "I believe it is a bad thing. You would be better off without it. Then people could see your true noble nature without magical deceit."

Keaf shook his head. Jarmon was as spellbound as the rest, but there was a truth in his words that the Templar could not see. The truth was that the Sword enslaved its owner as surely as it enchanted those around him. "For my own good."

"Yes," Jarmon said. "I have seen what it does to those who wield it."

"Servant Wend?"

"Servant Wend, Lord March. He was an unfortunate man, ordinary where you are extraordinary, and that magic blade brought him to ruin."

Keaf felt a shiver, not from the cold. Lord March! His land holdings were well known even in Palmora, and he conferred with kings and emperors. Such a man might have been able to rule the world with the Mindsword in his hands. Yet he now lay in an unmarked grave.

"Bury it before it harms you," Jarmon pleaded. "Bury it demon's deep where no one will dig."

Keaf heard footsteps on the road, and he forced himself to sit up straight. "Please, go home," he said quietly to Jarmon. "I release you from any service to me."

Out of the darkness, Dellawynn, Kaye, and old Lara arrived with clean cloths and a doctor's satchel. Kaye's hand had been bandaged, but Dellawynn's leg still seeped blood.

Lara muttered with each step. "I don't see why I couldn't

fix your leg. . . . And that hand needs more than a wrap of
linen. . . . Cold night to be out trapping wolves. . . ." She saw
Keaf, and her eyes grew wide for a moment before she returned to her interior dialogue. "Cold night for a lord to be
out. . . . Need a warm hearth and strong brandy. . . ."

She passed by Keaf on her way to the inn. Jarmon helped
him to his feet. Inside, Ganton appeared in his long night-
shirt, and he was mortified to see Keaf hurt. He offered drink
and food and had his servants stoke the fire as Lara began
her work. The old woman fussed over Keaf, crabbing to herself about kings and nobles and why hadn't anyone told her
it was Keaf. She tended Dellawynn and Kaye next, and came
back to fuss over Keaf some more. He finally insisted that he
was all right, and she left, still muttering.

A stiff drink of brandy loosened some of the knots, and
Keaf sent Ganton and the servants back to bed. Ganton offered anything from his considerable stores, and Keaf si-
lenced him by ordering a repayment to everyone who had
used their supplies over the last two days. After a dozen more
assurances that they had done everything they could to make
him comfortable, the staff retired.

Next, Keaf looked across the tavern bench at Jarmon.
"Go, now, Templar," he said, repeating his earlier dismissal.
You have duties to attend at your temple." He smiled at Dellawynn. He would miss her, but he knew she would leave as
soon as she was no longer Sword-bound, and he wanted to
set her on a better course than the one she might choose herself. "And you go with him. I think you could use some time
in a temple."

"But Master Keaf . . ." Jarmon said as he stood.

"A temple?" Dellawynn asked.

"You will be serving me by going," Keaf persisted. "I'm
counting on both of you."

Jarmon and Dellawynn looked injured, but neither could disobey a direct command. "As you wish," Jarmon said.

Dellawynn slid around the table next to Keaf and kissed him harder than she might. "I will miss you, Master Keaf. She turned to Jarmon and linked her arm in his. "Temples are quite wealthy, aren't they, Sir Jarmon?" Where she'd walked with no trouble a little earlier, she now let him ease her weight on her bad leg. Keaf hoped he wasn't sending Jarmon's temple too much trouble.

After they'd gone, Keaf turned to Kaye. "Thank you," he said.

"It was nothing," Kaye said. "I was out hunting the wolf that's been after the wool-beasts. I saw you were in trouble, and it was my duty to help."

Keaf held up his right hand and felt it throb. "It looks like we're both useless for a while."

Kaye raised his left hand. "One pair between us." His voice was flat, but his face showed worry. A man's hands were his living in these parts.

"Maybe we can work together," Keaf said. "I could use your help yet tonight."

"Anything, Master Keaf. I'm here to serve you."

"Not service," Keaf corrected. "I want your help working with me, not for me."

Kaye looked beyond tired, but his Sword-driven enthusiasm still ruled. "Command me."

Keaf shrugged. There was no stopping the power. "Jarmon made the mistake of not trusting me, but I won't do that to you. We're going to bury this Sword," he said softly, lifting the blade from the bench.

"It's a fine weapon," Kaye said. "Why throw away such a thing?"

Keaf pushed to his feet. "Let's head for the cemetery, and I'll tell you all about it."

Kaye nodded and stood. "I appreciate your confidence in me, Master Keaf."

Keaf smiled. "We'll be friends after tonight or not, but either way we'll share a trust." He slid the Sword carefully into a loop of his belt, and together he and Kaye headed out into what remained of the night.

Dragon Debt

Robert E. Vardeman

The gleaming, impossibly sharp sword slashed so close that Trav Gorman jumped back in panic. The blade swung around and the fifteen-year-old couldn't take his eyes off its steely meter-long length. For a brief instant it split sunlight into a delicate fan of colors, then came whirring back at him. This time he forced himself to remain rigidly immobile, no matter the cost to his nerves.

The little crowd of onlookers drew in breath, as the dragon-slaying blade lightly touched the young man's earlobe. Trav had thought it would be warm with its special Vulcan-forged magic. Instead, it was as cold as any ordinary metal blade.

"And that's how I slew the last of the great dragons preying on my village of Hues," Kennick Strongarm boasted loudly. The tall, muscular man twisted his wrist slightly and the god-forged Dragonslicer dropped heavily to Trav's shoulder, as if conferring knighthood.

But such was distant from Kennick's mind—and Trav's. Trav's face burned hotly with shame at showing any emotion. Kennick, to bolster his own image, seemed to do all he could to disgrace Trav, and today was the worst yet with half the village of Slake looking on. Worse than this, Trav's sister Juliana stood just behind Kennick, laughing at her brother's discomfort.

"You're so brave," Juliana said, hanging on to Kennick's sword arm. "Tell us again. How many dragons have you slain with this marvelous weapon?"

"Eight," Kennick said, puffing up and turning to slide the blade back into its gaudy sheath. Trav couldn't tear his eyes from the blade. Its length was encrusted with gems the size of his thumbnail, and the silver wire-wrapped handle seemed made for Kennick's huge grip.

"I thought you said nine," spoke up Trav's father, Merrow Gorman. "I definitely counted nine in your tale."

"Eight, nine, I lose count in the heat of battle. There has never been such a weapon as Dragonslicer," Kennick said, again whipping out the blade and holding it high in the autumn sun. His dramatic gesture quelled more questions, but Trav saw only reflected glory in the blade and nothing in the wielder. "And the gods have granted its power to *me!*"

"Juliana," Trav said, trying to pull attention from Kennick. "We were on our way to gather berries."

"You go," Merrow Gorman told his son. The man was slightly stooped from too many years of desperately hard work in fields that produced too little. His lined face, more leather than skin after the long sweltering summer, beamed with approbation for the newcomer. "Let Juliana have some time with the champion of Slake."

"Champion!" cried Trav. He spat angrily. "He's no champion. He's only—"

Merrow Gorman slapped his son and sent him reeling. "Don't speak of Kennick that way. Don't forget that he carries one of the Twelve Swords forged by Vulcan. For that alone, he deserves your respect."

Trav saw the fear in his father's muddy eyes—and hope,

hope that was seldom there of late. To marry his only daughter to a hero, a slayer of dragons, commanded his ambition and imagination. The opinion of a fifteen-year-old boy with no particular skill nor hope for apprenticeship mattered far less to him at the moment. And Trav had to admit the glow in Juliana's tanned face was more than adulation.

It might be love. That rankled more than any prolonged emptiness in his belly. He was the only one who saw Kennick for what he was.

An unexpected ally hobbled up, what remained of his left leg bound in dirty rags. Wyatt leaned heavily on his crutch as he shouldered through the small crowd.

"Did I hear someone mention Dragonslicer? I know that blade!" He looked about him, but Kennick had already resheathed his weapon. "Let me tell you of the time—"

"Not now, Wyatt. Spin your miserable tales some other time. We want to hear Kennick," interrupted Merrow Gorman.

"I have *seen* Vulcan's blade," protested the village storyspinner. "I—"

"Who wants to listen to made-up stories when we have a real champion to tell us what it is like fighting dragons?" Juliana's eyes were only for the paladin in his fine clothing. She ignored Wyatt as a man who told tall tales to supplement his meager income from cleaning the muddy streets of Slake and performing other, even less desirable jobs.

"I *know* dragons. I have seen them. What does this one know of the biggest dragons? Nothing. Come and listen. Sit and I shall tell you of glorious lands and magical weapons and . . ." Kennick, after giving the old man a glance of amused contempt, had turned away. No one else paid Wyatt any attention. The old man spat, the spittle hissing as it struck the ground.

"Why can't you see what a liar Kennick is?" Trav mut-

tered as he, too, backed away, bumping into Wyatt and almost knocking the one-legged man into the mud. No one else
heard his mumbled retort. The village of Slake was as short
on dreams as Merrow Gorman, and dreams were what Kennick offered with his wild tales. Trav ran through the village,
passing no great houses, no fine stores brimming with mer-
chandise such as in Westering and other big towns. Worst of
all, he passed too many deserted homes, miserable sod huts
left empty by the withering sickness that had held Slake hos-
tage for three long months.·

Tears welled in the corners of Trav's eyes as he thought of
his lost mother and three brothers. He brushed the wetness
away. There was work to do, and standing about lionizing a
stranger who had come to Slake only a week before accomplished nothing. Trav could only wish his sister saw with
clearer vision. He didn't want her hurt. She and his father
were the only family he had left.

"A braggart, that's all he is. Well fed because foolish people listen to his stories and believe them and give him food to
be lied to again!" Why was he the only one who heard the
hollowness of Kennick's tales?

Trav knew the answer and it burned inside him like a festering wound. The people needed a hero to take their minds
off their dreary, dangerous lives, and even Wyatt's wild tales
had turned stale and predictable over the years. The withering fever and poor crops and the demon that had ravaged
Slake a year earlier, all had broken spirits and made any diversion welcome. And Trav knew his father wanted Juliana
to marry well. No man under the age of forty remaining in
Slake qualified. Those unmarried were all dim, dirt poor, or
crippled. A wandering paladin expertly swinging one of the
Twelve Swords—the Sword of Heroes!—seemed a miracu-
lous opportunity.

"But he *lies*," moaned Trav, going over the conflicting tales Kennick had spun. The braggart had a story-teller's knack, all right. With each repetition the tales grew like tumors, and always so that the teller fought greater battles and triumphed more heroically.

Trav slowed his run and turned toward the chain of S-shaped lakes that gave the village its name. Half a hundred streams fed the lakes, and he had found his special place along a streamlet ignored by others in the village. Leaves were turning into a rainbow of shimmering colors, and a sharpness hung in the air from dying summer and birthing winter.

Walking along his special stream, he found the black- and red-striped berries that would supplement their meals for months after the snows came. Trav gathered slowly, picking with care, trying to forget his father and sister and Kennick and the entire village. Surrounded by the forest, he dared to imagine life being better.

Movement at the edge of his vision caused him to stop his work and whirl about. The gnarled, black-barked limbs of a walnut tree vibrated and a few dead leaves fluttered softly to the ground.

"Who's there?" he called. Trav put down his capful of berries when he heard a distant crashing sound, as if something heavy had fallen through the leafless tree limbs. Investigating, he moved forward warily through brambles, soon reaching the edge of a small clearing, where a streamlet came wandering through to form a glade of beauty.

And amid the beauty stalked death. Not thirty meters distant, its back fortunately to Trav, its long barbed tail twitching nervously, there lumbered a dragon of such immense size that Trav turned white with fear.

Shaken, he backed away for several meters, then turned

and ran. How long he ran, Trav couldn't say, but he eventually stumbled onto the Slake-Westering Road. He knew where help lay. With legs rubbery from fear and long exertion, he rushed into his village and found Kennick sitting with Juliana beside the public watering trough.

"Dragon!" he blurted, gasping. Kennick turned, gave him a sour look and continued his witty discussion with Juliana.

Trav's sister turned and gestured angrily at him. "Go away, Trav. You're bothering us. I must tell Kennick of available lodging. He intends to stay in Slake!"

Trav saw Dragonslicer in its hand-tooled leather sheath leaning against the trough and started to reach for the weapon. Kennick snatched up the magical sword and laid the long blade across his lap.

"Don't go telling stories, boy," Kennick chided. "There aren't any dragons in these woods. I've already killed them all." He laughed and returned to romancing Juliana.

Trav backed off, not knowing what to do, where to go. But some dark instinct drew him dragonward. He ran hard back into the woods, braving the gathering darkness and chill rising wind. He found the streamlet and worked his way up it. The closer he got to the meadow, the slower he crept and the harder his heart pounded.

At the edge of the clearing Trav looked around warily, suspicious of the silence. The huge dragon had departed. A milky whiteness in the sluggishly flowing stream caught his eye. Trav dropped to his knees and cupped his hands, scooping at the water's surface and coming away with dozens of small, slick-coated spheres. In the darkness, they shone with a cool opalescence that Trav had never seen before. Holding one up, he fancied he could see shadows drifting within. Opening his palm, he let one egg rest there, only to have it dance and roll about, impelled by inner magic.

Trav scooped more tiny globes from the streamlet and

broke open a few. A pungent yellow-and-white fluid gushed forth.

"Dragon eggs," he whispered. He had never seen one before, but he had heard the tales, the fearful warnings. "The she-dragon was laying eggs in the stream." Fish were feasting on them already.

He looked at the slick of millions of dragon eggs and saw not untold misery and destruction but opportunity. Trav carefully gathered a select small handful of the eggs and went looking for a cool, wet, hidden nest.

Winter wind whined past the tumble of rocks Trav had pulled into the mouth of the cave. Small sweeps of crystalline snow blew past the rock and stopped a few feet from the nest Trav had built. Cave mice had eaten most of the eggs, but he had saved a few. Keeping them damp had been easy for the first few weeks. Small drips running down the cave walls formed puddles deep enough to cover the eggs, but Trav had worried when, after a month, the eggs began drying out in spite of his care. The shells had turned a mottled brown and hardened—and a few weeks earlier, just before the first heavy storm brought blankets of clinging wet snow, the shells began cracking.

Trav sat on the cold floor and poked at the four dragons weakly tumbling over each other, looking more like bugs than the land behemoth that Trav knew had laid the eggs. He picked up the smallest of the clutch, a dragon hardly larger than the end of his thumb.

Holding it aloft, he peered into the unfocused yellow-slit eyes. Trav stroked over the dragon's head, marvelling at brown scales softer than fleece covering the miniature body. A tiny black tongue flicked out of a mouth too small for Trav to insert even his little finger.

"You're so tiny, you're a nothing," he said, cradling the

dragonlet in one hand. With more bitterness, he added, "You're just like me. Piddling. Nothing more. The runt of the clutch." Trav smiled slowly and said, "That's *your* name. Piddling." He laughed with delight and allowed himself to imagine that the yellow eyes had fixed on him with childlike adoration.

Trav put Piddling back into the tiny puddle and watched the dragon stumble and fall, splashing water everywhere in its uncoordinated attempts to stay upright on mouselike feet. Picking up another dragon, Trav recoiled when the beast made a savage snap at his finger. The small mouth failed to circle his finger, but he felt bony ridges scraping his skin. He dropped the green-and-gray dragon back into the puddle. The dragon glared at him, then turned and snapped at Piddling, frightening the smaller dragon.

"You are the biggest," Trav said, "and will grow up larger than the Great Worm Yilgarn." He pushed Piddling away from the more combative dragon. "I'll call you Yilg. And you," he said, poking another dragon, "you are ferocious and the stuff of legends. You will be the one to challenge Kennick Strongarm." Trav spat the name. "I'll call you Grendl."

The fourth dragon curled its long, thin tail around itself and went to sleep, oblivious to the struggles between Grendl and Yilg. Piddling stood to one side, watching its brothers fight, with what Trav interpreted as anticipation and anxiety on its expressive face.

"And you, sleepy one, I will name Drowsy." The sleeping dragon snorted and rolled over, never waking.

Trav got his feet under him, rubbing his freezing hindquarters. He worried that the cave was too cold for his small charges, yet they seemed to thrive. A small dark insect scuttled along the cave floor. Trav grabbed quickly, trapping the carnivorous pig-bug. The scavenger bug went into frenzied motion when he dropped it between Yilg and Grendl. The two newborns snapped at the pig-bug and each other. The larger Yilg won after a brief but fierce skirmish, gulping the bug down whole and looking for more.

Trav had already caught several more torpid pig-bugs and dumped them where the young dragons could feed. "Enjoy your dinner," Trav said, his own belly growling. He watched, marveling at how different the four dragons were. When they had finished their feast, Yilg and Grendl turned on the smaller Piddling.

"Hey, stop that," Trav said, picking up the small dragon and holding it close. Piddling hissed slightly, and Trav jerked in surprise. The dragon had burned him with a tiny spark from its nostrils.

"So, you're growing," Trav said, knowing a full-sized dragon could burn down a house with a single flare. "Let's see if this puts out your fire." He carried Piddling to the cave opening and dropped the young dragon into a snow bank. The dragon floundered about, legs thrashing. Then Piddling snorted real flames.

Trav grinned and finally applauded his small ward. A plume of steam rose from the superheated snow. Piddling lapped at the puddle he had created, backing off when it froze against his tongue. A second gust of flame was larger, stronger, and created a veiling curtain of steam.

Trav watched in silence. It would be some time before Piddling—or even Yilg or Grendl—grew to a size capable of battling Kennick, but the day would come. Dragons grew quickly. Trav would enjoy watching the swaggering dragon-killer face a real opponent.

Trav shivered hard, trying to keep his teeth from clacking. Juliana lay on the far side of the room, a blanket thrown over her quaking body. The way she shook gave the only sign that his sister still lived. The unnatural quiet after the storm had settled both inside and out, preventing them from getting outside for more than a day.

"Where is he?" muttered Merrow Gorman, walking painfully back and forth across the small room in a vain attempt to keep himself warm. "Kennick should have been here by now."

Trav tried to speak but his teeth began chattering. He wanted to tell his father that Kennick wasn't likely to return from Westering if it meant any discomfort. He might have promised to bring wood and much-needed food, but Trav would believe the dragon-killing paladin when he saw tangible proof. Warm proof. Food proof.

"We need wood for the stove," Trav got out. "We cannot last another night. It is still now, but cold, colder than I can remember."

"So fetch the wood," snapped his father. "There is no way to get to the woods and chop enough to last more than a few hours, not in this damned cold." He looked at their pot-bellied metal stove, long since cold from lack of fuel. "Why your mother wanted that monstrosity is a mystery to me. A good stone fireplace would serve us better."

Trav wanted to point out that any heat would be appreciated, but he lacked the strength to argue. He saw from the way his father's left leg increasingly dragged that he would be unable to gather firewood, even if a new storm wasn't threatening. And Juliana was in no condition to move. All she could do was lie under her inadequate blanket and mutter Kennick's name from between gray-blue lips.

Trav pushed to his feet and went to the door. Snow had drifted high, leaving only a small, open rectangle of wan daylight at the top. He burrowed a few minutes, ignoring his father's orders to shut the door. At last scrambling out onto the crusted snow, he looked out over a land that had been totally altered. Slake had vanished, save for a few chimneys sputtering fitful puffs of smoke. Gone was the poverty and the horror of the past months; replacing it was a blinding whiteness, a snowy renewal that brought beauty and threatened death.

Trav pulled his thin coat tighter around him and began trudging toward the distant woods. It was far to go, too far. The easy wood had been collected long since, and he had scant notion what he might do once he found decent forest. His father had traded their axe for two bushels of grain, on Kennick's advice. The grain had proven of poor quality and hadn't lasted nearly as long as Merrow Gorman had anticipated when making such an extravagant exchange.

Razor-edged wind began blowing, and ice crystals slashed Trav's exposed face. He pulled a long, woolen scarf woven by his mother over his mouth and nose. The cold still insinuated itself and slowly paralyzed both body and brain.

Hardly knowing where he walked, Trav blundered across the ice-encrusted lakes and up the streamlet toward the cave where, he was sure, his baby dragons must have frozen by now. It had been weeks since he had been able to tend them.

Trav broke through the tough rind of snow over the cave mouth and was met by a blast of hot air. He rocked back, the sudden heat painful against his frozen cheeks. For a moment, he thought some strange volcanic activity had warmed the cave. Then he realized the heat came from the dragons' own magical internal fire. The dragons huddled together, their considerable fiery breaths splashing against rocks until they glowed red-hot. The dragons then settled down and basked in the radiated warmth.

Trav scrambled gratefully into the warmth of the once-cold cave. He hunkered down and stared at the beasts. It had been a month since he had tended them, but they had thrived.

Trav reached out and waited for the cat-sized Piddling, identifiable only by facial markings, to waddle over to him and nuzzle his frozen hand.

"You've done well for yourselves," Trav said, picking up the dragon and stroking its head. The dragon snorted and made growly noises. Trav no longer felt softness in the nut-brown scales. Piddling made no move to wiggle free of his grip. The dragon turned its head up, as if begging to have its chin scratched. Trav started to run his fingers along the neck and belly but Piddling snapped, yellow eyes glaring.

"So, you've developed a personality," Trav marveled. He saw Yilg and Grendl sitting near their heated rock, but nowhere did he see Drowsy. He stood and walked around the cave, hunting for the fourth hatchling. He paused when he saw the tiny skeleton at the rear of the cave.

"The winter has been cruel," he told Piddling. The dragon growled and snorted again, this time snuggling closer to Trav's chest. The youth jumped when an unexpected spot of heat burned into his coat. Trav rubbed at the charred area Piddling's fire breathing had sparked. The dragon peered up at him again, and this time Trav at least imagined that he saw affection in its expression. Like a dog marking territory, Piddling marked its with fire.

An idea formed in Trav's cold-numbed brain. Of the dragons, Piddling was the smallest and most amenable to handling. Trav wasted no time stuffing Piddling under his coat. He winced as sharp scales nicked his flesh, but he didn't want the dragon exposed to the bitter cold outside—it would either kill the hatchling or provoke dangerous blasts of flame.

Darkness had settled over the still fall of snow and the wind had died, leaving behind a glacial temperature. Head down, Trav made his way back to his home, trying not to get turned around in the dark. Everything looked different with a meter of snow covering familiar landmarks. Hours later, his feet turned into numb lumps of frozen flesh, Trav found the cold chimney of his family's hut.

"In," called Trav, "let me in." He knocked on the closed door but got no answer. Again and again he banged, to no avail. Frantic, Trav burrowed down through snow until he reached the latch. The door opened with a suddenness that sent him tumbling into the still, cold interior.

For a ghastly moment, Trav thought both Juliana and his father were dead, but their slow, tortured breaths left faint, feathery trails in the air. Trav went to the iron stove and clanged open its door. He carefully drew Piddling from under his coat. The dragon shivered with the exposure and crouched inside the stove, eyes wide and questioning.

"Here, Piddling, try this," Trav said, giving the dragon a small amount of the household's remaining grain. The dragon sniffed at the kernels and turned away. Trav shivered with the cold and remembered dragons did not eat grain.

But what could he feed the carnivorous dragon? No bugs or mice were visible.

There was only one source for the needed meat. Dazedly Trav slumped to the floor and began pulling off his boots. His toes had turned blue from frostbite, too numb for any feeling. He had seen frozen digits on other folk, and these were dead. Trav placed a knife against his smallest toe, closed his eyes and shoved down hard. For a moment, he dared not look—it hardly seemed that anything had happened. Then Trav saw he had severed not one but two of his toes and had never felt the pain.

"Here," he said, placing his severed toes inside the stove next to Piddling. The dragon sniffed at them, then stared balefully at Trav, as if asking permission. Trav felt a giddiness from shock at what he had done. He waved a hand, hoping Piddling interpreted the gesture properly.

The dragon sniffed some more, then began daintily nibbling, using its rudimentary claws as hands to hold the frozen meal. Trav tried to turn away but watched in rapt horror and fascination as Piddling cleaned his toe-bones of all meat. Then the dragon belched a powerful flame that spread inside the stove. Not content with a single short blast, Piddling kept up the flame until the iron glowed dully. Then the small dragon settled down to eating the second digit Trav had given him.

Retreating a little from the glowing stove, Trav did his best to bind his foot. Then he pulled his father and sister closer to the stove. They stirred, then turned toward the heat. The hut would soon be warm enough, and would stay warm for a time.

Especially after Trav fed Piddling four more frozen toes.

"A great day, it is," said Merrow Gorman, briskly rubbing his hands together. "It is a truly great day for an engagement."

"Father, please," said Juliana, blushing. "Kennick doesn't want any fuss over our betrothal."

"I'm telling the entire town!" Merrow, despite his bad leg, almost danced about the small room, now lit with warm spring sun pouring through the door.

Trav stood painfully and hobbled outside. He couldn't bear the notion he had saved his sister from freezing—*Piddling* had saved her—just to marry Kennick Strongarm. The small dragon, nourished on occasional bugs and food scraps as well as frozen human flesh, had continued warming the iron stove for a week until the cold broke. Trav had not offered his father and sister any explanation of his heating system, nor had they demanded any. Neither did they seem curious about where Kennick had spent the winter.

Trav had returned Piddling to the small cave, where he had made sure his three remaining dragons were well fed with insects and a small rabbit that might have gone into his own stew pot. Those dragons would be Kennick's undoing. When they grew larger, Trav would use them to show the paladin's true colors. Dragonslicer was a fierce, magical blade, but the wielder was weak. Why couldn't Juliana see that? Why couldn't his father?

Trav hobbled out of his house into the sun, then paused. From behind the sod hut not twenty meters away, Trav saw a hunched-over figure watching him. The village smith and his family had all perished during the winter, and their house had been taken over by another. For some reason, Trav was startled to recognize the old story spinner, Wyatt.

"You hobble along, Trav," observed Wyatt. "You will end up like me." He spat, the gob hissing where it struck the ground. Trav retreated a pace, not wanting to be near the ragpicker. Sometime during the winter, Wyatt's face had become covered with thick, scaly patches, giving him a repulsive, almost reptilian aspect.

"My feet were frostbitten," Trav explained tersely, not wanting to engage in conversation with the old man.

"Wait, don't go." Wyatt's voice carried a startling snap of command. "You will be cursed if you continue on your course."

"Whatever are you saying? Is this another tale? I have no money, so save your breath."

"No tale, no tale. I, too, know Kennick for the liar he is. I know dragons, and I know Dragonslicer. Oh, how I know that blade!" Wyatt edged closer, his crutch making sucking sounds in the soft ground as he moved. In a conspiratorial whisper, he added: "Dragons will eat more than your flesh. They will steal your soul."

"What do you know about it?" Trav felt a growing uneasiness. Had Wyatt spied on him?

"I know more than you will ever know—I hope." Wyatt

tried to grab Trav's shoulder and hold him, but the youth slipped away. Wyatt called after him, "I know! Let me tell you a true tale for once. A dragon ate my leg! It ate my leg, and I killed it with Dragonslicer!"

Trav shook his head and walked as fast as he could to get away from the crazy old man. It was a shame Wyatt would say anything to regain the audience—and coins—stolen from him by Kennick's tales. In a way, Trav felt betrayed. Old Wyatt was the only one in Slake who also thought Kennick was a fraud. Still, some of the old story-spinner's words struck a chord in Trav's conscience.

What he intended to do with the dragons was dangerous, but he did it for a good reason. Trav was sure that if Kennick was faced with a dragon of any size, he would turn and run.

On his maimed feet Trav now needed a long time to make his way to the cave. Along the way he picked up a few choice bugs, special treats for the dragons. He approached the cave with some trepidation, worrying about Wyatt spying on him. He ducked in.

The dim light wasn't sufficient for him to see at first. Only slowly did his vision adjust. The musky smell of nesting reptiles came to him—and more, something he could not place.

Trav jumped when something hard and sharp rubbed against his leg. He helped and grabbed at the scratched place before seeing that it was Piddling rubbing against him.

"Piddling!" he cried in genuine glee. "You have grown so!" Trav knelt and held the dog-sized dragon's head in his hands, not moving to stroke or pet as he had once done. "I have a treat for you. And for Grendl and Yilg." He pulled the pig-bugs from his pocket and held them out.

Trav jerked back when Piddling snapped ferociously, one fang impaling the pig-bug before it hit the floor. The dragon ate noisily, then turned yellow eyes to him begging for more.

"I want you to share," Trav said, but he gave the hungry

dragon another bug. As Piddling ate, Trav hunted for the other dragons. He found one, small and huddled at the rear of the cave. Trav frowned and tried to identify the dragon. It might have been Grendl, but he thought it was Yilg. Of the third dragon, he saw no trace.

Trav dropped a few squeaking pig-bugs and the small dragon—he finally identified it as Yilg—avidly devoured them, but something was wrong.

"You are so small compared to Piddling," Trav said in wonder. The runt had grown twice as fast as his egg mates, leaving the once large Yilg far behind. Yilg was hardly bigger than he had been in the midst of the winter storms.

Trav winced as Piddling rubbed against him once more, begging for more bugs. Trav pulled the last one from his pocket, looked from Yilg to Piddling and back. He dropped the bug between them. Piddling snorted once and sent a gust of flame in Yilg's direction. The smaller dragon backed away and let Piddling eat uncontested.

Trav went to the mouth of the cave and looked around, concerned about possible hiding places a spy might use. Something crunched under his foot. White bones, well-chewed, were scattered around the mouth of the cave. Most had sunk in deep mud, partially hiding the remains, but it was obvious the dragons inside had begun foraging on their own.

A moment of fear surged through Trav, then passed. He had known how dangerous the dragons were when he had rescued their eggs from the stream. If they hadn't been, Kennick would never be shown for the coward Trav knew he was. The dragons were not as deadly as those allowed to grow up in the wild, away from human contact. These were—still, perhaps—more pets than predators. But had he really done the right thing nurturing Yilg and Piddling?

Trav didn't know.

* * *

"Please, Trav, listen to my words," Wyatt pleaded. His eyes, something inhuman about them, glowed a dull ocher that reminded Trav uncomfortably of his dragons. Trav looked at the tight knot of villagers gathered around Kennick and Juliana and wanted to join them, if only to shout denunciations.

Wyatt whispered to him, pleading. "Believe me. I might tell stories for a few pennies, but there is truth in much of what I say."

"What? That a dragon bit off your leg?" In other times, Trav might have been interested. Now he wanted only to get to his special cave and tend his reptilian wards.

"More. I lost the leg just as you did your toes."

"I told you, that was frostbite," Trav said in a flat voice.

Wyatt ignored the response. "I swung Dragonslicer. I used the true Sword to kill my dragon." He sniffed hard and wiggled his scaly nose as if scenting the air. "The Sword is magical."

"Yes, yes, I know," Trav said, distracted.

"I still have it," Wyatt said unexpectedly. Trav stared at him. Wyatt rushed on: "I was entrusted with the true Blade. The one Kennick calls Dragonslicer is a piece of trash. It looks no more like the real thing than I resemble Kennick." Wyatt spat out the words contemptuously.

"I must go." Trav's head was buzzing with wild stories. He had things to do and didn't want Wyatt around.

"They kill!" Wyatt shouted after him. "They are creatures of evil! I spent my life killing them, but they killed me. Look at me. Look!"

Trav gazed back over his shoulder. "I see an old fool, fit for nothing but to muck stables and clean privies. And now no one wants your yarns!" Trav's anger was directed inward as much as it was toward Wyatt. He was being forced to admit to himself that raising the dragons had been wrong.

The old man hobbled on after him, still speaking in low tones no one else could hear. "Trav, Trav, I *killed* dragons with Dragonslicer. That is no yarn. But the burden was too great." Trav, fascinated despite himself, could not tear himself away, as Wyatt pursued him. The old man sobbed: "In pride, in madness, I even thought to have a dragon for a pet. But the beasts cannot be controlled. I became like them. I killed dragons until I was no longer able, then I put aside the Sword."

"Enough!" Trav clenched his eyes shut, refusing to listen, refusing to think. "You are old, ancient. You have no business following me." He opened his eyes into a silence.

Wyatt was standing with his head cocked on one side. Bright eyes looked out of his hideous face. "You go to the cave? They're not there now. Both are out killing."

Trav felt a hand of ice clutch at his heart.

Wyatt went on: "They range farther now, out to slay humans. I have watched them growing this past week. Quick, very quick. Out on the road this morn, the bigger one killed a riding-beast—and its rider."

"None will believe you."

"Why do you nurture them? Why do you loose them on the country? Can't you see their evil? *Feel* it?" Wyatt straightened, surprising Trav with his height. The two were on a par in both height and girth. For the first time, Trav feared the old man.

"Whatever your reason, you are the one who must undo the evil you have created. The Sword—" Wyatt coughed and pointed, with a finger gnarled as an old tree root. "It is hidden—" He broke off, coughing so hard he couldn't stop.

Turning his back on the momentarily helpless man, Trav

hobbled away as fast as he could. Wyatt might destroy all he had worked for. Piddling and Yilg weren't killers. Not in the way Wyatt claimed. He, Trav, had raised them, and they were gentled to humans. That wouldn't stop the pair from intimidating anyone who lacked a backbone. Kennick would never stand and fight a pair of dragons, even ones hardly larger than a dog.

Instead of visiting the cave, Trav wandered for hours through the spring woodlands, thinking hard. Kennick might hear Wyatt's accusation of Trav raising dragons. No matter that Piddling and Yilg were still small. It was time for him to expose Kennick as the coward he must be.

Returning to Slake, Trav's resolve hardened when Kennick rode into the village on a fine new riding-beast and a tooled saddle chased with silver. Kennick jumped to the ground and embraced Juliana.

As Trav hobbled up, he heard the paladin say, "Juliana, my love! I am glad you are safe! There is a dragon marauding along the roadway. I feared for you."

"With you here, there can be no danger," Juliana said, adoration glowing in her eyes. She clung tightly to him.

Trav wanted to spit. Instead he hurried forward and said loudly, "I've seen the dragon. I know where it lairs."

"What? What's that you say?" Kennick spun, his face suddenly pale. He touched Dragonslicer's hilt, fingers drumming nervously. The fear in the champion's face was all Trav might have hoped for, but Juliana still did not see it.

"Less than a day's walk from here," said Trav.

"You do not joke?" Kennick tried to recover his composure. To Trav's critical eye, he failed. Trav dared not let the paladin escape now that he had set the hook. One look at a real dragon and only Kennick's dust would be seen in Slake.

"You must face the dragon, or Juliana will be in jeopardy. You spoke of depredation."

"But it was far from here. That way. The reports—" Kennick swallowed hard, and Trav reveled even more in the man's discomfort. Revenge was sweet.

"Only Dragonslicer can slay this dragon." Trav's voice prodded the reluctant hero. "I can show you the cave they—it—lives in."

"No, Kennick, don't go!" cried Juliana, true fear in her voice for the man she thought she loved.

"He must!" Trav prompted, as innocently as he could. "Otherwise, who can tell what the dragon might do to Slake?"

Kennick moved his lips as if his mouth were dry. But the man managed to summon up some courage. "Then come with me, youngling. Show me this dragon, and I'll slay it." He turned to Juliana. "I dedicate this creature's death to you, my love."

They kissed, and Trav for a moment was tempted to snatch Dragonslicer from Kennick's sheath and end the farce.

Moments later, Kennick had grabbed Trav's arm and was hoisting the youth behind him in the high-backed saddle. They charged off, Trav doing his best to hang on while he gave directions. He had to admit riding was superior to hobbling along on his mutilated feet.

In less than an hour, Trav and Kennick were dismounting in front of the dragons' cave.

Kennick Strongarm stared at the cave entrance but made no move to approach it more closely. In a low voice he said, "It hasn't the look of a dragon's lair about it. I know. I've seen dozens." The man struggled to keep the quaver from his voice. He fingered Dragonslicer again, then drew the sword and advanced on the cave. Kennick stopped outside and called, "Come meet your death, vile beast!"

"You'll have to go in after the dragon," Trav said, enjoying the paladin's fright. "I'm not sure a dragon understands our language."

"They are clever monsters," Kennick said, but he didn't argue. He edged forward, hand trembling on the sword's handle. Kennick looked back at Trav, a glare of hate and desperation, then plunged into the low cave. Trav saw fat blue sparks explode from the steel blade as Kennick swung wildly at nothing, striking rock.

Then there was only silence.

Trav frowned. Yilg ought to be growling and Piddling snorting fire—or Kennick screaming in abject fright. There was nothing. Trav shuffled toward the cave mouth and peered inside. It took a few seconds for him to understand what he saw.

Kennick stood over a dragon's skeleton, but plainly the champion had not killed the creature. The flesh had been stripped from these bones some time ago. Looking closer, Trav saw that one of the creatures he'd raised—perhaps Yilg?—had been eaten. The gnaw marks on the gleaming white bones were unmistakable.

"What did this?" Trav asked, confused.

Kennick's voice was hoarse, but had regained some strength. "It matters little. The dragon is dead. Once more I have triumphed!"

"You've done nothing!" cried Trav, outraged that Kennick would take credit for an accident. "You can't claim any honor in finding a dead dragon." He tried, physically, to stop Kennick from taking the skull as proof of death, but failed. The man was too strong for him.

"Walk back, youngling," Kennick ordered with satisfaction, hurrying from the cave and mounting his riding-beast. He never looked back as he held his trophy in his lap. Trav grumbled and started walking home as fast as his feet would take him. Anger burned away pain. He returned to Slake almost as quickly as if he had possessed a full set of toes.

But he did not return to the celebration he thought sure to be in progress. The village was deserted. Even during the withering fever, some people had been outside, wandering the muddy trails between the pitiful dwellings. Not now.

Frowning, Trav made his way to his home and stopped at a little distance. The roof had been burned off, leaving only a charred shell.

"Father!" he called. "Juliana! Where are you? What's happened?" Trav rushed to the door and peered into the charred husk of building. He blinked in surprise when he saw Kennick huddled in the far corner, arms curled around his knees and mewling pitifully. Taking a single step, Trav stopped and then vomited.

His father's body, burned and dismembered, had been partially eaten by monstrous jaws.

"It was a dragon, a big dragon," moaned Kennick, his voice unrecognizable. "When they eat human flesh they grow huge quickly."

"Where is Juliana?"

"I don't know, I don't know."

Trav spun when he heard feet pounding behind him. His relief was boundless when he saw Juliana. Her dark hair was disarranged, and she was flushed, but unharmed. It was up to him to tell her of their father's death.

"Juliana, wait," Trav said, trying to keep her out of their house.

"I know he's dead, Trav, I know. I saw it and I ran and hid. The dragon! It's half the size of this house, and it's coming back." Juliana pushed Trav out of the way and dropped to her knees in front of Kennick.

She grabbed him and shook him hard. "Kennick, you've

got to fight the dragon. It's vicious! Terrible! And it's coming
back!"

"No, no!" Kennick threw the sword from himself.

"Kennick, you must. You're our only hope. The dragon
feeds constantly on us. It . . . it's out there!"

Trav looked from Juliana to Kennick to the monstrous
dragon lumbering outside, heading toward them. It shocked
him to see, by the pattern of facial markings, that the marauding dragon was Piddling, the once-puny hatchling.

Giving a last frantic look at his father's half-eaten body,
Trav scooped up Kennick's fallen sword and ran outside,
screaming. He swung Dragonslicer as hard as he could,
counting on Vulcan's magic to pierce the thick brown scales
on Piddling's chest.

The blade glanced off, not even scratching the outer surface. The recoil staggered him and for a moment he stared up
into the dragon's yellow eyes. Trav wasn't sure what he read
there. Not anger. Not malevolence. It was more like surprise
or even delight.

Piddling roared and let out a long belch of flame that
surged above Trav's head. He ducked low and swung. Again
the blade bounced off the dragon's hide. This time Piddling
spun with startling speed and caught the blade between im-
posing jaws. The dragon's neck muscles tensed, and the
sword shattered like glass.

Trav stared at the sundered blade shining on the ground,
then backed off from the dragon. He stopped and stood his
ground.

"Piddling, here," Trav said, reaching into his pocket, pulling out a crushed pig-bug, and holding it in a surprisingly
steady hand. The dragon bent, and its darting black tongue
flicked across Trav's palm. The pig-bug vanished.

Trav didn't know what to feel. In the shock of his father's

death, all he could think of at the moment was that Piddling had probably killed Yilg, Grendl, and Drowsy, cannibalizing its own kind to grow this large.

"Trav, get back," called Juliana.

"No, wait, I—" Trav screamed when Piddling moved with dazzling quickness and caught Juliana in heavy jaws. The girl screamed once before being broken in half.

Trav's mind snapped. Dragonslicer had failed against Piddling; he beat at the dragon's haunches with his bare hands. Somehow, this attack made Piddling stop his feasting and turn his head with its bloody jaws, staring at him with wide, questioning yellow eyes. Then Piddling snorted flame and walked away slowly until he vanished into the gathering twilight.

Trav sobbed. He wanted to kill himself. He couldn't bear to look at the thing that had been Juliana. He was responsible—and all because of Kennick.

"Kennick!" he cried. Suddenly he had a target for his towering wrath. He hobbled to his burned-out house and looked around wildly, trying to find the object of his hatred.

"He's gone. Saw him running away toward Westering. Might be there by now, the way he was running."

"What?" Trav whipped around, fists balled and ready to fight, to confront Wyatt's hunched figure.

"That wasn't Dragonslicer. I carried the true Sword and know. He lied about everything." Wyatt spat a gray-green gob that hissed on the ground. He grimaced, displaying blackened, broken teeth, then coughed. The rattle sounded deep in his chest.

"Go away. Let me be." Trav wanted to strike out, and now there was nothing to hit.

"Kennick was a fool and liar, a blowhard who never saw Dragonslicer. That's not even a good copy. A jeweled blade—bah! Too long, not sharp enough—and lacking in any god-forged magic. And those gems. Fake. Fake, just like Kennick."

"You are as big a liar. You never held Dragonslicer."

"Take this," Wyatt said, shoving into Trav's hands a long package wrapped in old, cracked oilcloth.

Before Trav could reply, he heard Kennick's loud shout. "That's him. He's the one. He's a demon! He commanded the dragon to do his bidding!" Kennick, advancing, stumbled at the head of a dozen people, most from Slake but a few Trav had never seen before.

Trav jerked around to face Wyatt. "You? You're a demon?"

Wyatt coughed and spat. "Would a demon take such a sorry form? No, my young fool, he means you. He's damning you. You might not be a demon, but you're responsible." Wyatt sank down, amid a loud crackling of joints. He shivered, though the air was warm, and stared at Trav.

"You'd best run, my boy. They want someone to blame—and you know you are responsible. You *know* it—and so do I."

"I didn't mean for all this to happen." But Trav darted away as fast as his feet would take him, clutching the package Wyatt had forced upon him. The stumps of his toes, never well healed, turned bloody with his relentless flight, but he never stopped or looked behind him. If there was any pursuit, it fell behind. Slake was a world carried to the far side of the moon and beyond. His life was gone, his family, his friends, everything gone. He ran without knowing where his feet took him until he fell to the ground, exhausted.

It might have been the next morning or the next or even the next when he opened the package and realized where his destiny lay. The instant Trav touched the sword, he knew that Wyatt had told the truth.

On this plain, black hilt in bold relief there reared a small, white dragon, and the keen steel blade gleamed even in the pre-dawn darkness, catching the smallest ray of starlight and magnifying it until the weapon shone brightly. Even real jewels would have been superfluous. Trav, though no magician, could feel the latent power as he swung the Sword and listened to the shrill whine, a beautiful keening that tore at his senses and made him want to cry with pain. But he did not stop swinging the blade. Power flowed through him and grew until he knew he could stand against any beast, dragon or demon.

"Revenge," Trav said, then fell silent. He shook his head and amended this. "Justice. It will be nothing more than justice."

He whipped the blade, now feeling feather light, in a broad arc and created a new shrilling, a higher pitched wail that rose in frequency until he no longer heard it. But in the distance came a trumpeting reply he knew well.

"Piddling," he whispered. Trav continued to whirl Dragonslicer about, the shrilling an allurement for his monster. When his arms began to tire, a deep rumbling approached and Trav saw his one-time pet.

Piddling stood half again as large as in the village, the diet of human flesh augmenting both bulk and height. The dragon moved with a litheness that astounded Trav.

Juliana. Their father.

"Come here. Piddling, come to me," Trav urged. He swung Dragonslicer about his head and moved forward, his legs rubbery and feet bloody from the hard journey.

The dragon's head bobbed about, its long black tongue snaking forth as it sampled the air. Tiny sparks ignited in its nostrils and flames leaped out, only to die a few meters short of Trav. He paid no heed to the dragon's warning and surged forward, Dragonslicer moving with magic-driven power.

The blade touched Piddling's chest scales and did not bounce off. The Sword cut deeply into the dragon's body. Trav shoved as hard as he could, Dragonslicer gouging out a deep chunk of flesh. Piddling snorted, more in surprise than pain, and lowered his head, as if to butt Trav playfully.

The youth gripped the Sword of Heroes with both hands and drew the keening blade through a long swift arc that did not stop till it was more than halfway through the dragon's neck, devastating flesh and bone. Piddling twisted and tried to escape, then dropped to the ground, mortally wounded. The huge beast twitched and kicked, and the fires of its nostrils faded to dull-burning embers.

"Got you," Trav panted. "Damn you. You killed my father and sister and—"

Trav's voice trailed off. An eyelid twitched and opened; one large yellow eye fixed on him. Piddling tried to reach out a taloned forelimb—as if, Trav thought, to ask a question. But the move did not get far before the dragon died.

For what seemed a long time, Trav could not move. He stood staring at the great corpse, which was already drawing insects. There were the pig-bugs Piddling had loved as a hatchling.

At last Trav turned away, conscious of the fact that Dragonslicer weighed down his arms and made them tremble. He hurled the blade from him. It spun through the air and landed point-down in the dirt a dozen paces away.

But Trav kept looking at the Sword. Slowly he realized the burden he had assumed. He hobbled to Dragonslicer and pulled it from the ground, gripping the black hilt with tired but steady hands. Now he must work to slay all dragons—as Wyatt had before him.

The Sword of
Aren-Nath

Thomas Saberhagen

Aron felt the bite of the gray air in the openness where he perched. Head thrown back, he watched the gray clouds of the sky. They shifted and slid like silt heavy in the delta of the river of the gods. In a minute his head got light and he had to take his gaze downward for a moment to regain his balance. He locked his arms tighter about the Temple Icon and held to his spot. The Temple was the highest point of the town, and he sat upon the highest point of the Temple. But it was hard to feel too superior with the dark hill looking down. To his left the Grade rose steeply to the foot of the forest, where a mass of fat immovable trunks stood together in the fringes of a silent crowd of which no man could say he had seen the other side. But looking to the right and beneath him, Aron could see far. The soft earth fell gently downwards. Far down its side were only the gullies and rivulets made by the autumn rain. But closer up to where he perched he could see how the sparse walls of Aren-Nath were rooted in soft clay.

Thick splinters were starting to dig into the skin of his arm.

He unclasped his hands for a moment to push back his hair and kicked his foot one last time along the wall below. Then he scrambled down awkwardly and stuck his feet tentatively back into the mud of the town.

When he came to the edge of the Templeyard, a black bird swooped down from the heights of forest. He followed its slow path downward through the town. A bell gave three plaintive cries, as if annoyed for being hit, and he heard the distant clamor of his friends bursting out of the Schoolroom. He was supposed to be with them.

As he walked he looked over the squat brick wall of the Templeyard and saw the bald head and upraised hands of Takani the Sage. When townsmen came to the Temple with furrowed brows, it was no god they sought, but the friendship and counsel of this short man.

But today the faces that greeted him were small and smooth. From the Master's Stump, Takani told stories that no child of the town soon forgot. The Stump itself held a special meaning for each of them. It was the only sign that a tree had ever grown so far down the Grade, and the reason and time of its cutting remained mysterious.

Aron approached the garden and climbed up onto a bench so he could peek up over the wall. The buildings and the short quiet children who were gathered loosely about cast strange shadows in the faint daylight.

". . . but the peril of the town aroused in his Sword the fury of the gods, and the Sword sang keenly, and Vassal Yordenko tightened his grip; and the Sword led his strokes into the creature's spongy flesh; and the pieces of flesh flew out of the fray and burnt the flesh of the earth . . ."

Takani's open, limp hands circled the air, drawing in his audience. His sparkling eyes glanced quickly at Aron, and he incorporated a beckon into the gestures of the song. But a

Aron turned to come to the garden gate, the boys of the town swept through the street behind him and pulled him in their wake.

They ran so fast he knew that there was something they ran to see. He ran fast behind them, but couldn't catch up. He watched their tiny, mud-covered bodies slipping and tumbling their ways Earthward. Those in back were not looking where they were going, but turning and shouting to one another as they ran.

Aron's friend Klin led the pack, his head fixed forward in determination. Klin was always their leader, setting them into willful motion with a few quick threats or a few kind words. Klin would stand up to the meanest adults in the town and play tricks on anyone, even sometimes Takani.

Behind Klin and to one side easily loped the Tall Boy, unconcerned and never slipping.

As the pack came into the Town Square, Klin slid to a stop and held out his arms, keeping the others behind him. Then he anxiously strode ahead.

A black riding-beast draped with a strangely rich red-and-gold cloth stood neighing quietly to itself outside the Vassal's quarters. Renky the Idiot, who served as the Vassal's stableboy, was leading two smaller black beasts up beside it. Then from the small doorway, Grumo the Mason and Torstein the Wheelwright emerged. Their strong workers' hands awkwardly clasped pikes, and feathery, rusted helmets were perched atop their simple heads. They were acting as the Vassal's personal guard. Klin took a step towards them, but Torstein let him know with a worried glance that they had all better stay back.

They stood, shuffling their feet.

Yordenko the Vassal stepped from his door and surveyed the Square, then turned and ushered out a lean, dark man in

a green tunic—the Baron himself. A stirring of excitement
went through the boys at the sight of the rapier at his side.
Some of their fathers kept ancient heirloom weapons sealed
beneath wedding gowns and pewter in family chests. The
Vassal had taken his Sword on occasion from its wrappings
and shown it to each of them, letting them trace their fingers
along the cold steel Blade, the white emblem of its hilt, a
crenelated wall. But seldom would a man be seen in town
who had reason to carry such weapons at his side.

The Baron's lip was twisted with arrogance and with each
step his heel twisted into the mud of the town, as if to grind
some bit of foul food underfoot. He was flanked by two men
of his guard, also armed, who looked strong but slouched
carelessly as if this were their day off. The boys in the back of
the group exchanged awed whispers. Vassal Yordenko cast a
sidewise glance at the boys, and from the anguished expression on his face it looked like he knew there might be some
trouble.

Klin pelted the Baron in the back of the head with a pebble. Some of the boys giggled a little but most were too frightened. There was a sliding of metal. The Baron had spun
about and held his sword in the air ready to strike. Yordenko
cringed to one side and the men of the Baron's Guard
reached for their weapons. The Baron, seeing nothing but the
pack of boys, sneered, then sheathed his rapier and leapt
onto his riding-beast. The mount kicked wildly beneath his
harsh mastery but in a moment submitted. Frightened, it carried him downward from the Square, its rear legs buckling as
it slipped through puddles. The two men of the Baron's
Guard mounted their beasts more clumsily and followed
quickly.

Klin broke out laughing and the older boys started poking
him and laughing also once the Baron was gone. The young-

er boys were in awe, some of them turning to friends and whispering anxiously, *C'mon, let's go home now. . . .*

Yordenko did not so much as look at any of them. Aron thought he looked very tired and knew that it was very strange that the Vassal did not even come to reprimand them. Yordenko's face was drawn in resignation as Aron had never seen it before. His green eyes moist and empty, the Vassal retired to his quarters.

"You shouldn't have done that, Klin—I think something's really wrong. . . ." Aron said quietly, looking after the Vassal.

"Are you gonna start telling me when to throw rocks now? Uh?"

Their eyes locked. The other boys got quiet.

Klin came up to Aron, chest out, fists balled, and stood tall to look down on him. He was about five centimeters taller. The other boys cleared out. Klin gave Aron a shove. Aron kept his gaze but did nothing. Klin advanced again and gave another shove.

"You're just afraid of those fools. Yeah, that's what you are, *afraid!*"

Aron leapt on him and began pounding with his fists.

They tumbled to the ground and the other boys started cheering. Aron took a hard punch in the cheek then pummeled Klin's stomach. They got back to their feet and started boxing again. Klin gave Aron one quick kick in the teeth, nearly sending him into a rage. But through the blur of his teary eyes and through the pain in his mouth, which he was sure was bleeding now, Aron's eyes met those of the silent woman of the town. She stood on the far side of the Square, bastard child clinging at her breast. Crying, Aron took Klin down, hit him twice hard in the face, then ran downwards because that was the fastest way he could go.

*   *   *

Aren-Nath behind him, his quick feet followed the hoof-
churned trail to where it met the base of the High Road
where he would have to stop running and start climbing,
climbing far back up into the fat trees amongst which his parents had built their home. He took the final turn downward,
and though darkness had not yet set felt fleeting fears of ban-
dits and hooligans. His heart would not slow, it thumped
hard, then he was almost there. He could see the base of the
High Road just below.

He was tumbling down the hill. Something had grabbed
his leg from behind, and he was falling now, and there was
another body falling and rolling through the mud with him,
over him, then under him. He fought it off. It was Klin. At
the bottom of the hill, Aron got himself untangled, stood,
and started walking and slipping along the path again.

"C'mon, Aron," Klin called, getting up and running to his
side. Aron felt a hand clap him on the shoulder and rest
there. Silently they turned up onto the High Road together.
"That was a pretty good fight. You still got some blood on
your chin, though. Don't let your mom see that I did
that. . . ."

They talked. Aron said something was wrong with the
Vassal, and Klin shouldn't be messing with him right now.
Klin said maybe he was right, but he had no idea what was
wrong with the Vassal. "Beats me," he said, shrugging.

Aron knew that despite his foolery, Klin had a heart
greater than those of the other boys and worshiped the Vassal with all of it. But Klin's attention was elsewhere, he had
forgotten the whole issue and was telling some story about
what had happened in the workshop this afternoon, how so-
and-so had ripped the hammer off from the smith and so-
and-so was selling it. . . . Aron wasn't listening. He was

wiggling his teeth gingerly, wondering if they'd stay in place. He was still angry about the fight but at the same time glad to have his friend back.

When they got up to the fork that headed back toward town, Klin stopped Aron firmly and looked him over for a moment in silence.

"Tonight . . ." he breathed. Then he told Aron his plan. Always before had Aron refused to go on their nighttime excursions. He didn't like the things they did. He was afraid. But he would never let Klin tell him so again.

Aron lay in his bed that afternoon thinking about the girls in his class. There was one girl he thought about quite a bit more than the others. He had been hoping somehow he could be alone with her for a while, but then he heard one of the other boys talking about how ugly she was and he figured that he had better stay away because he didn't want to be seen with her.

Aron's house had only two rooms, the beds and the kitchen in one and Father's workbench in the other. The boards creaked under the thin stuffed mattress as he shifted around and opened his eyes a little to see what Mother was doing. She was at a stool by the window testily pulling handfuls of feathers out of a dark, dead bird and stuffing them into a bag. She was still young, her face just beginning to harden. Her thin but strong shoulders and arms had once been soft. She set the limp bird down on the floor and got up to ladle herself a cup of water from the waterbarrel.

At her feet beneath the table huddled sister Cainy, three years old, quiet, blonde, and with eyes that held a deep understanding. She was carving something into the floor with Father's pocketknife, as she occasionally would. At first the family had tried to stop her. Then they discovered it was useless. If they took the knife away she scratched with her fingers until they bled, and such a look of anguish came into her eyes that it made them worry more about not giving her the knife than giving it to her. They watched her carefully at first, but she had never hurt herself. Some of her carving was magnificent. Father would pick her up, take the knife gently from her grasp, and shake her up and down proudly. "At least we don't have to worry about what craft she'll choose," he would say, smiling.

When the bird was no more than a bag of bristly skin Mother set it on the counter, then got the broom to sweep up stray feathers. With the coming of the broom, Cainy dropped the knife and sat in place. When it was upon her she got up and scrambled out the back door.

Father came in the front door, axe gripped by the neck in one strong hand, a bundle of wood locked under his other arm.

Night had long fallen. The chill had dispersed the clouds, and the moon had already had time to make most of its long progress across the sky. His stomach still felt warm with his mother's stew. He lay perfectly still making shallow breaths and listening to every breath of his parents and every creak of the boards their bodies rested on. He waited. He heard the crickets. The chill crept in beneath him and around his covers. His stomach forgot about the stew and started rumbling.

A cold hand was on his shoulder. He sat up, startled. The back door was open to the night, but he had heard nothing. His heart was jumping, then he saw that the dark figure was Klin. He had known that all along, but the silence had startled him.

Klin raised a finger to lips which Aron was sure were smiling in the dark. He grabbed Aron by the arm, got him out of bed, and steered him toward the door. But now in the doorway was Cainy, her body tiny in the dark, her eyes looking silently up to them. Klin smiled and gave her a gentle *shush,* then took Aron out and closed the door with little Cainy safely inside.

The night was cold, terribly cold, but Aron thought at least he was out in it now and not trying to hide from it beneath his covers. They ran. At first Aron's knees felt weak and his steps were unsure. The air was cold. But they were outside, they were in the forest. It was night. They couldn't see a thing. His worries about what they were to do nagged at him only a little now, crying out to him from some region of his mind far removed from what his eyes saw and his skin felt.

They came upon Aren-Nath and slipped through its loosely bound wooden gates. The streets were black and muddy and empty. Aron could not stop looking around to see if anyone his parents knew would see him out here, away from his house at this hour. He thought he kept seeing people in the shadows, but they shrank back into darkness when he turned to look. Ahead there was one glow of light. It was the only light in the whole town at this hour. But Aron had never seen it before. He had never seen the town at this hour before. The light that shone out into the night came from the tavern.

When they came nearer, the darkness was no longer enough to stifle its eruptions of laughter and blasts of music. Outside its doors, a few figures shuffled together around the street, on the verge of collapse.

Aron glanced at Klin, then realized that his look might betray apprehension. But Klin merely nodded and gestured down an alleyway. They picked their way through its puddles in darkness and came up towards the rear of the tavern. The thin boards of its walls could not hold in its warm yellow glow or the raucous calling of its laughter and song. Aron wondered if he knew anyone who was inside, and was frightened.

Beside the tavern was the shack where the town's dead were kept on blocks of ice until their day of cremation. Klin used a crate to climb onto the roof of this shack. From there he hoisted himself to the roof of the tavern. Aron followed, wordlessly. What else would he do? For a moment he thought about telling Klin he would just wait outside, but then decided he couldn't. Not only did he fear standing alone in the alley, but a desire to see inside the tavern grew powerful within him and began to overpower his other concerns.

Standing on the roof of the tavern, he could see the whole town scattered like a bunch of broken pottery beneath him and rising up with solid-looking shapes to the forest above, but the only hint of the warm light of men was from beneath them. Klin was ducking into a hole in the roofing. Crouching, Aron found his way along the beam and ducked in after him.

Inside, the night was forgotten except that the feel of the lampglow told everyone that it could not possibly be daytime. The musicians completed a song, and cheers went up. Aron and Klin were in the rafters. Between thin boards and through knotholes of the ceiling they caught glimpses of rumpled hair and tables and the colors of women's dresses. A rat scurried across the beam beside them, then disappeared into the shadows around the perimeter. Klin got down on the beam and began inching his way carefully to the other side of the room. Most of the light was streaming in from over there, and Aron knew that Klin was going to get a better look. The musicians began anew with a song featuring the flutist. Klin lay down on the beam and bent his head down to and almost through a hand-sized hole in the boards. Aron squeezed up right behind him, so Klin got up to a crouch, holding on to a after for support and making a little space for his friend. There was just enough room beneath Klin's feet for Aron to slide up the beam and get a good look.

The hole was over a spot behind the bar. First Aron looked straight down the neck of the barmaid's tight dress. One man's laughter rolled out above the din. Then Aron saw the barmaid's hair, the stacks of grubby glasses behind her, kegs piled carelessly against the wall. He scooted forward another few centimeters, butting up against Klin's ankles, and turned his head to get a better look. The dust of the beam was on his face; it smelt like his mother's old dress. The bar was wet with beer, and it seated old men stirring their soup and young men laughing and throwing back their heads and downing pints. The young ones belched and put their hands on young, dirty ladies who pushed them away, while old, toothless hags rubbed the old men's heads. A smiling girl bounced through the room, then hopped into an older man's lap, threw an arm about his neck, and kicked back uproariously, nearly peeling him from his stool. She swung back up onto her feet, lifted her skirt off the floor and did a little jig, dancing off into a corner where Aron could not see her but from which he heard a great deal of laughter.

There in the corner were Kruman the Carpenter and Flores, the butcher's daughter. Feebin the Candlemaker sat at a table of quiet men, and the old hag who served as Matchmaker was being cornered by a tottering man who looked even older. An old man who sat at the bar slung his arm about his neighbor's neck and stood, pulling his chum up in a headlock. The man cried out grotesquely at the top of his wheezing lungs, *"Charlie's leaving!"*

All eyes turned to the chubby face of the man in the headlock. He smiled, and nodded. Charlie's chum gripped the fat neck tighter and called out, *"C'mon, boys!"*

Aron looked up at Klin to ask what was going on. Klin

rolled his eyes as if he'd seen this before. The musicians beneath them started a new song, and Aron looked through the hole again. The old man was leading the other regulars in a wheezing song, and slowly leading Charlie to the door. The music came, wheezing and staggering like its singers.

> *"Charlie's gone to fill our kegs,*
> *'Cause all that's left is stale dregs*
> *In the Town of Aren-Nath!*
> *In our little Town of Aren-Nath!*
>
> *Aren-Nath, Aren-Nath,*
> *Where mud is thick,*
> *The kids are sick,*
> *And God's plan gone awry . . .*
>
> *But we still serve the Vassal's will,*
> *And down we our last pints of swill,*
> *For Charlie's on his way!*
> *Charlie's on his merry way!"*

The song had ended and shouts rang out through the tavern.

"Long live the Vassal!"

"Long live the Vassal of Aren-Nath, and gods keep his Sword!"

"Hoorah! Hoorah!"

Charlie was pushed out into the dark and there was a short silence. There was the snort and whinny of a load-beast, and in his mind Aron could almost see the fog of its breath. Then there came a jingle, a creak, and a drunken *hiyah!* before the voices started their chatter again. The barmaid leaned far over the counter and gave one man a toothless smile.

Aron felt Klin's boot kicking into his calves; he looked up

from the hole. Klin gestured back the way from which they had come. Aron understood and got carefully to a crouch. He turned himself around and crept back towards the hole to the outside. He climbed out and was in night again and remembered that it was cold. The music was softer now. He found his way down the beam, onto the shed, and into the dark alley. Klin was on his heels the whole way, whispering for him to hurry it up.

They picked their way down the alley to the front of the bar. There, a tall figure stepped out of the shadows. It was rail thin. Aron knew it had to be Tall Boy.

"Did y'get it?" Klin asked hurriedly.

Tall Boy pulled a glass bottle halfway out of his coat pocket to show.

"Charlie always keeps this one beneath his seat," Klin explained. They all shuffled back into the alley. Tall Boy knocked the cork off the bottle with the back of his hand, took a swig, then wiped his mouth on his coat sleeve and passed the bottle to Klin. Klin followed, and offered it to Aron. He refused. Klin shrugged, and Tall Boy drank deeply again.

"We've got one more thing to do tonight, Aron," Klin explained. Aron looked to him in silence. "You don't know what that is, do you?"

Aron shook his head.

Tall Boy smiled and bit his lip and took another swig, exchanging a glance with Klin.

"Tonight we're going into Nero's house," Klin said flatly.

Aron's heart began to race. Nero was a man who lived in the forest, a man whom he had never seen but about whom he had heard much. The strength in his hands could tear the limbs off a man. In his mind and in his books he held strange powers barely under control. When forest winds whispered at night, it was said, they were angry spirits, looking for Nero. The sight of his black carriage approaching on a forest path gave men sleepless nights.

To go within his house would be suicide.

Klin and Tall Boy stood drinking for a few minutes and Aron did not know what he would do. He would not leave them here, now. Perhaps somewhere ahead he could slip off the path and return home. Anxiously he watched them drink, wondering how much more they would put down. Then Tall Boy corked and chucked the bottle into the shadows and the three of them emerged from the alleyway. Together they climbed to the top of the town, scrambled over the Temple wall and set off into the forest.

Upward they hiked, and then upward more and upward a few steps further, and still Aron could not see the house ahead. Tall Boy and Klin were moving slow and kept behind him. The fat trees stood like sleepy sentries in the dark. He looked up again and could not see the house. He looked down and thought of the bargirls, bright in the yellow glow of the tavern lamps, their toothless smiles and bright bosoms in tight dresses burnt into his mind.

Turning back, he tried to watch Klin's step, worrying that he must be terribly drunk. He didn't know how much it might take to get a man drunk. Klin's step seemed steady. Then Aron tripped.

"Look where you're going!" Klin shouted noisily.

Aron brought his attention back to the path beneath him, wondering if this was the time to escape.

It started coming out of the dark up ahead, a rough form darker and larger than all the rest. Weak fringes of light danced within it. They got closer and he could see that was candlelight dancing about the fringes of windblown curtains.

On the ground floor, all windows were dark. When they

came close they could tell that the house was white. In front it had a strange wooden deck, like the deck of a ship, and round white cylinders of wood reached high to the roof. On it there were dark wet shadows and whispers of ancient pain.

Evidently Klin could not hear these whispers. He pressed forward indomitably through the hedges. Aron shushed him, then picked his way painstakingly through the same bush. Suddenly he knew that he could not turn back. He did not know what would happen next, but he pressed onward, as in a dream, until the house was within his very reach. He touched it. Its side was cold. He turned and watched with horror as Klin rapped his knuckles on the strange, clear, flat glass which covered a window. Then with one swift punch Klin knocked out a pane. It tinkled to the floor inside, then all was quiet again.

"Now how do we get in?" Tall Boy whispered thickly.

He and Klin sniffed around the panes of glass. Finally Klin figured the bottom pane could be lifted so he pulled up on it for a while but it didn't move. Then he saw the latch and reached around inside. He opened it easily and the window stayed open. Then he was inside.

Then Tall Boy was inside. Aron heard his feet crushing the glass on the floor, and it was quiet again. So he hoisted himself onto the sill, then tumbled noisily in, then remembered the glass on the floor. His hands had missed it and he had not been cut. He got up, wondering where the other boys had gone. He could see very little in the darkness. It was all wood planks, like the deck of a boat. Around the room was furniture of strange thin wood that was curved and polished. There were shelves and cabinets made of wood and strange flat glass. The floor creaked beneath his every step. Cold breaths of outside air sighed from the open window behind him. His ears were pricked for any sound.

"Klin . . . Tall Boy . . ."

There was no answer. But the whisper had been so quiet he had hardly heard it himself. Everything was dark. Then it struck him.

Somewhere in these rooms was Nero. If Aron could bring himself to listen, he might hear Nero's breath, warm and determined, within this very hall.

There was a snap, the sharp sound of wood on wood, a young woman's laughter, then her laughter muffled, then silence and another breath of cold wind. Aron stood frozen in mid-step at the foot of the hall, listening, wanting to go forward and look into the open doors, afraid that at any moment some figure might emerge, afraid to turn around, and afraid that as he stood there he might feel an icy hand fall upon his shoulder.

He took a step forward, listening for the sounds of the woman. A door ahead opened swiftly and a robed figure stepped into the hallway. Aron saw only its swollen feet and the powerful balled muscles of its calves, white with moonlight from an opposite room. The figure shouted and ran towards him like a flying reptile swooping for its prey. Its bald head shone white.

"Klin!" Aron cried desperately, turning and bolting from the corridor. He heard pounding bare feet behind him and an angry cry.

He rounded the corner, into a big room. Klin was up on the balcony.

"Aron! Up here! Climb up!" His face was pale and worried, his eyes intent. Aron obeyed and broke for the shelves. There were books, so many books. . . .

Nero exploded into the room and stopped to survey it for his prey. He swung one arm up along the wall and bright light came down from a lamp suspended from the center of the ceiling.

"Come back here!" he barked, jabbing a finger at them. He marched fiercely towards them, his calves balled and fists clenched with tremendous energy. His eyes were blue, his skin dark, his head fringed with short coarse gray hairs.

Aron scrambled up the shelves, slipping with every step. Klin was at the top, screaming at him and reaching his hand down through the balusters to him. Nero was nearly within reach of Aron's feet now. Aron looked back and their eyes met. Then he lunged for the top though he had no solid footing. Nero leapt to seize a foot. Aron got his other foot on top of the biggest book on the shelf and shoved off of it, putting everything into one surge for the top. The big book tumbled out of the shelf as he pushed, but it had given him enough height to get his arms over the railing of the balcony. Klin grabbed him. Aron looked down, fighting to get his legs to the edge of the upper level.

Nero had turned his gaze abruptly from the boys and tried but failed to catch the book. It landed on its spine then parted, falling open. Nero grasped the fringes of his hair in tight fists as if about to rip it from his small round skull. He cried out, but no longer did his eyes seek out the intruders in his house. He looked down to the book, beside his swollen feet. On its yellow page stood a picture, jagged lines of the blackest ink.

It was a creature, gaping mouth draped with saliva, digging one bare claw into the almost empty carcass of a young boy on a rock.

Klin's hands pulled Aron up over the top. He fell hard on the floor of the balcony, then scrambled to his feet. Tall Boy led them through a window and into the night, onto the branches of a tree, and Aron jumped too soon for the ground, twisting his ankle and bruising his legs on the roots below.

Klin swung down beside him and picked him up. They were running, running, running. They did not look back once. From the house they could hear Nero's screams, screams of wrath and loss.

"Come back here you stupid boys!" they finally heard, then they could hear no more.

Aron's body ached everywhere and his heart was pounding out of control. He fell over a dead log in the path and collapsed on the forest floor, struggling just to breathe.

Klin and Tall Boy were crouched over him. He couldn't think of anything but trying to get his breath. There were hands on his chest and arms. He sucked one breath in, but could not remember how to exhale. Someone hit him and the air came out. He breathed again, then again. Now his breaths were coming fast and he started to hear their voices.

"Aron, Aron, it's okay. . . . Stand up! You gotta keep walking. . . ."

He stood but felt weak. His body was shaking. The other boys helped him for a few steps, then he pushed them away and fought his way alone. They kept anxiously by his side, and he pushed them angrily away. Slowly, he regained his breath and began to hear the wind and feel the chill of the forest. He had no idea where they were, but Tall Boy was leading them somewhere. Aron just kept following.

The moon was bright and cold and round.

Aron's house looked small when they came to it, and he thought of all the comfort that was inside. He wondered for a moment if Nero would follow them here. He wondered if Nero were somewhere amongst these trees.

The three boys squatted for a while on the hill, considering the events of the night. Aron thought the other boys might be laughing now, except that he had collapsed like that. Finally Tall Boy told them that his paw was going to get him up before dawn to skin some animals, and how his paw would probably skin him instead if he weren't around. His gaunt form wandered off into the forest, picking up rocks and nailing trees with them.

Klin smiled. "You doing all right?"

"Yeah."

"How'd you like it?" Klin questioned. His tone was quiet and sincere, threatening nothing for an erroneous answer.

Aron laughed a little, nervously. "Not too bad."

"You didn't do so bad. I've gotta tell you, starting off, I wasn't so sure you'd make it. When we were coming up on the house it looked like maybe you were about to bolt for the trees or something. But you did good. Got into a hell of a lot more trouble than me or Tall Boy."

"Have you ever gone in there before?"

"No."

"Were you scared?"

Klin smiled to himself, kicking at a root in the forest floor.

Aron said it was probably time that he went inside. Klin asked him if he was sure, and Aron told him yes, and Klin said okay. Aron started walking down the hill to his house. He walked a little nervously because he felt like Klin was watching him.

"Aron!" Klin called out, loudly enough so that Aron would worry if it had woken his parents.

He looked back and Klin was charging down the hill towards him. He came to Aron's side and grabbed the top of his arm tight.

"You asked me a question back there, are you gonna let me get away without an answer?" He was breathless. "Scared?" He let Aron's arm go. "Of course I was scared. But that isn't what matters. What matters is . . ."

Aron watched him silently.

"Aw, hell. Good night, Aron. Sleep tight. And be quiet getting in there! Don't want to wake the parents!"

He laughed and nudged Aron on his way. At the bottom of the hill Aron looked back once, and Klin was standing there where they had parted, and by his posture it was clear he was smiling.

When Aron got to the door of the house and looked back again, Klin was gone.

Quietly, he slipped inside.

His mind wandered and wandered in senseless circles. He heard sounds that were not sounds and saw strange things verging on dreams. He heard a knocking, a rapping at the door, then sat up, wondering if that one could have been real. But he heard nothing more. A scream from the forest.

The only sound was the cold fingers of the wind running through the earth's bristly hair.

He awoke to the sound of his sister's shrill scream. He rubbed his eyes and looked around the room, now bright with morning. His sister ran in the door bawling.

"What is it, baby?" he heard Father ask.

He got out of bed.

He saw his father slipping out the front door. His head poked back in.

"Son, stay with your sister," he commanded sternly.

Cainy stared up at him, her eyes brimming with fear. Aron stood motionless, still waking up, wondering if the night before had been anything more than strange dreams. He said nothing.

Father came back in. His face was like stone. Mother, drawn by Cainy's cries, came running in through the back door and went straight to her.

"What is it?" she asked Father.

"It's Klin," he spoke without moving his lips. "It looks like something's chewed him up."

Cainy screamed wildly but Aron did not hear her. He stared dumbly at his father.

Father was to go out to the field with a blanket to cover the body. Then he was to hike into town to tell the Vassal and his men what Cainy had found. Mother was to stay home and watch the children.

But Aron knew that with his sister throwing tantrums he'd be able to slip away soon. Cainy ran into the kitchen and Mother gave chase. Aron slipped out the back door into the open green field. He knew which way he had to run. At the top of the first hill, he heard his mother calling his name desperately. She must have thought she had lost him.

Klin was gone. In the mystery of the midnight forest winds, Aron might have believed it. In the strange light of the tavern, or with the shards of moonlit broken glass on Nero's floorboards, he could have felt something, he could have cried and understood that Klin was gone.

But the morning light was a cruel anesthetic.

In it the white house looked fragile, and Aron ran straight up and pounded on the door. What was inside could be no worse than what lurked in the forest. He screamed and pounded harder and kicked the door violently until his toes were all smashed up. Then it opened. A powerful fist came down, opened, and wrenched him inside.

The hand belonged to Nero. No other could be so strong. Now the sorcerer was clothed all in tight-fitting white garments and a white coat with a black ribbon tied neatly about his veinous neck. His powerful arms held Aron so tight against the wall that he could not swallow and could hardly breathe.

Piles of books were strewn everywhere.

Droplets of sweat ran down Nero's face and neck, then into his collar. He inhaled sharply through his mouth and pushed hot air back out through his nose. His eyes bulged wildly and stared at one of Aron's eyes, then the other, then shifting back and forth each half-second as he scrutinized the creature within his grasp.

"You stupid!"

He slammed Aron against the wall once, then again, knocking the breath out of him before letting him fall to the floor. Nero walked slowly, deliberately back to his books.

"I don't have time for this, I don't have time for this!" he screamed suddenly.

Aron lay motionless, panting, on the floor.

"Make it go away," he finally croaked.

"I can't!" Nero roared back and raged toward him once again. "The beast is out! You opened the book. That means he is hungry for *you!*" Nero had knelt by his side and was jabbing a finger hard into Aron's forehead with each word.

With the knowledge that he was hunted, Aron felt no greater fear, only agitation. Why Klin? Why had it not come directly for him, bursting into his house, casting his parents from their bed, picking his own body with one claw and stealing away into the night with it. . . .

"But it's eaten Klin!" Aron cried. He scurried from Nero to avoid his poking fingers.

Nero closed his eyes, then clenched his teeth and his fists tighter and tighter, turning his head up towards the ceiling with agonizing tension. Then he let go and opened one hand. "Yes! He will tear others limb from limb and devour them in a gulp. But it is you he will *stay* hungry for." He ground his teeth. "By the power of the gods he will not stop until your flesh is inside him!"

He stepped forward and grasped Aron's shirt, hoisting him

against the wall. This time Aron raged back with all his strength, kicking and flailing his arms.

"Make it stop! Make it stop!"

The old man threw him off.

"Begone!"

Nero turned, clutching at his chest, then fell, his face contorted in pain, onto one knee. "Begone I say. . . ." One quivering finger pointed to the door.

As Aron turned the knob and stepped outside he heard the old man sobbing quietly behind him.

The beast was in the forest and Aron could feel it smelling him. He could not go home. He did not want to know what he might find there anyway. By now Father would have given the news to the Vassal, and a party would be on its way back to the house. Soon Father would be crying with Mother because they did not know where he had gone. Mother would be sure he had been eaten. Father would try to tell her otherwise. He would stand fearless guard with the axe, watching the forest for any sign of motion, not knowing that it was the Power of the Gods with which he must contend and that the axe would be but a splinter in the side of the beast. It would eat them all. It would eat his sister.

Perhaps it had already happened. He could not go back. He held only one hope.

He had not run far on the path to town when he heard the rattling approach of a wagon around the bend. He ducked swiftly behind a tree. It did not matter who it was. He was not ready to face anyone at this time.

Guiding the load-beast was Charlie, his face broad and cheerful and sleepy. The beast picked its way along slowly and easily, pausing from time to time to sniff at roadside clover.

When the wagon came around, Aron slipped in back and

crouched amongst the heavy kegs. If the beast came out of the forest now, then it came, and he was dead. He held himself motionless and waited for the load-beast to make its lazy way into town.

There was the sound of the strong hooves of riding-beasts swiftly approaching, and a strong voice hailed Charlie. It sounded like Torstein. The slow load-beast came to a stop, and Aron heard the other party ride up beside them. He peeked out a hole in the cloth wagon-cover. Father was with them.

"Eh, we got some trouble a little deeper into the forest. . . . See anything, Charlie?"

"N-n-no, sir. . . ." Charlie mumbled.

"Well you better hurry on back to town as fast as you can get there. There's something funny going on in the forest, and we're advising everyone to come to safety. Come on, boys, let's get on up to the house and see how Aron an' his ma are doing! *Hiyah!*"

They were gone.

Charlie tapped his beast and it crept, pulling them onwards towards the town.

At last the wagon came to a stop. From the way it rocked and creaked, Aron knew that Charlie was stepping off. Peering out the hole in the cloth he could see the town wall stretching up into the distance. Charlie was swinging the gate open. His beast sputtered a little. He patted it and guided the wagon through to the other side, then came around back to close the gate. Aron ducked as low as he could amongst the kegs. Charlie put the latch carefully in place then turned, but didn't see him. He went back to the front, the wagon creaked and rocked, and the beast pulled them laboriously through the muddy streets.

"Charlie!" an anxious voice called out. The wagon ground to a halt. "Did'ya see anyone else on the road, Charlie? Well, good. Looks like you better stay put here for the time being. Something's up in the forest, not sure what yet. . . . Vassal's orders. . . . I'm gonna go guard that gate right now!"

Aron leapt from the wagon.

"The Vassal? Where?" he demanded.

"Why, at his quarters," the man he recognized as Grumo answered, bewildered. Aron sprinted. Charlie called out lethargically after him.

"Hey, wait a minute there, kid. . . ."

The Vassal's doorway looked small in the new, still cold sunlight, and Aron burst into the dark quarters without a knock or a wipe of his feet. The Vassal stood, his profile to Aron, his arms crossed, his gaze straight into the blank wall before him. He turned to face his visitor. His eyes widened when he saw that it was Aron who stood facing him.

"You have something to tell me?" he asked excitedly, coming forward and bending down to face Aron.

Aron said yes, but he could not find strength to begin his story. The words caught in his throat.

"How many men is it going to kill before we can kill it?" the Vassal asked, taking Aron by the collar.

"I don't know. . . . How can I know . . . ?"

"Do you know where it came from?" he pleaded, shaking Aron a little. Aron had not seen the Vassal like this.

"From Nero's house," he mumbled quickly. He felt himself on the verge of tears, and his throat began to hurt. "From a book at Nero's house."

Aron knew that it was stupid, but he expected the Vassal to ask what on earth they had been doing in Nero's house. But the Vassal said nothing for a long moment. Then he pushed Aron aside and stepped quickly to the door. He flung it open and called to the first man he saw.

"Feebin! Quick, to the Temple! Bring Takani to me at once! Quickly! Run, Feebin, run!"

He stepped back to Aron, leaving the door wide to the Square. He bent, facing Aron, but his gaze remained fixed on a brilliantly engraved cabinet in the corner of the room.

"Listen," he said. "Whatever you've done, whatever it is that happened last night, don't worry. No one's blaming you. There's a lot of things we can do out here if that thing is still hungry. Takani can probably fix us up right away. . . ."

He took two steps to the cabinet, seemingly oblivious of Aron's presence. With great care he turned its latch and swung open one door then the other. Blue velvet had been tacked onto its boxy interior. This upright bed kept the Sword, swaddled in blood-colored cloth, its steel blade naked only at the point.

The Vassal caught his breath for a moment, then took the black hilt into his hand. The red cloth fell away and lay limp in the cabinet as the Sword came to life within his grasp. He held it, and it danced with incredible lightness.

"You can be sure," the Vassal breathed to Aron, "that no harm will come to those in the town. I've often wondered if this day would come again, or if the Baron and his men would take this blade away first. But I have put them off, and the day has come. . . ."

"Maybe it won't come to the town. . . ." Aron said, not knowing what else to say. Then he remembered that the beast was hungry for him. The beast would come. He nearly cried, looking into the Vassal's eyes, but those cold green eyes stayed fixed on the blade before them. Unimaginable now was the resignation Aron had seen in those eyes not one day ago.

"Aron," he said, eyes unmoving. "You stay back here in case we need anything."

The back room was small and dark and filled by a short thick wood table and wet brown dust. There was just one small window. Aron sat, and suddenly was confined. There was nothing he could do here but play with his hands. His heart told him to rise and do something, or say something to the Vassal, but he stayed seated.

Sounds came from the other room.

"What has happened?" The words were from Takani. Aron heard no response. "So it is true?" Now he heard whispering. "Yes. Yes. Yes. . . ."

Takani slipped quietly into Aron's room. He shuffled hunching to the tableside, his body small and vulnerable in the dark morning.

"So . . ." he breathed. There was a long silence as he looked Aron over. "Your friend . . . I am very sorry, my child."

Aron remembered Klin. He said nothing.

"The Vassal tells me you have met Nero also."

Aron nodded mutely.

"For the sake of Aren-Nath, child, tell me, tell me what happened last night, and tell me the whole story."

Aron was silent for a long moment.

"It came out of a book," he finally choked.

"A book?"

"He heard us in his house. I was climbing over shelves of his books to get away. One book fell down to the floor and opened. I looked down. It was inside the book. . . ."

"What? The beast?"

"Yes. The book fell open and I saw it on the page."

"Then it is beast of magic!" Takani flew to his feet. "Vassal! Your riding-beasts! I must have them! I must reach Nero to know what manner of magic we face! If I cannot reach Nero we all are in peril!"

The Vassal stepped to the doorway, nodding slowly. Takani darted around him. The Vassal followed him out. There was whispering, an exchange.

"Send no man with me! By the power of the gods it would do no good! I must ride alone!"

"If your best men can do no good, what can we hope for, what can we hope for?" a woman's voice which Aron had not heard before cried out.

"Our boy had no chance . . ." a man sobbed.

Klin's parents were in the other room.

The Vassal stood silently, facing the wall.

"I am gone! Hold me back no longer!"

Takani fled the room.

Klin's mother shuffled slowly to the door of Aron's room. Her eyes were on the verge of tears.

Every able man of the town took a post about the perimeter. Some had brought axes or hoes or rusty heirloom swords forged for ancient wars long forgotten. The Vassal had told them that all these would be useless. If the beast came there would be no stopping it, and they should not even try, unless it got hold of a woman or a child. Then of course the men knew what they would do.

The townsfolk cried as they heard about what Cainy had found in the forest. There were few in the town who had not known Klin.

The men fingered their weapons nervously, resting the fighting ends in the mud and staring down thoughtfully. The older ones remembered the beast of Takani's song and thought of their friends who had died before Yordenko's Sword had bitten the hell-beast's spongy flesh.

They thought of the wounds Yordenko had sustained in that battle, and remembered seeing his young body gashed and burnt, being taken by flatwagon to those who knew the mysteries of Draffut.

Then the men of the town recalled their duty and turned their gazes outward to the forest again. They did not expect it would be over quickly. They could not even know that the beast would come. Aron had told no one for what it hungered. They waited.

"Where is he?"

It was Father's voice from the other room. Aron jumped and ran to see him, to fly into his arms. He stood tall in the doorway to the Square, his face haggard yet intent. Aron ran and grabbed him.

"But where is Mother?"

Then he saw her coming towards the door. Her strong arms carried Cainy, and the hard determination in her eyes did not soften until they met his own.

A woodsman emerging from the forest heard warning shouts from the watchful men on the town walls. The men crowded him as he came to the gate.

"I saw movement in the woods," he told them. "That thing you're looking for . . . well, it shouldn't be hard to find. . . ."

Not an hour had passed when the breach was made, just paces from that spot. A young man had seen some motion amongst the trunks of forest trees and called the others around to look.

"There it is! Gods!"

The young man's father had told him to run and get the Vassal. The young man had watched his father's gaze turn quietly back towards the vague hulking form which staggered from the trees and towards the town wall. He had seen his father fingering his ancient weapon, but the creature stood the height of two men, its body utterly unnatural, and even the young man knew that no ordinary sword could be enough. He turned and ran.

Aron heard the cries from the far side of town.

In a minute the young man was at the door panting.

"It's here," he gasped.

The Vassal looked up and took a step towards the young man at the door. Then he stopped himself and went to Aron.

"It's not your fault," he said firmly. The Sword was now on his belt. It hummed and began to sing in a high tone as keen as its edge. It jutted out behind him and bounced against his leg as he strode into the Square.

Aron's parents said nothing. Perhaps they were awed by the Vassal and his Sword. But Aron wanted to tell them that he knew it was himself the beast was after—that if only he gave his own life right now the town would be saved. He wanted to ask them if he should do it. He wanted to tell them he had just killed the Vassal. He had taken the beast here, led it here, it could smell him, and he had brought it, brought it for the selfish hope that the Vassal could kill it with an easy thrust of his Sword—or the hope that, at least, Aron would not have to face the beast's jaws alone, in the forest, with no one to die with him or hear him die. . . .

"I have to go," he said, and broke for the door. Again he had no choice but to keep running away from his mother's cries.

There was mud, slippery mud, and old men running.

"It's come, it's come, it's over by the Schoolroom. . . ." they cried out to him. One tried to pick him up and carry him in flight, but Aron easily broke free and ran toward the Schoolroom.

Women corralled children through the streets and away from danger. Aaron ran through them and around them.

In the distance stood the Schoolroom. Closer, to the right, the young man who had brought the news to the Vassal knelt by his father, who was fallen and bloody in the mud.

The Sword keened its constant song of fate, and below this Aron heard the earthly sounds of shouting men who waved poles and axes. Aron could see that the beast and the Vassal were about to engage.

The beast caught Aron's scent on the wind and looked straight up at him, its mouth gaping, its hideous black eyes embedded in dark flesh at the top of its broad head. It took one shuffling step in the direction of its prey. The Vassal circled to cut it off, the delicate Sword dancing in his ready hand.

The beast regarded him for a moment before its claws swung out on long arms in an effort to cast him aside. The Vassal leapt back and the Sword lashed out, screaming, gashing deeply the hand of the beast.

Nausea seized Aron's stomach, and he fell to the ground, trying to fight it off. The beast sensed his weakness and pressed towards where he lay with surprising speed. The Vassal rushed to cut it off. The Sword cried out and leapt in a broad arc and buried itself deep in its chest cavity. It howled, one of its claws tearing at the Vassal, gashing his side badly.

Aron came to his feet and took a step back. With a cracking of ribs, the Sword of Aren-Nath disentangled itself and swung again, then again, this time low. The legs of the beast buckled beneath it and gushed thick blood into the street. It turned to the Vassal, moaning. The Sword came down on its neck.

Nearly falling, the beast looked to Aron, its black eyes pleading, before turning to charge the Vassal and tear at the flesh of his face. It scampered over him and he crumpled beneath its claws like a rag doll. It hopped and shuffled on broken legs and the men flew from its path.

The Vassal lay motionless, the Sword still keening in his hand. Aron ran toward him, but as he approached the beast stopped its flight and grunted, panting.

"Yordenko!" Aron cried out.

The creature hopped towards the fallen body. Then the Vassal moved. He turned to his side and Aron saw that his face was covered with blood. The creature wheezed and bayed like a wounded pup. The men closed in a circle about it, and the Vassal rose with supreme effort to confront it.

With desperate strength it broke the circle, gashing two men, and stumbled up the Grade, away from the fury of the screaming blade. The Sword guided the Vassal after it, pulling his steps faster and faster in pursuit. Aron chased after them but could not keep up as they raced upwards towards the Temple in a hideous contest that neither could concede.

The beast broke into the Templeyard, the Vassal just behind it. There, it stopped to use its last strength in combat. When Aron could see over the wall, he saw them come together, two bloodied bodies colliding, both weak but compelled to combat by the power of the gods.

A claw came down and swiped the Vassal's right breast from his body. The Sword fell to the mud. He bent and raised it in his left hand. The creature shrunk down, moaning. The blade descended, splitting its side and spilling its innards to the ground. It fell, gurgling and clawing, to the ground beside the Master's Stump. The Vassal buried the Sword deep into its shuddering carcass, then came to his knees at its side. He laid his own body carefully down along it.

The men of the town rushed up with their axes and cautiously approached the bodies. Death was like a blanket over them both.

*　*　*

Mother ran a hand through his hair and hugged him for a long time. Then he told her that he wanted to go back to the Templeyard. With great and silent strength, she let him go.

He followed the road upward.

Aron looked uphill to see three men emerging from the Templeyard carrying a heavy sackcloth roll toward the ice-shed by the tavern. Here it would be kept until a pyre could be built, and hearts healed enough to do the dead man proper homage. The front man slipped once in the mud and the roll tumbled on top of him; he swore as they lifted the burden again.

As Aron drew closer he saw that the creature, wrapped in more sackcloth, had alrady been hoisted to a flatwagon. The vapors from its body were stinging men's eyes and making some vomit, even though cloths were wrapped round their mouths and noses. Renky the Idiot sat on the driver's plank, holding the reins and sobbing quietly.

"It's on there," a muffled voice called. Flies were beginning to swarm the flatwagon. Torstein stood up front, his face wrapped, his hand on Renky's shoulder.

"Take it to the Wells of Fire. You remember the Wells of Fire, Renky? You just go on the road, that way, out of town. . . ." Renky sobbed, nodding. "And push the whole thing in, then bring the load-beast back. There's lot of good stuff to eat in the bag. . . ."

Women had gathered around the edges of the scene and cried and held the children back.

Aron stood on the Master's Stump. The ground was still dark with blood here, and he imagined he could still see the two bodies lying peacefully beside each other, like tired lovers at a picnic.

Takani came up behind him.

"So . . ." he called out. Aron turned, and both were silent. They were silent for a long while, letting the wind whisper down to them from the forest.

"Nero was gone when I got there, child," Takani said at last, mounting the Stump. "And he had taken his books with him. There is nothing we could have done to help the poor Vassal."

Aron imagined Nero's house, boxy and empty like a broken milk crate in the forest daylight, its terror distant as a far-away song.

"You are . . . all right, my child?"

Aron nodded, swallowing.

"Takani!" a voice called and they turned to see Grumo hailing from across the street. He ran into the yard.

"The Baron has come," he panted. "He says we have to give him the Sword. But we were gonna leave it with the Vassal's things. Baron looks pretty angry. He's tearing up the Quarters looking for it. What do we do?"

"Let him have it," Takani said shortly. He stepped from the Stump and strode into the Temple without once looking at Aron.

Aron's gaze rose high to the Temple Icon.

He did not want to scale that height again.

Glad Yule

Pati Nagle

A young man sat brooding in the window of his chamber, gazing through snow-blurred glass at the windswept courtyard below. He was slender and dark, his curling black hair framing a face of striking beauty despite his slight frown. His clothing was simple, unadorned, though well made of rich cloth. The yard he watched was bathed in moonlight, deserted except for an occasional servant hurrying to finish some task and get out of the biting wind. For some reason this scene held his attention, keeping him by the window and away from the cheering fire on the hearth.

A quiet knock fell on the door, followed by the voice of a servant, saying "My Lord Paethor?"

The young man looked up. "Come in," he answered.

The servant entered, bowing deferentially. He wore the royal livery of blue and violet, and spoke with respect. "Your pardon, my Lord. His Majesty requests your attendance."

The young man slid from the window seat with a sigh and followed the servant out into the corridor, where three ladies, richly gowned and decked in jewels, paused in their chatter to gaze at him like startled deer. If he had met their eyes he would have seen frank appreciation of his comeliness, but he barely glanced their way, nodding politely, and continued in the servant's wake. Behind him the ladies resumed their conversation in whispered tones.

It was late, and the night's feasting and dancing were finished. King Nigel of Argonia had retired to his private chambers with a few of his most trusted lords, there to relax and enjoy a last cup of wine. The king, a strong, pleasant man with silver beginning to lighten his golden hair and beard, lounged in a chair, listening to his courtiers' raucous banter. When the servant announced Lord Paethor they fell silent, gazing at the newcomer in varying shades of curiosity.

"Lord Paethor, come in," said the king. "Have some wine. We missed you at dinner."

"Forgive me, Your Majesty," said Paethor, accepting a cup from a page. "I'm afraid I'm not very good company lately."

"The ladies have been asking after you, lad," said a lord, chuckling. "They're complaining that the best dancer in court has deserted them." Lord Paethor, who was sipping his wine, seemed not to have heard.

"Is there anything you want?" asked the king. "Anything that would make you more comfortable?"

"Thank you, no," said Paethor with a wisp of a smile. "Your Majesty is most generous. I have everything I need."

The king leaned back in his chair and gazed thoughtfully at the solemn young lord. "That's what I expected you to say." He swirled the wine around in the bottom of his goblet, then drained it. "Midwinter is approaching," he stated, setting the cup aside. "I wonder if you would consider doing me a small favor."

"Gladly, Sire," said Paethor.

"I presume, since you did not return to your father's keep for Midsummer, that you are not going now. Is that correct?"

"Correct, Majesty."

"Also that the coming Yule feast is of little interest to you," continued the king.

"Your Majesty is very observant," replied Lord Paethor, bowing.

"Yes, well. We needn't be quite so formal," said the king. "You're a gentleman, Paethor, and a fine addition to my court, but it doesn't take a wizard to guess you're not fond of festivals."

Paethor was silent for a moment, gazing abstractedly as he had done out the window, then returned his attention to the king. "What would you like me to do, Sire?"

The king dismissed the servants with a wave of his hand. When they'd gone he leaned forward, pressing his fingertips together. "There are skirmishes to the south," he said. "Along our border with Sabara. A few of their smaller baronies, squabbling over territory. King Asad is rumored to be ill."

Paethor nodded. The news had been spoken of in court for several days.

"It's also rumored that Farslayer has been busy down there."

At that the lords shifted and murmured among themselves, and Paethor glanced up at the king. The Sword of Vengeance was enough to frighten the bravest warrior; a merciless meter's length of steel that became flying death with a throw and a target's name.

"Needless to say I would like to know its whereabouts," continued the king. "I would like, in fact, to be sure it does not fall into the hands of an enemy."

Paethor nodded again. "You wish me to find news of it?"

"I wish you to retrieve it."

The lords stirred in response. "You want the thing here, Sire?" asked one dubiously.

"Better here in my keeping than flying around my borders," said the king.

"Or across them," murmured another.

The king stood. "I visited the treasury this morning," he said, going to a cupboard, which he opened with a small gilt key. He reached inside and withdrew a bundle of heavy cloth. This he unwrapped, revealing a sheathed sword.

"Wayfinder," he said, drawing the Sword. The lords crowded closer; it was known that King Nigel possessed a Sword of Power, but few had seen it. Its appearance was disappointing to some who had expected finely worked and gilded hilts; the simple black cruciform was unadorned except for a small arrow emblazoned in white on the hilt.

"Where is Farslayer?" said the king, and the Sword of Wisdom turned in his hand. The lords hastened to get out of the way of the unearthly-keen blade, which swung around southward, then quivered as though it would like to leap forward. "South and a little east," observed the king. "Ravenskeep, or Sun Mountain. A few days should get you there." He sheathed Wayfinder and held it out to Paethor. "Take this along to guide you."

Paethor accepted the Sword, bowing gravely. "Your Majesty honors me," he said.

"Honor?" said the king. "I've given you a damned nasty task is what I've done. Don't get yourself killed."

That drew the first real smile from the young lord. "I won't, Sire."

King Nigel clapped him on the back. "You'll have help," he added, and glanced around the small circle of lords. "I'd like two to go with him. Volunteers?"

"I'll go, Majesty," said a tall, dashing lord with steel-gray hair. "My lands lie near the southern border, I'll do my part to protect them."

"Thank you, Echevarian," said the king. "Who else?"

The lords hesitated, none of them anxious to leave the comforts of court for a lonely journey into danger, even for the chance to handle a Sword of Power and earn the king's gratitude. Finally one came forward, a young lord with merry eyes and light brown hair that fell in soft waves to his shoulders. "Oh, I'll go along," he said, with a lopsided smile.

"You, Trent?" said a lord. "Passing up the Yule feast?"

"Let him go," called another. "It's about time someone else got to be Lord of Misrule!"

Trent's smile widened. "Can I help it if I'm more charming than the rest of you?"

This earned him a round of buffets from his peers. He laughed as he fended them off. "Peace, peace! I'm going with Paethor, you can have the ladies to yourselves!"

"Are you sure you're feeling well, Trent?" asked a lord in mock concern.

Trent shrugged. "Maybe Don Echevarian will show me one of his sword-thrusts," he said, nodding to the elder lord.

"And maybe we'll happen by Sir Alfred's keep, and visit his pretty daughters," mused Echevarian, stroking his mustache.

Trent grinned. "Maybe."

"All right then," said the king, beckoning Trent and Echevarian closer. "Take three yeomen, and see the quartermaster for your needs. Go as soon as your affairs are in order."

Paethor looked at his new traveling companions. "I can leave tomorrow," he said.

"Me too," said Trent.

Echevarian nodded. "I'll send word to my steward tonight."

"Good," said the king. He took them each by the hand briefly. "Good speed to you." Though he smiled, it was plain to his lords that their ruler considered Farslayer a serious threat.

"Well," said Lord Trent. "We'd better have another cup to give us strength."

The solemn moment broke, and the lords resumed their chatter, shouting to the servants to bring in more wine. Paethor stayed beside the king.

"If Your Majesty will excuse me," he said quietly, "I'll retire and prepare for the journey."

The king nodded. "Come back safe," he said softly.

Paethor bowed and left, carrying Wayfinder back to his silent chamber. Once there he drew the Sword again to examine it more closely. The blade was perfectly balanced and deadly sharp, whispering as it left the sheath. There was little light in the room, the fire having burned down to embers, so Paethor carried the Sword to his seat in the window and peered at it in the moonlight, which lent a bluish cast to the polished steel. Whorls in the blade gave an illusion of depth that was almost dizzying, like swirling clouds of snow in the black of night. Paethor let the point come to rest at his feet, his eyes drawn back to the courtyard. No one stirred there now, but a few dry leaves danced in the corners, chased by the relentless wind. The frown descended on his brow again and his eyes seemed to gaze beyond the courtyard into some past shadow. Wayfinder stirred in his hand and he started, a look of dismay in his eyes as the Sword of Wisdom raised itself to point westward, its sudden quiver setting up an answering tremor in Paethor's arm. He hastily sheathed the blade and hid it in his closet. Whatever nameless query Wayfinder had responded to, it seemed Paethor had not intended to make it.

* * *

The next day dawned cold and bright, with clear skies and a dusting of snow on the ground. Paethor sent his packs down to the stables, then slid Wayfinder's sheath onto his sword-belt and fastened it about his waist. Throwing a cloak of dark wool over his shoulders he sought out the stableyard, where he found Don Echevarian overseeing the packing of their provisions. King Nigel had given the lords three of his best steeds for the journey; they stood saddled in the yard while three liveried yeomen strapped baggage to the load-beasts.

"Where's Lord Trent?" asked Paethor, his breath frosting in the crisp air.

"I haven't seen him," replied Echevarian.

A burst of laughter from a doorway drew their attention and they turned to find Trent staggering toward them, two large wineskins over one shoulder and his arms full of a gig-gling wench, who in turn clutched a pitcher and three silver goblets. When he saw his companions Trent set the girl on her feet and shushed her, saying "Remember, now." Her laughter subsided, and she made an effort to appear serious, which was slightly hampered by her noticing that some wine had spilled from her pitcher onto her apron. She stifled an-other giggle as she bent over and tried ineffectually to wipe it away. Trent had to grab the pitcher to keep her from spilling more. Finally she held up her goblets while Trent poured the remaining wine into them. He took one and nudged her to-ward his traveling companions. The wench carried the wine sedately to Paethor and Echevarian, her gravity hindered only by dimples that refused to be suppressed. A hiss from Trent reminded her to curtsy, and she offered up the goblets, saying "Good fortune on your journey, my Lords."

"Thank you," said Echevarian gravely, accepting a cup.

"Yes, thanks," added Paethor.

They drained the cups and handed them back, and the wench dropped another curtsy and scuttled back to where Trent lounged in the doorway. He rewarded her with a kiss, gave her his own empty goblet and the pitcher, and sent her on her way with a friendly spank. Her giggles echoed back from the corridor.

"A little warmth to run in our veins this cold morning," said Trent, smiling as he strolled forward to join the others. "Can't start a trip without a cup for good luck."

"You seem to have enough luck for the whole journey," said Echevarian, patting Trent's bulging wineskins.

"We may need it. Besides, it's very good wine. I have an understanding with the royal vintner."

"I'm sure you do," said Echevarian, gray eyes twinkling. He turned to survey the load-beasts. "Shall we be off?"

"Yes," said Paethor, and without waiting he strode to his mount, a great gray beast with black mane and tail, and swung himself up into the saddle. Echevarian mounted a handsome bay, and Trent gave a yeoman hasty directions for packing the wineskins before climbing onto his own coppery steed. With a few final shouted instructions the lords, yeomen, and load-beasts all moved forward to the main gates, which stood open under the watchful eye of the king's guards.

Crystal-clear air intensified the beauty of the lands around Argonhall, King Nigel's keep. The heavens were vibrant azure, echoed by the deeper blue of the Sandres Mountains, which had fresh snowdrifts blazing all along their crags. Their foothills were dotted with the bushy evergreens of the steppes; red soil already showed in patches through melting snow. Away to the west more mountains rode the horizon, but Paethor and his companions followed the highway southward, with the Sandres on their left. The bright sunlight cheered them, and soon they were stripping off heavy cloaks. They passed several villages but stopped only briefly to water their mounts, being anxious to make good time. The road narrowed, and the villages gave way to occasional farms and then empty plains. As they descended into a shallow ravine Trent raised his voice in a drinking song, his fine, clear tenor ringing back from the rock walls. Echevarian added a deep bass harmony, and Paethor joined in on the choruses.

Their good spirits lasted through midday heat and afternoon chill, but when a cold evening breeze rose and they stopped to pitch camp, Paethor fell silent, his frown returning as he hastened to build a fire. Echevarian went away to direct the yeomen in raising tents and seeing to the animals. Trent helped fetch water from a stream that trickled down a nearby gully, then unlimbered one of his wineskins and brought it to the fire where Paethor sat huddled in his cloak.

"Cup of cheer?" offered Trent.

Paethor shook his head, staring into the flames. Trent plopped down beside him and poured some wine into a drinking horn. He drank deeply, then leaned back against the skin, stretched his feet out toward the fire, and sighed. "The ladies at court have all lost their hearts to you," he said conversationally. "I suppose I'm a fool for not staying behind. I could have comforted them in your absence. Ah, well," he sighed, raising his cup. "Here's to good intentions."

Paethor didn't answer. He picked up a twig and began snapping it into small pieces, tossing them one by one into the flames. Trent glanced sidelong at him.

"They've decided," he went on, "that you're desperately in love with some lady you can never hope to win. Preferably one who lives at the other end of the world."

At that Paethor closed his eyes and shook his head, a sad smile on his lips. Trent watched him for a minute, then continued. "Each of them is sure she can heal your wounded heart, if only you would recognize the medicinal power of her love—"

"Enough," broke in Paethor.

Trent looked at him inquiringly.

"Thanks for your concern," said Paethor, "but I have to wrestle my own demons." Their gaze held briefly, dark eyes cautioning hazel, then Paethor looked back into the fire.

"All right," said Trent slowly. "Friends anyway?" He held out a hand.

After a moment Paethor shook it. "Friends," he said, a smile flickering across his face. "Guess I'll have some of that wine now," he added.

Trent refilled the horn and passed it to Paethor, watching him with candid curiosity. The quiet lord's sadness only served to enhance his dark beauty; his restless eyes gave him the look of a lost child.

"Perhaps it's just as well we'll miss the Yule feast," said Trent. "I'm not so sure I'd be chosen Lord of Misrule this year. The ladies might pick you instead, and then I'd have to kill myself."

That got a chuckle out of Paethor, but he shook his head.

"Do they have that custom in your father's keep?" asked Trent.

Paethor nodded and sipped at the wine, then passed the horn back to Trent.

"Ever been Lord of Misrule?" pursued Trent.

Paethor stared into the fire, his brows drawing together. "Once," he said softly.

Footsteps sounded behind them; Echevarian, carrying a platter piled with dried meat, cheese and bread. He handed it to Trent and sat down, rubbing his hands together over the fire. At the sight of the food Trent broke into a grin. "Why thanks, Echevarian," he said, picking up a hunk of cheese. "What are you and Paethor going to eat?"

For answer Echevarian pulled Trent's hood over his eyes and neatly plucked the wineskin from behind his shoulders. He poured wine into an elegant chalice while Trent struggled to sit up.

"Don't spill the food," warned Echevarian.

"Mrph," grunted Trent, pushing the hood back from his face.

Paethor came to his rescue, retrieving the precarious platter. Echevarian produced three apples and tossed one to each of the others. They ate hungrily, the long ride having sharpened their appetites. When the platter was empty they refilled their cups and built up the fire. The winter night had fallen quickly, blue sky darkening to star-scattered black. Dark gray shadows loomed; the southern end of the Sandres. Cold breezes bit at their faces and they crowded closer to the flames, risking a scorch for the sake of the warmth. A few meters away the yeomen could be heard murmuring around their own small blaze.

"What does Wayfinder say tonight?" asked Echevarian softly.

Paethor's hand went to the hilt, but he hesitated, frowning.

"We should check," urged the elder lord.

Paethor stood, throwing off his cloak, and drew the Sword. "Where is Farslayer?" he said aloud, though quietly. The blade came around from east to south, then continued a little farther before pausing.

"Southwest," murmured Trent. "It's moved."

A sharp cry, some predator's hunting call, made them look up. To the east the gibbous moon was rising over the Sandres, cold and white. Wayfinder trembled in Paethor's hand and edged westward, but he sheathed it again and sat down.

"Well," said Trent, "looks like we're riding into a merry party."

"Perhaps we should turn in," said Echevarian.

The fire snapped in the silence, its power to comfort diminished.

"One last round?" offered Trent.

Echevarian stood, gazing to the southwest. "Let's save our luck for tomorrow," he said.

Gray skies greeted them in the morning. After a hurried fistful of breakfast they broke camp and headed back to the road, now a rough track that followed a meandering river, muddy water low in its basin, sandbars dotting its surface. They passed the southern end of the Sandres and now a cold east wind drove at them across the plains. The travelers were silent, each with his own thoughts. At midday they halted to rest their beasts, and ate a cold lunch as they stood.

"Gods must be quarreling," said Trent. "They say that always makes bad weather."

"Don't joke about the gods," snapped Paethor.

Echevarian and Trent exchanged a glance.

"You religious, Paethor?" asked Trent. "I didn't mean to offend."

Paethor gave no answer. Instead he walked away toward the river.

"Let him be," said Echevarian.

They took to the road again and soon came upon a straggling band of wayfarers, mostly women and boys, walking northward beside two load-beasts that strained at an overburdened wagon. The little group looked up fearfully as the mounted party approached, one of the youths hefting a pike.

"You won't need that, lad," said Echevarian, reining his beast to a halt. "Where are you headed?"

"Argonia," answered the youth.

"Well, you're there. What now?"

A woman stepped forward. "We seek asylum from King Nigel," she said. "Can you tell us . . . how far is his keep?"

"On foot?" said Trent. "A good week, from here."

The little group's faces fell. In the wagon a child began to cry.

"Where are you from?" asked Echevarian.

"Sun Mountain," said the woman. "There was a terrible battle—our Baron was slain two days ago."

"Slain how?" asked Trent quickly.

The woman's face contorted, lines of grief furrowing her brow. "A Sword," she answered. "They said it was a magic Sword. It came from nowhere and struck him down—"

"Where is the Sword now?" demanded Echevarian.

"I don't know," said the woman, brushing tears from her cheeks with a sunburned hand. "There was an uproar, and then soldiers from Ravenskeep came—"

"We seek asylum," repeated the youth. "Will King Nigel help us?"

Echevarian gazed at the pitiful band, his stern eyes softening. "I'm sure he will, lad," he said gently, "but it's a hard journey to Argonhall. My hold is closer." He reached into his doublet and brought out a pencil and a bit of gray paper on which he scribbled a brief note. "Go back along the river to the wide shallows and the cottonwood grove, do you remember it?"

The youth nodded vigorously.

"Turn east and head for the bluffs. My house is in a little valley beyond them, you should reach it by nightfall. Give this note to my steward, Needham. He'll see you're cared for."

"Thank you, my Lord." The woman bowed as she took the note.

"Have you food enough?"

"Yes. We're not beggars," said the youth defiantly.

"We have enough for now," added the woman. "Bless you, sir."

"I'm afraid we can't escort you," said Echevarian. "We're on urgent business."

"We'll find it, my Lord. Thank you."

The riders moved on past the refugees, but after a few minutes Echevarian called a halt. He glanced at the road behind them to make sure the southerners were out of sight, then leaned toward Paethor.

"Check now," he said.

Paethor drew Wayfinder and softly asked "Where is Farslayer?" The blade swung to the southeast. It wouldn't settle, swaying back and forth in a small arc, but it was clearly pointing away from the refugees.

Trent sighed, and Echevarian nodded curtly. Paethor sheathed the Sword and they started forward again, urging their tired mounts to cover the dusty miles, and only stopped to make camp when failing light made the road dangerous. The lee of a small cliff near the river offered meager shelter from the wind. As the party rode up to it a flurry of wings burst from a twisted tree by the rock wall; an owl, shrieking its anger at being disturbed. Paethor cried out and his mount reared. He tumbled from the saddle, cowering wild-eyed between his beast and Trent's, then a moment later he swore and jerked at the animal's reins, leading it up to the cliff.

They made camp silently, pitching only one tent for the sake of shared warmth. A small cooking fire was kindled and the yeomen made hot soup from dried broth. Bread and cheese filled out the meal, but the previous night's banter was absent. Trent watched Paethor tear a piece of bread into small pieces, crumbs falling between long, graceful fingers to the ground. The handsome lord wore a haunted look, hollow eyes staring at nothing as the wind whipped his dark curls about his face.

The cooking fire smoked fitfully. Trent poked at it with a stick and added another log. Echevarian stirred and glanced at the yeomen huddled by the cliff wall.

"Let's stretch our legs a bit," said Echevarian as he rose. "I'd like to check the beasts."

Trent climbed to his feet, wrapping his cloak tighter against the wind, and nudged Paethor with a booted toe. "Come on," he said.

Paethor looked up, startled, then stood. The three lords wandered out of the shelter, buffeted by wind as they headed for the river's edge where the beasts were staked. The animals stood with heads down, tails to the wind, suffering mutely.

"All right, Paethor," said Echevarian. "Let's have it. Where's the blasted thing tonight?"

Paethor gave him a troubled glance before slowly drawing Wayfinder. "Where is Farslayer?" he said, his words swallowed by the wind. He stood facing south down the river bed, and the Sword wavered in his hands, moving from south to southeast. Finally it swung sharply to the west. Paethor gave a cry of frustration.

"This isn't getting us anywhere!" said Trent.

Paethor grabbed Echevarian's hand, pressing the hilt into it. "You do it," he said.

Echevarian faced south, squared his shoulders, and said "Where can we find Farslayer?" The Sword was still for a moment, then circled inexorably to point past Paethor's shoulder, west-northwest, into Argonian lands. Clouded moonlight shimmered on the blade as it quaked in Echevarian's grasp.

Three faces turned to follow the Sword's bearing. A shadow of gray marked a distant line of mountains.

"That's the Highmass," said Trent. "There's nothing up there, is there?"

"A few small holdings," answered Echevarian. "And our quarry, apparently."

"So we turn back? What if it's gone again by the time we get there?" complained Trent.

"We keep going till we've tracked it down," said Echevarian grimly. "Unless you have a better suggestion?"

Trent sighed. "I need a drink," he said, starting back toward the camp.

Echevarian held Wayfinder out to Paethor. He seemed reluctant to take it, but did so, sheathing it at once. Echevarian laid a hand on his shoulder as they followed Trent. "Looks like King Nigel gave you a heavier burden than he thought." Paethor turned a haggard face to him, and Echevarian glimpsed dread in his eyes. Then Paethor quickened his steps for the scant comfort of the cliffside, with Echevarian close behind.

At dawn they retraced their way northward, forded the river at the shallows, then headed cross-country toward the small cluster of mountains called the Highmass. Paethor was calm again, though silent, his fair face pale against the black hood of his cloak.

Travel was slower without a road, and it took them two days to reach the foothills. Wayfinder was consistent at last, pointing steadily to the lonely mountains regardless of which lord held it. Small comfort on the rough journey.

The Sword led them up a narrow valley through which ran a clear, ice-cold stream. The first of Trent's wineskins surrendered its last drop and was refilled with frosty water. Snow lay in deep drifts along the valley, and the short winter days were curtailed even more by the mountains blocking the sun.

Trent killed a hare with a well-slung stone, but even the fresh meat was of little help to lift chilled spirits. On the third morning after they entered the valley, it began to snow.

"Do we turn back?" asked Trent.

"No," said Echevarian. He looked at Paethor, who glanced at the ground rising ahead and sighed.

They struggled on, hampered by wet, heavy snow. One of the load-beasts blundered into a crevice hidden by a snow-drift and had to be pulled out; unhurt, luckily. The valley narrowed further and the party found themselves climbing toward a notch between two crests, barely visible through a gray wall of falling snow. Breathing was harder now, and they had to dismount and lead their animals up the treacher-ous slope, the yeomen using poles cut from trees to probe the way. The sky darkened as they neared the top, though whether from night falling or the storm thickening it was hard to tell. There was no place for a camp, so the weary group trudged ahead. Finally they entered the notch, which was level though deep in snow. Here only a few flakes were falling.

"We could camp here," gasped Trent, patting his weary beast.

"It's still light," said Echevarian. "Let's take a look at what's ahead."

"Sure," said Trent, handing his reins to a yeoman. "That ought to cheer us up."

The three lords dug their way through chest-high snow, pushing it aside with gloved hands. Soon they were puffing and sweating with the effort. Meter by meter they made their way to the far side of the pass, where they looked out over another valley, gentler in slope, and dotted with small dark lumps from which rose welcome plumes of smoke. Trent let out a laugh.

"Still want to camp up here?" asked Echevarian.

"I don't care if we're walking till midnight," said Trent.
"There's got to be a feather-bed in one of those houses!"

He turned back toward the beasts, but Paethor put a hand
on his shoulder, saying "Wait." With a glance at Echevarian
Paethor drew Wayfinder. "Where can we find Farslayer?" he
asked. The Sword's point lifted to aim up the valley, where a
manor-house stood out among the smaller dwellings.

"Whose hold is that?" asked Trent.

Echevarian shrugged. "We'll know soon."

Cheered by the prospect of shelter, the little party scrambled down into the valley. A spring not far from the pass
marked the head of a creek, which was followed down the
hillside by a narrow path. Dark was falling fast, and the little
lights of the cottages below seemed to twinkle a golden welcome. At the edge of the settlement they were met by two
sturdy men who asked their names and their business.

"We are emissaries from King Nigel," said Echevarian. "I
am Don Echevarian of Verdas, and these are lords Paethor
and Trent."

One of the men frowned. "From Argonhall? Why didn't
you come by the north road?"

"We were in the south," said Trent, "and wished to arrive
in time to present the king's Yule greetings to your master."

The guard seemed satisfied with this answer. "You'd better
come up to the Lodge, then. Squire will be sitting down to
supper soon." He led them to a wide yard in front of the
manor house, which consisted of a two-story structure built
of vast logs, with smaller wings running away on the south
and north. The yeomen were left to stable the beasts while the
lords went into the house. Warmth struck their faces in the
entryway and they sighed in unison. The guard led them into
the Hall, where firelight flickered on the polished logs of the
walls and gilded the rushes strewn over the floor. A long table

was set a few meters from a hearth at the room's north end, and servants were preparing it for the evening meal. The guard brought them to a stairwell from which narrow steps led to a gallery running along the east and south walls. At the foot of the stairs a stout man in faded green velvet was talking to a younger version of himself.

"Beg pardon, Squire," said the guard. "These men say they're from King Nigel. They're the ones we saw coming down from the pass."

The squire turned and stared down his craggy nose at the damp, bedraggled lords. Echevarian swept a bow. "Don Echevarian of Verdas," he said grandly. "These are my traveling companions, Lord Paethor of Mirador and Lord Trent Greyson. We thank you for your hospitality."

The youth beside the squire had the same shock of sandy hair, the same fearsome nose. His eyes opened wide and he said, "Did you really come over Dead Man's Pass?"

"We wouldn't have, if we'd known its name," muttered Trent.

"We were at my hold in Verdas when we were directed to come here," said Echevarian with a glance at his companions. "It seemed quickest to try the pass."

"Hmm, well you're lucky," said the squire. "It's usually snowed in at Midwinter, but the weather's been light this season. From Verdas, eh? There's a neighbor of yours here, Baron Carcham. Maybe you've come to speak to him?"

The lords stiffened at the name.

"Carcham of Ravenskeep, yes," said Echevarian. "You're very astute, Squire . . . ?"

"Fuller," replied the squire, breaking into a grin. "But everyone just calls me Squire. Carcham's in his room, he'll be down for supper. You can talk to him then, but you'd probably like to change first, eh?"

The lords, from whose shoulders melting snow had begun

to drip, agreed. The squire shouted orders right and left, calling for his guests' gear to be brought into the house and hot water to be fetched for them, then led them to a room in the south wing where a servant was already kindling a bright fire.

"Sorry to crowd you all in here," he said. "We don't often have so many visitors at once."

"No problem," said Trent, eyeing the mattresses being carried in.

"Come back to the Hall when you're ready," said the squire. "We'll hold supper for you."

"No need to do that," said Paethor.

"Pish. D'you think my women-folk would let me get away without waiting? They'll want a formal introduction to the king's lords." The squire raised an eyebrow as he surveyed Paethor's handsome countenance. "Lords from Argonhall, yes," he said. "We don't see your like around here too often!" He grinned, then headed out in the wake of the servants.

"Thank you, Squire," Echevarian called after him. "We won't be long."

The door closed and they listened to their host's cheery shouts fade down the hall. The lords looked at one another.

"Ravenskeep," hissed Trent. "What's he doing here?"

"Staying out of trouble, maybe," said Echevarian. "His barony's caught in the skirmishes."

"Then why isn't he there to defend it?" said Paethor.

No one answered.

"Come on," said Echevarian, stripping off his sodden doublet. "Let's make ourselves presentable for the squire's ladies."

They pulled off wet clothing and hastily washed themselves, then rummaged through their gear, deciding to honor their host with their one change of court dress. For Trent this was green suede trimmed with gold braid; for Echevarian, gray wool lined with red satin and edged in silver. Paethor wore dark brown velvet, unembellished. He pulled Wayfinder's sheath off of his traveling belt and stood frowning at the Sword.

"Would you rather I carried it?" offered Echevarian.

Paethor glanced up at him. "Yes," he said, then slid it onto his own fresh belt. "But it's my burden. Thanks anyway."

Echevarian softly smiled his understanding, and the three Lords hastened back to the Hall. The smell of roasted meat quickened their steps. They found Squire Fuller waiting with several young folk; one of them, a lovely redheaded girl, turned eager blue eyes toward the lords as they entered. The squire had changed his faded green velvet for a newer tunic, and the others also seemed to have put on their best for the strangers.

"Gentlemen, welcome," said the squire, coming forward. "You honor my humble Lodge. Allow me to present my household. This is my daughter Sylva," he said as the copper-haired girl curtsied and threw a saucy glance at Paethor. "Her cousin, Mari," indicating a slightly younger girl with dark, glossy curls and pansy-brown eyes. "My son, Damon," and he chucked the youth he'd been with earlier on the shoulder. "Oh, and this is Elian, my eldest," he added as a quiet, fair-haired young woman came forward. "Her mother's gone, alas, these seven winters."

"Greetings, gentle folk," said Echevarian, and introduced himself and his companions.

"Ah, and here's Baron Carcham," said the squire.

Carcham of Ravenskeep was known to the others by reputation as a fearsome lord, and his appearance as he stood in the doorway gave them no reason to doubt it. He was powerfully built and wore his long, blond hair in a warrior's queue, and the tips of his mustache were braided. Echevarian's hand fingered his own silvery whiskers.

"Carcham," said the squire, "these are the lords I told you about, from Argonhall."

As the baron approached a scabbard swung about the red skirts of his tunic, and the lords saw that the hilt above it was of rough black, identical to Wayfinder's. In that same moment Carcham's stride stuttered and his gaze fastened sharply on the weapon at Paethor's hip. For an instant he seemed alarmed, then a soldier's mask of discipline descended on his features. He bowed stiffly, clasping his Swordhilt, and Paethor's hand came unconsciously to rest on Wayfinder. Introductions were repeated, then the squire, perhaps sensing tension in the air, urged everyone to sit down to supper. He placed Baron Carcham at his right hand and Don Echevarian on his left, as befitted their rank. Paethor and Trent were seated on either side of Elian, who acted as hostess for her father. Sylva sat beside Trent and made eyes at both Paethor and Carcham across the table.

"A toast," said the squire, raising his goblet. "To our noble visitors."

"And to our kind host," said Echevarian. "May your goodwill return to you."

The words earned him a sharp glance from Carcham. Echevarian sipped calmly, seeming not to notice.

"Do you dance, my Lords?" asked Sylva, her eyes on Paethor.

"Yes," answered Trent, helping himself to a slab of meat from a heaping platter. "Everyone at King Nigel's court is required to dance or suffer harsh punishment."

The squire laughed heartily at this mild jest. Sylva looked confused for a moment, then added her piping laughter. "You will dance with us tonight, then!" she said.

Elian leaned forward to catch her eye. "Perhaps the gentle-men are tired," she said gently.

Sylva pouted. "But I want to dance!"

"You can dance with your brother, then," said the squire gruffly. Both Sylva and Damon grimaced. "These lords have had a hard journey, coming over the pass," added their father.

"All the more reason to celebrate," said Trent, which won him a beaming smile from Sylva.

"I would be happy to partner you, fair lady," added Carcham.

Sylva gave him a coy look. "Is there dancing in Ravenskeep?" she asked.

"Yes, and many other pleasures," said the baron, smiling.

Trent and Paethor exchanged a glance, each remembering the words of the refugee woman, "soldiers from Ravenskeep."

"There'll be dancing enough at the Yule feast tomorrow night," said the squire. "You'll have to be content till then. We've got no musicians, for one thing."

"Oh, Elian can play on the lute," said Sylva.

"But what if Elian wants to dance?" asked Echevarian gallantly.

"She doesn't mind," said Sylva, with the confidence of self-centered youth.

"Is that true?" asked Trent, turning to his hostess.

"Yes," said Elian. "I like to play."

"But you don't like to dance?" asked Paethor.

Elian glanced up at him with a gentle smile. "I like both."

"Well," said young Damon, "I'd rather dance to Elian's playing than to Sylva's."

Sylva stared daggers at him, then haughtily turned up her

nose. "You can dance by yourself, then. No one wants to dance with you."

"I do," said brown-eyed Mari. Then she blushed furiously and stared down at her plate. Damon looked mildly alarmed.

Sylva glared at her cousin, then seemed to realize her temper was not adding to her charm. She put on a smile again and turned to Trent. "You are staying for Yule, aren't you?"

Trent's lopsided grin broke out as he looked into her wide blue eyes. "How can we refuse?"

Echevarian glanced at the squire, who chuckled and said, "Yes, join us. The whole valley will be here for the feast."

"Thank you," said Echevarian, raising his cup. "We accept."

When everyone had eaten his fill Sylva again begged for dancing. Elian gave in to her pleas and agreed to play the lute. "But only for a little while," she said. "It's late already."

The Hall was big enough to hold twenty couples or more. As it was, there were only two. Damon had made himself scarce the minute the lute was brought out. Sylva claimed her dance from the baron, and flirted boldly with him. Trent danced with Mari, who blushed whenever the steps brought their hands together. Elian's fingers were nimble on the lute-strings, and as she strummed a quiet smile hovered on her lips.

"Your daughter plays well," said Echevarian, seated against the wall with the squire and Paethor.

"Hm? Oh, yes. She's very clever. Like her mother that way," said the squire. "Don't know what I'm going to do with her, though. She's had two offers of marriage, and turned 'em both down. May not get any more; the lads around here like their women robust, and well, you see how she is." He frowned in a puzzled way, as a gardener might upon discovering a frail lily in amongst his roses. "She's thinking she might join the White Temple," he added.

"Isn't she a bit young?" asked Echevarian.

A peal of laughter from Sylva signaled the end of the dance, and she curtsied to Baron Carcham, then skipped up to Paethor. "Now you!" she cried, holding out her hands.

Paethor looked up at her with a level gaze. "Not tonight, lady. Please forgive me."

Sylva stamped her foot. "But you have to!"

"Dance with me, Sylva," said Trent, coming up and bowing gallantly over her hand. She let herself be distracted, but a glance over her shoulder told Paethor she had not given up.

"I think I'll retire," he said, once the music had started. "Thank you again for your hospitality, Squire."

The squire nodded. "Rest well, m'lord."

Echevarian stayed to chat with their host, and in due course Sylva demanded a dance from him as well, though she behaved toward him much as she did toward her father. Echevarian was amused by this, and so, from the glint in his eyes, was Trent. Carcham danced with Mari. Echevarian stole a glance now and then at his Sword, but was unable to make out a marking on the hilt.

"That's enough," said Elian when the song ended. "We have a busy day tomorrow." The little party broke up, but not before Sylva secured promises of more dances at the Yule feast.

Returning to their chamber, Echevarian and Trent found Paethor musing by the hearth, his gaze fixed on the remains of the fire. He looked up, startled out of his reverie, and reached for another log. New flames threw golden light on his face and glinted back from his dark eyes and hair. Echevarian pulled a stool forward and stretched his hands toward the warmth, while Trent began searching through the baggage.

"Now where—aha!" Trent held up his second wineskin with a grin. "Let's drink the squire's health again for good measure. It's better wine, it ought to bring him better health." He carried the skin to the fire and filled his horn.

Paethor leaned his chin on one hand and regarded him. "You're never at a loss for something to celebrate, are you?" he murmured wistfully.

"We've got a roof over our heads and our bellies full of meat. I say that's cause enough," said Trent. He drank and passed the cup to Echevarian, who accepted it, smiling.

"Don't forget the young ladies," added Echevarian. "Looks like you'll be reveling on Yule after all."

"They're a pretty set, for country girls," said Trent. "That Sylva—"

"She's trouble, that one," said Echevarian, chuckling. "The sort who wants to be the queen bee."

"Bah, she's just a girl. She'll melt if I drop a little honey in her ear."

"Not she! You'll need a bucketful, and she'll ask for more. Besides, she's set her sights on Paethor here," said Echevarian, offering him the wine.

The look Paethor gave him was not appreciative, but he accepted the horn and took a sip, then passed it back to Trent. "If you'll pardon me," he said, "I think we have a more serious matter to discuss."

Trent sighed. "Ravenskeep." He swallowed the dregs and refilled the horn.

"*Is* that Farslayer he wears?" asked Paethor.

"I couldn't get a look at the hilt," said Echevarian.

"It has to be Farslayer," said Trent. "Why else would Wayfinder have brought us here?"

Paethor shifted on his chair and glanced over his shoulder at the moonlit window.

"We could ask Wayfinder again," said Echevarian.

"And walk up to Ravenskeep with a Sword of Power pointed at him?" said Trent. "He'll like that!"

"One moment," said Echevarian. He went softly to the door and opened it. The hall was empty, and after checking the window he returned to the fire. "We'd better be careful," he said, lowering his voice. "If Ravenskeep guesses which Sword we have, he'll know why we're here."

"What if he's already guessed?" muttered Trent.

The lords looked at one another. "Perhaps it's just as well we're all in one room," said Echevarian.

"There's another problem," said Paethor after a pause. "Assuming it is Farslayer, how do we get it away from him?"

"Challenge him?" suggested Trent.

"On what grounds?" said Echevarian. "He's done nothing to offend. Besides, he could probably beat any one of us."

"We have to do something," said Trent. "If we wait too long, he may use the thing, and we'll have lost our chance."

"Unless he uses it on one of us," said Paethor.

A look of horror crossed Trent's face. Paethor straightened and slowly said, "If he uses Farslayer to kill one of us, then it's the duty of the others to carry it back to Argonhall."

"Yes," said Echevarian after a moment. "You're right."

"Let's swear it," said Paethor. He unbuckled his belt and held Wayfinder between them by the sheath, placing a hand on its guard. The others grasped the hilt and pommel. "We swear by this Sword," said Paethor, "which our liege-lord entrusted to us, that if Farslayer comes into the possession of any of us we shall not use it in vengeance, but shall carry it back to our King at Argonhall. So say I, Paethor of Mirador."

"So say I, Echevarian of Verdas."

"So say I," whispered Trent, "Trenton Greyson." For once, he looked as solemn as Paethor.

Midwinter's Day dawned clear and bright. From first light the Lodge was bustling with preparations for the Yule feast.

Folk from the valley streamed in with foodstuffs to pile in the kitchen and evergreen boughs for the Hall. A red-faced servant brought cold meat and a pitcher of ale to the lords' room and hurried away again, begging them to shout if they wanted anything more. They ate a leisurely breakfast, and emerged to be met by their host, dressed for riding.

"Good morning, good morning," called the squire cheerily. "A Glad Yule to you, my lords! Came to see if you'd like to ride out with me, get away from all this bother. I could show you the valley," he offered.

The lords agreed, and soon they were mounted on sturdy beasts from the squire's stables, their own weary steeds being left to rest. Shading their eyes from sun-glaring snow, the lords followed the squire northward along the road, which had already been trampled clear by the feet of valley-folk. Some of these turned to marvel at the noble visitors, bowing as they passed. The squire waved a cheery greeting back.

"Won't Baron Carcham be joining us?" asked Echevarian, trotting beside the squire.

"He's seen the valley. I showed it to him when he arrived a few days ago, and besides, he's been here before."

"He has?" said Trent.

The Squire gave him a shrewd look. "Aye, he has. But you would know that, wouldn't you? Having come here to meet him."

Echevarian threw a warning glance at Trent, then said "To be honest, Squire, we did not come to meet him."

"Well, now, I didn't think so, after the way he looked at you last night."

"In fact, we are on an errand for the king, and found our way into your valley by chance," continued Echevarian.

"Did you, now?" Squire Fuller reined in at the crest of a small hill. They had passed the last of the houses, and now

the beasts were knee-deep in snow. "From here the road runs
north to the river, then turns east toward Argonhall," said
the squire. "Up there's a little shrine to Ardneh," he added,
pointing to a small structure on one of the valley's slopes.
"Elian likes to tend it. We haven't got a priest."

"It's a pretty holding," said Paethor, looking out over the
valley.

"Aye," nodded the squire. "And peaceful, too. Like to
think it'll stay that way," he added.

"Have you any reason to doubt it?" asked Echevarian.

"Well, now, I wonder," said the squire. "You gentlemen
will understand, I think, if I say I'm not overfond of Baron
Carcham. He came uninvited, and he's not an Argonian. At
first I thought he had just come to dally with my little Sylva,
like he did when he passed through here last summer." He
laughed. "She's a rare handful, my girl. Likes to make the
menfolk crazy. She's got half the valley lads green with envy
since Carcham showed up."

"Do you think she's set her heart on a baroness's coro-
net?" asked Trent.

"She's too young to set her heart on anything. Not that I'd
mind having a nobleman for a son-in-law," he said thoughtfully. "My late wife was a lord's daughter, so there's good
blood in my brood. She was a fine lady, she was." He sighed
and gazed down at his gloved hands resting on his saddle-
bow. "But I doubt any baron would take a squire's daughter
to wife. No, they're both just amusing themselves," he said.
"I thought that was all there was to it, but now you've arrived," he turned to Paethor, "and I can't help noticing that
fine Sword you wear that's so much like his own."

"Your eyes are sharp, Squire," said Paethor. "Indeed, we
have reason to believe they were forged in the same fire."

"That wouldn't be a magical fire, now, would it?"

The three lords were silent.

"Well, it's none of my business, I suppose. Pay no heed to me, gentlemen," said the squire. "We country-folk like to tell stories of magic. The old gods, and such. Never mind."

"We don't mean to be rude, sir," said Paethor. "Our king has charged us with a private errand, and knowing it would not comfort you, I fear."

The squire nodded. "Well, if it's king's business, I wish you good speed. My only hope is that no quarrel should disturb my little holding."

"If there's any quarrel it won't be of our making," Echevarian assured him.

The squire met his eyes with a perceptive gaze. "Can't ask for more than that, can I?" he said.

They rode back down to the Lodge, the squire describing the valley and its people, and introducing a few whom they passed on their way. In the yard they dismounted, waiting for attendance. The squire let out a bellow and a lone stable-hand hurried up. "Beg pardon, m'lords," he said, bobbing his head as he took the reins of the squire's and Echevarian's beasts. "I'll be back in just a minute for the others. Dan's been called to help in the kitchen."

"I'll lead these two for you," said Trent, taking Paethor's reins.

"Thank you, sir," said the stable-hand.

"Come upstairs to my study when you're done," said the squire. "We'll try the Midsummer's mead, make sure it's fit for tonight's feast."

Trent grinned. "I'll be there in a flash."

He led the beasts into a stall and was turning back toward the yard when he heard familiar voices from the depths of the stable. He walked quietly toward the sound and paused in the doorway of a tack room. One of the king's yeomen sat on a wooden chest cleaning a saddle, and before him stood

Baron Carcham, a golden coin gleaming between his fingers. Trent must have made some small noise, for Carcham looked up.

"Morning, Baron," said Trent, smiling amiably as he leaned against the door frame. "Happy Yule."

The baron turned to him, giving him a measuring glance as he tossed the coin idly in his hand. "Good morning," he said.

"I hear there's been trouble near Ravenskeep lately. I hope it won't spoil the celebration for you," said Trent.

Carcham scowled and his hand formed a fist as he caught the coin. "Mind your own business, boy, or there'll be trouble for you!" He brushed past Trent and strode out of the stable.

"Good advice," murmured Trent, watching him go. He looked back at the yeoman. "He could use it himself."

The yeoman glanced up at him with a bland face. "Aye, sir."

"What did he want from you?"

"Asked about that black-handled sword that Lord Paethor wears."

"And what did you tell him?"

"Told him I know nothing about it," said the yeoman, rubbing vigorously at the leather.

"Did he say anything else?" asked Trent.

"Asked if I'd ever seen m'lord draw it. Told him I couldn't recall." The yeoman stopped punishing the saddle and looked up with a grin. "He seemed to think the sight of gold would jog my memory."

"But it didn't," said Trent.

"King Nigel's good to us. I wouldn't give that prune-faced southerner the time of day, not for a year's wages!"

"Good. If he comes around again, report to me at once. Tell your comrades."

"Aye, sir," said the yeoman.

Trent gave him a pat on the shoulder and hurried back to the Lodge. He took the stairs two at a stride and walked along the gallery to an open doorway. In a small, comfortably cluttered room the squire was standing over a servant who was putting a tap into a small cask. Paethor and Echevarian stood by the window.

The squire glanced up. "Hello, lad. Careful, there," he warned the servant. "Don't spill any!"

Trent joined his friends by the window. "Carcham's been asking questions," he murmured. "I found him in the stable with one of our yeomen."

"What did he want?" asked Echevarian softly.

"Information about the Sword," whispered Trent.

"Ah, there we are!" said the squire. He held up a glass of amber liquid to the window's light. "Clear as summer rain! Come, try it, my lords."

They gathered around the little hide-topped table and accepted glasses of mead. The squire raised his in salute. "To his Majesty's health," he said.

"To the king," said Echevarian.

"The king," echoed the others.

They drank, the honey wine slipping smoothly down their throats. "Good mead," said Trent, regarding his empty glass with approval.

"But is it good enough?" said the squire, grinning. "I must serve only the best for the Yule feast."

Trent's eyes gleamed back at him. "Perhaps we'd better have another taste, to be sure."

Paethor set his glass down.

"Won't you have some more?" asked the squire.

"I'll leave it to more experienced palates to judge," said Paethor, smiling.

The squire shrugged and went back to business with the

cask. Paethor wandered out onto the gallery and looked down. Great swags of evergreen were being hung in the Hall, and the rushes had been swept from the stone floor so that fresh could be laid down for the evening. A whole goat was roasting on a roaring fire at the hearth, with two sweating lads turning the spit. The fire's heat rose to the gallery, and Paethor walked along to the south end where an open door led to a balcony. He stepped out and gazed at the snowbound valley, inhaling sharp, cool air. Tall pine trees nearby swayed in the breeze. At a sound Paethor turned to find Echevarian coming out to join him.

"Guarding my back?" said Paethor, smiling.

"And my sobriety," grinned Echevarian.

"Do you suppose they'll leave any for the feast?"

Echevarian laughed, then laid a hand on Paethor's shoulder. "Let me wear the Sword tonight," he said gently. "You could use a dance or two."

Paethor's smile dimmed. "You heard his Majesty. I'm not fond of festivals." He leaned on the balcony railing and stared out at the snow.

"Even Yule?" asked Echevarian.

"Especially Yule."

Echevarian studied Paethor, noting the frown that had reappeared on his handsome brow. "I wish I could lighten your burden, my friend," he said softly.

Paethor shook his head.

"Let me wear the Sword."

"No."

"If any of us must die, it should be me," reasoned Echevarian quietly. "I've lived long and happy. You've done neither."

Paethor glanced sharply up at him. "No need to talk of dying," he said. "We've promised not to quarrel."

"Not to start a quarrel," corrected Echevarian.

"You think Carcham might?"

"He might. He's been asking about the Sword."

Their gaze held for a moment. "Then so be it," said Paethor. "It may be the only way to fulfill our errand."

"I'm a better swordsman than you," argued Echevarian. "Let him challenge me."

"You said he could beat any of us," countered Paethor.

"But—"

"If he throws the Sword, you and Trent can claim it in the king's name. If he kills without throwing it, arrest him and take him to Argonhall. The squire will back you."

"Are you so anxious to die?" asked Echevarian.

Paethor swallowed, looking away over the valley. "If I die for this my life won't have been wasted," he said softly.

"Wasted?"

Paethor glanced up at him, a bitter smile on his lips. The next moment, a flap of wings made him flinch away from the balcony, his face a mask of terror. Echevarian moved to his side in one quick stride and caught hold of him. "It's nothing," he said into Paethor's ear. "Only an owl."

Paethor looked up at the large, snow-white bird that had come to rest on the railing. "I d-don't like owls," he said.

The owl stared at them, blinking its eyes against the bright sunlight. "Car-cham?" it called.

The lords looked back at the creature. Echevarian could feel Paethor's trembling.

"Car-cham?" repeated the bird, stepping closer along the railing and leaning forward to peer at Echevarian. Paethor shrank back, hiding his face against the older lord's shoulder.

"No," said Echevarian, the temptation to hear the bird's message outweighed by Paethor's panic.

The owl ruffled its feathers, then in a flurry of wings it departed.

"A messenger," said Echevarian. "It's gone now."

Paethor drew a shaky breath and raised his head. Echevarian led him to the far end of the balcony and made him lean against the sun-warmed wall. "Tell me," he said.

Paethor shook his head.

"Something or someone has hurt you," said Echevarian.

"Only myself," whispered Paethor.

"*Tell* me," Echevarian insisted.

Paethor looked up at him with eyes blinded by memory, then slid down the wall to sit in the snow. Echevarian knelt beside him, watching him intently.

"Ten years ago—ten years tonight," said Paethor, with a shiver, "I was just becoming a man, and I was proud. Too proud." He glanced up at Echevarian. "You know how Sylva is? The prettiest girl around, and knows it?"

Echevarian nodded.

"That was me. Only I went farther than she." He shifted and wrapped his arms around himself, though the sun beat down warmly. "In my father's keep they choose the Lord of Yule at sunset. All the women get to vote. It was the first year I was old enough, and of course they chose me." Paethor's voice grew bitter. "It went to my head, and I boasted—" He winced, and his voice became a whisper. "I boasted no woman could resist my comeliness, not even a goddess. And a goddess heard."

Echevarian frowned, puzzled, and leaned closer.

"I spent the evening surrounded by admiring women, dancing and carousing. I reveled in their attention—wallowed in it. Then someone called us outside to see the moon rise, and that's when she appeared to me."

Paethor paused to lick his lips. "She was the most glorious lady I'd ever seen, with light shining all around her. I thought it was Venus. She said she loved me and told me to follow her, and I did."

"Followed her where?"

"Into the woods. She kept telling me how beautiful I was, how much she adored me. I don't know how long we walked; hours, perhaps. Finally she stopped in a clearing. A beautiful clearing, full of moonlight. She said, 'I must see if your beauty goes beyond your face. Take off your clothes.' And I did."

Paethor covered his face with his hands. "I was entranced. I said 'Goddess of Love, teach me your art!' And she answered, 'I will teach you, but I am not Venus. I am Athena.' Then she vanished in a roar of wind, and there were owls flying all around me, carrying away my clothes. They left me there alone, naked."

Echevarian put a hand on his shoulder.

"I wandered around crying, calling to her to come back, not to leave me. Eventually my father's men came searching. They said they found me curled up in a snowbank, half-frozen; I don't remember it." He looked up at Echevarian with a pitiful smile. "Ever since I've been afraid she would come back."

"But she hasn't," said Echevarian.

"No," said Paethor, "and I've been careful to give her no reason."

"Paethor," said Echevarian, taking him gently by the shoulders. "It's past. She won't come back."

"Gods have long memories."

"Let it go, man."

"I've tried. Believe me, I've tried. I wish I could be—" he smiled, gesturing helplessly. "Carefree. Like Trent. But every time a woman smiles at me I can tell she's admiring my face, and suddenly I see Athena."

Echevarian put an arm around him, and Paethor let out one gasping sob. "So you see," he said, "it doesn't matter if I die. I only hope to die well."

"Hush. No one need die," said Echevarian. He hugged the younger lord, rocking him gently under the bright sunlight until he was calm again. Then Echevarian held Paethor at arm's length and looked deep into his eyes.

"Let me at least take one burden from you. Give me the Sword."

Paethor smiled wanly and shook his head. "The king gave it to me. I think some fate awaits me here," he said. "Wayfinder wanted me to come here, even when it said Farslayer was in the south." He stared into the distance for a moment, then gripped Echevarian's hand. "But thank you," he added. "I've never had a better friend."

Echevarian returned the clasp, then helped Paethor up. With hearts far from merry the two lords returned to the Hall.

Trent whistled as he strode down the gallery. The mead had been pronounced fit to drink, although it had taken three or four glasses to be sure, enough to take the edges off the world and make it necessary for Trent to keep a hand on the banister as he ran down the stairs. He rounded the foot and went up two stone steps to knock on a door tucked beneath the stairwell.

"Come in," called a feminine chorus.

Trent opened the door to a cozy chamber where a fire crackled on the hearth. Heavy curtains had been thrown back from tall windows to give the ladies of the house, seated around a table, light to work by. Elian and Mari were stitching golden trim to a half-cape of dark green, while Sylva fashioned a wreath out of sprigs of holly. They looked up at Trent, who smiled and swept them a bow. He knelt beside Elian's chair and kissed her hand. "Fair lady," he said, "your father sent me to tell you that the Midsummer mead is palatable."

She smiled down at him in amusement. "Oh, I'm so relieved," she said. "How much is left?"

"Plenty," said Trent. "Shall I bring you some?"

"Thanks, I'll wait till tonight."

Trent shrugged, smiling, and wandered over to sit beside Sylva. "What are you making? A crown?"

"Yes, for the Holly King," said Sylva with a sly glance at him.

"Who's that?" asked Trent.

"The Holly King," repeated Mari, opening her brown eyes wide. "Don't you know?"

Trent shook his head, his face all innocent puzzlement.

"It's one of our customs," said Elian. "Every Yule the young girls all share a cake with a bean baked into it. Whoever finds the bean gets to choose the Holly King, and he presides over the Yule festival."

"And he has to dance with all the girls, and be merry all night long," added Sylva.

"Ah," said Trent. "Sounds like hard work."

"Not for you, my Lord." Elian smiled.

Trent glanced up at her inquiringly.

"If King Nigel requires you to dance, you've had good training."

Trent laughed. "True. Do you think I would make a good Holly King, Sylva?"

"I don't know," said Sylva. "Let's see." She placed the wreath on his head, dark green leaves glinting against his soft brown hair. "Not bad," she said. "What do you think, Mari?"

"I think he's perfect," said Mari, then she blushed and looked down at her stitching.

Trent laughed again. "Thank you, kind lady," he said, coming around the table to kiss her hand. "If you find the bean and choose me, I'll dance with you all night long."

Mari giggled and smiled at him shyly.

"You would be a fine Holly King," said Elian, regarding him with her calm green eyes. "You can make anyone laugh, and you are always merry yourself."

"Not like Lord Paethor," said Sylva. "He never smiles."

"Oh, he does," said Trent. "You just have to be watching."

"Why is he so glum?" asked Sylva.

"Why? Well—it's because he's heartbroken, lady. All his life he has wished he had red hair."

The girls laughed.

"No," protested Trent. "It's true. And now he comes and meets you, Sylva, with the prettiest, reddest hair in all the world." Trent sat beside her again and picked up a strand of her hair, stroking it with his fingers. "Redder than sunset, and softer than a rabbit's fur. No wonder he's mad with grief."

Sylva laughed again and punched his arm. "Be serious!"

"I am!"

"No, I mean tell me! Why is he so sad? What's the *truth?*"

"Don't pry, Sylva," said Elian.

"The truth? The truth, dear lady, is that I don't know. I'm not in his confidence." Trent sighed. "He isn't always this gloomy. At King Nigel's court I've seen him dance through the night. The ladies there are all mad for him, but not one of them has ever touched his heart. Not that I know of, anyway." He looked up and found the girls watching him, even Elian, whose needle lay forgotten in her lap. He broke into a foolish grin. "You shouldn't listen to me, though," he said. "I never tell a tale the same way twice."

Sylva frowned, laughing, and took the wreath from his head.

"Have I displeased you?" said Trent in mock alarm. He

knelt beside her chair. "Tell me how to make amends. I want to be worthy of the holly crown!"

"Help me finish it, then," said Sylva. "Hand me that ribbon."

"I hear and obey," said Trent, jumping to his feet and snatching up a ribbon from the table, then presenting it to Sylva with an exaggerated bow. She laughed and took it from him.

"Now a piece of holly," she demanded, enjoying the game.

Trent scooped up a sprig and yelped as a thorn pricked his thumb. He squeezed it and a bright red drop appeared.

"You're supposed to take the thorns off first!" said Sylva.

"Are you all right, my Lord?" asked Elian.

Trent smiled sheepishly, sucking at the wound. "Fine," he said. "It's nothing but my own carelessness. My own stupid folly, for playing with holly—"

Sylva giggled, taking the sprig from him and snipping off the thorns with a little pair of scissors.

"Folly, lolly, lolly—" sang Trent, picking up two more sprigs by their stems and making them dance on the tabletop.

The girls laughed, and Trent kept them laughing until they'd finished their regalia. Then Sylva made him try it on, and he struck a royal pose, the cape lightly draping his shoulders, holly forming a halo around his head.

"I hereby decree that mistletoe shall hang in every doorway, and anyone who doesn't smile shall be sent to the kitchens to wash the dishes," he pronounced.

"Paethor, be warned!" said Elian, taking back the cape. "Come, Sylva. It's late, and we still have your dress to trim."

Sylva reached for the crown and Trent gave it to her, lifting her hand to his lips. She smiled coyly at him, picked up a leftover sprig of holly and stood on tiptoe to tuck it behind his ear. Then she and Mari tossed all their odds and ends into

a large basket and ran to the door where Elian waited.
"Thank you for your help, my Lord," she said. "We'll see
you this evening."

Trent bowed and watched them go, then grinned to himself and made his way back to his chamber. When he opened
the door he surprised Echevarian and Paethor, standing with
swords drawn in a space cleared in the middle of the floor.

"Come in, close the door," said Echevarian, beckoning.

Trent did so and leaned against it. "Funny place to practice sword-play," he said. "Funny time for it, too."

"Echevarian was just showing me a thrust," said Paethor.
He hefted Wayfinder and swung it back and forth a couple of
times to feel its weight, then made a feinting thrust toward
Echevarian, who parried and nodded.

"Expecting trouble?" asked Trent.

"No," said Echevarian. "Just being prepared."

Paethor sheathed the Sword, walked over to the fireplace
and leaned against the mantel.

"Well, that's not what you need to prepare," said Trent.
"For tonight you need to brush up your dancing and your
wit."

"I take it that's what you've been doing," said Echevarian.

"I," said Trent, strolling to his baggage and poking
through it, "have been entertaining the young ladies. One of
them will choose the Lord of Misrule—only here it's the
Holly King. I did my best to charm them. Have to, considering the competition!" He shot a grinning glance at Paethor
but got no response, Paethor being absorbed in stirring the
ashes on the hearth with his toe. Trent shrugged, found his
drinking horn and reached for his wineskin.

"Wasn't the mead good enough?" asked Echevarian.

"Yes, but I'm almost sober again," said Trent, filling his
horn.

"Sober might not be a bad idea."

Trent glanced up. "You *are* expecting trouble," he said, looking from Echevarian to Paethor. "What's happened?"

The others exchanged a glance, then Paethor said, "We saw a—a messenger."

"A talking owl," added Echevarian. "It mistook me for Carcham."

"What did it say?" asked Trent.

"I didn't hear the message. It flew away."

"News from the south," said Trent. "Damn! I wish you'd heard it."

"So we'd better be on guard tonight," said Echevarian, taking up the wineskin. "Let's give this to the squire. A Yule gift."

"That's all we have left," protested Trent. "That's our luck for the way home!"

"Haven't you ever heard the saying, 'Share your luck and double it'?" said Echevarian.

Trent sighed. "All right," he said, lifting his horn. "Here's good fortune to us." He sipped and handed the horn to Echevarian, who took a swallow. Trent carried the wine to Paethor. "Some luck for you?" he offered.

Paethor's face softened into a wistful smile. "Thanks," he said, accepting the cup. "I suppose I need all I can get."

Shadows lengthened as the shortest day of the year came to a close. Inside the Lodge torches were lit, fire blazed on the great hearth, and fresh candles glowed in all the sconces. Tables laden with food lined the east wall of the Hall, and valley-folk, all in their holiday best, thronged in. The three lords, dressed again in court clothes and each wearing his weapon, entered the Hall to find it already crowded. A trio of musicians sat in the south gallery, blaring away. In the little room under the stairs a group of young men were playing spinnikens, their occasional roar attesting to another victory. The squire bustled up, saying "Welcome, my lords, welcome! Merry Yule!"

"Merry Yule, Squire Fuller," said Echevarian, bowing. "Here's a small gift from the three of us." He handed the wineskin to the squire.

"It's wine from the King's cellars," added Trent. "His Majesty's best."

"Ho! Well, I'll put it away, or it'll be gone before I get a taste of it. Thank you, m'lords! Help yourselves to supper— no sitting down at table, I'm afraid, in this crowd." He waved them toward the food, and hurried away with the wineskin under his arm.

The lords took up plates and piled them with good, hearty fare. The valley-folk had brought out their best treasures, and besides the huge mounds of bread, meat, and cheese there were dishes of pickled vegetables, candied fruits, and even a steaming bowl of carrots that had been dug from the frozen ground that morning. The lords carried their supper to chairs along the south wall and sat watching the revelers. Baron Carcham came out of the gaming-room carrying a bulging pouch. He tossed it in one hand and the heavy chink of coins was heard. Carcham's tunic was scarlet and black, and he wore a wolf-pelt over his shoulders and heavy bronze bracelets at his wrists. He paused before Paethor's chair, a slow, unpleasant smile sliding onto his face as he glanced at Wayfinder.

"Good evening, your Excellency," said Paethor.

Carcham nodded, tucking the pouch into his belt, but his answer was stopped by a cheer that went up as the squire returned with his ladies. Sylva danced in on his arm, wearing a gown of deep burgundy trimmed across the shoulders with soft, white fur. A spray of holly berries was pinned to the trim, blood-red drops against the snowy white; winter colors. Her eyes were alight with festival fire, and the laughter on her lips enhanced her loveliness.

Mari, escorted by her cousin Damon, looked festive as well, chestnut curls glowing against her gold satin dress. Elian followed them, her fair tresses forming a pale waterfall over blue velvet. The squire, bellowing greetings, led them forward to meet the valley people. Carcham strode up to them, the crowd parting before him, and bowed over Sylva's hand. She beamed and curtsied, and let him lead her to the feast-table. The squire clapped his hands, the musicians blew a fanfare, and the chattering fell to a murmur.

"Welcome, good friends," shouted the squire. "I wish you all a Happy Yule!" He waited for the answering cheer to subside. "There's food and drink for all, and dancing afterward—" Here another cheer stopped him and he waved his hands for quiet. "But first, the Yule Cake!" A roar went up from the crowd as a servant brought out a great round platter on which lay a golden cake. All the young girls came forward to take some. Baron Carcham led Sylva up to the platter, holding her right hand close to his side as she chose a piece. There was a moment's hush as the young girls, colorful as a flock of summer birds, gobbled their cake eagerly. Then a cry went up and Sylva skipped into the center of the room, holding one hand aloft and still chewing, her eyes gleeful. "The bean, the bean!" yelled the crowd, applauding.

"Come on," said Trent, urging his companions to set aside their empty plates. A circle was forming around Sylva, this time of young men.

"You go," said Echevarian. "We'll watch."

"No," said Trent, grabbing him and Paethor by the hands, "I need you to remind them we're glorious lords from Argon-

all!" He dragged them forward to the circle. Echevarian and
aethor stood behind him, wedged between eager young val-
ey men. Sylva had traded her lucky bean for the holly-
wreath and cape, and prowled the edge of the circle, laughing
s the valley youths all begged her to choose them. Hushed
whispers and stifled mirth formed a background to the steady
rum beat provided by the minstrels. Sylva slowed her steps,
ausing to smile slyly up at Baron Carcham, then skipping
way from him to the laughter of the crowd. She made her
ay around the circle and stopped before Trent, who grinned
own at her. She glanced coyly at him through her eyelashes,
nd slowly raised the holly crown. Then she turned quick as
ghtning, and reached over his shoulder to set the wreath on
aethor's brow. Hoots and cheers rose from the revelers,
ome of whom grabbed the cape and threw it around Pae-
1or's shoulders.

"Now you *have* to dance with me!" cried Sylva.

Paethor stared at her in dismay, his face going pale be-
eath the holly, then he glanced up to see Carcham scowling
cross the circle. He pulled himself together, managing to
nile, and offered Sylva his arm. "Very well, lady," he said.
Let the dancing begin!" The crowd applauded as more cou-
les joined them and the musicians struck up a lively tune.

Echevarian turned to the crestfallen Trent. "Hard luck,"
e said, "but there are plenty of ladies to dance with."

"I think I'll cultivate a melancholy air instead," said Trent.
It worked for Paethor."

"Console yourself," said Echevarian. "He likes it less than
ou do."

They stepped back to make room for the dancers. Trent
atched with folded arms, but soon his feet were tapping to
1e music, and before long he spotted Mari standing shyly in
corner.

"She looks lonely," he said to Echevarian. "I'd better g ask her to dance. Just to be polite," he added.

Echevarian grinned at him, and Trent shrugged, smilin crookedly back. Then he went to lead Mari into the dance.

The revelry continued, Paethor dutifully dancing with a the young valley girls. Echevarian kept an eye on Carcham who leaned against the wall and glowered, his gaze followin Paethor. Midway through the evening the minstrels took break, and the revelers milled about the Hall, nibbling sweet and cheeses from the board and drinking the Midsumme mead. The valley folk crowded around Paethor, who ha recovered enough to assume his court manners, scatterin smiles among them and cutting a joke now and then. Sylv claimed his attention again, flirting furiously. Carcham, di gusted, marched back to the gaming room.

A small commotion attended the entrance of two servant bearing a holly-trimmed platter on which stood a huge brea pudding. Blue alcohol flames danced over it. Sylva and th others clapped their hands. Paethor took advantage of th diversion, slipping away to climb the stairs to the gallery Here he found Elian watching the revelers below. She turne to see him framed in the stairwell, golden torchlight gleamin on the holly leaves at his brow.

"Forgive me, lady," he said, pausing on the top step. " came up for some air. Shall I leave you?"

"No, no," she said. "Breathe while you can!"

Paethor smiled fleetingly. "Thank you."

"It's you who should be thanked, for being so patient, said Elian.

"Patient?"

"With Sylva. For making you the Holly King."

Paethor hesitated, then said, "I understand it's a grea honor."

Elian smiled softly. "For the valley-folk, yes. For you I imagine it's more of a trial." Then she glanced anxiously up at his startled face. "Forgive me, I didn't mean to be rude."

"You weren't," said Paethor. "But what did you mean? Have I seemed reluctant?"

"No." She shook her head. "You're very gracious." She flashed him a smile, and said, "Please pardon me. The mead must have made me giddy."

Elian picked up a cloak from a gallery bench and opened the door to the balcony. Paethor frowned, then followed her outside. She stood at the railing, her cloak wrapped around her, gazing up at the full moon. Wisps of gray cloud drifted softly, blue-white stars peeking out between them and moonlight setting cold fire to their edges. Elian turned as Paethor came up beside her.

"I do appreciate the honor," he said.

Elian met his gaze calmly. "But you don't enjoy it. You're a private person," she said. "You keep your thoughts to yourself, and you don't like being the center of attention." She looked out at the valley. "When you first came here I thought you were in mourning, but I see now it isn't so. Or if it is, the grief is old."

Paethor inhaled sharply, surprised at the accuracy of her insight.

"Anyway," she continued, "your courtesy does you great credit. I'm sure none of the valley people know how hard this is for you." She glanced up at Paethor, whose eyes seemed to stare through her, out at the trees. The holly berries in his hair shone black in the moonlight and the gay cloak fluttered about him, too light to keep away the cold.

"This is not your rightful role," said Elian softly, reaching up to take the holly from his brow. "For you this is a crown of thorns."

He blinked, but his eyes wandered away again, back into distant memory.

"My Lord," said Elian, "I pray that you will find a way to release whatever past disturbs you. It's Yule, the time of new beginnings." She paused, afraid she'd said too much, and stepped away from him to look at the moon.

"Stay," he cried softly, and Elian turned, surprised by the grief in his voice. She saw torment in the black depths of his eyes, and sensed he spoke not to her but to some bygone ghost. "Lady of Wisdom, you've taken my clothes," he whispered. "Don't leave me!"

"I've taken nothing," she said uneasily, holding out the holly crown. His hands came up to receive it, and as they touched he stirred, and looked into her eyes as if seeing her for the first time. Elian returned his wondering gaze, a slow blush darkening her cheeks.

"It was you," he whispered. "I thought I came to find my death, but it was you!"

Elian blinked in confusion. She wasn't frightened, but something in his eyes made her heart beat quickly.

"Forgive me," said Paethor, with a soft laugh. "You must think I'm insane."

"No—" said Elian uncertainly.

Paethor gazed at her for a moment, then seemed to reach a decision. His hand went to the sheath at his side and lifted the black Sword-hilt. "This is Wayfinder," he said. "Have you heard of it?"

Elian nodded. "The Sword of Wisdom," she said.

"Wisdom," said Paethor, his eyes wandering to the trees again. "Yes. And it led me to you."

"I don't understand," said Elian. "Why?"

Paethor's fingers caressed her hand. "Because you can see beyond my face, I think," he said softly. "I wish . . ." Then he shook his head and looked back at her, a strange mix of hunger and fear in his eyes. "King Nigel sent us to find another Sword. That's why he loaned us Wayfinder, and that task also led us here."

"Baron Carcham?" whispered Elian.

"We think so. Have you ever seen him draw that Sword, or seen a marking on its hilt?"

Elian shook her head. "He keeps it close." She laid a hand on his arm. "What Sword did the king send you for?"

Paethor met her anxious gaze. "Farslayer," he answered softly. "Don't be afraid," he added. "We'll get it away from him."

"How?" asked Elian.

"That's the trouble. If we try to take it from him, he'll throw it for certain. Our only hope . . ."

"Is for him to challenge you," whispered Elian. Her gaze drifted to Wayfinder's hilt. "Does he know which Sword you have?"

Paethor shook his head. "If he knew, he wouldn't hesitate. Wayfinder's no threat to him."

"Maybe I can help," murmured Elian. "I could tell Sylva I saw the arrow on your Sword. She loves to spread secrets. And from what I've seen of the baron, he'd be happy to collect another Sword of Power." She looked up at him, her face grave. "Can you defeat him?"

Paethor took both her hands in his and held them tightly. "I'll have to, won't I?" he said, searching her eyes. "You're willing to do this?"

"If it will help," whispered Elian.

"It will help," he said. They gazed at each other for a moment, then Paethor bent his head and kissed her hesitantly.

A commotion from the gallery made them step apart; the

musicians were returning to their places. A deeper blush sprang to Elian's face.

"You'd better go in," said Paethor, "before the dancing starts again. I'll follow you in a couple of minutes."

"Your crown," said Elian, bending to pick up the forgotten holly wreath. She started to brush the snow from it but Paethor took it out of her hands.

"Let me do that," he said. "I don't want you to be hurt." He shook the snow from the leaves and put on the wreath with a wistful smile. Elian smiled bravely back and Paethor squeezed her hand. "No matter what happens," he said softly, "I thank you. You've set me free."

Elian stood on tiptoe to brush her lips against his cheek, then with a final fleeting smile she hurried inside. Paethor looked up at the moon, riding clear above the pines. A gray shape perched in one of the treetops, and as he watched it spread wings and took flight, its haunting call echoing back; the white owl. He watched it circle and come to rest on a nearer tree. He felt no more fear of it; perhaps because of the more immediate threat of Baron Carcham. The bird gazed at him silently.

"Give your mistress my thanks for the lesson," he whispered, then turned to go inside.

He hurried past the musicians, who were tuning up their instruments, and ran down the stairs to the Hall. The crowd had thinned, many of the valley-folk having stepped outside to get away from the heat of the room. The squire and his family were by the hearth chatting over goblets of mead, and as Paethor entered the Hall he saw Carcham bending his head to Sylva, who whispered into his ear. Paethor glanced at Elian, standing with her father, and she nodded softly. He took a deep breath, then strode purposefully toward them.

As he approached Carcham stepped forward. "Stand back, King of Fools," he said, sneering.

"There's room for all," said Paethor calmly.

In one swift motion Carcham whipped his Sword from its sheath and flicked the holly from Paethor's head. "You've had your share of Sylva's charms," he said.

Paethor stood his ground. "I have no quarrel with you, sir," he said with a glance at the squire. "You are welcome to Sylva's charms—"

"No stomach for a fight, eh?" said Carcham. "I've heard that King Nigel's subjects are cowards."

Paethor's brows snapped into a frown, but he kept silent. From the corner of his eye he saw Echevarian stepping into place behind Carcham, and Trent hurrying up from the side.

"Come, come, Carcham," said the squire. "Put your Sword away. This is no time for brawling—"

"Stay out of this, old man, if you want to keep your pretty little valley," said Carcham.

"Squire Fuller is an Argonian subject and under King Nigel's protection," said Paethor.

"Protect him, then," said Carcham, stepping forward and leveling his Sword's point at Paethor's throat. "Come on, King of Fools," he said, with a nod toward Paethor's Sword. He beckoned with his free hand. "Winner take all."

Paethor met his gaze coldly, nodding his understanding, then tore the cape from his throat and threw it away behind him as he drew Wayfinder. Someone screamed; the crowd backed away. The squire started toward them, crying "My Lords!" Elian and her brother caught him by the arms, holding him back from the deadly blades, and Elian spoke into his ear.

Paethor and Carcham circled, the points of their Swords ringing softly as they tested their reach, each waiting for the other to make the first move. Carcham took the initiative and swung, Paethor moving swiftly to parry, and more screams went up from the crowd.

Carcham was stronger, but Paethor had speed and agility on his side. He stayed on the defensive, waiting for Carcham to drop his guard. He caught a glimpse of Elian standing against the wall with her father, then narrowed his focus to the Sword in Carcham's hand. Carcham swung his arm upward and for a heart-stopping moment Paethor thought he would throw the Sword, but he kept hold of it, bringing it crashing down toward Paethor's head. Paethor barely managed to parry the blow and skip back out of harm's way. He thought he saw an opening and stabbed, but his blade glanced off Carcham's metal bracelet and he felt a sharp bite on his left shoulder. He spun aside, avoiding the worst of the cut, but felt blood trickling down his arm. Carcham smirked, and pressed him harder.

Paethor knew his strength would fade quickly now. He held the Sword in both hands, and when he saw another opening he lunged forward, faithfully repeating the thrust Echevarian had taught him. But chance brought Carcham's blade between them on a backswing, and Paethor was flung back, losing his balance and falling heavily, wrenching his ankle in the process. Pain blinded him; he clenched his teeth to keep from crying out. Instinct commanded him to rise or be slain, then he heard Elian's voice calling "Stop!"

Paethor raised his head to see Elian stepping between him and Carcham, who wore a gloating smile. His throat tightened to see her within reach of the deadly Sword, and he uttered a strangled "No!"

"You've won," said Elian to Carcham. "Let that be enough. Don't mar this night with more bloodshed."

Carcham's eyes narrowed as he gazed at her, the smile growing into a sneer. He rested the point of his Sword on the ground and draped his hands over the hilt. "If I've won," he drawled, "then I have prizes to claim. Are you one of them?"

Elian ignored this, saying "You were fighting for this Sword, were you not?" She turned away from Carcham to kneel beside Paethor, looking into his eyes as she reached for Wayfinder's hilt. Her hands squeezed his gently and she whispered, "Trust me." Paethor gazed back at her and for an instant he saw her as Athena, light shining glory all around her head. Catching his breath, he released the Sword and let her take it by the hilt.

"The Sword of Wisdom? Yes, I'll claim it," said Carcham triumphantly.

Elian turned toward him, preparing to stand. "Take it then," she said, and as she rose she flung Wayfinder hilt-first toward Carcham. His hands shot up automatically to catch it, his own Sword clattering away across the floor and his face falling in horror even as he caught Wayfinder. Elian dove for the fallen Sword, Trent and Carcham doing the same, but before anyone reached it a flash of spectral light and an inhuman howl filled the Hall. Human cries answered, the revelers cringing away from the noise. The sound issued from a third Sword, which had appeared in midair, flying toward Carcham with deadly speed. He tried a desperate parry and then it was over; Carcham lay silent, eyes slowly glazing, the Sword of Vengeance embedded in his chest and his fingers curling away from Wayfinder's hilt.

Paethor struggled to his feet and took a step toward the dead man, but Echevarian was there ahead of him. The elder lord brushed his fingers over the white target pattern on the hilt that stood nearly erect, still thrumming with the force of impact.

"Farslayer," he murmured, then clasped the hilt with both hands: "I claim this Sword in the name of King Nigel," and he wrenched it from Carcham's body.

"So that's what you were after," said the squire, coming

forward. "Well, you're welcome to it. Take it out of my valley."

"We will," said Echevarian, "and the king will see that it doesn't return."

"If that's Farslayer, which is this?" asked Trent. He stooped to pick up the baron's Sword and examine the hilt. "Coinspinner!" he said, displaying the small white pattern of dice.

"He must have been counting on its luck to protect him," said Echevarian. "Keep his enemies from choosing him as a target."

"It worked, apparently," said Trent.

"Until he let it go." Echevarian wiped Farslayer clean on Carcham's tunic and pulled Coinspinner's scabbard from the dead man's belt, handing it to Trent. "You see?" he said. "Your luck came back to you."

"Doubled," said Trent, gazing in wonder at the Sword of Chance.

Paethor limped forward and looked down at Carcham. "Which of his enemies threw it?"

"Does it matter?" said Echevarian. "He must have had dozens."

Paethor bent down to retrieve Wayfinder, swaying dizzily as he straightened, then Elian was at his side. She put an arm around him and helped him to a chair by the hearth. Paethor clasped her hand tightly. "You took a great risk, coming between us," he said.

Elian smiled softly. "No greater than yours," she said. She urged him to sit, and called for water and bandages. Through a fire-gilt haze Paethor watched her calmly tend his wounded shoulder. A hand entered his sight holding a cup of wine, and Paethor looked up to see the squire, with Trent and Echevarian close behind and Sylva clinging to Trent's arm.

"Well fought," said the squire with a grim smile. Paethor accepted the cup, smiling weakly back. His ankle was throbbing, and his head had begun to ache. He sipped at the wine.

"Winner take all, eh?" said the squire, glancing at Sylva. "Don't suppose that means you'll have my daughter?" he joked.

Paethor gazed at him, a slow smile spreading over his face, and turned to look up at Elian.

"If she'll have me," he said to her.

Elian colored, and said, "We'll discuss it when you're better," but he read her answer in her gentle eyes. He leaned back, letting the wine dull his senses, and felt his past glide away from him on silent owl's wings.

Luck of the Draw

Michael A. Stackpole

As far back as I could remember, I'd never had a hangover this bad. Of course, with my brain pounding as if Vulcan himself were cold hammering it into a fit for my skull, my memory was decidedly unreliable. I did feel certain, however, that the heaving motion and the shrieking creaking of my bones were so remarkable that I would recall having been in such a sorry state before.

Knowing I was placing myself at risk for greater pain, I opened my eyes. The agonizing lightspikes I expected to pin my eyes to the back of my skull didn't come. I considered that a minor victory because I'd not been a willing participant in the drinking that left me so sorely used and addle-brained. It struck me as right and just that I not suffer as much as I might have, had I been the one pouring liquor down my throat.

The pallet on which I'd been laid out felt as if it were rising, and I decided to let it impel me into a sitting position. As I came upright, my forehead slammed into something above me in the dark. Sinking back on the pallet, I saw stars explode, each one shimmering away into a legion of aches. Then the hurt from the hit started to pulse through me.

Served me right, I supposed, since I *had* willingly participated in sitting upright. Something rustled above me, and I idly wondered if I should speak or just feign death—which was not much of a reach for me at that point.

The thing from above me landed solidly on the floor and unshuttered a lantern. I even faintly recollected having seen that dirty face before. I would have been certain, but he kept bobbing up and down and swaying ever so slightly from side to side.

"Where in the seven hells am I?" I croaked at him.

"M'lord, you are on your flagship."

"Flagship?"

"Aye, m'lord. She were the *Starfish,* but at the duke's order we renamed her the *Barhead Shark* to give her the proper aspect to frighten the pirates." The man—barely that by the curly wisp of beard at his jaws and the unseamed flesh of his face—smiled the proud smile of patriotic fervor. "We've got the *Leviathan* and the *Swordfish* in our wake, sir, and we're stealing up on the Pirate Isle same as the sun steals up on dawn. Just as planned, m'lord."

"As planned by the duke?" I looked at the boy imploringly.

"Aye, sir. I'm Marlin, m'lord." He smiled. "Me brothers Hal and Doc are topside tending sails and tiller. The duke entrusted you to our care, and we'll die before we let your mission fail."

I wanted to ask how many men my fleet had, but something deep down inside told me I really didn't want to know the answer. "Very good, Marlin."

"Count Callisto of Fishkylle will find his men stouthearted and brave, m'lord."

"Yes, lad, I mean aye. He, I mean I, I mean *we* have no doubt of your loyalty." I tried to think of some more nautical words to spew at him, but pain forked through my brain. "Now, how about your just turning this, ah, *Barhead Shark* around and head back to Fishkylle?"

Marlin grinned. "Good, m'lord, you're playing your part proper like, just as the duke said. I'll be refusing that order, sir, so it will look like you were kidnapped, as per the plan, sir."

"Marlin, that *is* an order from the Count of Fishkylle." I tried to put an imperious tone in my voice, but it just started my head aching horribly, so I gave up. I could not tell from the foolish grin on the man's face if he really understood the sort of danger into which we were sailing, or if he somehow thought—encouraged by Fabio, no doubt—that I would somehow keep him and his kin safe when we reached Pirate Isle. "Please. I, we, implore you. Put the ship about."

"Thank you for making it official, m'lord. Don't you go worrying about your men, m'lord, we'll not be causing you any trouble, nor will we get in your way." Marlin smiled as he headed for the cabin door. "You know, of course, we are doing this out of love for you, and not the reward his Duke-ness offered us. I'll go tell the men we're to hold steady on our course to Pirate Isle."

"Do your duty, lad." I shielded my eyes as he opened the—I gather *hatch* is the right word—and beyond his skinny outline I could see the first blue traces of dawn on the horizon. The hatch closed behind him, leaving me in the lantern-lit cabin. In the dim light I came upright, but ducked my head so I'd not again bash it on the bunk above mine.

Then again, mayhap I should have done just that, as cracking my head open would likely be less painful and just as fatal as the encounter toward which we sailed. "Duke Fabio actually got one up on you this time, Cal. Antonia will look wonderful in mourning gowns, and the duke will get the money he wants to build his fleet." I started to shake my head, but the drunken woozies warned me off.

I levered myself to my feet and noticed two things immediately, though they warred between themselves for supremacy in my spirit-steeped brain. The winner was the thought that the queasy disequilibrium I felt came more from the pitching and rolling of the ship than it did from my hangover. Though equally as unpleasant as being hung over, I found being seasick somehow more dignified—despite the fact it made me wish I was dead.

The second thought, which probably conceded victory to the first out of sheer perversity, was that I would likely have my wish come true. Fabio had taken great delight in laying out his plot for ridding himself of me, and had crowed about my sister's approval of same. I knew he tossed that in to hurt me, but I also knew Antonia had the sort of intellect that made each new dawn a wondrous experience, largely because she'd forgotten the previous one. Not terribly bright, my sister, but kind, loving, rich, and our father's heir by virtue of her birth coming four minutes before mine.

I took a staggered step forward, keeping my head ducked. The fact that I kept my head down was more a commentary on the cosy closeness of the cabin than on my size. Indeed, had the cabin been in scale to the rest of the world, I would have been a giant and would never have found myself in this predicament.

Alas, I am not a physical giant, and therefore I found myself on a moaning fisher boat bobbing my way to a confrontation with pirates who plied the coast and demanded tribute from the Duchy of Newgrave. All my life some sort of pirates had raided in the area, but these corsairs had become a substantial threat to Newgrave commerce roughly around the time my father died and Antonia's husband Fabio became Duke-Regent.

Fabio *is* a giant—at least physically—and the sort of son my father wishes I had been. My sister had been given the size, charm, and beauty to make her a perfect match for Fabio. On the day they wed my father commissioned a portrait of the wedding party, featuring the happy couple standing tall, blond, and unblemished in the center, and the rest of us gathered around them.

You can see me back behind the dogs, peeking out from a display of orchids.

I'm not ugly—I don't make most children cry when they see me—but I'm just not artistic. And, I will concede, I'm not terribly coordinated, nor am I skillful at arms. I've studied all manner of martial skills—my appetite for books is voracious—but have for little time to practice or practically apply what I have learned. Fabio brought this shortcoming to my attention when he used a butter knife to disarm and best me in a sword fight.

The defeat proved problematic for me in more than the obvious way. What little vanity I have—and my broomstick limbs and thinning hair allow me very little of it indeed—comes from my dignity. I hate being made to play the fool, especially by a man who showed more skill with the knife in our fight than he ever had at a dinner table. The infant dreams I had about somehow, one day, being seen as an epic hero died right there—and only my sister's heartfelt commiseration over their deaths made the incident bearable.

I was not so much interested in being a hero for the glory of it all—my studies had showed glory to be, if not fleeting, certainly grossly malleable. I had become unforgivably enamored of folklore and the way things passed into legend. I imagined my grand adventure as being a fantastic experiment because I would know what the truth had been and I could see how it changed and warped with retellings and dissemination. My defeat at Fabio's hands would likely become a thing of legend; one I could monitor, but one that I had no real desire to follow.

Reaching out, I steadied myself against a ceiling beam and took a step toward the hatch. I knew, ultimately, my current predicament had been my fault because I had avenged myself on Fabio. While he was regent and able to administer the duchy, the matter of taxation had been left in my sister's hands. Fabio approached her numerous times with plans to raise an army for this reason or that, each of them requiring a special levy. Having my sister's ear, I managed to convince her that a tax at this time would be crippling, but maybe next month or the one after it would be permissible.

If I felt any twinge of regret in thwarting him, it came when he hit upon a plan to build a fleet to destroy the pirate Red Rinaldo. The pirate had managed to consolidate a number of corsair groups by slaying their leaders and accepting the other pirates' vows of fealty to him. Other leaders had tried the same thing in the past, without success.

Rinaldo had an edge. He had one of the Swords. He bore Shieldbreaker.

I knew something of the legend of the Swords, but my information was far from complete—largely because Newgrave is really something of a backwater. Of the reported dozen I could name eight, and Shieldbreaker had to be the most famous. The most fearsome and feared of all, it was supposed to make its owner invincible. The verse concerning it was explicit enough to justify the blade's reputation.

> *I shatter Swords and splinter spears:*
> *None stands to Shieldbreaker.*
> *My point's the fount of orphans' tears*
> *My edge the widowmaker.*

I had hoped—though it would have pained my sister—that Rinaldo might make a run at Fabio at some point. Fabio likely feared the same, and he astutely noted that if Newgrave had a fleet, it would be possible to sink Rinaldo's ship, *Sea Slayer,* before Rinaldo got a chance to use the Sword in combat. This struck me as an inventive solution to the situation—making me wonder who gave it to Fabio—and solved the puzzle of how so powerful a Sword could be parted from the person wielding it. There were other solutions to that puzzle, were I to take rumors of rumors to be fact—but one and all they struck me as suicidal, especially for someone like me who is more likely to injure himself by fighting unarmed than he is with a weapon in hand.

I convinced my sister that directly opposing Rinaldo could lead to a slaughter of Newgraveans, if the effort failed, and that some sort of negotiation should be tried first. No one at court was fool enough to volunteer for that sort of diplomatic duty—Rinaldo had a reputation for being something of a sociopath—so Fabio's brilliant plan ended up in the grave along with my heroic dreams. Satisfied, I considered us even, and therein made a terrible error.

The thought of having underestimated Fabio combined with the roiling ocean ride to make me nauseous. I dropped to my knees and vomited into a bucket, then pulled myself around to the bulkhead and pressed my back to it. I closed my eyes, then pulled the bucket in between my knees and spit until my mouth lost its sour taste.

Fabio had convinced my sister that I wanted to be the one to approach Rinaldo. After all, I had suggested the mission. Antonia knew of my dreams about adventure, and Fabio suggested I had been too modest to put myself forward. He had admitted to me that he had deceived Antonia into thinking I had come to him with a plan, begging him not to reveal it to her. He told her that because of his love for her and his knowledge that she would worry about me, he could not keep my plan confidential, and she covertly granted him permission to help me face down Red Rinaldo.

As they had shoved the funnel in my mouth and started pouring juniper juice into me—a precaution against my thinking of a way out of this before I was at sea—he had laughed and noted that Antonia would obviously give him his fleet to avenge my death at the hands of Red Rinaldo. Not only had he won, but my death would lead to the vindication of his plan. To make matters worse, he had taken volunteers from the fishing village of Fishkylle—a people whose loyalty to me stemmed from the belief that I looked a bit like a mullet—and pressed them into service to convey me to Rinaldo and my death. Adding injury to insult, he took my rapier from me—noting Rinaldo was not known for his skill with a butter knife—and left me with a flaccid scabbard belted around my waist.

With my elbows resting on the insides of my knees, I ground the heels of my hands into my eye-sockets. Alone, sick, and sent on a mission to a homicidal maniac with a magic Sword. I decided things could not possibly get worse.

Then the ship listed badly.

A sword banged me on the knee.

Swearing, I opened my eyes and snatched at the hilt. I wanted to toss the sword across the cabin, but I lacked the strength or determination to do even that. I rubbed at my knee and realized that I had been less hurt than surprised by the flat of the sword hitting my leg. The blade looked substantial enough that it should have hurt more when it landed on me, and I didn't think my light, woolen hose enough to pad the kneecap. "Just like Fabio to give me some toy, tin blade," I thought aloud, and managed to put down to drunkenness the fact that I'd not seen the blade in the cabin before.

I turned the sword over and brought it into the lantern light. I knew instantly I had something very special in my hands. Despite drink-lees still slowing my brain, I realized the steel in the blade had been forged by someone whose abilities dwarfed those of my father's master metalworkers. The mottling on the blade and the device worked into the flat of the blade made the weapon appear far thicker than it was.

Fabio would have puzzled over *that* fact for a month, but I accepted it because I was beginning to realize I held one of the *Swords!* On the hilt, two cubic symbols stood out in white. I knew they did not form a hammer, for that was the device borne only by Shieldbreaker. I canted my head to the right and twisted the blade to the left to figure out what the symbols were.

I flipped the blade over and saw a change, but initially missed its significance. On one side the two squares had single dots in the middle, but on the other they had six pips a piece. This puzzled me, because the only things I knew to look like that were dice. That knowledge did not help me identify the Sword I held.

Despair washed over me as I realized how heartily the gods had conspired with Fabio to mock me. They launched me on a heroic quest and gave me a heroic weapon, yet neither I nor the blade was suited to the task at hand. I knew, I just *knew,* the story of my fool's question would go down in history. The only consolation I could draw from the situation was that I'd not live to suffer my own mortification.

I stood and slid the blade into my scabbard. Settling its weight snugly at my left hip, I felt my mouth twist into the sort of grin I imagined on the faces of countless heroes facing hopeless odds. While I found it utterly uncharacteristic for myself, I let it remain. "I may not be a hero, and I may be about to die, but that doesn't mean I have to be afraid. That's the one shred of dignity I won't let Fabio tear away from me."

In keeping with my newfound bravado, I slid the Sword from the scabbard and let it hang easily from my right hand. A meter long, the blade had a balance that settled in right at the hilt. I made a little cut and heard the blade whistle as it clove the air. My wrist came around in a practice parry, and the Sword moved with me instead of lagging like a dead lump of metal. The blade's weight was not excessive, and the balance made the parry feel effortless. My mind filled with various diagrams of fencing styles about which I had read, and I knew this blade would slip through each technique with an élan that could make even me seem competent.

I slowly nodded. "I always wanted to be a legend, and now I hold a legend in my hand. I don't know why some god hated you so to consign you to die with me on the edge of Shieldbreaker. But I'm happy to have so fine a companion in my misfortune."

I wasn't expecting a reply, and getting none only disappointed me in that I had briefly hoped the blade could tell me its name. For a moment it struck me that the Sword might be too embarrassed to identify itself, given present company, but I dismissed that idea instantly. I flipped the blade through a complex Aurochian parry, and smiled. "I'd rather you speak with actions than words."

From the deck I heard Marlin yell, "Admiral, island ho!" I resheathed my anonymous companion before striding through the hatch and out to the deck. My mind filled with the images of countless nautical heroes of legend, and I determined to strike a pose worthy of any of them. *Might inspire the men.*

They could have used it. Marlin, if my eye did not betray

me, was senior in age and experience, not only in my crew but
in my fleet. Actually, I decided, the boats themselves were
older than any of the boys crewing them. The *Barhead Shark*
by far looked the most seaworthy, while the other two ships
wallowed in the troughs like flotsam and jetsam that had not
yet broken apart.

The boys in my crew, being Marlin, his two brothers, and
three other boys who looked like their cousins, had all armed
themselves, and I regretted their being fishermen. Had they
been farmers I would at least have had men armed with flails
and mattocks, pitchforks, axes, and scythes. As fishermen all
they carried were gaffing hooks and filleting knives, no doubt
fearsome weapons to a fish, but less than terrifying to the
kind of pirates lining the gunwales of the frigate heading out
of Pirate Isle's harbor.

If the sight of the big ship were not enough to daunt me,
Pirate Isle would have admirably served. A white stone castle
had been built there, all towers and turrets, atop a massive
outcropping of rock. It reminded me of coral trees I'd seen
for sale in Newgrave Town, for it sprouted towers at unusual
places and they all rose to differing heights. Had it not been
the stronghold of an enemy who bore a weapon that made
him invincible, I would have thought it a grand place.

But stronghold it was, and hostile as well. I could see people moving around and watched ballistae mounted on walls
and in towers being readied for use, as if the castle's defenders thought my fleet could somehow defeat the ship bearing
down on us beneath full sails. "Just hoping they'll be lucky
enough to have us for target practice in the harbor," I sighed
as the frigate sliced through the swells and came round the
breakwater. "I'd consider it right good luck if they got their
chance."

Marlin appeared at my side, gaffing hook in hand. "The

Devourer will be slow to beat back up wind, Admiral. We can cut across her bows and come around for a run at the harbor."

He pointed as he explained, and I grasped what he intended. It seemed a suitably heroic thing to do. "You read my mind, lad. Do it."

As small as our boats were, they came smartly about and managed to force their way through the waves at right angles to the pirates' course. I saw seamen on the frigate mount the rigging and start shifting sails, but we were across her bows before she could cut us off. Marlin bellowed orders at his brothers, and the *Barhead Shark* came about to shoot into the harbor, with the *Leviathan* and *Swordfish* abeam on either side.

I looked back at the *Devourer,* knowing she would be coming about to cork the harbor and keep us in, but then I never expected to get back out, so that did not concern me overmuch. As we cleared the breakwater I saw her bow again pointed in our direction, but an oddity appeared toward the stern. The frigate appeared to be trailing smoke, and as I watched, the cloud grew thicker, and black as a raven's wing. "Marlin, what's happening to the *Devourer?*"

The lad turned and squinted, then smiled. "They came about too fast! The cookstove in the galley must have gone over."

Pandemonium broke out on the frigate. Men started rushing back and forth over the deck. I saw canvas hoses unfurled as men started to work pumps to pull water up to quench the fire. The ship heeled leeward, dipping down toward the breakwater, and the bow swung around as the man at the tiller abandoned his post, escaping the flames nibbling at the quarterdeck. I saw a great spray of water gush out of the hoses on deck, then nothing, as the ship rocked back and forth in the wave troughs, pulling first one hose, then another from the ocean.

"She's going aground!" Marlin pointed back at the *Devourer* as a large wave picked the ship up and dashed her down on the breakwater. The wall of stone stove in the bottom of the ship and snapped the keel in half. It dumped the stern bubbling and steaming into the Isle's harbor. The crewmen still on board leaped free before the bow slid back out toward the sea. The waves seduced the ship into them, then collapsed its wooden walls, as the ocean jammed it against the sea wall again. Planks splintered and masts snapped, shrouding the ship in canvas as the sea used it to batter the breakwater repeatedly.

That threat fortuitously removed, my fleet bore in through the harbor. I moved to the prow and drew my Sword in an effort to make myself appear as heroic as possible. I laughed aloud, my drunken headache serendipitously banished. While the frigate's destruction did not tempt me even to dream of possible success, it did raise the hope that my death might not be as ignominious as I had feared.

The other large ship at anchor—the *Sea Slayer*—remained in place, though pirates did line the deck. I knew at once they were not going to weigh anchor, because the first of the castle's trebuchets splashed a stone off *our* port bow. Water geysered up and wet me, but I swept thin, wet hair from my face and hooted back at the defenders. I opened my arms wide and invited them to aim for me.

That might have seemed courage to some and madness to others, but it was neither. The siege machines might have been effective against the sort of fleet Fabio had hoped to raise, a flotilla filling the harbor with wood from wharf to seawall. My fleet was too small to provide anything close to a good target. Stones and timbers, chains and rubbish, an unnatural hail whirled through the air, but the *Barhead Shark* passed through it all unscathed. The *Leviathan* lost its spinnaker to a length of chain, and a stone crushed the figurehead on the *Swordfish,* but both boats kept coming.

The ship at anchor lowered a boat, but even with all eight men aboard pulling hard, they could not reach the dock before the *Barhead Shark.* To port the *Leviathan* sped on despite having lost a sail, and on the starboard the *Swordfish* rammed the longboat and sank it. Behind me Doc and Hal furled the sails, while Marlin brought the fishing boat close in to the dock.

Too close, as it turned out. The *Barhead Shark*'s prow hit the dock dead on, splitting the first half-dozen planks before pilings squeezed it to a stop. I know this because the sudden cessation of our forward movement catapulted me through the air. During my first somersault I realized I had been lucky in that my course remained true and that when I hit, I would still be on the dock. During my second revolution I acknowledged a less heartening fact: my landing would bring me perilously close to the first three men running out to oppose my fleet.

While my martial training, especially that involving equestrian pursuits, had never been the sort of success my father had wished for, it *had* endowed me with a knowledge of how to fall and bounce to minimize injury. I curled up into a ball, holding the pommel of my Sword in both hands, with the blade extended to the side rather like a scythe, so I would not impale myself if I hit wrong.

The blade turned out to be held more like a scythe than I had hoped. I landed hard on my shoulderblades and bounced through a roll toward my feet. My Sword-blade caught on something. I twisted to the left, felt my left hip bump something else, and heard a couple of yelps. Then the dock was firmly beneath my feet.

A splashing noise prompted me to open my eyes and turn slightly to the left. As I did so, I brought the bloodied Sword across in a short arc in front of my face. *Chang!* It blocked a thrown dagger, dropping the lesser weapon to the pier beside the unconscious form of the man whose legs I'd slashed during my roll.

Of course, I knew instantly that what I had done—which included blindly bumping the center man into the third man and sending them both into the bay—was highly improbable. Parrying the thrown dagger was nothing more than luck, and my fingers still tingled with the impact of the knife against my Sword. Still, the men now standing a dozen meters away clearly took the carnage as a result of purposeful action, and their reluctance to engage me showed.

Before they could persuade themselves, the wind shifted and the gods again intervened on my behalf. The *Leviathan* flashed past on my left, its speed unabated as it drove straight at the pirates' wharf. The man at the tiller tried to bring the ship around and back out to sea, but the changeling wind shoved the ship to starboard. With a horrendous cracking and crashing, the *Leviathan* broadsided the dock ahead of me, tumbling me to my knees. Near the point of impact, the dock tipped up, launching a full dozen pirates into the bay.

The impact vaulted the *Leviathan*'s fishing nets up and over the gunnels as neatly as if cast by a master fisherman. By the time I had regained my feet, the ship had already rebounded from the collision and made headway while pulling out to port. The nets, which had draped themselves over a number of recumbent pirates, dragged their catch off with them. Hastily, I estimated that more than a third of the men facing me had succumbed to the *Leviathan*'s misadventure.

I drove forward, wanting to reach the rammed section of the dock before the pirates could cross it. I knew, from countless legends of epic battles, that defending the uneven territory would be far simpler than allowing my foes to stand on equal footing. It did not really occur to me until I came close enough to cross blades with the pirates that the valiant defenders upon which I had chosen to model myself usually died at the end of their fights. I also realized that defending in a situation that clearly called for offense was less than satisfactory, but attacking would have pressed my luck even further than it had been pressed so far!

A swordsman I am not, so I steeled myself against my eventual steeling by the pirates and determined to give as good as I got. By the strangest coincidence, though, their thrusts missed me by centimeters while my Blade slipped fortuitously beneath guards or over parries. As part of me tried to catalog each cut and each block for my experiment in folklore, another part identified fencing styles and suggested simple strategies that succeeded in even the most improbable situations.

As much damage as I did to them, I believe that they did more. Rinaldo's men seemed as adept at sticking each other as they were at missing me. Pressed forward by the men behind them and tripped up by the wounded in the front, their blades spilled more pirate blood than mine, and it almost seemed as if letting them surround me would prove more devastating to their number than the advent of Fabio's future fleet.

Bleeding and howling men fell from the dock or went staggering back through the press of their companions. Before I knew it I had crossed the treacherous length of canted dock and was actually forcing the pirates into a general retreat! It was impossible, unbelievable, but I was doing it. I looked at them saw fear in their eyes. For the barest of moments I knew what Fabio had read in my eyes during our duel, and in that burning second of shame, I faltered in my advance.

Even as I paused, my momentum lost, a giant of a man bearing a cutlass in each colossal fist pushed forward through the crowd to demand my attention. He looked like Fabio, except that he was taller, stronger, and had a wolfish intelligence in his dark eyes. Most disturbing of all, I noted as he set himself, he bore no deformities or scars. That fact told me that my time as a hero was over. When he squinted at me, then contemptuously cast aside the sword in his right hand, I got all the confirmation I needed of my impending opportunity to solve the mystery of life after death.

A gull wheeled overhead and ridiculed me mightily—or so I interpreted his raucous cry, before a splotch of white washed my enemy's left eye away. The man pulled his left hand up to swipe at the guano in a reaction automatically reflexive. The dull edge of his cutlass smacked him squarely between the eyes, momentarily stunning him. Off balance and still half-blind, a staggering misstep sent him off the edge of the dock and into the ocean.

I assumed the gape-jawed look of surprise on the pirates' faces mirrored the one on my own. Coincidence after coincidence had piled one on top of another high enough to have toppled over faster than the man now sputtering in water. I knew the chances of my having gotten as far as I had were slimmer than none.

There was no reasonable, no possible, explanation, except one. I glanced at the Sword I held. *This has got to be* Coinspinner, *the Sword of Chance! It is known to move about by its own volition, entrusting itself to those who need it.* I saw a brief flash of white on the hilt, and observed three and four pips on the dice respectively.

Hope exploded in my chest. I glanced sidelong, slyly, at the knot of men facing me, and gave especial attention to the heavyset one in red and yellow at the edge of the dock. "It would be very lucky for me," I murmured, "if he were to lose his footing and fall off the dock."

The forward movement of an impatient man behind him sent my target tottering into the ocean. I smiled, and shifted my gaze. "And if that lean weasel hit a weak spot in a board . . ."

The impatient man's foot went through the dock, quickly followed by his body and most of his teeth.

My smile became generous.

I brought my sword—my very special Sword—up into a guard. "Come on, gentlemen. As luck would have it, I'm in the mood to take you all!" With the boldness of a berserker, I leaped over the missing board and stabbed out as two blades passed on either side of my body. Pulling my Sword free of one man's shoulder, I parried the other, then slapped the flat of the blade across his ample belly. The two men fell to either side, leaving me a straight avenue to their comrades.

They broke, and I chased them with laughter. I pointed Coinspinner at one and imagined how happenstance might make him run blindly off the dock. Before he hit the water I shifted my attention to another, thinking to myself that it would be well within the vicissitudes of life for him to faint dead away in terror of me. His limp body tripped the man following close on his heels, tumbling that man into one yet further forward. They both crashed to the ground, narrowly missing the last man. It almost appeared that he would get away, but it was *my* lucky day, not his, so he suffered the misfortune of having his boot heel catch in the space between planks on the dock. This pitched him sideways and wrapped his middle around the upper end of the pilings that supported the dock.

Looking up as I strutted along the wharf, I saw a host of pirate reinforcements pouring out of the castle. I laughed nonchalantly and, somewhat disturbingly, much akin to the way Fabio had when I had vowed to avenge myself for the butter knife duel. These men, these *luckless* men were mine for the harvesting.

I watched the line of them scurrying down the narrow stairs carved into the side of the island's stone face. I was moved to pity the fourth man in line as he took an unfortunate misstep in his haste and fell into the man in front of him. The fifth man vaulted him, but hit the second man, turning the whole front end of the procession into a roiling mass of jumbled bodies.

Dame Fortune smiled on me when another pirate caught his halberd at a narrow point in the trail, slamming running men into his back until the weapon's haft gave way and they all spilled to the ground. Lady Luck seduced loose stones from the rocky face above to crash down among the defenders of Pirate Isle. As I advanced to the foot of the steps, I considered it the greatest of luck that the confident man picking his way down toward me suddenly suffered an anxiety attack over the lack of approval his father has shown for him as a child. Equally as fortunate, from my point of view, was that when he laid down his sword and began to weep another man slipped on the blade and bumped his way down a length of granite stairs on his tailbone.

My glee knew no bounds as I picked out one enemy after another for special treatment. One doomed fellow caught his spurs—bad luck for a pirate to be wearing them, it seems—on the tunic of a downed man and crashed head-first onto a landing. Another star-crossed corsair attracted the attention of a passing seahawk, rendering himself *hors de combat* as he dove for cover from its slashing talons.

"And you," I noted as I pointed Coinspinner at an archer preparing to shoot me, "your bow will attract lightning . . ." I stopped because lightning struck me as too improbable and the rapid gathering of dark clouds on the horizon scared me. Coinspinner handled him itself when the bowstring snapped in mid-draw and the arrow tipped down to stick the man in the leg.

I mounted the steps like a conquering hero, graciously nodding in response to the whimpers for mercy rising from around my knees. "You are a Commodore now, Marlin," I announced over my shoulder to the fisherman following me. "Into your care we commend these prisoners." I made certain to keep my voice pleasant, yet infused it with an imperial tone in a synthesis that Fabio had never managed to produce.

"Aye, sir."

The respect in his voice played like soft music in my ears. Never had anyone spoken to *me* with that hushed tone of awe. I'd heard it used many times when men and, oh, so many women spoke to or about Fabio, but until Marlin addressed me with it, I did not realize how much the veneration of Fabio had annoyed me. He, by accident of birth, by being tall and strong and handsome, was beloved by many and envied by even more.

Including *me*, I discovered. *No more!* I had earned through my deeds what he had been given by the gods. Marlin's respect for me, the pirates' cowering in fear, all this had been won by my actions. I *deserved* exaltation, and before I was through I would have accomplished enough that even Fabio would come to me on bended knee.

I slid Coinspinner home in my scabbard and stalked upward. Even with the Blade out of my hands, men pulled back away from me. Those who were still ambulatory, or at least conscious, bowed in my direction. They watched me cautiously, in case I chose to capriciously strike out at them.

They knew they could not stand against me, and they wanted to provide me with no reason to demonstrate my superiority.

"Who dares assault my people so?"

Though the shout from the top of the stairs surprised me, I conquered my reaction and continued to pace up the last two steps to a landing before I looked up at him. I forced and suppressed a yawn, then folded my arms across my chest. *"Your* people?" I glanced about at the pirates huddling in fear below and above me. "Then you must be this scurvy sea-bandit, this wharf-rat in pantaloons who calls himself Red Rinaldo." I echoed Fabio's contempt for me in the tone I used to address him.

"And who is the fool who dares address me in so dismissive a manner?"

I wished I had a hat so I could doff it as part of my exaggerated bow. "I am Count Callisto of Fishkylle, Protector of the Duchy of Newgrave." I wanted to make up another title or two to throw at him, but my mind betrayed me as I looked up at Red Rinaldo. He was tall enough and thick enough of limb to be an even bet in a wrestling match with a bear. I felt a familiar jolt of fear run through me, but I overcame it and thrust my jaw as far forward as it would go. "I have been sent to end your dominion of the seas and restore peace to the coast."

"Have you now? You bear a sword, good. I will not sully my blade by slaying an unarmed man." Rinaldo smiled as he drew the Sword he wore. Immediately I heard a slow, dull thudding sound reverberate down the stairway between us. The men crouched there looked at me and then back at him, many moaning, more slinking down past me and a few even going up and over the wall for the drop to the wharf. "This blade is Shieldbreaker, and none may stand before it."

I knew he meant his comment to terrify me but it did not—

quite. Actually, even in my exalted state, it did make me uneasy. The rhyme did say that Shieldbreaker shattered Swords, which I wanted to take as a generic use of the word. Still, all the translations and iterations of the verse *did* capitalize Sword, and that could be taken as a portent of dire difficulties on the horizon. Still, I refused to let my confidence in Coinspinner flag.

"That may be, Reedy Rinaldo, but I think you will have the misfortune of falling down the stairs and cracking your skull." I stared at his feet as he began his descent, willing him to slip, or for granite stones to crumble, but nothing happened, save for the pounding thunder of his Sword growing louder and more swift.

Down another step he came and down another, moving as inexorably as an executioner approaching a victim on the block. His eyes had darkened except for a gray glint, and I marked that as the reflection of Shieldbreaker. The hammerfall sound thudded through me, a bass counter to the staccato fluttering of my heart.

Perhaps I had somehow misconstructed my first destructive wish. "Wouldn't it be lucky if your heart seized up and you suffered a stroke?"

He slowed not a whit, nor did the sound.

"It would be incredibly, unbelievably lucky *for me* if lightning would strike you."

Nothing, not even a cloud on the horizon. Not a wisp of fog, not even a lightning bug. Nothing, nothing but his mechanical advance down the stairs. Barely a dozen steps separated us and I felt panic rip through me.

No! I forced myself to dominate my fear. I knew in an instant what I had done wrong, why the Sword refused me, and I named it *hubris!* I had dared claim *its* victories as my own. I had placed myself on the level of Fabio, and I had reveled in it. Coinspinner had chosen me because I had been an underdog in a hopeless situation. It had come to me to give me a chance at survival.

And why? Clearly it was so I could stand as an example to all who would otherwise despair and for that reason never realize their potential. Coinspinner, I imagined, wanted to give me the opportunity to overcome the sort of adversity that had beset me for all my days. Red Rinaldo obviously stood as surrogate for Fabio and all those like him who dismissed me because of my physical limitations. With the Sword of Chance in battle against Red Rinaldo and Shieldbreaker, I, *we,* would show humanity that the only true failure is to surrender to adversity instead of fighting it.

I took a step back as Shieldbreaker's thunderous voice slammed through my chest. Red Rinaldo reached the landing, his long strides hungrily devouring the distance between us. I let him come on, even as he raised his right hand, elevating the Sword of Force for a blow that he doubtless believed would cleave me in twain. Unbridled confidence and battle-madness shone from his eyes—he knew he could not lose, and wanted me terrified of that fact.

I knew no fear. My left hand held Coinspinner's scabbard rock still. I knew this battle had been predestined and the name of the victor had been written in stone since before the gods themselves were born.

Shieldbreaker started to fall, the cacophony building until it even drowned out the pounding of my heartbeat.

My right hand yanked on the hilt of Coinspinner. I slid the blade free of the scabbard, brandishing it with a flourish. I meant Rinaldo to see it and see the design worked into it. I wanted him to know he was vulnerable to my attack. Even as his blade arced in toward my left shoulder, I knew the Sword would not fail me and nothing could stop me from defeating Rinaldo.

· Nothing but the fact that Coinspinner twisted in my hand

and flew from my grasp! It shot out from within my clutching fingers, the pommel brushing my fingertips as the Sword rose into the air. I watched it become a black silhouette in the heart of the sun, then saw it evaporate as soon I knew my life would.

Many chronicles have noted the elastic property of time, allowing it to stretch to infinity in times of horror. It seems the gods, while tending to ignore the most fervent entreaties for long life or happiness, take a perverse delight in granting humans more than enough time to experience the mortification and embarrassment spawned when their dreams run headlong into reality.

The hollow ludicrousness of everything I had surmised about Coinspinner and its mission for me sucked my stomach in on itself. My arrogance tasted bitter in my mouth, and the truth about my pitiful condition filled me with disgust. The whole world would mock me, for once my head bounced down the steps Red Rinaldo would strike out at Newgrave, pillaging and slaughtering innocent people in payment for my audacity. The base stupidity of my thinking about Coinspinner likewise pilloried me—the Sword had no intention of using me as a lesson for humanity. The verse had said it all, exactly, that no Sword could stand against Shieldbreaker. Had I left it in my belt, Coinspinner would have survived me. Because I drew it, because I doomed it, the Sword of Chance had fled as I would have done were my luck not all run out.

Defeated and dishonored before I died, I collapsed in on myself. In that frozen moment, it struck me as laughable that I couldn't even die properly, for Rinaldo's blow struck me on the left shoulder and carried on down through my body to exit at my right hip. Anyone else would have dropped into two pieces, but not me. Bisected by the most powerful of all the Swords, I felt no agony, heard no angels singing, saw no visions of a glorious afterlife. Aside from the chill sea air pouring through the gaping rent cut through my clothes by the Sword, I felt nothing to confirm my death. There was not even a drop of blood. Though the irony of the thought would not occur to me until later. I decided that the failure that defined my life culminated in my failure to die.

Angry and resentful at Rinaldo for making apparent to all that last failure, I leaped forward, weaponless, and grabbed double-handfuls of his tunic. Clinging to his chest like a mad squirrel on an oak, I pushed him with one hand and pulled with the other. Rage at my ultimate humiliation fueled me, and I wrestled him around as if I were his size and he were nothing but a doll.

The rhythm of Shieldbreaker's thunder broke as the frenzied pulse of my heartbeat pounded in my ears.

I knew men stood behind me and was certain they were laughing at my humiliating plight. I pulled Rinaldo toward me and turned to interpose his body between them and me. As I did so, my right hip caught his left and sent him spilling. Rinaldo's heels went up and his head went down, smacking hard on the stone. Shieldbreaker started to fall from his nerveless grip, but my right hand stripped it from him before gravity could wrestle it free.

The hammer-thud faded as Rinaldo lay limp at my feet. Without a thought to the consequences of my action, I raised Shieldbreaker and prayed against the possibility that *now* I might succumb to the wound he had inflicted. I half-expected battle-madness to fill me, but as I looked out at the men gathered on the stairs and wharf, I did not sense a single *foe* among them. Supplanting the thunder I had thought I would hear, a great cry rose up from the men on the island. It took me a moment to sort it out, for I'd never heard my name shouted outside of a curse before.

"Hail Callisto, Corsair Supreme and Master of Pirate Isle!"

"What?" My voice revealed my surprise, but no one seemed to notice. "What do you mean?"

Marlin dropped to one knee before me. "It is the way of the pirates, m'lord. You have defeated their leader, and now they are sworn to your service. They know a great leader and fearsome fighter when they see one, and so do I, m'lord, I'm hoping me and my men can serve you as well."

"Yes, yes, Marlin—*Commodore* Marlin, of course." I slid Shieldbreaker home in the scabbard that had contained its brother, and I noticed a general lessening in the anxiety on the faces of the corsairs. All in all they didn't look like a bad lot, and it struck me that I could convince my sister to raise enough of a tax from the Merchants' Guild to let us rebuild the *Devourer* and turn the whole pirate company into Newgrave's own Navy.

Then again, if we remained outlaws . . . I shrugged. There would be plenty of time to decide if I wanted my legend to be that of Callisto the Corsair or Count Callisto, Lord of the Sea. I had other things to do before that choice had to be made.

I forced my voice as low as I could make it and scowled fiercely. "Get up, you scurvy seadogs, and make this island ship-shape. I want everything ready for when Commodore Marlin returns from Newgrave. He'll be bringing my sister Antonia with him, *and* her husband, and I want them even *more* impressed with Pirate Isle than they already are."

Smiling I turned to Marlin. "Go to Newgrave and tell them exactly what—" I hesitated for a moment. "—you *saw* happen. But no need to mention Shieldbreaker."

"Aye, sir." Marlin shot me a wink. "Anyway, m'lord, no one would believe me if I said you threw your sword away so's you could engage Rinaldo bare-handed."

"No, no, they probably wouldn't, would they?" I shook my head. "Ask my sister to visit me here, and conduct her yourself."

"My pleasure, m'lord." Marlin bowed and started back down the steps, collecting his brothers as he went. He stopped when I called to him.

"Marlin, one more thing."

"Yes, m'lord?"

"Extend the invitation to my brother-in-law, of course." I dropped my left hand to Shieldbreaker's hilt. "And see to it he brings his butter knife when he comes."

Stealth and the Lady

Sage Walker

The boy wore a traveler's cloak and carried a staff. In the dark tent, Tegan held up a small shuttered lantern and looked closely at his face.

He carried the stone. She read the signs of it in the faint trace of gray under his pale skin, in the subtle dysphoria that showed in the fine tremor of his hands.

The boy blinked at the riches in the tent, a chest of carved oak gleaming with the shine brought by pots of beeswax and hours of labor, satins and furs piled on the cot where Tegan would sleep. And he would not lift his eyes to her, Tegan the Courtesan, who held the Duke Osyr in the palm of her hand, and the duchy as well, in all but name.

"You have brought me something," Tegan said.

"Uh. Uh . . ." He gripped his staff with white-knuckled fingers. It seemed to be the only thing that kept him from falling to his knees before her.

"You've done well. You could hand it to me, I think."

He fumbled inside the folds of his cloak and produced a grubby leather pouch tied with a thong.

"Thank you." Tegan took the pouch in her cupped palm. She smiled, feeling the nascent power of it even through the leather, and teased the lacings apart to look inside. The pouch held a small, heavy object, a misshapen black lump, black as the rotted fuels of the Old World, at its heart a sparkling bit of greenish glass. The wizard Greenapple had not lied to her. This was a demonsoul.

The thing throbbed in her hand. She must inform the demon who it was that held her without calling the demon forth. Tegan was no wizard. All she could do was to say what Greenapple had told her to say, and hope.

Tegan held the stone close to her lips. Would that she had years to learn a wizard's art before she held a demon in her hand, but there was no time! Would that the boy were not at risk, but she did not have the knowledge to shield him if the demon appeared.

"Ninidh," she whispered. "I am Tegan, who holds your soul in my hand. Know this, Ninidh, but do not wake."

A tiny warmth escaped the stone. Tegan waited for possession, for the unleashing of a demon's powers. She felt a slight shift in the weight of the world, as if a power had turned in its sleep, the demon responding to her name.

Then, thank Ardneh, the stone was only a stone, inert in her palm.

Her fear disappeared in fierce joy. She held a demonsoul in her hand! This stone held Ninidh, who was ever enamoured of gems.

Tegan wrapped the stone in gold foil to mask its power, and dropped it in a little pocket stitched into her bodice.

The boy tried not to watch, but he did; he stared at her hand touching the warm creamy skin between her breasts. Tegan could see dreams rise in his eyes, dreams that he had never dreamed before. She hoped that someday he'd find a woman to make them true.

"You'll feel better in just a little while. Here." Tegan

opened the oak chest and picked up a moneybelt, weighty with gold.

"Put this on. It's for your master."

The boy held the moneybelt in his hands, all of Tegan's wealth, though she would risk much to not to have that fact known.

"Do it *now.* This much gold might tempt the loyalty even of *my* servants."

Obedient, he started to lift his robe, then stopped.

"I won't look," Tegan said.

He got the straps tied round his waist, but he stood swaying on his feet, exhausted and dazed, sickened by his long journey and the restless miasma of the stone.

"Your master will give you a share of it when you're safely home. He's promised me that." She picked up a small purse, coppers and silver, and put it into his hand. "This is for you. I would have you comfortable on your journey." He looked like he was going to faint. Tegan took the boy's arm and led him out of the tent.

"Give him mulled wine," she said to the guard. "And find a cot where he can rest. When he's strong enough, he'll leave."

Tegan hurried through the maze of tents. She saw something move in the shadows, one of the guards, perhaps. No matter. She entered the tent where Osyr and his advisors had gathered for the evening meal.

Osyr and his coterie sipped porter and cracked walnuts. They plotted tomorrow's battles while they digested tonight's cold dinner. No cookfires had been lighted, lest an Idris scout see them.

"Tegan!" Osyr said. "Join us!"

She bowed to him and edged her way past the men crowded along the trestle table.

Osyr sat slump-shouldered, his colors of bronze and black yellowing his sallow skin. He held an opal in his fingers, an Idris opal, gleaming like a pearl but full of hidden colors. They were beautiful stones, Idris opals, filled with mystery. Osyr owned one, and craved them all.

The air around Osyr was thick with tension. He had planned, interminably, the conquest of Idris, but the day had never been right, the weather, the omens. Only the news that the Idris Duke would leave his stronghold had brought him out to battle. Tegan smoothed her expression into a mask of tender concern and sat at her place on Osyr's left.

Osyr's right side was flanked, as always, by Seagus, his weaponsmaster, red of beard and slow to anger. Seagus, who drilled Tegan in swordplay and kept her strength up and her reflexes tuned to a fine pitch. Seagus, whose bed she shared at times, for his guilty pleasure and her own sanity, lest she kill Osyr too soon.

"Beautiful, is it not?" Osyr held the gem between his thumb and forefinger, displaying it to his advisors. "Such power is wasted on Idris."

A border skirmish had cost Osyr's father his life, struck down by the man who held Idris now. The old duke had left the boy Osyr alive to rule his father's duchy, thinking it of little value to anyone. Osyr still smarted at his charity. In his way of thinking, death would almost have been a better outcome, at least a more honorable one.

"Idris will be conquered." Old Blacknail spoke in prophetic, wizardly tones.

"You're sure the duke will journey out tomorrow?" Osyr asked.

"Idris is taking a shipment of opals to Wellfleet," Blacknail said. His thumbnail was not really black, nor was his real name Blacknail. His wore a black robe, always, and it was embroidered with white symbols that were too often stained with splattered potions. "Idris is going himself, to make sure these gems reach the proper ship. He will be disguised as a pilgrim to the White Temple, and lightly guarded, only a few strong men with him. But he has arranged that the hills along his route will be thick with armed men."

"We can cut through them. Then the duke falls." Osyr leaned forward and clasped his hands together as if to squeeze a throat. "Idris is ours!"

Dorn, the beastmaster, seemed as relaxed as if he sat in the hall at Osyr. "This much is he hated," Dorn said. "Not for years has the Lord Idris"—the ferretsnake draped around Dorn's shoulders snarled at the name and showed a mouthful of needle teeth—"shown his face beyond the boundaries of his lands. Even the beasts find him vile." Osyr's beastmaster stroked at the ferretsnake's soft white fur to soothe it.

"We'll send out our knights in small groups to drive the Idris soldiers to the road," Seagus said. "Then we take them."

"We are agreed," the Duke Osyr said, and it was the royal we he used, a voice of authority.

"Ay," his advisors said, for once in unison. The formal response boomed out and the shadows in the low tent seemed suddenly ghosted with battles and glories past. Tegan felt the stirrings of battle lust in herself, a foolish thing for any woman to feel.

"I still say we should take the castle," Seagus said.

"Ah, but with the mine in our hands, then the money, the lifeblood of Idris dries up. We have no need of that drafty castle, that heap of stone. It will empty itself in a year. Is that not so, my wisdom?" Osyr's fingers sought for Tegan's wrist.

He stroked it in a way that he thought was sensual, his cold, sweaty fingertips tracing damp lines across her skin.

"Just so, my Lord," Tegan murmured. Osyr would be aroused tonight. He would want to escape his fears and his greedy anticipation of the treasures he might gain, and hide from them in the deep heedlessness of coupling. She would tire him if she could, accept his embraces with grace. She cautioned herself, as always, not to let her distaste show to him, ever. Never, never in these seven years, had she ever let him think he gave her less than joy.

"The castle holds the high pass that leads to the mine. From the castle, the duke's men can come at the mine again and again. I still think at least a sortie against it—"

"No." Osyr stopped Seagus with a sharp word. "We kill Idris. He has no heir, no one to step into his place, and his men will have some confusion about that. We announce that the lands are now held by Osyr, and we offer better pay than Idris gave. The soldiers will come to us. I have said all I have to say on this, Seagus."

Osyr stood, and perforce the others did, from courtesy.

"Ready the troops, gentlemen. We ride at dawn. Come, Tegan."

Duke Osyr led his courtesan out into the night.

The camp was restless with the energy of men thinking of battle and trying to rest. The riding-beasts stamped in their corral. Tegan pulled the hood of her cloak up over her hair and shivered. It seemed to her that the noise and the energy of the camp would send an alarm that would carry all the way to Idris.

And if it did? No matter. Osyr was committed now, win or lose.

Osyr fiddled with the ties on the flap of his tent.

"Seagus is right about the castle."

A woman spoke in a low voice, nearby and unexpected. Osyr jumped and his hand fumbled for the dagger at his belt.

She stepped out of the shadows, a shadowed figure, brown skinned and clad in gray leather, and with a bow slung across her back. "But you don't have enough men to breach its gates. Put your knife away, Osyr. You sent for me."

Tegan pulled the folds of her hood across her face. She knew this woman. Noya's voice, her easy walk, had not changed, but she spoke with authority now, with presence. Oh, Noya! Envy fought with anger and Tegan pushed them both aside. If Noya would send the Gray Archers to help Osyr, then all would be well.

"You come late," Osyr said. He turned back to the tent and got the door unfastened. He motioned Noya inside, but she shook her head.

"You asked for our help. A change in the rule of Idris means nothing to us, as long as the mine is not closed. You don't plan to seal it, I think."

"No," Osyr said.

"We won't join you," Noya said. Her narrowed eyes swept over Tegan.

Then she was gone.

Tegan followed Osyr into his tent.

"You're pale," Osyr said.

"It must be the salt meat we had for dinner. I didn't know you had sent for the Gray Archers," Tegan said.

"I hoped to hire them as allies," Osyr said. "She didn't even stay long enough to see what I would have offered in pay."

Coins could not buy the services of these women. Osyr would never understand. Tegan turned away from Osyr lest he see the grief in her face. Almost she would have put aside her pride and sought out Noya, but no one would find the archer unless she chose to be found.

"Come to bed, my Lord," Tegan said.

She accepted Osyr's nervous caresses. After their coupling, she lay next to him and stroked his thinning, colorless hair. His evil was only the weakness of greed. Almost, she pitied him.

He might die tomorrow. She might die. She wondered if Noya would watch the battle, if her archers would scout it to see who fell, who triumphed. Did Idane still live? Was Noya now in command?

Stop it, Tegan told herself. Don't think about her, or wonder about the health of the Lady Idane.

The demonsoul lay safe in the bodice of the gown that she had tossed, as if carelessly, beside the cot. It held the power to call Ninidh from her exile. If Ninidh could be bound to the mine, then the cursed stones would stay in their poisoned earth, for no miner, however crazed, would dare a demon's wrath.

The stone would call Ninidh, but would she stay confined?

Greenapple had hedged when she asked him. Ninidh was a particularly virulent demon, he'd said. Any one of the Twelve Swords could command a demon. A child of the Emperor had power over demons. A mortal? Well, given enough protective magic—

Tegan was no Emperor's child, and she had no Sword. But she would risk her life on the hope that Ninidh loved gems beyond all else, and would stay near them.

Hopes, Tegan had those, even though the risks were great. She hoped that the Idris guard she had bribed had told the right stories to the children in the mine. If he had, then Ardneh willing, they would flee when the time came. The crofters had made shelters for them, places in stables and haystacks.

"When you see the lady in red, run! Run away, scatter, run for your very lives!"

If the guard had not betrayed her, then the children had been taught she was a witch. That fear might break through the fear they had of their guards.

Terror sometimes worked where love could not. The wizard's messenger boy had been so terrified. I have never seen a more frightened face, Tegan thought. Well, once. But that was so long ago.

There had been a time, not long ago as this tired and tattered world knows time, when dawn's cool air sighed clean mysteries across a young girl's shoulders, when every spiderweb was jeweled with dew.

Just so, the oak tree, the little clearing. It was walled with wildrose and crowded with summer's blackberries, ripe as garnets. The mist fleeing the sun hid a dancing faun, a faun in spotted goatskin breeches grown of his own hide. The distant sound was his syrinx, the song of an innocent goatboy piping out his lewd joy at the first morning he had ever known, for a faun wakes with no memory, and has no guilt.

Or so Meraud said, who was as wise a woman as lived in Small Aldwyn. Meraud told stories of princesses in high towers all dressed in silk and jewels, of kingdoms lost with the loss of a bauble, or duchies gained with a kiss. Perhaps, behind the screen of leaves, a prince waited, or a young god as beautiful as polished marble who had searched all over this ancient land for an innocent girl to help renew the world.

But a bird stopped singing. It flew from the branch and out of the mist, a plain brown bird, and the blackberry Tegan reached for was guarded by a thorn that poked her in the fat of her thumb. The blackberry was not ripe, the mist and the light had lied to her.

She remembered, years later, the prick of the thorn, the

taste of the sour berry she threw away. She remembered that
on that morning of mornings she had been cold, her feet were
wet, and the light had lied. How else to explain what she had
seen that morning?

Beside Tegan in the tent, Osyr snored gently. He would sleep
until dawn, sleep restless if she left him. Tegan slipped away
from him and went to her tent. She needed rest, not memories, memories that Noya had stirred up, memories from a
time that Tegan had pushed into the back of her mind. Damn
Noya, anyway. Tegan thumped at her pillow and remembered a distant time, a scent of crushed, tender leaves.

In that long-ago clearing, a man crashed backward through
the roses, landed on his shoulders, rolled to his feet and
turned to face his pursuer.

By then, Tegan was in the absolute center of the blackberry patch, crouched in the smallest heap she could make of
herself.

The man held a sword and carried a shield. The sword's
point made tiny circles in the air.

Tegan peered out from between blackberry branches. The
swordsman concentrated his attention on the wildrose and
the pathway he'd just torn through it.

"Give over, Lennor. You didn't kill the old man; you
won't kill me. Go home."

It was a woman's voice, highpitched and hard-breathing, a
woman hidden from Tegan by blackberries and wildrose.

"Duke Osyr is an evil man, but his son is weak, and that's
worse. It is not time for the old man to die. The Red Temple
would have paid you for his death in the coin of sorrow, silver bits and pennies garnered from restless husbands and
from wives dreaming of wealth."

The man advanced toward the voice, struck at the wild-rose, retreated.

"You tire? Give over, then. Would you die to steal from gamblers like your father, who came to the tables hoping to regain the losses of a bad season, a failed crop? Go home. Your father has a pair of fine colts this year, and you are a trainer of riding-beasts by nature, not a mercenary."

The boy—a boy, not a man, and thin except for his hands and forearms, he would be good with riding-beasts, yes. His red livery did not fit him. He shook his head, staring at an empty wall of wildrose. Wild-eyed, his eyes squinted at a dull red glare as if a furnace of Hell blazed in the shadows. His hair fell across his face and Tegan winced, for he was helpless at that moment, blinded. He tossed his forelock aside and blinked away sweat or tears. The circles his sword made in the air were from fatigue, not skill.

He tensed, showing his intent before he moved, and raised his sword. He brought it down with all his strength.

It flew from his hand and spun through the air at the counterblow of an unseen blade. He tripped, reaching for empty air where his lost sword was not, and sprawled on his back with his head not far from Tegan's hiding place. He panted like a winded riding-beast.

As motionless as flies in amber, the boy, Tegan, the clearing.

She stepped into the light. Tegan knew her. She was Diana, the huntress with a bow slung over her shoulders, the guardian of wild things. How could she be here? The gods had faded in these late days; withdrawn to the far corners of the world; Diana of the wild forests and Athena of the gray owls had gone away into the far lands where there was no time.

She could not be here. She wore red, or snowy white, a chi-

ton that foamed around her bare arms as she came forward,
or she wore silver armor that reflected red from the boy's
cheek, the blackberries. Something in her hand left a space in
the air, a space where falling stars streaked across the night, a
space of utter silence. Her face was terrible and beautiful.

Tegan loved her, worshiped her, could not have turned her
eyes away if she died for it. Tegan wanted the power she saw,
the majesty. She felt a terrible strength rise in her, a strength
lent by the goddess herself, a feeling that she could do anything, go anywhere, be whatever she chose to be.

"Go," the goddess said.

The boy fled, scrambling through the wildrose.

The goddess sighed. "Poor fool," she whispered. She
sheathed the Sword. It had a plain, beautiful blade marked
with patterns in its dark and glossy metal, or the patterns
were Tegan's eyes playing tricks and they not there at all. The
Sword's plain hilt was marked with the white outline of a
human eye.

There had never been a goddess. There was only a woman,
not tall, in gray linen breeks and a tunic. She had a shirt tied
round her waist by the sleeves. The woman reached down
and picked up the boy's discarded sword. She was not beautiful, but she had hair the color of ripe wheat, heavy hair
bound in a knot at the back of her neck.

And in bending, she caught sight of Tegan, huddled in her
thicket.

Now she'll kill me, Tegan thought. And she thought,
mother spins better linen than *she* wears; the weave is rough.

"Oh, bother," the woman said. She stood up and pointed a
finger at Tegan. "You. Come out of there."

Tegan did, pushing away blackberry canes and catching
the hem of her skirt behind her. She jerked it free.

"What did you see?" the woman asked.

"Darkness. Light. A boy overmatched."

The woman frowned. "He wasn't overmatched. He tired me, and I used a weapon that sent his own fears to threaten him. I shouldn't have used it, but I didn't want to kill him. You have a good eye for swordplay, though." She examined the boy's discarded sword, running her eyes and fingers along its length. Tegan felt dismissed, ignored.

"A goddess," Tegan whispered.

"Oh, *bother!*" The woman held the boy's sword and swung it twice, testing its heft, and seemed to decide to keep it. She untied the shirt from her waist and wrapped the sword in it. "Look, kid. The Red Temple may send guards to find out why Lennor doesn't show up. Your story is, nothing happened. You picked some berries, that's all. You didn't see anything, hear me?"

She was a plain woman, not a goddess, but around her the morning light crackled with power.

"That's a Sword! It's real!"

"It's a weapon," the woman said. "Only that."

"I'll help you. I'll come with you. Please."

She had heard of women like this, women warriors who fought with swords and bows, who traveled in small bands and went wherever they chose to go, through the wild lands, into the towns, free as birds. They earned their bread by the sword, some said. The emperor paid them, others said, paid them to play tricks. No, to avenge the wronged. Both. Their leader carried one of the Swords? How wonderful.

The woman looked at Tegan with appraisal and Tegan wished a hole would open in the ground and swallow her, mousy hair, scratched knuckles, nails bitten to the quick, a nothing girl with freckles. She was too big all over, big nose, big hips, legs like a riding-beast's and feet that were meant for workboots, perhaps, but never for slippers. Tegan hid one foot under the other one, both of them bare.

"You're a widow's child?"

Tegan nodded.

"Good at your letters." The woman was not the goddess, but her eyes pierced Tegan like knives. Hazel eyes, cat eyes. "Skilled at needlework, strong. A dreamer. A dreamer who wants the wide world, and beautiful lovers, and silks to wear, and glory. You want to be a great lady, loved for your honor, your generosity. But you have a dark side, a part of you that wants too much."

How did she know? Tegan swallowed back tears and bowed her head.

"You must choose your life yourself. Remember that."

The woman's eyes dismissed her. She turned away, and Tegan could not bear it, to be left behind, to have seen wonder and never to see it again. She reached out, to hold the hem of the woman's tunic, to beg her.

The woman's hand moved to unsheathe the Sword she carried. The clearing filled with the sound of beating wings, with the face of a harpy, with terror.

"Pick your berries," a voice said. "You will *not* remember what you have seen."

Tegan dressed in red for the battle, a divided skirt rather than the breeches she favored, but the children would look for a *lady* in red, and breeks on women might confuse them. She fastened her sword at her hip and covered it with a dun cloak, for she had riding to do, and best she were dull of color for it.

And she took a little pendant from its jewelcase, a tiny silver arrow on a chain. She had not touched it since—

That's over, Tegan told herself. I wear it now on a whim, without anger. But on this morning of all mornings, I will trust my whims, my intuitions. It's a bauble my hand has reached for, and perhaps my hand knows more than I am willing to know. So be it.

Tegan fastened the pendant around her neck and hurried out into the bright morning.

Osyr's mount danced with the nervousness his master transmitted. Osyr on a riding-beast was a near-disaster at best, his thin legs never meant to control a mount, his hands too jerky on the reins. The beast he rode was of necessity thick of lip, but stolid enough to follow Seagus.

"You are dressed to ride, Tegan?" Osyr asked.

"I would see you triumph," Tegan said.

In the fields outside camp, Osyr's troops mustered in good order, a hundred men mounted, two hundred more on foot, armed with pikes and spears. Their riding-beasts breathed clouds of excitement into the chill air of early spring. The day was threatening to dawn bright, and Blacknail muttered weather-spells as urgently as he could from his perch on a dumpy load-beast.

"Keep safe. When this is done, you must choose a proper princess for me," Osyr said.

"Just so," Tegan said, thinking, never, my Lord, would I saddle any woman born of woman with such a burden. Tegan mounted her riding-beast and fell into place beside Dorn, the lanky beastmaster carrying his pet ferretsnake, as usual. He squinted at a nearby sycamore, where a mated pair of great owls waited to scout out the land. The owls had been coerced out of day-sleep this morning. They would be unhappy about it, and offer their complaints to Dorn with each message they brought him.

Always, there were plans within plans. If Idris died today, then his lands would have at least a new master. That accomplished, Tegan hoped for so much more. That Osyr might die, too, well, that might happen or it might not.

The bigger hope was to free the children, and for that, the mine would have to be not just closed, but destroyed. The greed the gems caused could be closed away, but unless the stones that lurked in its depths could be hidden forever, Tegan could buy only a few years of peace from its evil. Someone else would crave them.

The opals were laid in narrow strips of clean earth between bands of poisons from the Old World. Matana had learned that, and told the Duke Idris so, before the sight of one of the gems had ensorceled him.

"It is possible to bring them out," Matana said, "without killing the miners directly. But only a child, a small child, can get into the passages between the poisons. Even then, the children would sicken and die if they were kept for more than a third of a year at such work. The price of these stones is too great, my Lord Idris."

He had agreed, and sought out dwarves to investigate the mine. The dwarves, being fellows of good sense, had refused to work the place.

"The humors are evil," they had told him, and left.

But gems began to appear in the markets, polychrome opals with enchantment in their depths. The Lord Idris had paid his crofters well for the use of their children, and returned them, pale but seeming well, at the end of a year. The crofters, by and large, had taken their money and moved from Idris. They went into the towns, or to different lands. The duke brought other families to his farms, and other children to the mines. They sickened and died in time, but of different things, wasting sicknesses, weak blood. It had been a decade of years before the White Temple related the cases one to the other.

But the duke persisted, and there were always some who didn't believe the stories, but did believe that the Duke Idris paid well. Memory was a slippery thing, easily pushed aside with coin and dreams of coin. Forgetting was so easy.

Tegan would not have heeded the stories, save that her

niece, Lyse's child, had died in a collapsed tunnel. It was after that that Lyse, grieving, had heard of other deaths, and told Tegan of them, and that Tegan had learned what really killed the children of Idris. She learned then to bless the hatred that gave her courage, the hatred that had begun with an order to forget, an order she had disobeyed.

The memory of it flooded through her, a memory that Noya had wakened.

Tegan stood alone in the little clearing walled with wildrose, guarded by the old oak, filled with blackberries ripe as garnets, where a bird sang sleepy half-songs in a drowsy mid-morning. She settled her basket on her hip and reached for a blackberry, ripe and juicy. It stained her fingers with the color of garnets and blood.

I *will* remember, she told herself. Remember . . . what?

Had she heard someone whistle up a riding-beast, the creak of leather as someone mounted?

I *will* remember, she thought later, her basket full, the sun hot on her neck, and old Rollo's spotted kid munching blackberry canes beside her. Funny, Tegan thought. Silly little boy goat, for a minute this morning I thought I saw a faun, with spots like yours.

The great owl spiraled down toward the line of riding-beasts. Dorn pulled his mount out of formation and galloped toward the tree where the owl waited. Tegan followed the beastmaster.

"Hungry," the owl said.

"What news?" Dorn asked. "Earn your mouse." He dangled one by its tail. The ferretsnake darted for it. Dorn batted at the snake and it settled back around Dorn's neck. "What travels on the road, owl?"

"White," the owl said.

"Idris rides, then. I think," Dorn said.

"Mean owls," the great owl said.

"Idris has sent out his owls?"

The owl turned his head half around. Maybe that meant yes.

Idris was warned, then.

"Small mouse," the owl said.

"You'll have a bucket of mice when we're done," Dorn said. "I promise."

"If you live," the owl said. He stretched out his beak and took the mouse.

Tegan wheeled her mount and galloped for Seagus, for the head of the column. Behind her, she heard the cry go up, "Forewarned! Forewarned! Close ranks!"

I will take Idris, Tegan thought. I will kill him myself, if I can.

She crested a little hill. On the road below, a procession all in white, twenty or more mounted men, rode single-file. She spied Idris in the center of the column. So innocent he looks, this old man, Tegan thought, but as the Osyr riders appeared, the old man found a sword and bared it, spitting curses through his few remaining teeth. Tegan heard Seagus yelling beside her before his mount pulled ahead of hers. She spurred her beast forward, her sword raised. The world had filled with mounted men in the Idris colors of green and gray.

Seagus parried the duke's blow and skewered the old man. The Idris Duke's riding-beast stumbled and the corpse went flying. Osyr, close behind Tegan, reined up sharply. Tegan cut at a 'pilgrim' beside her. His chainmail glittered beneath his loose white robe. The bright sun suddenly ducked behind a cloud, Blacknail's spells successful at last, or the clouds simply a whim of weather. Tegan fought through the clot of pilgrim soldiers and raced up the road. She glanced back and saw Osyr, off his mount, kneeling beside the duke's body. He clutched a sack in his hand, lifted it aloft, and remounted.

Well, let him have those stones for his own. If this day went well, they were the last the world would ever see.

Seagus caught up with her, and behind him, she heard the thunder of riding-beasts, a century of Osyr knights who howled like banshees.

At the outskirts of the charging formation, she could see gray and green riders cut toward Osyr's ranks, and be cut down. There, at the pass, Castle Idris loomed, but Tegan and her army sped past it, almost out of range of the archers on the ramparts. Seagus raised an arm as if to shield her from the arrows. Some clattered against mail, some struck at the ranks. None of Osyr's men fell, but a few of their mounts now sported flesh wounds.

To the mine, Tegan thought. To the mine, and to hell with what's behind us.

She found she was laughing, but it sounded more like a shriek. Her riding-beast stretched her neck and ran flat out, as battle-maddened as her mistress. Between Tegan's breasts, the foil-wrapped stone nestled safe. She bent forward into the wind. Her tiny silver arrow swung free on its chain, as sharp as the day she had found it.

Tegan's mother plied a hoe around the sweetgourds, and wisewoman Meraud had come to help her, for a share of the gourds when the frost came and turned them gold. Chop, talk, chop, gossip, it made the work go not faster, but with less boredom.

The heavy basket weighed against her hip. Tegan was proud of her labors, enough to make a tart with just a touch of hoarded honey, hot enough to burn and cooled with sweet milk poured over, and plenty of berries left to put in the crock for a winter's wine. Tegan was hungry.

"I said, you may have some of those stringbeans, take them, lest she come back at night and empty the field, or so I feared, but she smiled and gave me a coin for them." Tegan's mother whacked at a weed and it flew through the air, its roots white.

"The warrior woman? I am not surprised, Edda," Meraud said. "She is a lady, after all."

"That one? Brown as an elk's hide, no lady would let her skin brown like that. Tegan, where is your hat?"

"I forgot it," Tegan said.

"The Lady Idane," Meraud said. "The Lady Idane herself has paid you a visit, and you thought she would steal your beans."

"Is that her name? Do you know her?" Mother asked.

"So, we had words last night, and she listened to my tale, and she went out to the highroad this morning, I think."

I am already gone from here, Tegan thought. These two are already part of my past. I will miss them.

"Which way did she go?" Tegan asked. The words flew out with urgency, with pleading.

Her mother looked up. "Tegan? Is something wrong?" Edda straightened slowly. Meraud had said she had rough spots on her bones, and had given her simples for the pain.

"I'm fine, Mother. Meraud, which way did she go?"

"Where she had business, I expect," Mother said. "Business far from here; it's nothing of ours what those women do."

Tegan promised herself she would come back, someday. Whenever she could, yes, and bring gifts.

Meraud planted her hoe and leaned on it as if it were a crutch. She looked at Tegan, at the berries. "You met her."

"I would follow her."

"So," Meraud said. "So."

Tegan would remember her mother's face as long as she lived, the love, the grief.

"I must, Mother. You know I don't fit here, I don't belong, Lyse, you'll have Lyse, and grandchildren soon. I'll never be as good a wife as Lyse is, or skilled with herbs like Meraud, or—" Or happy to stay in this village, where nothing changes, ever, not now that I have seen a goddess in her power.

"Or beautiful? Or loved? Oh, child."

"Many go to them," Meraud said. "Most come home."

"I will not," Tegan said.

"Take the berries to the porch," Mother said. "They will get hot here in the sun."

"I will go, Mother." Not to the porch. Far away. Far away from here.

Mother struck a vicious blow at a tiny weed, as if Tegan had not spoken at all. The hoe made a grating sound, metal on metal. "What's this, now? Something to break my hoe?" She knelt, quick enough in spite of the pain in her bones. Her fingers grubbed in the earth.

"Don't, Mother." Tegan put the basket down and knelt beside her. "Let me help you."

Coins. Not a hoard of gold, no, worn thin coppers and coins of silver.

"Well," Mother said. "Well." Her gnarled fingers cupped earth and metal.

Meraud rocked back and forth, braced by her hoe. She hissed at the sight of the coins and drew away from the tiny black arrow Tegan held like a needle. Tegan scratched at it with her close-bitten thumbnail. It was silver.

"It's for you," Meraud said. "For you, Tegan."

They seemed so far away, these two goodwomen with their beans and their long, busy days.

"A sign," Mother said. "Go if you must. I would not keep you here against your will." There were tears in her eyes.

Meraud beckoned, and Tegan came to the old woman's side.

"West," Meraud whispered. "The Lady Idane has gone west. But comfort your mother before you leave. Will you do that?"

"Yes," Tegan said. "I will try."

But she left in the night, left with good-byes unsaid, anxious for the journey.

The entrance to the mine was well-guarded. Tegan led the Osyr knights into a rain of javelins. Above the mouth of the cave, she spied a rank of men with crossbows. She pointed to them, screaming warning.

Seagus left her side, calling up twenty men who veered from the charge, speeding toward a side path that led up past the cave's mouth.

Bolts from above chattered on armor. Two of Tegan's men fell. Her riding-beast dodged aside, but Tegan urged her forward again. The beast seemed as enraged as the woman felt. There had been fear. Now there was only rage, rage at the sight of that low tunnel faced with sagging timbers, that black mouth into hell. The entrance was barred by an iron grate, a cruel doorway to let foul air out, to keep the miners in.

Tegan's sword seemed to strike of its own will. She slashed at an outstretched arm, cut down at an unprotected shoulder, heard a sigh as the man beside her gutted an Idris spearman.

Her protector went down, felled by a bolt. Tegan heard Seagus bellowing above her, and the hissing of the bolts began to slacken.

"Bring up the ram!" Tegan yelled.

An aisle formed behind her, centered on the grate. Twenty Osyr men hauled up a huge oaken log mounted on straps.

"Not at the center! The timbers! Hit the timbers!"

The new-cut log crashed into old wood. The grate fell.

Tegan dismounted and slapped at the flank of her riding-beast. The war-trained beast reared, twisting to bring her steel-clad hooves down on an Idris man. The tip of his falling sword cut a long gash through the cloak on Tegan's back. Tegan tore at its fastenings and threw it aside.

She turned at the ruined grate and saw, below her on the mountain's dark flank, a melée of green and gray fighting Osyr's bronze and black, a knot of Osyr men surrounding their duke and his banner.

Tegan ducked under the sagging timbers, into the mine itself. She held her bloody sword like a beacon.

The woman had left the tiny silver arrow, how else could it have got in Edda's field? She had buried it for Tegan to find. But the little weed had grown in undisturbed earth. It could have been an old thing, a bauble tossed away centuries before.

No, Tegan told herself. She called me. She left a sign.

All through that journey, west, she clutched at her talisman, polished bright and tied round her neck with a length of green ribbon. The coins were gone, save for four thin coppers. Cold and tired, Tegan stumbled along a stream that came down from the high pass in the western mountains.

At dusk. She had some plan to make a fire, to curl up beside it, to try to remember why she was here and not at home. She was making too much noise, clumsy-footed and hungry. She feared, or expected, dark men and danger in the high places, for Meraud had told tales of such things, but there had been no danger that she had been able to spy out, and no

men at all except for fat inn-keepers who had told her she
reminded them of their daughters.

She slipped on a mossy rock, unseen in the dark, and sat
down, splat, in the middle of the stream.

"Shit!"

Tegan hauled herself out of the water, sobbing like a wet-
nosed baby, and over her sobs, she heard a giggle.

A girl. Giggling.

Then silence.

"Come out where I can see you, damn it!" Tegan yelled.

Nothing.

A single twig snapped, uphill from the stream, yes. Behind—that rock. Tegan pulled off her shoes, wet and useless
anyway, and stalked the noise. A girl, giggling, in the high
mountains, unafraid, must be one of them, one of the Gray
Archers, the women who wore trousers and kept flocks of
stunted griffins as flying steeds—although that tale might be
only a wishful tale told to children, for no one had seen a
griffin in living memory.

Not behind the rock. Tegan sank into its shadow and
waited. If the elusive girl wasn't one of the warriors, she was
at least a girl, and she must know where food was, and shelter.

Click, a pebble disturbed.

Tegan moved toward the sound, back toward the water. A
fish splashed, once, upstream.

There, beyond that stand of quiverleaf saplings. There was
a glow from a small fire, above it the silhouette of an archer
poised on a high cliff, her arrow nocked. Under the shadow
of the cliff, the silent welling of a deep sourcespring reflected
early stars. Women sat around the fire, dark shapes, unconcerned. One of them wore her heavy hair in a knot at the
back of her neck. Tegan walked flat-footed to the circle of

firelight. She pulled her ribbon over her neck, with its four copper coins tied in a twist of cloth and the tiny silver arrow all gleaming, and laid them at the feet of the Lady Idane.

"It's all I have to give you," she said.

"Oh, *bother*," the Lady Idane said. "Someone get her some food, would you?"

Fear me, Tegan thought. Fear me, little ones. Fear is all I have to give you now.

In her red skirts, holding her dripping sword, Tegan entered the stench of urine and poison, a low space roofed with and floored with earth. Rows of cots stretched into the shadows. This was where her niece had slept, chained to her cot at night, freed only to be crushed in the earth.

If the pale squat man who was this room's last guard meant to beg mercy, he moved too late. Tegan sliced a two-handed blow at his neck as he stepped forward. He fell, a mountain of pale flesh. In the shadows, Tegan saw the gleam of terrified eyes. The children had fled into the tunnels.

"The witch!" a child screamed.

"The Lady in Red. She'll hurt us!"

"Run!" Tegan yelled. "Ardneh, help them! Run, I say!"

She stepped aside from the opened grate. As they ran past her, scrambling around the fallen guard, Tegan saw a welter of thin legs, of flailing arms. The children were as covered with earth as grubs. Some of them screamed. Most were silent.

They boiled out of the mine in a rush. One limped, and might have been left behind. Tegan grabbed the little boy and thrust him into the arms of a larger urchin.

Were they gone? Were all of them gone? Against the roar of the battle outside, she strained to hear any whimper, any scuffling sound at all. She searched in the low tunnels where

they had hidden, her eyes wide to try to see in the dark. There
was nothing, no one.

Ahead of her, a smoky lamp guttered and went out. The
air reeked with malice, not a true scent, a trace of heaviness,
of old evil. Between her breasts, the foil-wrapped stone gave
off a dull, nauseating heat. Tegan clutched it tight in her left
hand. She must call Ninidh here. If the demon devoured her,
would the Lady Idane hear that Tegan had battled here, and
lost? Would she be happy, knowing that Noya had been the
better choice to train as her successor?

Noya was the best, the brightest, the girl who had gone out to
lead Tegan into camp. Tiny Noya, so fast, whose quick at-
tacks darted through Tegan's guard. Caedrun, who coached
the girls at swordplay, matched them often in those hot hours
of drilling, slow Tegan, fast Noya, the reward for the exercises a jug of cool water in the shade, so precious.

Always, Noya, the winner, drank first.

Sometimes there were four, or six, women summering in
the high country, sometimes there were twenty. Waking,
Tegan learned to count bedrolls, to look for new faces, and
later, to see who had slipped away in the night, off on some
errand that might last days or longer—two of the women
round the fire that first night were gone by morning, and still
gone in autumn.

There were no griffins here.

There was no Sword. Tegan had not seen it again, the
Lady Idane's blade serviceable and plain, as ordinary as her
unremarkable riding-beast grazing in the alpine meadows.

There were, sometimes, women with babies slung on their
backs who walked into camp and stayed a day or two, laughing in the deep shade and yelping in the cold water of
the stream where Tegan had fallen. Others came to other

streams; they moved camp five times that summer. Some of
the women wore long skirts or brocade, and those seemed
never to have carried swords at all, but came to sit beside the
Lady Idane in the long afternoons, to speak to her in quiet,
rambling phrases, or to listen. All of them wore tiny silver
arrows around their necks, a match to the one Tegan had
found in the earth and given to the lady.

The women talked of voyages, of the proper churning of
butter, of the wiles that would hold a man, or send him away.
Tegan listened, soaked up what she heard as if she were a dry
sponge returned to water.

They came from everywhere, these women, seldom taking
up the sword but keeping their skills honed in summer camps
or winter caves, a network of women that spanned the kingdoms. And when they did bring out their bows or their
blades, at necessity, they fought well.

The Lady Idane pulled them to her like a lodestone pulls
iron. She said little, but when she spoke it seemed she had
distilled a rambling bucketful of talk into a few drops of
strong brandy. Quiet, calm, she seemed uninvolved in the activities around her, distanced from them. But when she said a
word here, put her muscle to a task there, questions got answered, things fell into place as if even stones and trees hastened to do her bidding. Tegan watched her, fascinated,
envious.

Sometimes she felt the lady's eyes on her, her measuring,
skeptical evaluation. What did she measure? What did she
want?

Tegan grew shy around the lady. She hung back from the
others, she said little. She watched and listened.

The world, seen from these high mountains, seemed laid
out like a board game. Men, duchies, kingdoms, all were
pieces to be moved if only the hand that moved them was

skillful enough for the task. Swords were one move in the games these women played, but they were only used when other moves were blocked.

"There's too much to learn," Tegan whispered one night, sore from a drubbing Noya had given her. Tegan's head swam with the Lady Idane's explanation of the true cost of a bumper crop of barley. As the Lady Idane had it, a loaf of bread in Small Aldwyn would be dear in two years, when those who had sold their grain too cheap planted other crops, unless certain merchants in the foggy cities to the north could be persuaded to pay a fair price for this year's barley. It made a sort of sense, but only if Tegan held the pieces in her mind in a certain way. Good crops can cause famine?

"Nobody can learn everything," Noya said. "You want too much."

"The lady said that the first time I met her. She was right."

"She likes you, Tegan." Noya yawned and pulled her blankets up over her nose.

"She's never pleased with anything I do."

"That's how I know she likes you," Noya said. She smiled, tucked in her bedroll like a brunette caterpillar, and blinked up at the stars. "Get some rest, Tegan. All of this thinking is making you skinny."

Skinny? Tegan pulled her arm out from under her blanket and looked at it. It wasn't skinny, it was slender. Well.

In two breaths, Noya was asleep.

Tegan backed out of the tunnel. What needed doing now needed doing at the mouth of the cave. When she opened the foil and released the demon's soul, her life would hang on a thread of slimmest chance. She had no armor against the demon Ninidh, against any demon.

At least she could stand in sight of daylight for this task.

Beyond the fallen grate, a cold spring drizzle wetted the fighters. The men of Idris fought better than Osyr had planned. Green and gray mingled with bronze and black, and over it all lay the screams of riding-beasts and men, the stink of fresh blood. Bodies lay trampled in the mud, but Tegan saw no children. They would have fled the battleground, and if the gods were kind, they had scattered.

Her arm ached with the demon's longing. Now, before Osyr's battle was won or lost. Now.

Tegan held the foil-wrapped stone close to her lips. "Ninidh?" she whispered. "Ninidh, do you hear me?"

Noya came to sit beside the Lady Idane when the silver quiverleaves were going gold on the high slopes, Noya sent out in skirts for provisions but was back in her breeks now, and happier for it.

"What news from the pass, Noya?" the Lady Idane asked.

Noya settled close to her feet of her lady, snuggling in like a puppy, and the lady stroked her hair. She has never stroked mine, Tegan thought. She finds more fault with me than with anyone here. Tegan looked down to hide the envy that might show on her face, and resolutely picked through the beans that would be tonight's dinner, discarding the odd pebble or twig here and there.

"Men are leaving the lands of the Lord Idris, for his wizard has found a mine there and they say that strange humors rise from the ore. Others are traveling there to work the mines, having heard that the pay is good."

The Lady Idane nodded, and Tegan knew that Matana, who had a gift for alchemy, would not be in camp by morning, but on her way to test the ores for safety or for useful essences.

"In far Salton-on-Fen," Noya said, "they say a Nereid

lives near a spring, and has enchanted it so that all who come
there tell her secret things."

"Nereid? Hmph. Meredith is setting herself up as a Nereid,
is she? A flashy one, for news to travel here this fast. Well,
that's an old name for us, and not so far off," the Lady Idane
said. "True, we need water and stay close to it, but any creature does. Water stays low to the ground and goes around
what it can't go over. It follows whatever course it must take,
but it wears away the strongest stone, in time."

"It works by stealth, then," Tegan said.

"Yes, stealth," the Lady Idane asked, her eyes not on
Tegan, but on a pattern of light and shadow cast by the
branches overhead. "Stealth, deception, the skill to turn
aside a blow and direct it elsewhere, the ability to let an
enemy see what she fears most, and fight herself rather than
you."

The lady carried the Sword of Stealth, one of the twelve,
Sightblinder, its story told one night by the fire, Matana singing of all the half-remembered Swords of legend.

Hidden or no, the Lady Idane carried it, wielded it at
times. Tegan closed the knowledge in herself, the questions.
How did you come by this? For what purpose do you carry
it?

Tegan felt the lady's attention focused on her. She felt as
exposed as a bug turned up from under a stone. Noya had
gone off on some task, had slipped away without a sound.
Her absence left an intimacy between them, Tegan and the
lady.

"Ask yourself. What did the boy in the clearing really
see?"

The lanky boy had stared at a green wall, and seen—

Reflected in a haze of red, crimson livery, the brotherhood
he had not yet chosen. He had seen himself a Red Temple

guard, drug-crazed and desperate for the next coin, terrified that the man beside him might be more crazed than himself, that his "brothers" would turn on him and cut him down.

When I fight against Noya, I see—grace like a darting swallow flying at sunset, speed I will never have. I see my faults, not hers.

"He saw his own faults, my Lady."

Idane smiled and stayed silent for a time.

"The seasons change so quickly. It's almost time for some of us to move back into the lowlands for the winter," the Lady Idane said.

Some of us. Not all of us. A few girls came to the summer camps every year, fewer remained for a winter's training. So Tegan had learned. Noya would stay, certainly, and Havoise and little Jibben. But would she be with them when they went to the winter caves and learned letters and lacework, and things of leechcraft that a visitor from the White Temple taught?

Tegan's fingers found a pebble, rough in the smooth beans. She tossed it toward the stream, got up and walked away, feeling the Lady Idane's measuring gaze on her back.

Outside the mine, Osyr's banner wavered, dipped, and fell. A shout went up and the banner rose again. Tegan caught sight of Seagus, his red beard red with blood. He threw Osyr's banner to one of his men and roared with triumph.

Release the demon now, if ever she were to be released. She felt power gathering, drawn to the beacon in her hand.

"Come forth, Ninidh," Tegan whispered.

The demonstone grew hot. It burned against Tegan's palm like a coal. She struggled to hold it and opened her hand. A puff of smoke rose from her singed flesh.

The smoke drifted upward. Tegan could not take her eyes

from it, from the swirling forces that circled the confines of the cave. They drifted on currents of desire and release, and centered themselves in the fetid air.

Transparent as blown crystal, a woman's form took shape in the mouth of the tunnel. It floated above the filthy floor of the cave, and laughed a laugh like shattered ice.

Ninidh. It *was* Ninidh. The demon spun like a whirlwind. She darted into one of the tunnels. Tegan heard her cooing at what she found there. Ninidh returned, her ghostly hands filled with raw gems in all the colors of moonlight.

The demon glided toward the shattered grate, and freedom.

"Stay!" Tegan shouted.

A demon's voice laughed and a demon's wild joy filled the cave.

Stay? With all the wide world before me, and all these gems in my hands? Almost, mortal, I would let you live, for the joy you have given me when you unlocked my powers.

Tegan gripped the demonstone in her fist. It had grown cold as ice.

That bauble? The demon danced around Tegan like a whirlwind. *I'm not in it now! You have freed me!*

Tegan slashed at the transparent form with her sword, a foolish weapon against a demon. The sword would not serve her for this.

What would?

Tegan had sought strength in skills of seduction garnered from the Red Temple. She knew the way power moved among the world's divided kingdoms. She knew how to use the weaknesses of men or women as needs be. Nothing she had learned could help her leash this demon, this evil wraith that Tegan had hoped to bind against a greater evil.

*   *   *

Blow after countered blow, the sword growing heavy as lead, the heat of the autumn sun on her shoulders, and old Caedrun's voice grating in her ears, "Strength! Strength and speed, Tegan, make the sword light in your mind and you will find it easier to wield." Until Tegan wanted to cry, and would not, because the Lady Idane had come to the edge of the clearing and was watching, seeming not to watch.

Had the lady sighed, shaking her head in frustration? Tegan couldn't really see anything in the shade but the brown on brown of autumn leaves. There had been frost at the edge of her blanket this morning.

In a match against Noya, thinking, this is useless. I will never best her, I will never fit in here, with these women of grace and laughter who are always at ease, always accepted, ever the gentle word comes to their lips and at times I can't speak at all.

Noya will stay and I will go back to the beanfields. I will carry my sister's baby on my hip, not a sword.

A man in gray stood beside the Lady Idane. The two of them turned away.

There was only the clearing, the heat, Noya bringing her sword once more toward Tegan's guard in this last match, this final time, this last time for losing.

I outreach her, Tegan thought. I always did. She is fast, but there is a pattern that she follows. If I move *here,* turn her on her own path, then, then—

A calm came upon her, the world slowed down for her to use, for the lady had turned away and there was only Tegan, centered in a still place born of despair and loss where nothing mattered except the blade's edge, the pattern of its reaching.

See, how slow this is, the back of Noya's knee exposed, the dark sureness welling up within me, a touch there. So! So slowly, I turn as she trips, my sword a part of my arm, weightless, a hawk stooping from this far and distant sky where I'm alone—

Noya lay on her back, the point of Tegan's sword at her throat.

Well. Well, Tegan thought.

Noya rolled away, laughing at the expression on Tegan's face.

Tegan was only human, no emperor's child. She held no magic except a demonsoul stone, and no enchanted sword. She could never win against a demon. She kept her back to the outside world, trying to create a barrier of mortal flesh between Ninidh and freedom. Her grip on the sword began to loosen. She fought to hold it, useless though it seemed to be.

Ninidh, laughing, held a king's ransom of opals in her hands. What weakness in that, that a mortal could use?

Tegan reached for a calm place that she had once found, a still place born of despair where nothing mattered except the blade's edge, the pattern of its reaching—

Tegan struck at the demon's hands. Her sword could not cut demonflesh, but it struck the gems. Raw opals scattered across the cave.

The invisible substance that was Ninidh shrieked in outrage. The demon sank toward the floor. Her insubstantial fingers plucked at the tossed gems. The stones drew themselves into little heaps as Ninidh tried to pick them up again. Tegan let herself feel the smallest bit of hope.

"Well fought," old Caedrun said. "Well fought."

Noya, on her feet again and still smiling, handed over the water jug.

It was so good, so wet, Tegan's thirst had been like a fire in her throat. She drank, and drank again, and handed the jug to Noya. Far to the west, thunderheads were growing, black at their bases and moving quickly.

"Tegan! Come here, please." The Lady Idane called. "Caedrun, see to the packing, if you would, and Noya. We will be leaving sooner than I expected."

Tegan rushed to keep up with her, the lady speeding along a path through the crackling leaves, this once careless of their noise. The man in gray—had he been real? Tegan felt eyes on her, appraising eyes, but when she looked, she saw bare branches, bright evergreens waiting for snow. No man anywhere.

The lady carried a wrapped bundle on her back. It contained, Tegan knew, the Sword.

They reached the sourcespring. The stream that welled from it led down toward the pass, the road back into the lowlands.

Beside it, crouched, an impossible beast lapped at the water with its long tongue, its bronze wings furled tightly on the length of its huge back. The beast backed away from the spring and growled. The lady shoved at it with her shoulder and scratched a spot behind its ears.

"This is Tegan," she told the beast. "Take her scent. Tegan, come closer."

Reek of giant cat, hot breath, the beast reached out its long neck and sniffed at Tegan's hand. Its rough tongue flicked lightly along the skin of her wrist, taking a delicate taste.

"Stand still," the lady cautioned.

Tegan stood still. It had never occurred to her to move. She was almost too awed to be frightened.

The Lady Idane mounted the griffin and settled the weight of the Sword over her shoulders.

"This is not to be your life. You will leave us now."

The protests that rose in Tegan's throat died at the look on Idane's face.

"Here." Idane tossed a small sack tied with a familiar green ribbon. Tegan caught it. It was heavy.

"You won't understand, not for a long, long time. Nothing I can say will—Oh, bother! Go quickly. We are hunted."

The Lady Idane touched her heels to the beast's side. The griffin stretched its wings and rose toward the western pass, toward the gathering storm.

Rejected, cast aside, named unworthy. Tegan had hated the Lady Idane with deep hatred, and tried to mask it in disdain. Who did she think she was, this uncaring woman, but a surrogate mother to a bunch of foolish women who lived in tents? They were fools, fools who saw themselves as knights-errant for the weak. Feh. Their schemes and manipulations seemed to do so little in the world.

Tegan despised them. They were petty, and cruel, to cast her aside.

I'll show you! Tegan thought. She clenched her fist at the sky and choked back tears. I'll show you!

Wealth and power, and satins, and kingdoms to do her bidding, that was what Tegan had decided would be hers, in that moment when the griffin vanished forever. How were they gained in this world? How did a woman gain them? Not by eating beans and wearing rough linen in a mountain camp.

She went to the Red Temple at Wellfleet. She listened to the random bragging of her clients. She kept the coins that were her due, and avoided the gaming tables. She spent some of them on lessons in swordplay, telling herself it was only to keep her body hard and tight, for she sought clients who liked hard, tight bodies, and found them.

The deceptions that the world called beauty, she learned those, too, cosmetic arts, gestures, the uses of a low and murmuring voice. Even among the wrecked souls of the Red Temple, there were skills to be gained.

If the women of Small Aldwyn, her mother, her sister, knew how she had gained her wealth in those visits she made them, they pretended not to know. Then Lyse's husband vanished, Lyse's child with him. Lyse's grief had led Tegan in a search for knowledge of the lands around Idris—and she found Osyr, a fitting tool to use against Idris.

Osyr now used, now dead.

As she would be, soon, and for naught.

In the mine, Ninidh's presence seemed stronger, as if each stone she gathered from the floor added to her substance. Laughter filled the cave and echoed back from the tunnels.

Did you think to hold me? the demon asked. *Oh, foolish mortal.*

Tegan struck again at the gems, scattering them to the far corners of the cave.

The demon's breath washed across Tegan, a wave of ice, of terror. Cold sweat drenched Tegan's face.

Ninidh would be loosed to do as she would, and her theft of whatever gems she wanted would only make the ones yet to be found more valuable. Another duke would hold power in Idris, in Osyr, and the mine would be restocked with little ones. Ninidh would like that, an ever renewed source of innocent souls to chew up and spit out.

The demon's malice leached away the last of Tegan's strength. She fell to her knees, weakness bringing her down as if she were made of melting wax. Darkness rose from within her, darkness that filled the cave and left her helpless, paralyzed. Her sword slipped from her hand. Her breath sighed out and she knew that her muscles would not move to draw in another.

Was this how dying felt? Where were the bright memories, the peace that the priests of Ardneh promised? Where?

The cave filled with a space where falling stars streaked across the night, a space of utter silence in which Ninidh's shriek of immortal terror tore at the hills themselves.

Ninidh shrank away from a sword wielded by a goddess in silver armor that reflected the red of Tegan's dress, or it was a chiton she wore, gauzy draperies spun of unearthly silk.

Ninidh retreated, her substance torn by the invisible path of the terrible blade. Tegan got to her knees, released from the demon's attention by the onslaught of the Sword of Stealth.

"Tegan! Get out!" the goddess cried.

Idane struck with the Sword, a blow that divided one Ninidh into many and flung her divided selves to the ground where her treasures lay—a Ninidh shown as she truly was, a creature made of wisps of greed, of puerile pleasure in baubles and sparkles and groveling incarnations of persistent, immortal vanity, a vanity that reflected only its own image and spiraled inward, forever. Ninidh screamed at what she saw, a thousand tiny Ninidhs reflected in a thousand tiny mirrors, Ninidhs that clung to the opals on the filthy floor, to grains of faceted sand, to dust. Ninidhs the size of gnats burrowed into the earth, sifting it like flour.

Tegan stood, wobbly on her feet. She took a position by the lady's side, guarding her as best she could. The two of them backed toward outside air, toward the useless iron grate.

"Bury her, Idane!" Tegan yelled.

"She buries herself!" Idane shouted. "Look!"

The floor of the cave shifted, its stones loosened by a demon's greed. Sand and pebbles, then stones, fell from the walls. One of the timbers at the entrance cracked and sagged.

"I have her soul!" Tegan shouted.

"Bury it with her, then!" Idane ducked through the narrowed space at the mouth of the cave and pulled Tegan with her. "Throw it, Tegan!"

Tegan tossed the ugly soulstone into the dirt, into the rainbow colors of the opals that lay scattered on the churning earth.

Idane's Sword scribed out a circle around the mouth of the cave. "You are bound here, Ninidh," Idane cried. "Sleep well."

From the soiled earth, a multitude of tiny shrieks rose. A rumbling began deep in the tunnels. Its soil loosened by restless demons, the cave fell in on itself, on vanity and greed, on gems buried forever and forever guarded by a presence that forced the two women back, back, toward a battle won.

Side by side, Tegan and the Lady Idane fought free of the dust cloud that rose from the cave's buried mouth. Weaponless, for her sword was buried in the mountain, Tegan looked for danger, but the battle had moved down the mountainside and seemed to be over. The afternoon's gray light showed changes in Idane. Her hair had gone gray, and she seemed shorter. Or was it only that Tegan had thought her to be taller than she was?

"Noya said you would not help us," Tegan said.

"We didn't come to Osyr." The Lady's deeply lined face was pale with exhaustion. "We came to you."

Idane took a step forward. Her hands trembled on the hilt of the Sword she carried.

"Hold this for me, Tegan. It is so heavy." Idane held out the hilt of the Sword and Tegan took it in her hand.

"Sheathe it," Idane said.

The great Sword's invisible blade lighted the lady's face, a
face that Tegan saw clearly, a face she thought she had
known and had never really seen until this moment. Idane
was old, and kind, and her face held compassion and love,
and pity. Why does she pity me? Tegan wondered.

Tegan, obedient, lifted the blade and sheathed Sightblinder, the Sword of Stealth, whose power showed its enemies
what they truly feared. Or truly loved.

The Lady Idane straightened her shoulders and walked
away from the sealed mine. Tegan followed her, bearing the
heavy burden of the lady's Sword.

Halfway down the slope, Seagus and his men surrounded the
Osyr banner, bronze and black victorious against green and
gray. The ferretsnake had wrapped its long body under
Dorn's collar to keep out of the wet. It flicked its tongue at
the women as they approached. The fighters stood helpless
now, bewildered by the churning in the earth. Spring rain
pattered in the sudden silence.

It seemed the men would stand in the rain forever. Had
they lost their wits? Tegan stepped forward so they could see
her.

"Seagus!" she called.

He looked up at her, all the battle lust drained now from
his honest, homely face, replaced by fatigue and wonder. The
Lady Idane stood aside.

"You have gained a duchy today! Hold it safe!"

The tired men around him raised a cheer, and seeming to
find strength in it, raised another.

He left them and climbed the slope to where she stood.

"You'll be with me?" he asked.

Would she? No. Not as a consort to Seagus, although she
wished him well. The lands in Osyr and Idris were good farm-

ing lands, and the foothills of the mountains fine pasturage. Given no gems to twist his soul, and good farmers, Seagus would be a careful guardian of what he held.

"Sometimes," Tegan said. *Yes, sometimes, I'll come to you and laugh, and we'll make love. We'll comfort each other again, as we have before. But you'll need a wife in time, a dutiful wife, and children. I'm not for that.*

The wiry, gray-haired woman had taken shelter beneath the branches of a new-leafed tree. Tegan watched her, afraid Idane would slip away. The lady was almost invisible, gray in the world's gray rain. "We'll talk about this, Seagus. Soon. Your men are waiting. Go to them."

He hesitated.

"You're the duke. Be a good one. Your men are tired and wet, and hungry."

Seagus blinked as if he'd just been awakened. He turned and looked at his new charges. "Dorn! Set out guards!" he shouted. "Blacknail, do something about this damned rain! All of you! Get the wounded to shelter!"

He walked down the mountainside toward his men, his future. In these brief moments, he had gained a lordly set to his shoulders.

Tegan went to the Lady Idane.

"Your Sword. Take it," Tegan said.

The woman folded her arms one in the other.

"Of all those who came to me, you alone could bear it in my stead," Idane said.

"You sent me away!"

"Yes. But the Sword is yours. I will not take it up again."

Idane had sent Tegan away, hurt and angry. Because of that anger, an untrained girl had learned the uses of loyalty, of power, of weapons of steel and of weapons that had no physical being but were useful in skilled hands. Of patience, of misdirected purpose. Of stealth, even if used to force someone to become what she, on her own, would not.

"Did Noya watch me buy the stone?" Tegan asked.

"Yes. She did not understand how you planned to use it."

Neither did I, Tegan thought.

"It was a clever ruse, scattering the gems," Idane said.

A clever ruse that had almost failed. Tegan had not been wise, or devious. She had only been desperate. Had she hoped the lady would come to her, and bring the Sword?

Yes. Tegan had hidden her hope even from herself. She had taken a foolish risk, but she had won.

Was she a fit successor to the woman she had seen in the cave, a woman of deadly wisdom, who fought even demons? She saw the answer in the Lady Idane's tired, compassionate face.

Tegan raised the sheathed Sword to her forehead in salute to her mentor.

"Oh, bother," the Lady Idane said. The fatigue of battle seemed to have left her. She looked as brisk as a spring wind. "It's not going to be all fun, you know. You have a bit to learn about wizardry, for starts. I thought for a minute there that you didn't know what you were about."

Infuriating woman! Was she smiling?

"You'll learn," Idane said. "I did."

Idane stepped to a thicket and reached inside it with a fast swoop of her arms. She brought out a little girl, earth-stained, terrified, who clung to Idane and whimpered. Idane crooned to her.

Beyond the Lady Idane and the child she held, half-hidden in spring leaves, a griffin whuffed in impatience. Close by the creature's side, a man in gray waited with his instructions.

About the Authors

Gene Bostwick is a 1992 graduate of the Clarion West Writers' Workshop in Seattle, Washington. His short-story sales include the *Writers of the Future* anthologies and *Tomorrow* magazine. He's married (14 years) to his number-one fan, critic, and copy editor. He has practiced architecture and built most everything from doghouses to shopping malls. Creating a good story, he has discovered, demands as much and rewards as much as creating a good design.

Pati Nagle, native and life-long resident of New Mexico, has been writing fiction since she could hold a pencil. Her work has appeared in *The Magazine of Fantasy & Science Fiction* and in *Infinite Loop,* an anthology of science fiction by computer professionals. She has a special interest in the outdoors, particularly New Mexico's wilds, where many of her stories are born.

Fred Saberhagen has been writing—and sometimes editing—science fiction and fantasy for more than thirty years. He lives and works in New Mexico with his wife, Joan.

Tom Saberhagen grew up in New Mexico where his passions were hiking, reading, and playing the piano. He graduated from Rice University with a degree in mathematics and philosophy. As a business systems consultant, he is engaged in battle with the berserkers of corporate America.

Michael A. Stackpole is a writer and game designer who moved from Vermont to Arizona in 1979 after graduating from the University of Vermont. He's best known for his novels in the BattleTech line and his fantasy novel *Once a Hero.* In his spare time he plays indoor soccer and defends the game industry from allegations of Satanism, murder, and mayhem. Future projects include another fantasy novel, *Eyes of Silver,* and four *Star Wars*™ *X-Wing*™ novels for Bantam Books.

Robert E. Vardeman has lived in the Southwest since 1956, a resident of Albuquerque, New Mexico, for most of that time, and is the author of thirty-five fantasy novels, including Tor® Books' *The Demon Crown* series (titles: *The Glass Warrior, Phantoms on the Wind,* and *A Symphony of Storms*). Short stories have appeared in many horror anthologies including *Greystone Bay, Doom City, SeaHarp Hotel,* and most recently in Robert Bloch's anthologies, *Psycho Paths* and *Monsters in Our Midst.* Vardeman is a longtime fan of the *Swords* books and is delighted to have a story in the current anthology.

[Editor's note: Sage Walker offers two biographical paragraphs. One of them—she claims—is a fantasy.]

Sage Walker has survived an Oklahoma childhood, the Sixties, medical school, and seventeen years of practice in emergency medicine. Tor has scheduled her first novel for publication in April 1996. She is currently working on a fantasy set in Norway and first-century Britain. Sage lives in New Mexico and has been known to sing along with coyotes.

Raven-haired, hard-bodied *Sage Walker* never has to do dishes. She writes three novels a year, all best-sellers. She is twenty-nine years old and attributes her unquenchable good spirits to a diet of champagne, buttered lobster, and Godiva chocolates.

Walter Jon Williams lives in New Mexico. His books include *Hardwired, Days of Atonement,* and *Aristoi.* Many of his stories, including the novellas "Surfacing" and "Wall, Stone, Craft" were nominated for Hugo and Nebula awards. In addition to the *Swords* shared-world project, Walter has also written for George R. R. Martin's *Wild Cards.* Walter's pastimes include kenpo karate, scuba, and small boat sailing.

THE BEST OF FANTASY FROM TOR

THE BEST OF FANTASY FROM TOR

"So are you still spouse-hunting in Riviera waters, Olivia?" Luc asked.

"I would be if you hadn't robbed us of our trip!" she replied. "It's only fair you make up for it now. Who knows? I might meet an exciting playboy with husband potential! But the point is, when your brother finds out I've gone on a vacation with you, he'll give up any idea he had about marriage to me."

"Why is that?" His voice had taken on a darker tone.

Olivia's impulsive nature had once again caused her to leap before she looked.

But this was serious business. The most serious of her existence.

It was Luc she loved with every fiber of her being. The longer he didn't say anything, the more she realized that if she didn't give him the right answer, she might just lose him forever....

Dear Reader,

I came from a family of five sisters and one brother. The four oldest girls were my parents' first family. There was a space before my baby sister and baby brother came along.

My mother called the first four her little women, and gave each of us a Madame Alexander doll from the *Little Women* series based on the famous book by Louisa May Alcott. We may not have been quadruplets, but we were close in age and definitely felt a connection to each other.

In our early twenties, I recall a time when I took the train from Paris, France, where I'd been studying, to meet one of my sisters at the port in Genoa, Italy, where her ship came in from New York. Some of my choicest memories are our glorious adventures as two blond American sisters on vacation along the French and Italian Rivieras, dodging Mediterranean playboys.

When I conceived THE HUSBAND FUND trilogy for Harlequin Romance®, I have no doubt the idea of triplet sisters coming to Europe on a lark to intentionally meet some gorgeous Riviera playboys sprang to life from my own family experiences at home and abroad.

Meet Greer, Olivia and Piper, three characters drawn from my imagination who probably have traits from all four of my wonderful, intelligent, talented sisters in their makeup.

Enjoy!

Rebecca Winters

Book 3: *To Marry for Duty,* Harlequin Romance #3835, on sale March 2005
www.rebeccawinters-author.com

TO WIN HIS HEART

Rebecca Winters

HARLEQUIN®

TORONTO • NEW YORK • LONDON
AMSTERDAM • PARIS • SYDNEY • HAMBURG
STOCKHOLM • ATHENS • TOKYO • MILAN • MADRID
PRAGUE • WARSAW • BUDAPEST • AUCKLAND

ISBN 0-373-18173-6

TO WIN HIS HEART

First North American Publication 2005.

This edition published by arrangement with Harlequin Books S.A.

® and TM are trademarks of the publisher. Trademarks indicated with
® are registered in the United States Patent and Trademark Office, the
Canadian Trade Marks Office and in other countries.

www.eHarlequin.com

Printed in U.S.A.

CHAPTER ONE

August 2nd
Monza, Italy

"GOOD night, Cesar. I've had a spectacular time."

After the party downstairs with his Formula I racing team, Cesar walked Olivia to her hotel room, but it irritated her when he looped his arms around her neck outside the door.

Since he never drank before a race, she knew for a fact it couldn't be the effect of alcohol making him amorous all of a sudden.

Twenty-nine-year-old Cesar de Falcon, known as Cesar Villon when he used his paternal grandmother's maiden name Villon to race, was all flash and excitement, the ultimate charmer, albeit one who was still too obsessed with his career to be taken seriously.

Neither during the night of the Monaco Grand Prix in June, or throughout the last two days in Monza prior to tomorrow's race had

Olivia led him to believe there was anything but friendship between them. There couldn't be.

She was painfully in love with his elder brother, Lucien de Falcon.

Though that love wasn't reciprocated, it didn't matter. With her emotions involved elsewhere, she couldn't let go with Cesar and kiss him for the sheer fun of being out with one of Europe's most eligible and sought after playboys. Especially not this particular one.

When she'd come to Europe with her sisters in June, the highlight for Olivia had been to watch the Monaco Grand Prix where the legendary Cesar Villon had taken second place.

It was an absolute fluke that Cesar's cousin, Max, had ended up marrying Greer, one of Olivia's sisters, thus throwing their families together under the most unlikely and unexpected circumstances.

Because of her fascination with Formula I racing before meeting Cesar, she'd been thrilled and flattered by the famous driver's eagerness to show her around. How many times in life did one get a chance to see firsthand what went on behind the scenes of the racing world? Especially with someone as well-known?

"I've had an even more wonderful time, *ma*

belle. There's no reason why it can't continue now that we're alone.''

"Yes, there is.'' She averted her face in an attempt to prevent him from kissing her. "You have a big race tomorrow and need your beauty sleep.''

"Beauty sleep?'' He chuckled before brushing his lips against the side of her cheek. "I intend to get some, but not by myself.'' So saying, he trapped her against the door and kissed her.

Cesar was an attractive man, very persuasive, but she broke away before he could deepen the kiss. The look of surprise on his face let her know few women had ever resisted him.

"You're not going to invite me in?'' He gave her that wounded look so typical of Max, her new, all-Italian brother-in-law.

She smiled, needing to handle this with grace and discretion considering the fact that he was now Greer's cousin-in-law. It wasn't as if she could risk offending him by her rejection, knowing she would never see him again in this lifetime.

"No, *cousin*,'' she said the word deliberately. "I'm not. I always sleep alone.''

"Always?'' He looked shocked to the foundations.

"Always."

"Not even with Fred?"

The mention of her ex-boyfriend, the one who'd followed Formula I racing on TV and had gotten her interested in the sport in the first place, made her chuckle. "Especially not Fred."

"But this is unbelievable."

Olivia burst into laughter. She couldn't help it. "My sisters and I were taught to wait for marriage."

"You mean to tell me Greer and Max—"

"Didn't until their wedding night," she finished the sentence for him.

Now it was his turn to laugh. "Then she lied to you."

"No." Olivia shook her head. "I would stake my life on it." When she could see he wasn't convinced she said, "Tell you what. After they're back from their honeymoon, you can ask Max. He'll tell you the truth."

Cesar grinned. "What if you're wrong?"

"I won't be."

"For the sake of argument, let's assume you are," he teased. "We'll make this a bet. If I win—"

"You won't!" she declared in a note of finality.

He was such a tease, it surprised her when he grasped her upper arms. "The German team thinks they're going to win the Italian Grand Prix tomorrow, but by the end of the race *I* will be the one standing at the podium.

"After a race I always spend a week at the family villa in Positano on the Amalfi Coast where I can be alone. This time I'm taking you there with me to celebrate my victory, so be warned."

No, Cesar, I won't be going anywhere with you.

The man had an ego that wouldn't quit. Any other woman would probably jump at the chance to go off alone with him, but Olivia wasn't one of them.

"You would have to be my husband first."

He flashed her a disarming smile. "Then I guess we'll have to pick out a ring while we're in Positano."

"You're full of it, Cesar, but I like you anyway. I'll be rooting for you tomorrow." She raised up on tiptoe and kissed his cheek, then eased out of his arms. "Good night and good luck," she said before escaping to her room for the night.

Though he represented the epitome of most women's desires, he wasn't the man who'd dominated Olivia's every thought after she and her sisters had flown home to New York to get ready for Greer's wedding.

There was only one man's kiss she wanted. She'd worked herself up into a breathless state just waiting to see Luc again at the wedding, but he'd shot her down within the first moments of their meeting.

You may come off the innocent and have Cesar fooled, Olivia, but I see right through you. You're nothing more than what you Americans call a "groupie."

Really...well if I'm a groupie, then that makes you the jealous older brother with what we Americans call a "game" leg. It must be galling to know you wouldn't be able to climb into Cesar's race car, let alone drive it!

Her body still bristled from the ugly words they'd thrown at each other. He'd actually had the audacity to call her a *groupie!*

How dare he liken her to a sycophant, one of a cast of a thousand hopefuls...those grasping, opportunistic women who hung around the track and flung themselves at idols like Cesar who was single, famous and wealthy.

Luc had made her so furious, she'd been glad to take Cesar up on his invitation to watch him race in the Italian Grand Prix. However it had given off the wrong signal to Cesar who now assumed she was his for the taking.

Everything was Luc's fault. Just thinking about their fiery confrontation outside the chapel caused Olivia's heart to thud painfully.

If he hadn't thrown that final insult at her, she wouldn't have done anything so impulsive.

Unlike his brother, Luc didn't need or crave the limelight, a fact that made him much more appealing to her. Though she found his aloofness disturbing, she was also fascinated that he didn't seem to need anyone. He was a man who lit his own fires and moved in an orbit all his own.

According to Cesar, Luc's energy was tied up in his work as a robotics engineer. She found herself wanting to know everything about him, but Cesar had been strangely silent when it came to details about Luc's life, whether professional or personal.

The most she'd learned was that seven months earlier he'd almost lost his leg in the same tragic ski tram accident that had killed his cousin Nic's fiancée.

Olivia already knew from Greer that Luc had never been married.

It certainly wouldn't have been for lack of opportunity. His serious gray eyes beneath black hair and brows were startlingly beautiful and unexpected when contrasted with the olive complexion of his hard-boned features.

She'd only seen him smile once and thought there couldn't be another man as gorgeous, not even Cesar. But after their bitter quarrel, Olivia had given up hope of ever witnessing that rare sight again.

She imagined the pain from his injured leg had something to do with his saturnine disposition. However Olivia suspected his morose moods were the result of problems that went deeper than the physical.

Some woman must have gotten to him... Whoever it was, she'd done a good job of ruining him for anyone else.

The Falcon men were tall, dark and dashing in that irresistible Mediterranean way. If it were Luc's goal, he could be surrounded by stunning beauties all the time. But he obviously had other things on his mind and was too intelligent and self-confident to need constant attention from the opposite sex.

He definitely didn't want Olivia's. She'd never been so hurt, and was still suffering from the wounds. Yet the more she pondered it, the more she refused to accept his biting remarks as final. That jaded, aloof, thirty-three-year-old brother of Cesar's had misjudged her, and she was going to prove it!

Pounding her pillow, she lay her head back down willing sleep to come, afraid it wouldn't.

"You're not going to see your brother race in the morning?"

Non, Dieu merci.

"I'm afraid not, *maman.* The doctor plans to drain my knee day after tomorrow, so I'm taking it easy until then." Luc was glad to have a legitimate excuse to give his mother. She would pass it on to his father and Cesar.

"Then take care, *mon fils.* I'll be by in a few days to see how you are doing."

"That won't be necessary. I'll come to see you."

If the doctor's prognosis was correct, Luc's leg was in the last stage of healing. After seven ghastly months of pure physical hell, the end was in sight. He only wished he could say the same about his mental torment, but no medical procedure could fix that.

"Talk to you soon, *maman.*" He hung up and sat back in the swivel chair of his private study, staring blindly at the monitor screen.

Normally the math required to do his latest project kept his darkest thoughts at bay, but not tonight. An image of Olivia Duchess in his brother's bed made the bile rise in his throat.

He reached for his cell phone and punched one of the digits. After three rings his cousin picked up.

"Luc? I was wondering if it might be you."

"Who else bothers you at this time of night? Were you in bed?"

"No. I'm in my library working on this blasted manuscript."

"I was just going to ask how it was progressing. Now I won't."

Nic had been going through his own personal hell since Nina's death. On top of his grief that the accident had happened, he was suffering guilt. All because he'd broken his engagement to her an hour before she'd taken that last tram ride up the mountain without him.

Luc would never know if Nic had discovered she'd been unfaithful to his cousin, and that's why he'd called the wedding off. As close as Luc and Nic were, his cousin had never once hinted that Nina had been seeing another man.

But Luc knew she had.

By chance he'd decided to take one more ski run late that day. When he'd gone outside the lodge to get his skis, he'd witnessed a sight that had torn him apart.

Over in the trees he'd seen a stranger with thick, dark blond hair kissing Nina. She gave him her full cooperation before she broke away and hurried toward the tram with her skis.

Having always loved Nic like a brother, Luc intended to confront her and followed her onto the tram. But before he had a chance to take her aside, tragedy struck, killing her and injuring him.

During the long talks at the hospital while Luc underwent several surgeries, Nic finally admitted that he'd never been in love with Nina the way he should have been. He'd agreed to the engagement because of pressure from his parents, particularly his father, who'd wanted the marriage to take place.

But as Nic explained, once the wedding date was set, he realized he couldn't marry her.

His confession hadn't surprised Luc or Max. Nic had never acted like a man madly in love. But since Nic had never breathed a word about Nina's betrayal, Luc decided his cousin hadn't known anything about it.

After discussing it with Max, the two of them thought it best Nic be kept in the dark since it wouldn't have served any purpose. Nina was dead. Why make it any uglier.

In Luc's mind, whether you were engaged or

married, it was adultery if your partner proved to be unfaithful. Luc knew firsthand what it felt like to be betrayed, by his own brother no less. He wouldn't wish the feeling on his worst enemy, let alone Nic of all people.

Thousands of spectators screamed and jumped around when the announcement came over the loud speaker in four different languages that Cesar Villon, the brilliant Formula I race car driver representing Monaco, had claimed the coveted first place at Monza.

Olivia had come to the stands early to watch the race. Now she was on her feet, clapping and cheering like so many of his other fans.

The two days before his race had been an instructive time for her as she'd watched him go through the testing and qualifying trials prior to the big event that he'd just conquered.

Being the fierce competitor he was, he'd made his own prophecy come true. Hopefully he'd forgotten what he'd said about taking her away afterward. But in case he hadn't, she decided to leave Monza so she wouldn't be around for him to collect later in the day, giving him another wrong impression.

Blessed with many gifts, including the fact that he was the younger son of the Duc de

Falcon of Monaco, he could be excused for assuming no woman was immune to him. If there were depths to him not yet visible, only time would tell, probably after he was too old to compete anymore.

Half Italian, half Monegasque, Cesar's movie star looks made him the supreme favorite with the crowd. Filled with the matchless optimism of a man who knows he's number one, he'd arranged for Olivia to sit near the podium. But she didn't try to reach him after the ceremony was over. Even if she'd wanted to, it would have been a physical impossibility.

Not only was he basking in the adulation of thousands of screaming fans while he drank champagne and pressed his lips to the winner's cup—at least a dozen gorgeous female admirers were now crowding him, hanging on his arm, lifting their mouths for his kiss which he passed around with obvious relish.

Naturally the spectacle provided hundreds of photo ops for the many international journalists covering the race. By tomorrow morning pictures of him embracing one beauty after another would grace the front page of a thousand newspapers and magazine covers.

For Olivia, the whole scene was a huge turn-off. Her sense of distaste for such a lifestyle deepened as she watched the women battling for position, hoping to be the one he took home for the night. Little did they know that last night Olivia had been his target.

Scenes like the one going on in front of her right now happened to Cesar before and after every race. Women would continue to swarm around him like bees, and he would respond for as long as racing fever was in his blood.

Olivia recognized that any woman unfortunate enough to fall in love with an international sports celebrity would have to put up with a mistress more merciless than any flesh-and-blood female.

While she stood there staring blindly in Cesar's direction, the idea that had taken root in her mind last night had turned into a fully fledged plan. She couldn't leave the grandstand fast enough to put it into action.

Without hesitation she worked her way through the crowds to reach the cue of taxis outside the race track. "The Accademia Hotel," she told the driver.

"Si, signorina."

Once back in her room, she would phone her sister Piper, who was already in Genoa, Italy, on business.

Some mockups of their calendars in Italian

were ready for them to examine. If they thought the finished products looked good, she'd run off a bunch for Signore Tozetti to distribute in the Parma region. Provided they sold well, it could mean a lot more orders down the road.

Olivia was supposed to be there to help make the decision before they flew home to New York together. But she'd changed her mind about leaving Europe just yet, and she trusted Piper's judgment completely.

Her sister wouldn't approve of Olivia's plan to go after Luc. Neither would Greer. Luckily she wasn't around to quash Olivia's idea. Thanks to Maximilliano di Varano, the love of Greer's life, Greer was on her honeymoon.

It had taken a very special man to break up the Duchess triplets, three blond sisters who caused a minor sensation at birth and bore a strong resemblance to each other without being identical.

Max had taken one look at Greer with her amethyst eyes, and the dedicated bachelor had fallen so hard, Olivia knew he would never recover.

Since their nuptials four days ago in the private chapel of the Varano family palace in Parma, the two lovers had been honeymooning at an intimate hideaway somewhere in Greece.

The look of desire and adoration in Max's eyes after kissing his bride at the altar revealed to the whole world how he felt about Greer. There was no telling how long he planned to keep her to himself, but Olivia had a hunch it would be at least a month before she and Piper heard from their sister. Long enough for Olivia to follow through with her daring scheme...

With Greer married off, Olivia's world had changed. She was feeling a heady new sense of freedom both physical and psychological. She figured Piper was enjoying the freedom, too. Without Greer around to tell them how to think and what they were going to do next, Olivia could finally be master of her own destiny.

It wasn't that she didn't love Greer. On the contrary, she adored her. Still, it was a relief not to have to face her and hear her say, *I told you it would be a mistake to go off with Cesar. If you do that, then you're the kind of stupid, naive, dumb blond he seduces after every race.*

Despite the fact that Luc's antipathy toward Olivia had made her do it, heat filled Olivia's cheeks to realize that once Greer had left on her honeymoon, Olivia had gone off and done the exact, stupid thing Greer had warned her not to do.

In fact it was Greer who'd told Olivia she

wasn't in love with Fred. Olivia had already figured that out after meeting Luc, but she'd gone on dating Fred for the six weeks prior to Greer's wedding in an effort to forget Luc and prove that Greer's power over her wasn't absolute.

Unfortunately she'd paid for it in the end when she'd been forced to tell Fred that it was really over. She'd been very unfair to him by leading him on, and was still smarting from the pain she'd caused him. One piercing glance from Greer with that "I told you so, now you've really done it" look, hadn't helped matters.

What really miffed Olivia was the fact that even though Max had claimed Greer for his wife and taken her away, Olivia was still battling her sister's powerful influence over her. She could just imagine Greer's reaction if she knew what Olivia was planning now.

You're what? Are you insane? Didn't we all learn a very important lesson the first time around?

"*Signorina?*" the driver called over his shoulder. They'd arrived at the hotel. She'd been so immersed in her new strategy, she hadn't even noticed!

After paying him a bundle of Euros she didn't even bother to count, she got out of the taxi and rushed inside, anxious to set things in motion.

Once she'd confirmed tickets on a flight to Nice leaving in two hours, she phoned Piper at her hotel in Genoa.

After relating the spectacular news that Cesar had won the Italian Grand Prix, Olivia told Piper what she was intending to do.

"You're *what?*" Her sister sounded suspiciously like Greer just then, which didn't help matters.

"I'm going back to Monaco to force Luc to make my trip good. It's payback time."

"Say that again?"

"You heard me," Olivia answered defiantly. "We were cheated out of our first trip to Europe because Max and his cousins thought we were jewel thieves and they ruined everything!

"By the time the whole business got straightened out, our vacation had to be aborted because Max wanted to be alone with Greer on the *Piccione*. Luc owes me ten days on that boat!"

"It's Fabio Moretti's boat! August is still high season. Some other tourists have probably chartered it. Don't forget it's the Moretti's livelihood."

"I'm sure Luc will be able to work something out with Fabio. We paid three thousand dollars each for a trip along the Riviera that never happened!''

''Technically you're right, Olivia. But in return we acquired Max, the dream brother-in-law who has treated us like the Duchess of Parma herself while we stayed at his family's royal palace. That beats any vacation I can think of.

''Besides, what are you complaining about? Your dream came true when Cesar whisked you off to Monza for the last three days. I thought you were crazy about *him*. At least that's what you told Fred.''

Conscience made Olivia bite her lip. ''I had to tell Fred something that would help him retain his pride. If I'd been truthful and said I couldn't picture him as my husband, it would have hurt him a lot more.''

''Okay... I can buy that, but what about Cesar?''

''He's a friend. Even if he weren't, he's spoken for.''

''By whom?''

''By the entire female population of Europe!''

''Yeah, well Greer already told you that.''

Olivia ground her teeth. ''Greer doesn't know everything.''

"Yes, she does."

"She didn't know we talked Daddy into setting up that phony Husband Fund that brought us to Europe in the first place."

After a moment of quiet, "That's true. It's probably the only secret we ever kept from her."

"Yup. And it worked!" A satisfied smile broke out on Olivia's face. "We finally got her married off. Now we can do what we want, and I want to go on the vacation that never happened. Don't you?"

"Maybe one day. At the moment we've got a calendar business to run."

"Has Signore Tozzeti decided if he wants to take us on as a client?"

"Not yet. He says there are a few other people in his company he needs to talk to, but they're on vacation, so he won't be able to get back to us for a while."

"Great."

"That's why we've got to go home and see about enlarging the market there. Otherwise we're not going to be able to pay the rent. We need to do it now!"

"You sound just like Greer!"

Greer was the oldest triplet by a matter of minutes. Yet Olivia, who'd been born last with

Piper in the middle, had always been dominated by Greer, their natural born leader.

Over the years she *had* made the decisions about everything, whether Olivia or Piper liked them or not. For the first time ever, Olivia could do what she wanted without having to hear Greer's opinion.

"With Greer gone, someone needs to talk sense into you. What's the *real* reason you want to stay? You and Luc looked like mortal enemies after the wedding ceremony, so I don't understand why you would dare confront him again—oh, no—tell me it isn't true."

"What?"

"Tell me you haven't fallen for Luc de Falcon—"

Her cheeks turned to flame.

"Olivia? You *can't!*"

"What do you mean, I can't?"

"Because you just can't, that's all."

"Why?"

"Think of Greer."

"That's all I've ever done. We've had to do everything her way because she always took charge. Now she's married, I want to think about *moi* for a change."

"Then you need to think again because Luc is Max's first cousin."

"So?"

"So, Greer married Max, and Luc has become her family, too. You can't horn in!"

"Excuse me?"

"Look, Olivia. She's found her heart's desire in Max. This is her world, her turf. We need to leave well enough alone."

"It's a free country," she retorted.

"No, it's not, and you know exactly what I mean." Olivia did know, but she didn't like Piper reminding her. "Greer needs time to make a new life with Max. He married a triplet, and don't think he isn't worried about it!

"At the wedding feast he didn't make that crack about the three of us being joined at the hip, heart and brain for nothing. We have to help Greer cut the apron strings, which means we need to back off and give our sister her space."

"Luc lives in Monaco, not Colorno, Italy."

"That's not the point. The cousins are super close. Besides, it just wouldn't work for you to get involved with Luc, even if he were interested, which he…isn't."

The slight hesitation before the last word set off alarm bells inside Olivia. "How do you know?"

"Because…I just do."

"What do you know that I don't?" she fired.

"More than you want to hear."

She blinked. "How come?"

"Because it might hurt you."

Hurt? "You mean you're not going to tell me?"

"No. I promised someone I wouldn't," Piper's voice trailed.

"I see." She slid off the side of the bed and stood up. "Well in that case I plan to proceed as if you hadn't warned me. With a little hard work I'll make him change his mind."

"You'll be playing with fire."

"Then that's my problem isn't it."

"Don't snap at me, Olivia. I know you're feeling as lost without Greer as I am. You simply don't want to admit it."

She tossed her head back. "I admit it feels strange to be two-thirds of a whole. In time I trust we'll both get over it."

"Until we do, please come home with me."

"Not yet, Piper."

"Listen to me. You don't mess with a man like Luc. In more ways than one he's a different breed from anyone you've ever known. Besides, and this is probably the most important point, he has the distinction of being the only male who never fell under your spell. You can't win them all, Olivia. Trust me on this.''

"Are you through, *Greer?*"

"That wasn't very nice," Piper came back in a quiet voice.

Olivia clutched the phone tighter. "I'm sorry. It's just that I'm tired of people telling me what to do."

"Translated you mean, Greer and me."

Since the answer was obvious, Olivia didn't say anything.

"Whatever happened to all for one, and one for all?"

"There's no more *all.*" She prided herself on keeping a steady voice.

"You and I have each other. I don't want to see you in any more pain. It's been hard enough on us to lose Daddy."

At the mention of their father who'd died in April, Olivia's eyes smarted. "I don't intend to stay in pain. My plan is foolproof."

There was a long, resigned silence. "What is it exactly you're intending to do?"

"Get him to propose, at which time I will say *yes.*"

"Not that again! Luc already knows about the Husband Fund scheme, so it won't work on him."

"Yes, it will. He thinks I'm interested in Cesar, so he'll jump at the chance to save his brother from a fate worse than death by taking me on Fabio's boat. While we're basking in the sun, I'll find ways to thaw out his heart until he's unable to resist me. By the time we dock at Vernazza, he'll have proposed."

"You'll never break him down, Olivia."

She clutched the phone tighter. "Want to bet?"

After a pause, "I don't bet when I already know the outcome. I repeat. You'll live to regret this." Piper's voice sounded like Greer's at her most prophetic. "Come home with me and we'll find you a nice American guy to date."

"After Fred, no thank you."

"Not like Fred. Europe doesn't have the monopoly on exciting men."

"Sounds like you're trying to convince yourself!"

"Don't be ridiculous."

"I've already met the man I want for my husband, Piper. There's no talking me out of it."

"You think he's hurt you now...you just wait!"

Olivia refused to let the secret Piper was withholding about Luc get to her. "We'll see."

"It's your funeral, but whatever happens, call

me tomorrow. I have to know where you are and where I can reach you or I won't have any peace. I should be in Kingston by noon at the latest.''

"I promise to phone," Olivia vowed. "Have a safe flight. I'm glad Tom will be there to meet you. Be sure he takes a look around the apartment for you first."

"Don't worry about me."

Now Olivia was doing what she'd accused Piper of doing—telling her what to do. Running her life. "Okay, I won't. Talk to you later. Love you."

"Love you, too."

After Olivia hung up, she sat down to write a letter to Cesar. She needed to couch her words carefully.

"Dear cousin-in-law," she began. Once she'd explained that her heart belonged to another, she thanked him profusely for the wonderful time he'd shown her, thanked him for his kindness and generosity and praised him for his latest win.

"May all your wins in the coming years be as successful. I remain your friend and greatest fan from the U.S. Olivia Duchess."

Pleased with her message, she sealed it in the

envelope and took it downstairs to leave with the concierge.

"I don't know when Monsieur Villon will come back to the hotel to check out, but as soon as he does, will you make certain he gets this?"

"Si, signorina."

"Grazie."

After paying her bill, she carried her suitcase outside to the limo. The hotel provided transportation to the airport. Hopefully she was leaving soon enough to avoid the mass of tourists who probably wouldn't jam the terminal until tomorrow after a night of nonstop partying.

Once she reached Nice, she would take a taxi to the Falcon Villa in Monaco and surprise Luc. If her plan was going to work, it was imperative she catch him off guard. Forewarned and he might disappear on her. She couldn't let that happen.

CHAPTER TWO

"PLEASE wait for me."

The chauffeur de taxi nodded while Olivia approached the front door of the villa. It was seven-thirty on a hot August evening. She could still feel the heat rising from the street.

A maid answered. She recognized Olivia from her previous visit in June. When Olivia asked if she could see Luc, the other woman explained he didn't live there with his parents, yet Olivia distinctly remembered Luc claiming that he did!

Cross because it had been a deliberate ploy on his part to keep his private life private, she was forced to ask the maid where to find him. She learned he had his own home, the Mas de Falcon. Olivia wasn't familiar with the word.

The maid wrote down the address for her. Olivia thanked her, then gave it to the taxi driver. He nodded and they took off once more, heading for the region above the city.

In a few minutes they drove down a private

road that opened up into a charming courtyard filled with pots of flowers. There she discovered an exquisite pale pink, two-story villa with light blue shutters at all the windows. Apparently this was the back of the house.

Like an eagle's eyrie, the *mas* sat perched on a hill overlooking Monaco-Ville. The view would be magnificent.

In front of the garage at the side of the house were two vehicles: a truck that had to be several years old, and a black sports car. Hopefully that meant Luc was home, but she wouldn't know until she rang the doorbell.

Assuming he employed staff who could call another taxi for her in case he wasn't there, she paid the driver, then waved him off.

Determined as she'd ever been in her life, she walked up to the back entrance with her suitcase. "Be home, Luc."

With her heart pounding out of rhythm, she pushed the buzzer and waited. When there was no answer, she rang again.

On the third try, she heard noise like someone swearing. Shivering a little, she was glad she didn't understand French.

Then the door opened to reveal Luc himself, dressed in low-slung cutoff jeans and nothing else. Though she could see scarring on the shin bone of his leg beneath the knee, he looked so blatantly male with the dusting of black hair on his well cut chest and physique, she couldn't think or talk.

In that dizzying moment, she didn't notice that his mouth had formed a white line of anger. Not until her eyes wandered helplessly up his hard-muscled body to his striking face.

"What in the hell are *you* doing here?" Despite the anger in that low, grating voice, she loved his French accent when he spoke English.

"What are you doing answering the door without your cane?" Olivia fired back. She wasn't about to be intimidated by him. "You don't have to prove how macho you are in front of people, especially me. We're family now," she added just to irritate him.

His hands went to his hips, a gesture that emphasized his total masculinity. "Is that your unsubtle way of telling me you and Cesar ran off and got married after the race?"

She laughed. "Wouldn't you hate it if I said yes, thereby proving that I'm the ultimate groupie who was out for everything I could get from your brother, and did!"

His silvery eyes had narrowed to slits. "Why are you here?"

"What?" Her expressive brows lifted in

question. "Not even a 'won't you come in and make yourself comfortable'?"

"You're not an invited guest."

"Not even when we're related through marriage?"

He stiffened. "Whatever it is you have to say, make it fast. I'm in a hurry."

"Is that why you were cursing on your way to the door?" she taunted him with relish. "If you don't have the time to be civil to me right now, I'll be happy to wait."

If looks could kill... "Then you'll have a long one because I'm on my way out and don't know when I'll be back."

"That's no problem. I'll go with you and keep you company. As you can see, I brought my suitcase with me so I'm ready to travel."

He rubbed his chest in a motion he probably wasn't aware of. The fact that his first cousin Max was married to her sister was undoubtedly the only reason he hadn't slammed the door in her face yet.

"What's this all about?" Talk about a forbidding tone—

Standing her ground she said, "The trip my sisters and I never went on of course! The trip you and your cousins ruined for us. The trip that cost us over twenty thousand dollars after the bills we incurred by being forced to buy new bikes to try to get away from you.

"Shall I count the ways you destroyed the dream?" Her fingers started to tick everything off. "First, Max had us detained by the police in Genoa the second we got off the plane, then he stalked us while we walked around Portofino.

"After that, he inveigled you and Nic to take over as the crew aboard the *Piccione*. At that point the three of you sabotaged our itinerary, stole the family pendants our parents gave us on our sixteenth birthday, threw us in jail, prevented us from boarding a plane home and then forced us to show up at your family's villa to help draw out the real jewel thief.

"The thief you didn't catch by the way!" she mocked. "All this because you *thought* we'd stolen an identical pendant from the palace, which we didn't!"

Her fists went to her waist, drawing his piercing gaze to the curves beneath the leaf green cotton dress molding her body. "You were totally unfair to us, and now I'm here to collect. Since Max is on his honeymoon, and Nic left for London after the wedding, that leaves *you* to pay up.

"You owe me, Luc! So I've arrived to inform

you that you're taking me for a ten-day trip on the *Piccione* before I go back to New York.''

He shifted his weight, a sign his leg was probably bothering him. ''You make a compelling case, but I don't buy any of it. Why don't you try telling me the truth for a change. What's the real reason you've come to my home on a Sunday night, uninvited? Where's Cesar?''

''I haven't a clue. Well, that's not exactly true. The last time I saw him, he was at the winner's podium kissing one beautiful groupie after another, having the time of his life.''

For just a moment she thought she saw a shadow cross over his face, but maybe it was a light plane passing overhead, hiding the rays of a setting sun for a moment. Then he smirked. ''What's the matter? Couldn't you take the competition?''

''That question doesn't deserve an answer. The truth is, I had other things on my mind. Remember the Husband Fund?''

''What about it?'' he practically snapped.

''I'm afraid I may have hooked the wrong playboy without meaning to, and I need an out.''

''Which playboy would that be? There've been so many.'' His insulting remark was meant to sting. Well, she would sting him back!

"Cesar," she admitted.

Luc eyed her with disdain. "I don't see him anywhere around. Now you'll have to excuse me." He started to close the door.

"Last night he said something about buying me an engagement ring after the race."

She'd purposely slipped in that last tidbit before he could shut her out completely. Olivia was a hundred percent sure Cesar had been joking, but Luc didn't know that.

"I left Monza as soon as it was over and came straight here."

To her satisfaction she didn't hear the click that would have severed all contact. The door opened wider again. A stillness had stolen over Luc.

"He asked you to marry him?" his voice grated with incredulity.

Her instincts had been right. The idea of her becoming Luc's sister-in-law was so repugnant to him, he was caught in a vise.

"Isn't that what an engagement ring means? Or is your younger brother in the habit of promising one to every groupie he fancies without any intention of delivering..."

He raked a hand through his vibrant black hair, a gesture that indicated the news had disturbed him. Good. She hoped his concern to protect his brother from a predator like herself was great enough to agree to her plan.

"What kind of game are you playing with him?" came the voice of ice.

"Game?" She feigned innocence. "I admit it was exciting to be wined and dined by him for a little while. Fred got me interested in Formula I racing and I followed Cesar's success for a long time before we ever met.

"Meeting your brother was a great thrill. He's a wonderful man, and he's done everything to show me a fantastic time, but—"

"But all along it's been dull, boring Fred you wanted, and now you're afraid to tell Cesar?" She felt his question like the tip of a whip against her skin.

"No," she came back, intrigued to discover he'd remembered an offhand comment she'd made about Fred in his hearing. "I ended it with Fred before I flew here for Greer's wedding."

"How many dead bodies are lying around in that colorful past of yours?" he muttered in an acerbic tone. The wounds were growing.

"My past is none of your business, but Cesar *is*."

A nerve ticked at the corner of his sensual mouth. "Go on!"

"Well...Cesar knows I'm not seeing Fred

anymore. So he's not going to believe there's another man in my life, and he would be right. But that's not what I told him in the note I left for him at the hotel in Monza.''

''That was like waving a red flag,'' Luc drawled with contempt.

''I thought I was being polite,'' Olivia asserted. ''After the race I went back to the Accademia in a taxi and dashed off a letter before checking out. It was a combination good-bye–thank you note.

''I left it with the concierge to give to him when he came in. In it I explained that my heart belonged to another, but I wished him success in the future. Since Cesar is aware that other person isn't Fred, I'm afraid I've painted myself into a corner, and now I need help.''

Lines marred his features. ''You should have thought of that before you went to bed with him.''

''The Duchess girls don't sleep around!''

''That's an interesting fairy tale.''

She bridled. ''Cesar said the same thing, so I told him to ask Max when he gets back from his honeymoon if he doesn't believe me. Theirs was a *white* wedding. Why do you think they got married so fast?''

He folded his arms. ''Why are you digressing? If I'm to be of assistance to you, you have to tell me exactly how far things have progressed between you two. The truth this time.''

''You won't believe me if I tell you, so why should I bother.''

''You're still avoiding answering my question,'' Luc reminded her testily. ''I can assure I'm not asking out of a prurient desire to know the intimate details, just the facts. But if you don't want my help after all...'' He was a breath away from shutting the door on her.

She had to tamp down her euphoria. Obviously the thought of his brother marrying her disgusted him enough to listen.

''After the way you spoke to me at the wedding, do you honestly think I would darken your doorstep if I didn't?'' she challenged.

A war was waging inside him. She knew it by the tautness of his Gallic features. ''I repeat. How far did you go to accomplish what no other groupie has managed to do?'' he persisted.

''I didn't have to do anything. He's the one who kissed me outside my hotel room before I told him I had to go in.''

''And you expect me to believe he did *all* the work?''

Her brows knit together. ''Why do you have to know that?''

"So you *did* respond," he muttered, "which means he'll believe you were being a provocative tease."

She gave him a vexed look. "I couldn't help but respond a little bit. Your brother's the stuff a woman's dreams are made of. But the truth is, I have no interest in being his wife. For one thing, he won't make a good husband until his racing days are over. I've a feeling that day won't come for years yet."

"So you're still spouse hunting in Riviera waters?"

"I would be if you and your cousins hadn't robbed us of our trip! It's only fair you make up for it now. Who knows? I might meet an exciting playboy with husband potential while I'm waterskiing or exploring some island.

"The point is, when Cesar finds out I've gone on a vacation with you, he'll give up any idea he had about marriage to me."

"Why is that?" His voice had taken on a darker tone.

"You don't know?"

His face closed up. "I wouldn't have asked otherwise."

"Since the first time I met Cesar, I've discovered you're the only man in the world who intimidates him. You're kind of like Greer incarnate." Luc's black brows furrowed. "You know—the *oldest* one in the family. The one who rules by divine right?"

"No, I didn't know." He looked like thunder.

"Well you wouldn't! You don't have to. You were just born in charge. The one who knows everything, even if you don't!" She paused to catch her breath.

"Anyway, Cesar will think you must be the man who stole my heart after I came to the Riviera the first time. He wouldn't dare come after me knowing I was under your protection, so to speak."

Like the day she and her sisters dove off the *Piccione* into the warm blue water of the Mediterranean to get away from Luc and his cousins, Olivia's impulsive nature had once again caused her to leap before she looked.

But this was serious business. The most serious of her existence.

It was Luc she loved with every fiber of her being. The longer he didn't say anything, the more she realized that if he didn't give her the right answer, she would be in permanent mourning.

His eyes looked dark in the fading light. "Nothing's sacred to a woman like you, is it."

A woman like me? "Haven't you realized by now you can't play at life without paying too great a price?"

Those words were meant to debilitate her. They reminded her of Piper's warning on the phone earlier in the day that Luc could hurt her if she let him.

She struggled for breath. "My parents raised my sisters and me to believe fairy tales do come true. I can't help it if they were divinely happy and everything worked out for them.

"You have to admit the Husband Fund they set up managed to get Greer and Max together. I've never seen a more besotted couple."

"You're straying from the point again. It's a bad tendency of yours."

"No stronger than your tendency to ridicule everything," she fired back. "Can you think of a better way to put your brother off so he gets the message without causing damage? He *is* Greer's cousin-in-law through marriage. So are you of course.

"I don't want to be the one responsible for some kind of rift in our families before they've even come home from their honeymoon."

"You should have thought of that before you leaped into Cesar's Ferrari."

"You would have leaped too if you'd never

been in one before. How many people will ever get the opportunity to drive in such a car with a world-class Formula I race car pro like your brother? It's an experience not to be missed. But I'm forgetting this is a sensitive issue for you since you can't drive.''

His eyes glittered dangerously.

''The sooner you phone Fabio Moretti and tell him I'm ready to go on my trip now, the trip you stole from me, the sooner we can leave Monaco where Cesar won't be able to find me.''

Luc gave a careless shrug of his broad shoulders. ''I'm afraid a trip for me is out of the question. I'm due at the hospital in the morning for a procedure on my knee. For the next week I'll have to stay off it except to do some exercises and water therapy.''

''Perfect!'' she blurted excitedly. ''The *Piccione* is pure luxury. You can recuperate on it at your leisure while I enjoy myself. The first mate also acts as steward, so he can wait on you. Call Fabio right now! Tell him I want the same itinerary Greer planned for us before.''

''He'll be booked solid for August,'' Luc declared as if the final word had been spoken. But Olivia wasn't about to let him wriggle out of this.

''Even if he is, there are accommodations for

six guests aboard the catamaran. Probably not all the bedrooms are taken. If you don't want to phone him and arrange it, I will. He *knows* you owe me, and he won't turn me down.'' After a slight pause, ''Even if Cesar wanted to come after me, he wouldn't relish being confined with a boatload of tourists in such close quarters.''

She'd thrown out that last salvo for leverage, but nothing seemed to be working. Just when she thought they'd reached gridlock, he surprised her by wheeling around to reach for his cane lying in the middle of the foyer. He must have tripped on it answering the door, which would account for his cursing earlier.

Though he didn't ask her to follow him, she assumed he wouldn't have left the door open if he'd expected her to remain on the porch.

Consumed by curiosity to see his home, she trailed after him with her suitcase, noticing his limp was barely noticeable anymore. The minute she stepped over the threshold, she was enchanted.

This was *real* French country with a mix of period furniture. The authentic kind of fabulous treasures belonging to a man with a royal heritage.

Alcoves, beamed ceilings, inlaid parquet

floors, hand-carved furniture, flowers in copper pots, wrought iron fixtures, books, paintings. Sheer elegance that could only be created and enjoyed by someone of Luc's aristocratic status.

Once again Olivia was reminded that Luc's father was a duc, and his mother a Varano who was one of the direct descendents of the House of Parma-Bourbon in Italy.

Greer was now married to Max, the son of the Duc of Parma-Bourbon. After their honeymoon, she would be living with her husband in Colorno, a town near Parma, in an Italian villa so fantastic, words failed Olivia.

They failed her now. She looked around in wonder as they passed through to a study off the entrance hall where a stairway of hand-painted Provence tiles rose in a graceful curve to the second floor.

Surely Luc employed staff to keep the villa in such perfect condition, but she could see no sign of them right now.

After being in the hot sun most of the day, his house felt blessedly cool to Olivia. Since he was ignoring her, she entered his inner sanctum without being asked, and sank down in one of two fat Louis XV chairs upholstered in a fabric with the Falcon crest.

Luc moved around his huge oak desk with an

ancient porcelain clock placed on top. What a striking contrast to see the master of this small palace of a villa dressed in nothing more than a pair of well-worn cutoffs.

Still standing, he reached for the house phone. Before long she heard him say, *"Ciao, Fabio."* The next thing she knew he was speaking fluent Italian.

The multilingual Varano cousins were close as brothers and exceptional men in their own right. More than ever Olivia was determined to get Luc to fall in love with her. She was so crazy about him she would do whatever it took.

Olivia wasn't under any delusion that Luc wanted to be with her. On the contrary. The fact that he was trying to arrange a trip with Fabio only proved he would do anything to save Cesar from her clutches.

The situation couldn't be working out better. *Please make it happen, Fabio.*

"I wish I could accommodate you, Luc, but the boat is fully chartered for August. There's one bedroom left for you if you were to join us in Monterosso on Tuesday. Signorina Duchess could use it until Saturday. You could have my berth in the crew's quarters and I could sleep on deck."

"You're a good friend, Fabio, but I would never ask such a favor of you."

While they were talking, Luc kept his eye on Olivia, wondering what in the devil she was really up to. He'd learned not to trust one word that came out of that treacherously beautiful mouth of hers. However he didn't believe that even *she* would lie about Cesar's intention to give her an engagement ring.

Life hadn't been the same since the Duchess triplets had exploded into Luc's world with the force of a colliding meteor. They'd done the unexpected at every turn, driving him and his cousins crazy.

But because Cesar had entered into this latest equation, Luc had been hesitant to shut the door on her half an hour ago and leave her to her own cunning devices.

"I wish I could help you," Fabio murmured, "but the other charter companies in the Cinq Terre region are as busy as I am. If I had more time, and you didn't need a luxury craft, I could probably arrange something for you."

A luxury craft...

Luc's thoughts shot ahead. "What about your friend, Giovanni? Does he still have that old sailboat?"

"Of course, but it needs a paint and has no sail at the moment."

That was even better. "Would he let me use it? I'll pay him what the Duchess triplets paid you."

"You mean just to putt around Vernazza's bay while you do a little fishing? You must be joking! Twelve thousand dollars is more money than he makes in five months at the trattoria in Vernazza.

"He'll be overjoyed to let you borrow it for as long as you want, but I seriously doubt Signorina Duchess will step foot on it. She paid for a luxury boat to take her as far as the Spanish Riviera, and she expects a crew to wait on her."

A diabolical smile broke the corners of Luc's mouth. When she found out she was the designated crew who had to do all the work, that spoiled, mercenary, scheming female would leave Vernazza on the first train out of there.

If Cesar wanted her so much, he'd have to go after her. As for Luc, she'd be out of his life forever. By tomorrow afternoon, he'd be liberated. In a week he'd be able to drive a car again, and life would get back to normal as he knew it before the advent of the Duchess sisters.

It didn't matter that his skiing days were

over. The alpine sport he'd enjoyed from child-hood was now a thing of the past. But because of modern medical science, he'd be able to walk again without the assistance of a cane. When the week was up, he'd celebrate by burning it.

"Luc? Are you still there?"

"Forgive me, Fabio. I was distracted for a moment. To answer your question, Signorina Duchess won't have a choice if she wants to get in a Mediterranean trip before she flies back to New York. If you'll give me Giovanni's phone number, I'll call him and see if he's willing to let me use it starting tomorrow. I know this is short notice."

"No problem. *I'll* take care of everything, Luc. You can consider it a fait accompli. The *Gabbiano* will be waiting for you at the Vernazza dock."

"Excellent. *Grazie,* Fabio. *Ciao.*" Mademoiselle Olivier was in for the surprise of her life!

The second he hung up, his gaze locked with a pair of flame-blue eyes.

"Well?" she prodded. "What did Signore Moretti have to say?"

"He told me to tell you that for the Duchess of Kingston, he would move heaven and earth to accommodate you."

"I knew Fabio would pull through! But the next time you talk to him, tell him I like heaven and earth right where they are. All I'm asking is to go on the vacation Daddy paid for."

Ah yes. The famous Husband Fund. Who could forget? It proved that truth *was* stranger than fiction.

According to Max, the Duchess sisters had come to Europe the first time around on the money their father had willed to them, money he called the "Husband Fund." They could only use it to try to snag a husband.

Absurd and ridiculous as the plan had sounded, it had worked. Greer Duchess was now Signora di Varano, with Max her blissful groom.

Both Luc and Nic had been stunned by the way their cousin had run to his own wedding with such eagerness. In fact he'd gotten engaged to Greer four days after meeting her, which had to be some kind of record.

Luc studied her for a moment. "It seems you're going to get your wish. The boat will be ready for us tomorrow."

"But you said you have to go to the hospital in the morning. Won't you need a day of rest first?"

What was she playing at now, feigning concern. "I thought the main point of this exercise was to remove you from Cesar's grasp as soon as possible."

"Well of course it is, but not at the expense of your leg."

"I had no idea you cared."

From their first meeting, Olivia had seemed to take particular delight in mocking him over anything to do with his injury. Her last taunt about his not being able to get in Cesar's race car, let alone drive it, still rankled. Being prohibited from driving for the last seven months had served as its own prison.

"Of course I care," she blurted. "You *are* a human being, even if you don't display the normal set of emotions. Cesar told me you were into robotics engineering. How very *apropos*."

"I'm glad we understand each other."

She eyed him suspiciously. "Why?"

"You're going to have to fetch and carry for me."

"The *Piccione* is a luxury boat. The crew will help you. I'll be too busy swimming."

"You mean fishing for men."

"That's right. I understand from Cesar that the Prince of Monaco is scuba diving off the coast of Ischia at the moment. His mother was an American. We would have a lot in common.

I'm going to tell the captain to set sail for Ischia as soon as we leave port.''

"You do that.''

"I will!'' She tossed her head before wandering over to the window to look out at the view. The gesture brought attention to her cap of gleaming gold curls which was a new hairstyle for her. Over six weeks ago when they'd first met, she'd been wearing it longer.

Short like this, it brought out the classic mold of her facial features. Her eyes looked larger than ever.

Luc found himself looking forward to tomorrow when she discovered that she and the steward were one in the same person.

It was hard to believe that only an hour ago Luc had assumed his younger brother had already whisked her off to the Amalfi Coast where the family had a small villa above Positano. It sat high on a cliff overlooking the Mediterranean, one of Cesar's favorite haunts to take his flavor of the month.

When Luc thought of Olivia standing near the altar in some filmy white bridesmaid concoction where she'd caught the golden light from the stained glass windows pouring into the chapel, the image of luscious, succulent golden peaches in rich crème came to mind.

Definitely an enticing taste treat. Cesar could be forgiven for not being able to take his eyes off her during the ceremony.

Since Luc had been the one to introduce her to his brother, he shouldn't have been surprised she would take one look at Cesar and go after him with a vengeance. The ultimate playboy with a title. Just what she'd come to Europe for.

Watching a laughing Olivia drive away from the Varano estate in the Ferrari with Cesar after the wedding was a case in point.

Now she was pretending to run away from his brother, but it was a ploy to sink her hooks deeper until he was caught. Unfortunately she'd come to the wrong man for help. No way was Luc going to allow a treacherous opportunist like Olivia Duchess to succeed at her game, even if she and Cesar deserved each other...

Suddenly she wheeled around. "I don't suppose there'll be a *real* French chef on board this time."

Luc pretended to look in his desk drawer for something. "Fabio employs various locals. I didn't think to ask him which one. You should have taken advantage of my cooking when you had the chance."

"Give me a break. I found out it was your

parents' chef who prepared the food before it
was brought aboard the *Piccione.*''

He darted her a quick glance. "I concede to
that happening on one occasion because I was
otherwise occupied."

"You mean you and your cousins were too
busy playing undercover cop. How come you
haven't found your thief yet?"

"Give us a little more time and we will."

Earlier in the day Nic had called Luc, asking
him to fly to England. The police had stumbled
across a new lead in the case of the family's
missing jewelry collection from the Colorno
palace in Italy. One of the pieces had turned up
at an auction in London. Nic wanted to discuss
the new development with him.

Luc had been forced to turn him down because of his hospital visit in the morning, but
after his week of recuperation was up, he promised to join Nic in Marbella, Spain, where he
lived and they'd discuss new ideas to track
down the culprits.

The disappointment in his cousin's voice was
understandable. Luc suspected his cousin was
looking for an excuse to get together because,
like Luc, he was feeling deserted now that the
wedding was over. Their cousin Max, who'd

been a best friend and brother to them, was now a married man.

"Luc? In case you hadn't noticed, your phone's ringing. From the sound of it, they're not going to hang up. I would imagine it's Cesar looking for me.

"The maid at your parents' house had to give me your address and probably told him I was here. Maybe I should answer it. That way he'll believe you're the man I was referring to in my note. What do you think?"

Luc didn't have to think. She obviously had Cesar eating out of her hand. "Be my guest."

CHAPTER THREE

FULL of confidence, Olivia took the receiver Luc handed to her and said hello. When there was no answer she said hello again, a little louder this time. If it was Cesar on the other end, no doubt he was debating whether to hang up or not.

Suddenly a familiar female voice came over the wires. "Olivia Duchess!"

Oh, no. It was *Greer!*

"I didn't want to believe what Piper told me," her sister started in without preamble. "What in heaven's name are you doing at Luc's house, let alone answering his phone? I can't believe you actually followed through with this outrageous plan of yours!"

Olivia spun around so her back faced Luc. She couldn't fathom that her sister was calling all the way from Greece when she was supposed to be in Max's arms right now. Greer could ruin everything!

Think fast, Olivia. "Are you still in Monza?"

"Monza— Oh, I get it. Luc's standing right there next to you. Piper told me about this crazy scheme of yours and begged me to stop you, but I can see it's already too late."

"I'm afraid it is."

"Listen to me—there's something you need to know about Luc. I was hoping I would never have to tell you, but after Piper's emergency phone call, I've decided it's necessary."

"There's nothing else to be said. Please understand. Besides this isn't the time with Luc going into the hospital first thing in the morning for surgery on his leg. It's time for bed right now and he needs a good night's sleep."

"What surgery? Luc never told Max about that!"

"Luc assures me it's nothing serious, but he won't want visitors for a while. In the meantime, I'm going to nurse him while he recuperates. When he's feeling better the two of you can talk."

"Olivia Duchess—don't you dare hang up on me! I haven't finished with yo—"

"Congratulations again on your win. You were fabulous. No doubt the German team has left Italy to re-strategize for the next Grand Prix on the schedule. But between you and me they don't stand a chance against you. I'm proud to know you.''

"Oliviaaaaaaaaaaaaa?"

"I'll tell him. Good night."

She turned around and put the receiver back on the hook too fast for Luc to hear her sister's alarmed cry. When she looked up, their eyes collided.

His merciless gaze unnerved her. "Tell me what?" he demanded.

"Cesar's worried about your leg and hopes the operation goes well."

"It's not as much an operation as a procedure done under a local anesthetic."

She gave a feminine shrug of her shoulders. "The important thing is, I think I put him off. He's concerned about you, and he isn't going to come charging after me."

"You expect me to believe that?" he asked in an urbane voice, but she felt his underlying contempt. "You kissed him back, remember?"

"At least a dozen women did the same thing to him today after his big win. I don't know how he keeps his girlfriends straight in his mind. The point is, if he does show up, it probably won't be before tomorrow. We'll be long gone from the hospital by then.

"However should he come looking me, I'll

tell him that the pity I felt for you on the *Piccione* turned to love, but that I didn't realize it until I went to Monza with him and he started kissing me.''

"He'll never buy it.'' His words dropped like rocks.

"You mean because he knows you're not in love with *me?*'' she fired. "Well if everyone didn't know it before the wedding, you made certain they figured it out by the time it was over!

"But it doesn't matter how you feel about me. All that's important is that Cesar realizes I'm here and that I've made my choice, so ther—''

The phone rang again. She grabbed for it, fearing Greer was calling her back, but Luc's hand was faster on the receiver. His smile was wicked as he picked up the receiver.

"Allo?'' she heard him say. She held her breath, fearing the worst. *"Bonsoir,* Cesar.''

Oh, no. Cesar! This was turning into a nightmare.

"Congratulations on another brilliant win.'' He'd switched to English. Olivia stood stock still, waiting for the bomb to drop. "She's right here.''

With a penetrating glance that kept her rooted

to the spot, Luc handed her the phone. "You'll have to do a better job of getting rid of him this time around," he whispered. "He's not the grand champion of Formula I racing for nothing."

Feeling as if she was walking on the edge of a cliff that was about to give way at any moment, she put the receiver to her ear. "What is it, Cesar?"

"*Eh bien,* what a greeting! You really do know how to wound. It wasn't until a few minutes ago that I learned you'd been to our parents' house asking to see Luc.

"I expected you to come to the podium after the race today. With so much going on, it was several hours before I could get away to meet you at the hotel. When I did, all I found was your note."

"I really am sorry."

"Now I discover you at my brother's house— Tell me, *ma belle.* What does he have that I don't?"

For once she couldn't figure out if it was his male pride talking, or if he truly had feelings for her.

"Can't we leave it alone and just be friends?"

"So it was love at first sight for you when you met him in June?"

"Yes." She could answer that question honestly.

There was a long silence on his end. "He's a lucky man. By the time I see you again, I hope to God he has realized it." There was a distinct tremor in his voice. *"A bientôt, cherie."*

Another solemn warning about Luc, this time from a different Cesar than the one he presented to the world. She'd heard real pain underlying his words. What on earth?

Piper hadn't been kidding when she'd said she knew a terrible secret and Olivia sensed that it was to do with Luc, not her. Greer had tried to tell Olivia, but she'd refused to listen.

Luc took the phone from her hand. "You'd better sit down. You've gone a little pale. It appears my brother is having trouble accepting your rejection."

"I'm all right, however I have to admit he did sound a little shaken." But it was because of *you,* Luc. Not me...

"How soon will he be arriving?"

She bit her lip. "What does *a bientôt* mean?"

Lines darkened his features. "See you soon. Coming from Cesar, it probably means tomorrow."

She swallowed hard, not wanting anything to interfere with her plan. "What time do you have to show up at outpatient in the morning?"

"Six-thirty a.m. The doctor explained it should take about twenty minutes. If all goes well, I should be released by eight-thirty at the latest. I'll arrange for the helicopter to fly us from the hospital to Vernazza."

"That'll be perfect." Perfect. Cesar didn't know anything about the operation. If by any chance he did decide to pay a visit to Luc's home, the two of them would be long gone.

"You're sure you want to disappear on him?" came the sinuous voice.

"Of course!" She turned aside so Luc couldn't tell how excited she was about going away with him. "A clean break is better. I've already said everything I wanted to say in the note I left for him."

Needing to maintain the lie that Cesar was the person who'd phoned twice she added, "I just wish I hadn't told him about your operation. Do you think he'll come to the hospital?"

"Isn't that exactly what you were hoping for?" Luc's expression was grim.

Her chin lifted defiantly. "Think what you want."

"It's not what *I* think." His wintry smile cut

o the quick. "It's my brother who thinks he's n love with you."

"He couldn't be! As Greer would say, he's ust in the first throes of lust."

Caustic laughter erupted from Luc, but she gnored him. Her thoughts were on her conversation with Cesar who'd emitted strong emotion while they'd been discussing Luc.

Piper knew a secret about Luc, and had been concerned enough to call Greer. For Piper to bother their sister while she was on her honeymoon meant the situation was more serious han Olivia had thought. She needed to have a ong talk with Piper without Luc being anywhere around.

She faced him once more. "If you'll phone or a taxi, I'll stay in town tonight and meet you at the hospital in the morning."

"So you can join him at prearranged location?" His eyes glittered dangerously. "I'm afraid not. With five bedrooms upstairs, there's no need for you to go anywhere. In fact I insist you stay so you can help me pack for our trip. My staff isn't here on weekends."

The thought of remaining at the *mas* with him made her almost sick with excitement. She could always call Piper from an upstairs phone after she'd gone to bed.

Olivia eyed him speculatively. "It shouldn'
take long. You're not going to need man
clothes if you're just going to be lying aroun
in the sun. A few shirts, a couple of pairs o
cutoffs like you're wearing, plus a swimsuit fo
your water therapy ought to be plenty. Come t
think of it, I packed very little for the weddin
myself."

She'd only brought one pair of shorts and he
bathing suit for swimming in Max's pool. I
would do for starters. When the *Piccione* pu
into port at various towns, she could go ashor
and pick up some more casual clothes so sh
would look beautiful for Luc.

"A woman who travels light is worth he
weight in gold."

"Why do men always say that?"

"Do I really need to explain why a ma
would rather see a woman in less than more?"

Wasn't it Max who'd told Greer he lived fo
the moment when she appeared to him au na
turel, like Venus Rising From the Sea?

Olivia would give anything to know if Lu
ever had fantasies like that about her, even if h
did despise her.

"Funny about that. A woman would rathe
see a man in uniform."

"You mean like Fred, your military man

Apparently he didn't look that good in his after all," he inserted silkily.

"He looked terrific, but on a scale of one to ten, ten being irresistible, he rated a three."

"What scale is this?"

"The one my sisters and I use to rate the men we date."

"Obviously Max—"

"Was off the charts!" she finished for him. "Cesar came in a nine. All he lacks is husband skills." Taking a risk she said, "If you're interested in knowing where you weigh in, I'm afraid to tell you."

"You mean I'm dull and boring like Fred."

"It's not so much that you're boring as you're morose and very aloof most of the time compared to your brother for example. You don't know how to play, and you take your responsibilities so seriously I've only heard you laugh when you were mocking me."

In an effort not to give away the plot in front of him, she deliberately gazed at him like he was some kind of alien species. "In fact you're not like any other man I know. The normal labels don't apply. Like I said, robotics pretty well sums you up. You're the exact opposite of the exciting playboy I planned to win a proposal from when I came to Europe."

"Tout ce qui brille n'est pas d'or," he muttered.

"I give up. What does that mean?"

One black brow quirked. "All that glitters isn't gold."

"Spoken like the bona fide cynic you are! If you'll show me where to go, I'll get started on your packing."

"Follow me."

She fell in line behind him, feasting her eyes on his sensational male body. He handled the stairs very well with his cane. His was a powerful physique. Olivia wouldn't be at all surprised to learn he'd been a world-class skier before his accident.

According to Cesar, Luc had been in excruciating pain for several months after getting out of the hospital. She'd listened in horror as he'd told her about the ghastly accident in Cortina that had almost severed Luc's leg.

No wonder she'd seen deep lines of strain carved on Luc's handsome features when she'd first been introduced to him aboard the *Piccione*.

This close to him she could tell he'd healed to the point that the shadows under his eyes and the slightly gaunt look to his cheeks were disappearing. But he hadn't lost the remote quality that put a wall between them. She wanted to tear it down and find out what had caused it in the first place.

When they reached the large master bedroom with its semi-contemporary decor, she thought the shades of blue and burgundy against neutral walls stunning. She lowered her suitcase next to the king-size bed.

Luc sat back against the headboard and rested his leg. "You'll find a valise on the wardrobe shelf. Everything else I'll need should be in that long dresser beneath the window."

She forced her eyes away from the incredible sight he made, then let out a quiet gasp when she looked out the vitrines. It was like getting a bird's-eye view of the whole principality of Monaco. She almost forgot she was supposed to be packing.

The thrill of being here with Luc, of handling his personal clothes, caused her body to tremble, especially with him watching her movements. She soon found everything he would need; a few sport shirts, T-shirts, boxers, cargo pants, cutoffs and a black bathing suit.

"Done." She smiled at him as she closed the lid.

It was a mistake to take another look at him. She might never recover. He resembled some gorgeous virile god lying there on the bed studying her through shuttered eyes.

That's how Greer had first described Max when she'd seen him climb out of the swimming pool at the Splendido Hotel in Portofino. Now Olivia understood why her sister had looked like she'd been shaken to the foundations the night she came back to their hotel room.

Clearing her throat she said, "We'll pack your grooming items in the morning before we leave for the hospital. Anything else I can do for you before I find a room to sleep in?"

Images of crawling on the bed next to him and lying in his arms sent her pulse rate off the charts.

"When we reach the boat, I'll need my leg muscle massaged, but we'll give it a pass for tonight. Do you have an alarm clock?"

She could hardly breathe thinking about touching him and having the right to do it. "I never travel without one."

"Then I'll need to be wakened at six. A limo will be here to take us to the hospital at quarter past the hour."

"I'll be happy to do that."

"If you're hungry, make yourself at home in the kitchen."

"Thank you, but I ate on the plane. Would you like something to eat?"

"I was just finishing my meal when you arrived at the door."

Uh-oh. "Since I interrupted you, I'll go downstairs and clean up."

"That's what I employ a housekeeper for. You're being suspiciously meek and humble all of a sudden."

"It's my true nature coming out."

A burst of mocking laughter escaped his throat. "I have to wonder if you lied to me, and Cesar is on his way over as we speak."

That stung. "While you wonder all you want, I'm going to pick out a bedroom to sleep in."

"*Bonne nuit*, Mademoiselle Olivier. If you would be so kind as to turn off the light and shut the door on your way out. Note that I said shut, not slam."

She could still hear his low evil chuckle after she'd left the room carrying her suitcase. Once she'd peeked in the various bedrooms, each one more elegant and inviting than the last, she chose the room next to Luc's with the same view.

The warm yellow and cream decor delighted her. Substitute the dark furniture for a baby crib and dresser, and it would make a heavenly nursery. All you would have to do is create a connecting door between it and the master bedroom.

Filled with thoughts of what Luc's baby would look like with her as the mother, she got ready for bed in the en suite bathroom.

After setting her travel alarm, she slipped between the sheets of the queen-sized bed, still pinching herself that her plan had worked to the point she was sleeping beneath Luc's roof, next to his own room.

But there was one more thing she had to do, or she wouldn't be able to relax. Turning on her side she picked up the receiver on the nightstand to make a credit card call to Piper. After giving the hotel operator her sister's room number, she waited, then was told Piper had checked out.

While the operator was speaking, Olivia heard a click, like the kind when someone else picks up the phone from another extension.

Luc had his own cell phone to make calls. He was probably spying on her to see if she was trying to reach Cesar. The man in the next room had serious trust issues.

Olivia frowned before thanking the operator and hanging up. Apparently Piper had decided to take a night flight to New York instead of waiting until morning.

Unless Olivia tried to get a number through Greer's new in-laws to reach her in Greece, it looked like she would have to wait until tomorrow for Piper to enlighten her about Luc. While he was in surgery, she would make the call.

Unable to do anything else for the moment, she sank back against the pillows, afraid she would never get to sleep. Luc lay on the other side of the wall. The knowledge that he was awake and might be thinking about her, even if they were negative thoughts, left her breathless.

Visions of him sprawled on top of his mattress were the last images in her mind before her alarm went off seven hours later.

The ground came rushing up to meet the helicopter. Olivia felt slightly unsteady during the rapid descent. This was Luc's normal mode of travel, but it was the first time she'd ridden in one. Way back in Monaco she'd lost her stomach as it took off from the roof of the hospital.

But for most of the flight she forgot to be frightened or sick when her eyes beheld the glorious French and Italian Riviera from the air.

People actually lived here, were born here in this paradise!

Olivia couldn't imagine what it would be like to wake up to such beauty every day of her life. To be able to work here, to play, to eat, to go bed and start the whole process all over again the next day in surroundings captured on canvas by the great Impressionists—

Her mind could scarcely comprehend what kind of joy that would bring. But of course Luc would have to be part of that picture, or the magic wouldn't be there no matter how captivating the ambience.

Since she hadn't been able to reach Piper from the hospital, the mystery surrounding Luc loomed larger than ever. Thank goodness Cesar hadn't shown up at the house early to make a liar out of her. Besides, today was not the day for any kind of confrontation.

Though Luc managed to sail through the medical procedure, the doctor had given him a heavy dose of painkiller. She noticed it made him quieter than usual, but other than that he still took charge.

An orderly had helped him from the wheelchair into the helicopter. After they'd landed at the small waterfront area in Vernazza, and he'd been assisted to the ground by the pilot, he was able to walk by leaning on his cane.

Olivia looked all around. The *Piccione*, named for the stylized pigeons on the sails, wasn't in its berth or anywhere else. Puzzled, she turned to Luc. ''I don't understand. Where's the catamaran?''

Noise from the rotors of the helicopter must have drowned out her question. After it lifted in the air he moved closer. ''What did you say?''

''Why isn't Fabio here to meet us?''

''I forgot to tell you he phoned me while I was in the recovery room. He explained that one of the engines went out, so he had to pull into port at Monterosso. It might take a few days to fix, so he made an arrangement with his friend Giovanni.''

Olivia blinked. ''What arrangement?''

CHAPTER FOUR

Luc inclined his dark head toward a pathetic-looking sailboat tied up next to the *Piccione*'s berth.

"That dinky thing? You have to be kidding! It looks like something that barely survived the wreck of the *Hesperus*."

He stared at her through veiled eyes. "I've sailed the *Gabbiano* before."

"*Gabbiano?*"

"It means 'seagull.' She's a worthy vessel."

"In other words, we're lucky it floats."

"Fabio tried his best." Luc remained unflappable. "It seems every available boat along this part of the coast has been booked months in advance. I'm afraid it's this or nothing."

His mouth looked taut. Probably the painkiller they'd given him in the hospital was wearing off and he needed to take more. Olivia felt guilty about keeping him standing there, especially when no one was available to help. Worse, the helicopter had disappeared.

''You need to lie down. Come on. We'll get on board while we wait for Giovanni to help us make some other arrangement.''

Luc didn't seem to need any urging. It meant his pain level was greater than she'd supposed.

She gathered their bags. Together they walked along the pier. When they reached the boat, she put them down again and told him to use her shoulders for balance. The contact sent little darts of delight through her system.

Slowly he lowered himself into the boat. Even to her uneducated eye it needed an over-haul and paint job inside and out.

In this end of it she saw some fishing gear and one oar, but there were no water skis, no sun mattresses or jet skis—none of the kinds of water sport equipment that came with the lux-urious *Piccione*.

She jumped down after Luc, leaving the suit-cases on the pier. He held on to her as they descended the steps to the galley below that contained a miniscule kitchen and bathroom with a stall shower. Everything fit together like sardines in a can.

Luc opened the cabin door on the right, with its small window above the dresser and ward-robe. Bunk beds for two took up the rest of the space, leaving little room to maneuver.

Olivia had to confess the place looked clean, yet it was a far cry from the luxury she'd paid for the first time around.

Still, she'd accomplished her first objective. Except for Giovanni, who would probably sleep on one of the padded benches on deck if he couldn't manage to find them something better, she would have Luc to herself for the next ten days.

If it had to be on this sailboat rather than the *Piccione,* she wasn't about to complain. Secretly she was overjoyed to be with him at all.

What she'd give for Piper and Greer to see her now. They hadn't thought she would get this far with him, but they'd underestimated her love for Luc, her determination to win his heart.

The object of her thoughts let go of her and eased himself onto the bottom bunk. After she helped lift his bandaged leg on top of the spread, he lay back with a deep sigh and closed his eyes.

Quickly she left the cabin and hurried into the kitchen. To her surprise the small fridge was fairly well stocked. She pulled out a bottle of mineral water, then rushed back to him.

The doctor had sent him home with some pills. She drew the bottle from her purse.

According to the directions, he could take two every four hours.

"Luc? I've got something for your pain."

His eyelids opened. In the dim light his normal silvery gaze had dimmed to pewter. "Ah...just what the doctor ordered."

Rising up on his elbow he swallowed the pills and drained the bottle. He was thirstier than she realized. It had to be the heat.

"Thank you." He fell back against the pillow and closed his eyes once more.

"When do you think Giovanni will come?"

"I have no idea."

"Could we call him on your cell phone?"

"Of course."

"It's in your trouser pocket."

"No. I gave it to you."

"You did?"

"Hmm. Along with the pills."

"I didn't notice it in my purse." She moved over to the dresser where she'd left it on the top. After rummaging through the contents she turned around. "It's not here."

"Then I have to assume it was left at the hospital by mistake."

Oh, no— Now she couldn't call Piper, either.

"Well—if Giovanni doesn't come soon, I'll

walk to a shop near the waterfront and ask to use one of their phones to call him.''

''That sounds like a good idea. If you don't mind, I'm going to sleep for a while.''

''Good. I need to unpack the suitcases anyway.'' Oops. She'd left them on the pier.

She retraced her steps to the deck. Thankfully no one had walked off with them. Inside of twenty minutes she'd put everything away. Luc continued to sleep soundly. As Olivia tiptoed around finding places to stash their things, she derived great pleasure watching over him. It was like they were husband and wife.

When she'd arranged everything to her satisfaction, she acquainted herself with the kitchen. There was a tiny cupboard that held some condiments including olive oil. Against the wall was a table and stools you could pull down when you wanted to eat.

A further inspection of the fridge revealed bread, eggs, cheese and ham slices, fruit, wine, soda and some yogurt. Until Giovanni arrived to take over, she could fix Luc the latter. She doubted he would want anything heavier until tomorrow.

As for herself, she was hungry, so she made herself a sandwich and ate it accompanied by a cold orange soda. She loved Italian bread and could make a meal out of it. American bread was squishy and tasteless by comparison.

Once she'd cleaned up her mess, she checked on Luc, who was still out like a light. Helpless to do otherwise, she bent over to look at him.

The arrangement of his strong male features combined with his black hair and olive skin made him a striking man. Unforgettable. She studied him for a long time before tearing herself away to go up on deck and wait for Giovanni.

Most of the boats were out. That was probably the reason why there were so few people walking around. She sat down on one of the benches to take in the view of Vernazza, the same view she'd seen from the cabin window of the *Piccione* over six weeks ago.

Once before she'd marveled at the colorful port village with its cluster of tower-shaped houses, palaces and castles nestled against a backdrop of emerald green steep cliffs. Little had she known then that one Lucien de Falcon would come into her life.

Just knowing he slept below sent a delicious shiver through her body. There was nowhere else in the world she wanted to be. It hurt to realize this was probably the last place he wanted to be, that she was the last woman he wanted to be with. Cesar was the sole reason Luc had been willing to recuperate here instead of his house.

But this was only the first day of their trip. They had nine to go. In that amount of time she intended to make her patient forget all about the brother he'd felt forced to protect from the female he'd branded a groupie.

By the time the boat returned to Vernazza, Luc would be in love with her, no matter what she had to do to make it happen.

A few more minutes of sitting in the hot sun and she felt perspiration break out on her skin beneath her blouse and skirt. Europe was suffering a heat wave right now. She would love to change into her bathing suit and go for a quick swim, but she wanted to wait until Giovanni had come and they'd left the port.

So far no one walking on the pier approached her. Something had to be holding him up. She decided to check on Luc. If he was awake, she would get the phone number from him and go ashore to make her calls.

As she started for the stairs she heard, *"Signorina—Signorina—"*

Olivia turned in time to see a boy of eleven or twelve waving to her from the pier. She moved closer to him. "Yes?"

"You are waiting for Giovanni?" he asked
in heavily accented English.

"Yes!"

"He is not coming."

"How do you know?"

"I know everything!"

"Where is Giovanni?"

"San Remo."

"Is he coming back?"

"No."

"But we need him to sail the boat!"

"His wife. She has a baby!"

A baby— Good heavens.

Her plan to go sailing with Luc had just gone
up in smoke!

"Thank you. *Grazie*," she said to him with
a heavy heart.

He smiled. *"Ciao!"*

Devastated by this turn of events, she needed
to think up a new plan before Luc found out
and had her phone for the helicopter to come
and get them. The next thing she knew she'd be
deposited at the airport in Nice, left to her own
devices.

She could hear Luc now. "Under the circumstances I suggest you go home to New York
and make plans with Fabio for another trip.

Next summer perhaps? By then Cesar's ardor should have cooled.''

No way was she going to let him dispatch her as if she were so much baggage!

She could go ashore and ask around for someone who knew how to sail and wanted a job on the spot. She would pay them out of her own pocket if she had to. But she didn't have that kind of time. Luc might wake up at any minute.

What to do?

She could hear Greer's voice on their last trip. *What did the Von Trapp Family do when they wanted to get out of Austria and the borders were closed?*

That was it!

Olivia would take the boat out herself. It had a motor. The Mediterranean was smooth as glass right now. She'd run the outboard motor on her dad's rowboat many a time. For that matter she'd driven Fred's boat dozens of times while they'd taken turns waterskiing. How hard could it be?

Later on she would worry about working the sail which was probably in one of the lockers. For now it was imperative she get them away from shore before Luc knew what was happening and sent her packing.

Without wasting another second, she climbed onto the pier and undid the ropes. Once that was accomplished, she got back in the boat and walked to the other end.

She studied the outboard motor and gear shift. It all looked straightforward to her. After seating herself on the bench, she turned the key and pressed the button. The motor revved on cue.

So far so good.

She put the gear in reverse. Luckily there weren't any boats nearby for her to run into. The boat slowly inched away from the pier. With her hand on the tiller, she made an experimental circle to get the hang of it.

Okay. Here goes.

She pressed on the forward throttle. Off the boat flew. Knowing she should be traveling at a wakeless speed, she decreased the power and headed straight out to sea past the buoys.

Her thoughts flew ahead.

The island of Ischia off of Naples was southeast of Vernazza. All she had to do was head east as far as Lerici where Luc and his cousins had taken them on the *Piccione*. She knew what to look for. After all, it was in those waters she and her sisters had jumped ship in order to get away from the crew. From there she'd head south.

She opened up the throttle. This was a piece of cake.

When she glimpsed other pleasure boats, she gave them wide berth as she navigated through the calm waters. Luc was still asleep. That was good. He needed it.

The motor gave her no trouble. She relaxed and enjoyed the breathtaking view of jewel-like villages dotting the coastline in the far distance.

Olivia decided this was much better than being on the *Piccione*. She had Luc all to herself at last.

A smile curved her lips upward remembering the first time she'd met him. He'd passed himself off as a French chef who cooked for royalty, but to Olivia he'd looked like some sort of dangerous French Adonis.

They'd clashed mightily. Deep down she'd never been so exhilarated in her life. Now they were clashing again. This time it was a battle to the death, and all the spoils would go to Olivia.

Hunger brought Luc awake. Still disoriented from a drug-induced sleep, he opened his eyes and was surprised to discover it was dark in the cabin.

He checked the time on his watch. Eight-fifteen. He'd been passed out for six hours— Where was Olivia? How come she'd let him sleep this long?

Easing his leg slowly off the bed, he stood up, then had to clutch the upper bunk for a moment. Either he was having serious side effects, or a wind had come up, causing the boat to bob up and down in its berth.

Had Olivia decided Giovanni wasn't coming?

If she'd realized Luc had tricked her, she might have phoned Cesar for help. Luc had no doubts the two of them would have gone off together, leaving him to deal with the situation he'd created.

He felt for his cane resting against the wardrobe and looked out the window expecting to see the lights of Vernazza. To his shock, water surrounded the boat. The *Gabbiano* was at sea!

Who was at the helm?

For one thing, any experienced sailor would have turned on the boat's lights by now. For another, they weren't moving, and there was no sound of the motor.

Leaving the cabin, he used the braille method to make his way to the stairs and ran into a soft,

feminine body hurrying down the steps. The im
pact knocked the cane out of his hand.

"Luc—"

Beneath her surprised cry he detected an un
derlying note of anxiety. He held on to her i
an effort to steady them both. Her heart wa
pounding so fast he couldn't count the beats
His was thudding, too, but not for the same rea
son.

During their brief moment of contact, hi
body became aware of every enticing line an
curve molded against him. Her skin still radi
ated warmth from a hot Mediterranean sun tha
had gone down some time ago. With his fac
helplessly buried in her golden curls, he foun
himself intoxicated by the fresh peach scent em
anating from her.

Sensation after sensation bombarded him
Having been in a deep sleep and then suddenl
awakened, he felt alive to the primitive side o
his male nature. The part of him that recognize
this particular female could have been made fo
him.

*If it weren't for the fact that she was a cal
culating liar and cheat, incapable of bein
faithful to any man.*

He let her go abruptly, then felt for the pane

above the stairs to switch on the power and lights.

"So *that's* where they were," she moaned the words. "I looked everywhere but up." She reached for his cane and handed it to him as if that moment in his arms had never happened.

Mon Dieu. Like pure revelation it came to him *she'd* been playing captain of the *Gabbiano*. Once again he'd underestimated her. This would be the last time...

"Unless there's a reserve tank on board, we're out of gas. That's what I was coming down to tell you."

Her voice sounded steady enough now, but he hadn't imagined her nervousness seconds earlier. He would never forget the way she'd clung to him for that infinitesimal moment when the darkness had stripped away her bravado.

He found himself drawn to the alluring design of her mouth whose shape reminded him of a half-opened rose. Something told him that if he were ever fool enough to taste it, then it meant he hadn't learned life's most important lesson.

"When did you decide to take matters into your own hands?"

"This afternoon a young boy ran along the

pier and informed me Giovanni wasn't coming.''

Luc had to give her credit for not pretending that she didn't know what he was talking about.

''Why couldn't he make it?''

She folded her arms. ''Suppose you tell me? If I didn't know better, I would think you'd set me up so I'd go back to New York and forget about my Riviera trip. You would love to see the last of me. Admit it!''

''I admit it would be better for my brother who's too blindsided by you and his latest win to see through to the real Mademoiselle Duchess.''

Her eyes narrowed. ''The *real* me?''

''That's right. A heartless, materialistic, ambitious vixen who does whatever comes naturally to her without any compunction. I could tell you more about yourself, but first I need to switch tanks. In the meantime you can bring me a hot dinner while I find us a cove to spend the night.''

Vixen my foot!

Olivia banged things around in the tiny kitchen. Heartless? Materialistic? Ambitious?

A seer wasn't required for Olivia to figure out what kind of women had thrown themselves at him over the years. She supposed being born a Falcon had made him and Cesar natural targets for the type of avaricious female he'd accused her of being. It had turned Luc mean and hurtful, and so suspicious of the opposite sex his natural feelings were buried.

That's why her sisters had tried so hard to dissuade her from chasing after him. She could understand why. He was a thirty-three-year-old misogynist more hardened than Max before Greer came into his life.

But not all women were opportunistic. Far from it. Whether a prince or a pauper, the majority wanted to find a great and lasting love and remain true to that one man.

Somehow she would show Luc she was the latter.

Instead of retaliating because of his cruel attack, she would ignore every barb and salvo intended to destroy her. When he realized she could take whatever he dished out, and that she wasn't about to go away, he would be forced to see that her heart was pure. In time she would wear him down with her love until he had no choice but to love her back.

Tonight he wanted a hot meal. She would get busy and give him the most scrumptious dinner she could prepare with the ingredients at hand.

Now that he'd turned on the power, she could make him an omelet à la Olivia, and homemade bruschetta with the olive oil she'd seen in the cupboard.

If he could play a French chef, so could she. Turnabout was fair play. She bet he thought she couldn't cook worth a darn, especially not under these circumstances. Well he could think again.

While she was preparing cappuccino, she heard the engine rev. Soon she felt the boat moving through the water once more. Thankful he'd sailed this boat before and knew where and how to navigate in the darkness, she got his plate ready and carried everything up on deck.

He sat on the bench with the tiller in one hand, his long powerful legs extended in front of him. She noted he was still dressed in chinos and the tan sport shirt he'd worn to the hospital.

The collar flapped against his firm jawline where she could see the shadow of his dark beard. Combined with his black hair disheveled by the sea breeze, his potent sexuality turned her insides to liquid.

"Here you go." She put everything on the bench next to him. His gaze darted to the food she'd fixed as if he couldn't believe his eyes. When he finally looked up at her, she turned away and said she'd be right back. Olivia didn't dare gloat in front of him.

In a minute she'd rejoined him with her food and took a sip of the steaming brew. It tasted even better than she'd thought. Putting in extra sugar gave it that extra punch they could use.

To her satisfaction she saw that he'd already swallowed half his food. Most of his coffee was gone, too.

"More bruschetta?" She piled another couple of rounds on his plate while he finished munching the last of his.

He flicked her penetrating glance. "How did you learn to make it?" Upon asking the question, he devoured the ones she'd given him.

"Greer found out Max loves it, so she practiced fixing it at home. Piper and I helped." She had to bite her lip to keep from asking him if he liked it.

Once he'd drained the last of his coffee, he put everything aside. She expected to see some softening of his features after the feast she'd just prepared for his royal highness. Instead they'd gone all chiseled looking. His eyes pierced hers. "Do you have any idea where we are?"

"Sort of. I was headed for Ischia."

"You mean you just took off and hoped for the best."

"Well...yes. I mean, how hard is it? The sun sets in the west, so I went east and kept the coastline in view."

He rubbed his eyes with his palms. She half wondered if he hadn't wanted to shake her unconscious, and didn't know what else to do with them. Taking out the sailboat without his knowledge had been a foolhardy, if not dangerous thing to do, and she knew it. But she'd been desperate.

"Relax, Luc. We're alive, safe and well fed." If he wasn't going to compliment her on her culinary skills, then she would.

He lifted his head with a grimace. "You took advantage of a calm sea and ran the boat at full throttle. It drained the first tank of gas. The other one is only a reserve tank and doesn't hold nearly as much. We'll be damn lucky if we make it to Monte Cristo."

Her eyes opened wide. "You're kidding! I've always wanted to go there." She smiled. "I didn't realize I'd brought the boat this far!"

"As I said earlier, life is just one big game to you, but in this case it could have cost lives if another boat hadn't seen us in the fading light. When you're on the water, the ability to judge distances is hampered and can present serious problems.''

She ate the last of her omelet before responding. ''I came down to get you as soon as I realized we might be hard to spot. Don't worry. I wouldn't have let anything happen to you in your condition. If we'd run out of gas, I would have figured out how to put up the sail.''

''There *is* no sail.''

No sail?

''But I thought that locker container—''

''You should have looked before you took our lives into your own inexperienced hands.''

It was the story of her life, and a reminder of her impulsive trip to Monza with Cesar. But Luc didn't have any room to talk. ''If I leaped, it's because you led me to believe this sailboat was a worthy vessel. Your exact words!

''If you already knew there wasn't a sail, it means you never planned for this trip to come off in the first place, so it's your fault if we're stuck out here.''

He didn't bother to deny her accusation. To her chagrin he stared at her like she was a child having a temper tantrum. ''You may end up having to row us to safety. In fact you'll have to slip overboard and tow us to shore should we be fortunate enough to reach the island before we're running on fumes.''

His gaze produced a breathless sensation inside her as it wandered the length of her body still clad in the skirt and blouse she'd worn to the hospital. ''I suggest you put on something more practical for the ordeal ahead.''

Olivia's first instinct was to engage him in another verbal skirmish, but that's what he wanted. To make her so mad she'd go away forever at the first opportunity.

She rose to her feet, gathering their plates and mugs. ''How's your pain? Can I bring you another pill?''

''I'm fine right now.''

Even if he wasn't, he wouldn't admit to it. The medication had made him sleep so soundly, he'd been unaware of what she'd done until it was too late. Naturally he didn't plan on taking any more risks with her around.

''How about another cappuccino?''

''Later.''

''That's probably a better idea. I'll be able to give your leg muscles a massage at the same time,'' she said before disappearing below with a secret grin.

Once she'd cleaned up the kitchen, she entered the cabin and changed into her emerald green bathing suit. It was the most modest two-piece she'd been able to find in Kingston, but that wasn't saying much.

On impulse she drew a navy T-shirt out of Luc's drawer and pulled it on over her suit. It fell to mid-thigh and made her feel less exposed. After removing her sandals, she put on her sneakers.

According to Greer who'd done the research, Monte Cristo was a rocky, uninhabited island. If she had to jump off the boat, she needed something to protect her feet.

On the way up the stairs she heard the engine start to act up. It kind of sputtered, ran, then sputtered again before stopping altogether. She swallowed hard. They were out of gas.

The idea of rowing didn't appeal, but they had no choice now. She walked over to one of the benches and lifted the top.

"What are you doing?" he asked grimly.

"I was hoping I might find some gloves in one of these lockers. I used to do a lot of rowing with Daddy on the river and can already feel the blisters forming."

"You must live under a lucky star because the island's about forty yards straight ahead. Here!" He threw her a life jacket from the bench locker where he'd been sitting. "Put it on, then grab the rope at the front end of the boat and jump in the water.

"You'll feel the bottom at about twenty yards. It shouldn't be difficult to pull the boat after you and find a place to secure the rope."

She supposed she deserved his cavalier treatment of her. Besides, he knew she was a strong swimmer. He'd seen her dive off the *Piccione* to swim twenty times that distance in order to reach the port of Lerici.

"What about sharks?"

He cocked his head. "I don't recall you worrying about them before."

"You told me there'd been a sighting of a great white near the Marche/Abruzzo border when we were on the *Piccione*. It wasn't until later I found out it wasn't a lie."

"I'm glad you remembered our little chat. Be sure to slip into the water quietly. If I should see one, I'll tell you to let go of the rope and swim like the devil for shore."

"That's very reassuring."

It was a warm night, even with the breeze blowing from the northwest. If there was a moon, she couldn't see it in the mist that seemed to hover around them. In fact she could barely distinguish between the water and the outline of land exposed like the back of a turtle.

"Tell me when you're ready and I'll light a flare to help you see."

She reached for the end of the rope and made her way to the edge of the boat. "I'm waiting—"

There was a hissing sound before light illuminated his handsome features and the water surrounding the boat. It was a surreal sight.

She climbed up on the side and jumped, pleasantly surprised to discover the water wasn't as cold as she'd feared. Once she'd surfaced, she struck out for the island doing the side stroke. It enabled her to tug the boat along behind her without getting tangled in it. At first she had to pull hard, but little by little she made progress.

Luc must have known these waters well to have gauged how soon she'd be able to touch the sea floor with her sneakers. Though she would never admit it to him, once she walked on dry land, she was glad she hadn't met with anything out there in search of prey.

Quickly while the flare lasted, she found a good-sized rock and tied the rope the best she could. Then she shouted to Luc to toss the other rope end in the water. Within a few minutes, she'd pulled the boat around to secure it to another rock. Hopefully she'd done a good enough job that the boat wouldn't float away from the shore during the night.

At least here they would be protected from the many cruise ships and large ocean-going yachts and tankers passing back and forth in the night.

By the time she'd swum to the boat, the flare had burned out. Luc lowered the ladder over the side for her. She grabbed hold of it and swung herself up. He surprised her by gripping her waist to ease her to the deck.

"You shouldn't have done that!" she cried in a shaky voice. His touch had sent what felt like an electric current running through her body. "Your leg!"

As he slowly removed his hands, they seemed to trail over her hips before letting her go. "No harm was done. I put all the weight on my good one."

"Nevertheless you shouldn't have had so much activity this soon after leaving the hospital. Let's get you off your feet and back to bed." She handed him his cane and followed him below.

He nodded toward the bathroom. "You use the shower first." There was an underlying tone of authority in his suggestion that tolerated no argument.

"I'll get my things."

When she went to move past him, the confines of the passageway were so tight, her body brushed against the hardness of his. Her breath caught to feel his flesh and blood warmth. She didn't let it out until she reached the cabin and rummaged in the drawer for a pair of shorts and a white T-shirt she would wear to bed.

On her way back out, Luc had cleared the doorway leaving space between them. She moaned inwardly, wishing he were still in the way so she could experience the thrill of the contact of their bodies again, no matter how brief.

Once she reached the bathroom and closed the door, she clung to the sink for something to hold on to until her trembling stopped.

Earlier in the day she'd put their toiletries in the cabinet. After a few minutes of attempting to get herself under some semblance of control, she took a shower and washed the seawater out of her hair.

Several towels were folded above the cabinet. She pulled one down and wrapped it around her wet curls. Then she rinsed out her swimsuit and Luc's T-shirt before leaving them over the towel rack to dry.

The last thing she did was brush her teeth

before going to the kitchen to fix Luc another cappuccino. When she entered the bedroom, she discovered he'd changed out of his clothes and was half-lying on the bottom bunk wearing one of the pairs of cutoffs she'd packed for him.

''Here you go.''

He took the mug from her. ''You're not having any?''

''Too much caffeine makes me restless this time of night.'' She got down on her haunches. It put their eyes at the same level. His gleamed like sterling silver in the cabin light. ''Where shall I begin your massage? How does it have to be done? I don't want to hurt you.''

Before answering her, he drank his coffee, then set the mug on the floor. ''I think I'll forego the experience tonight.''

She eyed him anxiously. ''Because you're in too much pain?''

He seemed to hesitate, as if choosing his words carefully. ''Because you've done enough for one night.''

Olivia sucked in her breath. ''What you really mean is, I put our lives in danger today and you wish me thousands of miles away from here.''

His head went back against the pillow, but

his eyes remained trained on her. "Since it's a moot point, what I wish doesn't matter."

Luc was covering up for his discomfiture. "You're hurting, aren't you," she persisted.

"No. It's only a mild irritation." He sounded as if he meant it, but she would never know for sure. "The doctor drew fluid out of my knee in several places. It relieved pressure that's been building, *Dieu merci.*"

She inspected the visible signs of the operation done on him months earlier, then raised her eyes to his once more. "Cesar said you almost lost your leg. Thank God you didn't!"

"I was very fortunate." He put one arm behind his head. "The doctors were able to reattach the severed nerves, restoring circulation. Exercise and massages did the rest."

"Are you sure I can't rub your leg down?"

"Tomorrow will be soon enough."

Olivia shook her head. "What a ghastly ordeal that must have been for you."

"It was worse for Nic."

She shuddered. "Cesar told me about his fiancée. I can't imagine losing someone I loved, let alone in such a horrible accident."

Luc didn't respond to that, but she felt his

emotional withdrawal. "I'd rather not talk about it."

"Of course not. I'm sorry. Is there anything else I can do for you before I go to bed?"

"Shut off the light."

CHAPTER FIVE

FOR a few moments there they'd actually been conversing without her feeling Luc's animosity. But as soon as Olivia had brought Cesar into the conversation, a barrier slid into place like one of those cloaking devices in a science fiction movie.

It hurt to be shut out so totally. As she started to get up, her towel unraveled, revealing a head of damp, unruly curls before it fell to the floor. When she reached for it, she heard him whisper something unintelligible.

"You *are* in pain."

"Give it a rest, Olivia."

He'd delivered his last comment with an edge intended to warn her off. She wouldn't be learning anything more from him tonight. Defeated for the time being, she retraced her steps to the bathroom and hung up her towel.

On the way back to the cabin, she made a detour to the kitchen for more mineral water and his pills. "I'll put these on the floor by your bed in case you need them."

Without expecting a response, she shut off the cabin light. There was a ladder at the end of the beds. She climbed it to the top bunk and eased herself beneath the covers.

"Luc?"

When she heard the expletive that came out of him, she winced.

"Doesn't that wild Duchess brain of yours ever shut down for one second?"

"It can't when I know we're out of gas."

"Someone will come by eventually."

"To this deserted place? What if we run out of food first?"

"You saw Giovanni's fishing gear. You can catch us our meals. If that doesn't appeal, you could always swim to Elba for help."

Olivia blinked. "How far away is it?"

"It might take you an hour."

An hour—

"If it's too much of a challenge—"

"I'll do it if I have to, but first I think we should try to flag down a passing boat. I know—we'll set off another flare to get their attention."

"I'm afraid I used the only one left to help you see what you were doing."

"I already knew what I was doing! You should have saved it for an emergency," she grumbled.

A taunting laugh escaped his throat. "*That* from the woman who stole out of Vernazza without a map, compass, or a clue as to what you were doing."

"I got us this far didn't I?"

"You don't really want me to answer that question, do you?"

She turned on her other side and pounded her pillow.

"Look on the bright side, *mademoiselle.* Tomorrow you can hunt for buried treasure. Your Riviera trip doesn't have to be a complete loss."

"The Count of Monte Cristo already found it." She fumed. "Besides, I saw the movie, and it was filmed in the Maltese Islands."

"I've been there on the *Piccione.*"

She lifted her head, alert because he'd offered something without her having to pry it out of him. "When?"

"Several years ago."

Olivia tried to sit up all the way, but her head bumped the ceiling of the cabin. She lay back down again. "You and Fabio must go back a long way."

"The *Piccione* was Max's boat before he gave it to Fabio."

Gave it— She bumped her head again. "He must have had a good reason to part with anything so fabulous."

"The best of reasons. Fabio and his whole family fished for a living. His parents, their fishing boat, everything was lost at sea during a violent storm. Max was close friends with him growing up. Knowing he had a pregnant wife and two brothers to support, he let him have the boat to establish a charter business."

Olivia's throat closed up with raw emotion. Did Greer know that piece of information about her remarkable husband?

"By your silence, I realize that kind of generosity is anathema to you. It may surprise you even more to learn that Fabio has paid Max back every lire for it through hard work."

Luc's stinging barbs found their mark, but she'd promised herself she wouldn't rise to the bait.

"Thank you for confiding in me. Before you gave me this insight into Max, I loved him because my sister loved him. But now, I love my new brother-in-law for my own reasons. You've given me a priceless gift. It has been worth taking all the abuse you've heaped my way."

''Material things matter much more to you than I thought. Work it right, and you'll be able to benefit from Max's generosity for years to come, Cesar or no Cesar.''

It was such a heartless comment, she groaned into her pillow.

There had to be a way to reach Luc. He wasn't born believing the worst about people. That world-weary derisiveness he wore like a shroud was the result of one terrible act against him.

Piper had been told what it was, but there was no way to reach her without a phone.

Greer knew the truth, yet until she returned from her honeymoon and could enlighten Olivia, the status quo would continue to prevail with Luc who was well ensconced in his invisible fortress, withdrawn and utterly impervious.

She flipped over on her back, wide awake. Her immediate problem was to figure out how they were going to get off this island anytime soon. If no one came by to help them tomorrow, they could always start out the next day by rowing.

It would be hard going with only one oar, but they might not have any other choice. Unless she could find something on the island she could use for another paddle...

As she took mental stock of their provisions, she realized they only had enough food for a couple of days, if they were careful. Part of the excitement of a trip like this was to go ashore each day at a different heavenly spot. She'd planned to buy various items in the local markets of the ports and bring them back to the boat to cook and eat.

In the event that it might be several days before they could get more gas and food, she would act on Luc's suggestion and fish for their breakfast in the morning.

She was no novice to the sport. Her dad had been an expert fly fisherman. He'd taught a lot of tricks to his daughters, his precious pigeons as he'd loved to call them.

Along with their mom they'd done a lot of outdoor activities at one of his favorite lakes in the Adirondacks. Tomorrow she would get up with the sun and find out just how good a pupil she'd been.

Relieved to have a plan, any plan, Olivia rolled over on her stomach praying sleep would come so she wouldn't be tempted to climb down the ladder and seek comfort from Luc. In the mood he was in, she could easily imagine him strangling her with his bare hands.

Hands that had grasped her waist and hips

earlier tonight to haul her into the boat. Hands she could have sworn had lingered for an overly long moment against her wet skin. She still felt feverish from their warmth.

"Knock, knock. Ready or not, I've brought you breakfast in bed."

Luc had been in that hazy place where one hovered between waking and sleeping. When he opened his eyes, he discovered the sun was already well up in the sky. Olivia walked toward him with a mug in one hand, a plate of food in the other. Even out of the sun, her curls gleamed like spun gold.

"On a scale of one to ten, ten being highest, what's your pain level this morning?" Her cheery disposition irritated the hell out of him.

"Minus one."

"If that's true, then why the scowl on your face? Don't you know it takes more muscles to frown than smile?"

Ciel! On a scale of one to ten, ten being the highest for the most exasperating, impossible female he'd ever known, she rated a twenty!

That tantalizing body of hers was dressed in the same shorts and shirt she'd worn to bed last night. Among their many gifts, the Duchess triplets were blessed with long shapely legs. No one was more aware of that fact than Luc as she approached looking wide-awake, and for want of a better word…exhilarated.

"It's another gorgeous day." She put his coffee on the floor next to him. "I've been up for hours watching for a passing boat to wave down, but so far no luck."

He eased his back against the wall so he could take the plate from her. The mouthwatering aroma of grilled fish hot off the skillet wafted past his nostrils. His eyes took in the expert presentation of toast points and orange slices arranged as if he'd just been served the pièce de résistance at a five-star restaurant.

One bite of the delicious, light flaky meat expertly filleted, seasoned and sauteed in olive oil, and he shot her a questioning glance. "This is fresh sea bass!"

"That's right. I caught it a little while ago. There was a school of juvenile fish playing around the rocks. We don't have to worry about starving to death before we're rescued."

If he didn't know for a fact there was no freezer on board to keep fish on ice, he wouldn't have believed her. She'd actually found food for them and could prepare it like a master chef?

"There are four more fillets in the pan, so if you want refills just holler. I'll be in the kitchen cleaning up.'' She took away the mineral water bottle he'd drained during the night.

With the combined flavor of the oranges, fish had never tasted so good to him before. Even the coffee was different. She'd added cocoa. He devoured everything between mouthfuls of the steaming brew, stunned by her resourcefulness and a lot of other things he wasn't disposed to examine right now.

A few minutes later she reappeared in the doorway. ''More?''

''No. I'll eat the rest for lunch.''

''Whatever you say. When I come back, I'll give you that massage.''

His muscles had tightened up on him during the night. A massage would feel good. He removed the covers and turned over on his stomach so his injured leg would be closest to her.

Soon he felt her presence as she knelt at the side of the bunk. The subtle flowery fragrance from the soap she used in the shower drifted in his direction, intoxicating him.

''Okay. I'm ready for your instructions.''

''Start with my foot and knead your way up my calf, but no farther.''

''All right.'' She molded her hand to his heel and began to caress the pad with gentle insistence. Her nimble fingers seemed to know instinctively where to rub using the right pressure. With slow deliberation, she worked her magic from his toes to his calf.

He didn't have to tell her to use the flat of her palm to wiggle the fleshy part, thereby loosening those muscles. Her touch was instinctive. He could feel its healing effect as his whole body began to relax.

"How am I doing?"

Luc was afraid to tell her. He didn't dare admit it to himself. "If you did this service for Cesar before the race, then I can understand why he would want you around."

"I'll take that as a compliment," she said without missing a breath. Her glib response frustrated him no end. "Would you like your neck and shoulders massaged, too?"

She'd probably done all this and more for his brother. Luc sucked in his breath. "Just keep up what you're doing for a minute longer, and I won't require another session until bedtime."

"What about your water therapy?"

"I'll go for a brief swim later in the day after my lunch has digested."

"We'll both swim. In the meantime, you can read the latest thriller I brought with me while I go hunting for treasure."

He lifted his head. "Owing to the fact that

the fabulous fortune buried in the grotto of Monte Cristo didn't exist outside Dumas's imagination, I thought you'd given up on the idea.''

''Wasn't it you who told me 'all that glitters isn't gold'?'' Her hand gave him a final pat. ''There may be treasure lurking here not instantly recognizable to the naked eye.''

To his chagrin she stood up, thereby ending these few moments of sheer physical pleasure. ''I understand from Greer the island only takes up six square miles. I probably won't be gone exploring for more than a couple of hours. While I'm away, you can shower and read at your leisure. I've left the book on the dresser.''

Olivia Duchess never did anything without an agenda. What was she up to now? ''Good luck spouse hunting,'' he muttered as she started to leave the cabin.

She paused in the doorway. ''Thanks. Maybe I'll run into a heartthrob who's scuba diving off his yacht.''

After she disappeared, he eased himself out of bed with the help of his cane and walked over to the window to survey the situation.

In a minute he saw her splashing through the water to the shore. She took the time to inspect the ropes still tied by the rocks before she began her jog around the desolate island.

It didn't matter that the surface resembled the moonscape. At this point Luc was beginning to realize this woman was a self-starter who made her own luck. Nothing kept her down. No hill was too hard for her to climb.

Her resilience under stress was almost as astounding as her fearless predilection for attempting the impossible and getting away with it. Only the Duchess sisters could have made their escape out the second-story window of his parents' villa in the middle of the night without making a sound or injuring themselves.

He might even have admired her daring if he hadn't known she'd risked life and limb to watch Cesar race in the Grand Prix a few hours later.

Luc's brother had been so flattered to learn that he was the sole reason she'd come to Monaco—that she'd tossed her American lover aside for him—it was no wonder he couldn't see through her master plan which had been to become Madame Cesar de Falcon.

It was a stroke of genius on her part to run away from him after his win at Monza, pretending she really wasn't interested in him after all.

Knowing how many other women had tried and failed to get his ring on their finger, she'd done the one thing guaranteed to bring him to his knees.

Beautiful, amoral Olivia Duchess was the perfect match for Luc's dashing, amoral brother.

Little did Cesar know that while she was waiting for him to catch up to her, she'd made for Ischia last night while Luc had been asleep, hoping to catch a prince. There was no limit to her ambition, as Cesar would find out one of these days. Luc wished them the joy of each other.

But in the meantime they were stuck on Monte Cristo, and she was unable to be a temptation to anyone since no one in the world knew where she was except Luc.

While they were marooned here, it might be an interesting experiment to see how long she could keep up this adventurous facade before she started to crack. Every human had a breaking point. More than anyone else, Luc would appreciate learning what it was. Even better, he'd enjoy watching it happen.

Curious to know if Cesar was hot on the trail yet, he walked back to the bunk and reached inside the pillowcase for his cell phone. He wasn't surprised to see a list of callers that included everyone close to him except his brother.

Taking advantage of Olivia's absence, he phoned Nic, who'd left half a dozen messages.

"Luc—it's a relief to hear your voice. How's the leg?"

"Couldn't be better. What's the real reason behind all your calls?"

"Max phoned to find out if I knew where Olivia is. I thought she was in Monza with Cesar, but apparently he said she left after the race and went to see you. Later I found out that Greer spoke to her at your house night before last. What's going on?"

Good question.

Night before last Luc had listened in while Olivia had tried to reach Piper in Genoa. That meant the first phone call to the house had been from Greer, not Cesar. Why had Olivia pretended otherwise?

"Greer and Piper are both upset because they've had no contact with Olivia since," Nic explained further. "If you know where she is, tell her to do everyone a favor and get in touch with her sisters so they'll stop worrying. Max would like to enjoy his honeymoon."

Luc chewed on his lower lip for a moment.

"Right now she's playing a very dangerous game."

"What do you mean?"

He glanced out the window once more. There was no sign of Olivia yet. "How much time have you got?"

"It's been a half hour since we ate lunch. Time for your water therapy."

After finishing off the fish, Luc had sat in the sun to read, effectively shutting Olivia out. Since she'd returned from her exploration of the island, something about him had been different. She couldn't put her finger on it, but he was less approachable, which didn't come as any great surprise. He'd removed the elastic wrap and bandages where the doctor had drawn off the fluid. Olivia couldn't tell the procedure had even been done.

But maybe his leg was hurting him, and he didn't want her to know.

If that was the case, hopefully a swim might make it feel better. He'd donned his black suit in anticipation. The trick was to get him in and out of the boat without injury.

Olivia stood up from the padded bench and removed the T-shirt she'd been wearing over her swimsuit to protect her shoulders. Because the sun was so strong, Luc had also put on a shirt he'd left unbuttoned.

She walked over to him and took the book from his hands. By the way his features seemed to harden as his narrowed gaze swept up her body to confront hers, it had been the wrong thing to do. But it was too late to worry about that now.

"Ready?"

He rose to his full height and started to remove his shirt. She put the book on the bench so she could help him. He had an extraordinary male physique. The desire to touch him had become a driving need, but he shrugged out of his shirt so fast, she was denied the pleasure of physical contact.

Before she could catch her breath, he dove off the side of the boat into the water which was at a depth of about twelve feet. She followed him in and swam circles around him while he tread water.

The sun had warmed his olive skin, bringing color to the surface. His eyes glinted silver. With his wet black hair sleeked back, and drops of water beading his dark brows and eyelashes, he was the personification of male beauty. As she looked at him an ache passed through Olivia's body so intense, she looked away.

When she felt she was under control again, she swam over to him. "If you'll lie back and let me support your head and shoulders, you'll be able to exercise your leg the way you need to."

"Since when did you become a physical therapist?"

Olivia forced herself not to react to his rancor. "In the early stages of cancer, mother enjoyed a swim if we girls helped her. She tired easily."

In the silence that followed her remark, she could feel him digesting what she'd said. Then without her having to say anything else, he turned over on his back as a signal she should help him.

Hoping he couldn't tell she was trembling, she slid her hands under his arms and steadied him while he propelled them around with his legs. Cocooned as he was in her arms, she could bury her face in his hair and he was none the wiser that she was in a state of ecstasy.

"Was skiing your favorite sport?" she asked, trying to keep her voice steady.

"One of them."

"How soon does the doctor say you can ski again?"

"Never again." There was a wealth of emotion in those words.

"Knowing you, you'll probably end up an Olympic swimmer."

Before she could blink, he'd jerked out of her arms and had turned so he was treading water in front of her. "You don't know anything about me."

"I know *of* you," she fought against the bitterness in his accusation. "Despite the fact that you almost lost your leg in that accident, Cesar told me how you gave CPR to several of the injured skiers and kept them alive until the paramedics arrived. Your action saved their lives. That kind of heroism is rare."

His eyes clouded with emotion she couldn't decipher. "It couldn't save Nina's."

"According to Cesar, no one could have done anything for Nic's fiancée. Your little brother lives in awe of you, you know."

She thought his face lost color. "Then we're not talking about the same person."

The next thing she knew, Luc had rolled over on his stomach. Like a torpedo, he took off for deeper water, leaving Olivia to ponder his words.

She felt the weight of them as she headed for the boat and pulled herself up the rungs of the ladder. Joy had gone out of her day because she realized that something terrible had torn the two brothers apart.

If Luc had serious issues with Cesar, then it explained why Cesar was so intimidated by his elder brother despite his hero worship of him. And somewhere in the middle of all this sat Olivia.

It killed her that two wonderful, remarkable brothers had reached such a terrible impasse in their lives. Though her sisters irritated her at times, Olivia couldn't comprehend being estranged from them. Life wouldn't be worth living if that were the case. No wonder Luc and his brother were both suffering.

She could see him in the distance. It didn't look as if he would be coming back for a while. Since she couldn't bear to sit around on the boat in agony because of all the things she didn't know about the Falcon brothers' complicated relationship, she decided to get started on her latest project.

Once she'd pulled on Luc's navy T-shirt and had found her sneakers, she grabbed another of her own T-shirts and went ashore to hunt for rocks. There were all kinds with interesting pink and red colors the size of Ping-Pong balls strewn across the island.

It took her a couple of hours to gather them into a sizable pile. She carried them in the T-shirt she'd made into a pouch, and took it down to the water's edge to wash them off.

If they were polished, they'd be quite pretty. Pleased with the results, she lugged them back to the boat. To her surprise, the sun had dropped a lot lower in the sky. She'd been out longer than she'd realized.

When Luc saw her on the ladder, he put the book aside and took the pouch from her while she climbed into the boat.

He lifted it up and down, as if trying to guess its weight. That mocking smile was in evidence once more. "What have we got here?"

"Treasure. Want to take a peek?" She plucked the pouch from his hand and put it on the bench to open it.

He stared at the contents. "I don't see anything but a pile of rocks."

"Your psyche's too scarred to see their individual beauty."

She felt his body stiffen and rejoiced that she'd hit a nerve. It was about time she won one round in the battle for his love.

"For your information, I'm going to start a new business with these."

"What happened to your calendar business?"

"It was Greer's idea, and Piper's the artist. I've decided I want to do something solely on my own for a change."

"These stones are too big to make into pendants."

She let that intentional dig go by. "Not pendants. Paperweights. The perfect gift for the discerning customer."

A deep chuckle rolled out of Luc.

"Laugh now, but one day I'll be laughing all the way to the bank."

"You're hoping to make a fortune on these?" he taunted.

"I *know* I will."

"Why bother when the Prince of Monaco will be able to shower you with everything you could ever want."

Good. Luc hadn't forgotten. He possessed a mind that worked like a steel trap.

"I'd rather marry for love, and earn my own money. There's tons to be made on the Internet. My sisters and I found that out when we advertised our calendars online."

His hands went to his hips in a totally masculine gesture. "Just how are you going to get people to buy your rocks?"

"If you had any romance in your soul, you wouldn't have to ask that question."

"Romance..." He made it sound like an evil word.

"Yes. There's probably no more famous adventure novel in the whole world than the Count of Monte Cristo. Even if people haven't read the book, they've heard of it.

"My hook will read, 'Enjoy a piece of living history. Treasure straight from the Island of Monte Cristo. Every paperweight is different in size, shape and color. Beneath its polished surface lives the story of two men: Abbe Faria who loved God, Edmond Dantes who loved revenge more.'"

Luc was so quiet at this point she said, "I'm thinking of charging fifty dollars a piece. It's not too steep for the person looking for that perfect gift for the discerning shopper.

"In a way I hope we're not rescued for another day because I need to gather as many rocks as I can. After we leave here, I'd like to head to Elba and collect rocks from there. In case my business takes off, I could sell them as mementos of Napoleon's exile. History buffs would love them!"

"I thought you were anxious to get to Ischia."

"I am, but a few more days delay shouldn't matter."

"What if the Prince is gone when we arrive?"

"Then I'll use you and your connections to find out where he went." She smiled and stretched. "This trip is turning out a lot better than I'd hoped. In a way I'm glad Fabio's boat wasn't available. If we'd gone with him, we wouldn't have come here, and I wouldn't have stumbled onto my future."

He frowned. "Aren't you getting ahead of yourself? These rocks might turn out to be a weight around your neck."

"No." She shook her head. "I can feel success in my bones. It has made me hungry. What do you want for dinner?"

"Surprise me."

"Would you like it served on deck, or below?"

"Below."

"I don't blame you. To think the Mediterranean is known for its unmatched beauty, and here we are marooned on the only ugly, flat rock pile out in the middle of nowhere."

His lips twitched. He was gorgeous when he even halfway smiled.

Relieved that the dark mood he'd been in earlier seemed to have passed, she headed for the galley determined that one day soon she would break him down enough to learn his secrets.

Half an hour later she told him dinner was ready. They ate a meal of ham and cheese melts at the little drop-down table. She found a bottle of wine, and threw in some plums for dessert.

"Tell me about these robots of yours," she said after biting into the fruit. "If we brought one out here, could it pick up rocks for me?"

He drank some more wine. "The one I'm working on is an automobile that can drive itself and enter a war zone to deliver supplies in hostile territory. If you want a worker robot, the Japanese have developed ones that pick fruit, scour sewers, clean the windows of skyscrapers. The list is endless."

Totally fascinated, she leaned closer to him. "I want to hear more about your invention. How long have you been working on it?"

"While I was at the University of Parma a few years ago, I designed a prototype of an intelligent vehicle. The hardware and software platform enabled it to drive automatically in real traffic conditions."

"How far did your car end up traveling without a driver?"

"Two thousand miles of Italian motorways and back roads."

"No accidents?"

"None."

She shook her head. "How incredible! I would love to have seen it. Like a remote-control car without the remote."

"That's a good way to put it. Inside it's interfaced with many layers of sensors, cameras and computers that react on multiple levels."

"Something like the human brain?"

"Close."

"What made you go into that aspect of engineering?"

"I grew up reading science fiction, and imagined myself creating a world of robots to do my bidding."

"Since Cesar dreamed of being at the wheel to drive fast cars himself, he obviously didn't share your interest."

The comment had just slipped out because the joy of interacting with Luc had made her forget how much he despised her. But the mere mention of Cesar and the tension was back. She could tell by the way his hard-muscled body stiffened.

"Why is it that whenever his name is brought into the conversation, you act as if I'd committed high treason?"

When he refused to answer her, something snapped inside her. "Would you rather we talked about the reason why you're so certain he doesn't worship the ground you walk on?"

CHAPTER SIX

Luc's eyes pierced hers like lasers. "Have you always gone where angels feared to tread?"

"My sisters would tell you yes."

"If you're that curious, why don't you discuss it with Cesar the next time you see him."

"You mean I have your permission?"

"Would it stop you if I said no?"

She let his question hang in the air and got up to clear the table. "Tell me something. Are you just naturally bitter because it's a trait inherited through your Falcon genes? Or was it the tragedy that turned you into a dark facsimile of your former self?"

He bit out something unintelligible while she washed the dishes and straightened up the kitchen. When she reached the doorway, she paused. "Do you need another massage before we turn in?"

"I've exercised it enough for one day."

You have your answer, Olivia. "I'll go up on deck and get the book."

"I finished it."

Her eyes closed tightly for a minute. "Good. Now I'll have something to read before I go to sleep. Anything else you need from above?"

"No."

Olivia had thought she could withstand whatever verbal blows he thrust at her, no matter how mean or cruel. But she was wrong... His hateful remarks were slowly crucifying her.

Wretched, wretched man. She would love to throw something at him, but she could hear her father whisper, "Handle it like a Duchess."

"Then I'll say good night."

She made a detour to the bathroom to brush her teeth. He was still seated at the table drinking the rest of his wine when she passed the kitchen on her way to the stairs.

If he craved his solitude so much, then she would let him have all he wanted. There were several more bottles of wine in the cupboard. He could drink himself into oblivion for all she cared.

The darkness had brought an even heavier mist than last night. Clouds she'd seen in the far horizon had moved much faster than she would have imagined. She shivered involuntarily, glad the boat was moored to the island since there was virtually no visibility at the moment.

By sitting next to the light at the end of the boat, she was able to read. It was almost impossible to concentrate, but she was determined to stay away from Luc until he'd gone to bed and had passed out for the night.

After an hour she noticed the breeze had kicked up. There was a drop in the temperature. Without anything covering her bare legs beneath her shorts, she was starting to get uncomfortable, but she kept on reading.

In another few minutes she felt the first drops of rain. Unable to lie there any longer, she got off the bench with her book and headed for the stairs. No sooner had she passed the kitchen than the lights flickered several times before going out. Great!

Luc must have heard her surprised cry because he called to her from the cabin. "Did you just shut off the power?"

"No."

"The rain must have shorted out some wiring. I'll take a look at it in the morning. Do you need help coming to bed?"

It was pitch black. "No. Just keep talking and I'll follow your voice."

"Don't move! There's a flashlight in the locker where I found the flare. I'll get it."

But Olivia ignored him and darted across the expanse where she could feel the ladder. In the time it would take him to slide out of bed, she'd climbed beneath the covers of her bunk.

"Olivia?" The alarm in his voice was incredibly satisfying to hear. It proved he wasn't totally devoid of concern for her.

"I'm up here, cozy and warm."

He cursed in French again. "Then stay there! I won't be long."

"Please don't bother with a light tonight," she begged him. "The stairs might be slippery. If you fell and injured yourself after all you've endured, I'd never be able to forgive myself. I'm the reason we're stranded here. This whole situation is my fault," her voice shook.

"In case it's a heavy rain, I need to shut the doors at the top and bottom of the stairs to keep the galley area watertight."

"I'll do that! You get back in bed!"

"For the love of heaven— Can't you once in your hedonistic life think of someone else besides yourself and do as your told?"

Hedonistic? He really saw her as a woman in pursuit of pleasure, devoid of conscience or concern for anyone else?

Hadn't everything she'd done for him today counted for anything?

While she lay there wounded and seething with fresh indignation, she could hear him battening down the hatch.

She prayed he would make it back to bed in one piece. But as soon as she heard him enter the room and get in his bunk, she was waiting for him and leaned her head over the side, armed with a new tactic.

"You're right about me, Luc. I'm not the kind of woman who can be faithful to one man. It isn't in me. I love men too much. I thought I liked Fred and a dozen others before him. Then I met Cesar. It was fun for a while. But then I found myself attracted to his mechanic who wanted to spend time with me after the race."

"Etienne."

"I don't remember his name. If he's the one with the dark blond hair like Fabio, then yes."

"He's married with three children."

"I found that out from one of the other mechanics. Whatever else you may think of me, I draw the line at getting involved with married men. So...I've been thinking about...us."

"Us?" he mouthed the word silkily.

Her heart throbbed so hard in her throat, she

almost choked. "Yes. You and me. Since Cesar knows I turned to you, and we're probably not going to make it to Ischia after all, what do you say we take advantage of our situation for the duration of our trip."

"You mean you've decided you're attracted to me now."

"Well, yes. Strictly on a physical level."

"Are you that desperate for a man?"

If he happens to be you...

"Not desperate. But we're both here, and we're alone. Why not make these moments as pleasurable as possible. No one else ever has to know."

She waited to hear his answer. When none was forthcoming, she took it as a yes and scrambled down the ladder with her heart pounding like a jackhammer.

It was taking a gamble, the biggest of her life. But if she could just get him to kiss her, then maybe he would break down enough to admit he loved her. Greer had ended up proposing to Max. Olivia would do the same with Luc. She would confess she was painfully in love with him and wanted to marry him if he would have her. Whatever was in his past, they would deal with it together.

The darkness gave her an edge. She couldn't

see Luc's expression, and it seemed to bring her senses alive.

Something told her it wasn't pain that made his breath catch before it turned shallow the second she touched him. The skin on his upper arm felt warm to the touch. It pulsated with life.

This close to his body she breathed in his own male scent. Intoxicated, she leaned over and brushed her lips against his hair-roughened chest. She'd wanted to do this for such a long, long time.

He made no move to touch her back. She didn't mind doing all the work. From the beginning he'd been a challenge. Like a wild stallion that had never known a rope around its neck, he'd put up an enormous fight.

Gentling him was taking time and patience, but she was winning the fight. Even a thoroughbred who ran alone was vulnerable to a little comfort once in a while.

She started to massage his shoulders, marveling at their strength and breadth. "Doesn't this feel good?" she whispered. Being able to play with those corded muscles was ecstasy. A man and a woman had been designed with opposites in mind. Beautiful opposites that were meant to fit together as one pulsating entity.

"Do you have any idea how desirable you

are to me?'' Unable to resist, she found his chin with her lips. ''Um. You have a little beard growing there.''

She felt the rasp of his jaw over and over again before her lips slowly moved to his ear. ''I love everything about you, Lucien de Falcon. In fact I think I need to take a little bite out of you.''

Her teeth grazed his earlobe. She relished the sensation of his hair brushing against her nose. In the next breath she buried her face in its vibrant texture. Maybe it was because she was so blond, but there was something erotic about kissing hair as black as midnight.

Instinct caused her mouth to travel over his forehead to well-formed brows as dark and luxuriant as his hair. ''Your eyelashes are tickling my cheek.'' She smiled before kissing each eyelid, then his aquiline nose. The kind that added a hawk-like quality to his features, denoting his aristocratic Falcon heritage. It set him apart from other men.

''You're the most breathtaking man I've ever known,'' she confessed. Still on her knees at the side of the bunk, she cradled his face in her hands and started nibbling at the corner of his mouth.

The journey to get this close to Luc had been

long and arduous. Almost two months in all.
Now that she'd arrived, she intended to take her
time and savor what she'd been yearning for.

"I didn't know you had a little scar there,"
she said when she felt the tiny ridge at the other
corner. "It's not visible, but it tells me something about you, even if you won't. So does the
tiny nick on your neck."

She kissed both spots again, then closed her
mouth fully over his, aching for him to sweep
her away. "Darling? Help me out," she begged,
feeling feverish at this point.

Just when she was afraid the miracle would
never happen, a tremor passed through his powerful body. Suddenly she wasn't doing all the
work anymore. His mouth began to respond.

At first it was like the soft, experimental caress of love's first kiss between two young teens
who'd been anticipating the moment, yet
couldn't quite believe it was really here.

Olivia was running on primal instinct now.
Her lips opened of their own accord, unaware
of what she was unleashing. Beyond control, all
she knew was that the driving force of her desire was coaxing him to take their kiss deeper.

With her mouth fastened on his, she climbed
on the mattress, needing to get closer to him.
She would be careful not to hurt his leg.

"Finally," she murmured in rapture when she felt his arms close around her. "I've waited so lo—"

Her cry was replaced by little moans because the startling hunger of his kiss had engulfed her. He caught her to him in an explosion of need. The pleasure was so exquisite she felt it to the tiniest nerve ending in her body.

They moved and breathed together, arms, mouths and bodies locked in a melding as old as time itself. She forgot where she was. Time…place…nothing had any meaning except to go up in flames with the man she loved beyond reason.

Suddenly he shifted her away from him. Caught up in a frenzy of overwhelming passion, she was slow to understand she might have done something to injure him. In a clumsy movement, she rolled off the bed and stood up, but her legs were trembling like jelly.

"Forgive me if I hurt you. I didn't mean to."

"No harm was done," came his answer in a voice devoid of emotion. Without light she couldn't tell what he was thinking, but she sensed a stunning change in him. The blood pounded in her ears.

"What's wrong?"

"Playtime is over."

She weaved on her feet. "I don't understand."

"Of course you do, but a woman like you chooses not to pick up on the signals. I don't recall inviting you to join me in my bed. Because of your history with men, you just assumed you would be welcome.

"Perhaps your 'one for all, all for one' motto is the by-product of being the youngest in a set of triplets, but to be frank, the thought of making love to my brother's latest *pit babe* sickens me. I don't know how I can make myself any clearer than that."

A thousand knives seemed to be stabbing her heart at once. She held back scalding tears only through the greatest strength of will.

"I don't know, either. How come you didn't push me away sooner?"

"I must admit I was curious to see if there was a conscience hiding somewhere inside that tempting body of yours that would stop you before I did."

Her breath caught. "I noticed you waited until you'd kissed me back first!"

"You're a delicious flavor treat. The trick is to enjoy a small taste rather than to sate one's self with fruit from the basket others have picked over first. When I decide to fully indulge myself, I will pluck the sweetest fruit of my choosing from off the tree and swallow it whole.''

Both sisters had warned her Luc wasn't like other men. They were right. His demons were too daunting for her to fight without more information.

But he *had* responded to her.

No man could have kissed her with such soul-destroying intensity if she'd sickened him that much. He would never have let her get that far otherwise.

What she needed was input. The kind only an insider could provide, *if* he was willing...

She climbed back up to her bunk and spent the rest of the torturous night huddled under the covers while she thought out her new plan. Toward morning the elements decided to cooperate. The storm passed over, and the light patter of the rain ceased.

As soon as the first light of dawn filtered into the cabin, she stole out of bed and climbed down the ladder, careful not to make a sound. Luc was in a deep sleep. She could tell by his breathing.

It was vital he stay unconscious for a while longer since she intended to undo the ropes and start rowing toward the mainland. Her impetu-

osity had gotten them into this predicament.
Now she needed to rely on her ingenuity to get
them out on the double quick in order for her
latest strategy to work.

She tiptoed to the bathroom. After putting on
her bathing suit and T-shirt, she slipped into her
sneakers. Quietly opening the doors at the bottom and top of the stairs, she climbed out on a
deck still damp from the night's storm.
However the mist had lifted enough to give her
the visibility she needed.

In a few minutes she'd untied the ropes and
had climbed back in the boat. She used the oar
to shove off, giving it a hard push for maximum
glide. When she couldn't touch bottom anymore, she started paddling, first on one side,
then the other.

Within ten minutes every muscle in her body
was killing her, but her determination to put her
new plan into action had become a driving
force. Though progress was slow, even after she
got the hang of it, the island had almost disappeared from view. That was a good omen.

She rested for two minutes, then began the
backbreaking process all over again.

Within a half hour she'd reached her exhaustion level and sank down on the bench for a
breather. That's when she heard the sound of an

engine off to the left. Pretty soon she saw a light plane flying over the water. As it came closer, she noticed it had pontoons.

Olivia started jumping up and down, waving her arms.

The plane circled, then landed and taxied toward the boat. A man dove overboard and swam toward the *Gabbiano*. When he reached it and climbed the ladder, she let out a surprised cry.

"Nic! What are you doing here? How did you know we were in trouble?"

His captivating white smile was reassuringly familiar. "Giovanni forgot to tell Fabio that when the wiring gets wet, it causes a short and the power goes off."

She rolled her eyes. "We already found that out last night."

"He called Fabio because he was worried you and Luc might be caught in the storm, so Fabio called me. According to one of the children near the dock, they saw you head east when you left Vernazza.

"Since you girls were so fascinated by Monte Cristo's history on your first trip, I figured it might be your destination. Therefore I instructed the pilot to search this area first."

"Luc and I came across it by accident.

Between you and me, the fascination has worn off. It's just a pile of rocks.''

He grinned. ''Where *is* my cousin?''

''Right here,'' came Luc's deep, grating voice. Olivia looked over her shoulder and found herself trapped by his enigmatic gaze. ''The question is, what are we doing out in the middle of the Mediterranean this time around?''

Nic folded his arms, eyeing both of them with speculation. ''I found Señorita Olivo rowing the boat for all she was worth with one oar. That's quite a feat, even for several sailors twice her size and strength.''

''I was looking for help.''

Luc stood there in cutoffs, disheveled and unshaven, yet hateful as he was, she'd never seen a more attractive man in her life. After being kissed by him last night, after experiencing his embrace if only for a little while, she would never be the same again.

But his grim demeanor reminded her she was a long way from being able to claim victory.

''Well we couldn't just sit on Monte Cristo and do nothing!''

''I'll get the rope attached to the tether,'' Nic interjected. ''We'll tow the boat back to Vernazza for electrical repairs.''

Olivia smiled at him. "I've never been in a seaplane before. Are we riding with you?"

"Of course."

"Terrific!"

Ignoring Luc, she climbed up on the side and leaped into the water to make her escape from him.

Within a few minutes she and Luc were seated comfortably behind the pilot and Nic. The seaplane fairly skated across the surface of the water with the *Gabbiano* in tow. While Olivia drank her hot coffee, Nic looked over his shoulder at her.

"What do you think?" No doubt he felt tension emanating from Luc and was trying his best to neutralize it.

"I haven't had this much fun in years. I feel like I'm at Disneyland on one of those children's rides." The two men in front burst into laughter. "This is the only way to see the Riviera. How much would you charge to escort me around on a ten-day trip?"

"More than you could ever afford," Luc muttered, his tone as black as the stubble on his jaw. She couldn't understand his grim disposition. They'd been rescued and he was about to be rid of her. What more did he want from life?

"When I've made my fortune, I'll be able to

afford anything I want and I'll buy one of these. In fact I think I'll take flying lessons so I can do everything myself.''

''You'll have to sell a lot of rocks first.''

''Your encouragement to one who wasn't born being fed by a silver spoon with the Falcon coat of arms does you great credit.''

For the rest of the ride back, Olivia pretended Luc hadn't come along. She concentrated instead on the magnificent view of the coastline. The rain had refreshed everything. The greens of the foliage, the pinks and yellows of the flowers were more vivid than usual.

Vernazza was beginning to look like home. The pilot of the seaplane skimmed the harbor in a circle and came to a stop. He'd brought the *Gabbiano* close enough to the pier for some local fisherman to secure it at the end of the dock.

Olivia was first out of her seat. ''Nic? Luc shouldn't use his leg anymore today. Last night he strained it unintentionally,'' she deliberately stated in order to remind him of those moments he wanted to forget. She hoped he was tortured by them. ''I'll go aboard and pack up our things.''

Pleased when she heard Luc's protest overruled by Nic in no uncertain terms, she dove from the open door into the water and swam for the boat. Once on deck she went below and changed into a blouse and skirt.

After packing both suitcases, she went back up the stairs. Nic had come aboard. He stood by and watched as she reopened her bag and put the pouch of rocks on top of her clothes and toiletries. But when she lowered the lid, it wouldn't close all the way.

He smiled. "Whatever that is, I don't think it's going to fit."

"Yes it will."

She sat down on the lid and that did the trick. Gathering her purse in one hand, she took hold of her suitcase in the other. It weighed a lot more than before, but she didn't mind.

"Let me transport those bags to the plane."

"Only Luc's," she said when Nic started to reach for them. "He's the one who needs to get back to Monaco and rest. Otherwise he'll blame me when it takes his leg longer to heal. I couldn't bear that on my conscience along with everything else."

"Everything else?" Nic shot her a questioning glance.

With her emotions so close to the surface, she was in danger of giving herself away. "I—it was just a figure of speech," she stammered. "I was starting to get nervous out there. Without power I wouldn't have been able to cook us more fish even if I'd been lucky enough to catch another one.''

He looked shocked. ''You caught fish?''

''Yes. Who would have believed?'' She gave him a tired smile. ''Thank you for everything, Nic. You've been a real lifesaver.''

''Where are you going?'' he questioned after she'd kissed his cheek.

''Greer made me promise to take the train to Colorno and spend a few days at Max's villa before I fly home to New York.''

It wasn't a lie. Her sister had told her she and Piper would always have a home with them. They would never have to wait for an invitation.

Of course Olivia had no such intention of traveling to Colorno. There was only one detour she planned to make before leaving Italy, but nobody else needed to know about that, least of all Luc. She just hoped she wasn't too late.

''Bye.'' With a little wave she stepped off the boat with her suitcase and headed for the town. It was only a five-minute walk to the train station.

''I'd like a one-way ticket to Positano, please.''

''*Si, signorina.*''

Before she left for Kingston, she wanted to

know why Luc hated her so much. She had a gut instinct the younger Falcon brother could provide her with the answer. Not that it would take away her pain. Nothing could do that, but she wouldn't be able to go on functioning without some kind of explanation.

Nic climbed into the seaplane with the valise. He stashed it behind the seat before his gaze flicked to Luc. "Olivia's not coming."

"Tell me something I don't already know." Luc had seen her march off with her suitcase toward the town, her gleaming blond head held high, her curvaceous body the cynosure of every male eye in the port. "Let's go."

While Nic strapped himself in the co-pilot's seat and told the pilot to take off for Monaco, Luc phoned Signore Galli. The head of security at Genoa airport had dealt with the Duchess sisters before. If Olivia did check in for her overseas flight, the other man would spot her immediately and contact Luc.

Nic didn't try to make further conversation until they were alone in the back of the limo headed for Luc's house. "Why the call to Signore Galli?"

"If she's flying home from Genoa, I plan to

put her on the plane myself. I want proof she has left the continent.''

Another experiment like last night and he'd never be able to hold out. The things she'd done to him, the way she'd made him feel... He couldn't believe he'd come so close to being the amoral bastard he'd accused his brother of being. Olivia was poison disguised.

''The sooner thousands of miles separate us, the better.''

''I hate to tell you this, but she said she was going to Colorno for a couple of days first.''

Luc made an angry sound in his throat. ''Neither of her sisters is there which means she lied to you.''

''Why would she do that?''

''Because she's probably running to Cesar.'' In fact he was sure of it. She'd couldn't last twelve hours without a man. ''Her next trip on water will probably be a honeymoon cruise. In that case I wish them Godspeed on their way to hell.''

A shadow crossed over his cousin's face. ''Luc—''

''If you're going to tell me she's not like Genevieve, don't waste your breath. Last night put any doubts about that to rest. I've decided all women are alike, offering themselves to the highest bidder.'' Even Nina, Nic's deceased fiancée. But that was a secret Luc and Max would take to their graves.

"I think you're mistaken about Olivia.''

"You don't know what I know,'' Luc lashed out, then lowered his head. "Sorry I snapped, but even the most luscious-looking peach can have a rotten pit at its core. Should she end up becoming Madame Cesar de Falcon, how would you like a permanent new neighbor?''

Nic looked stunned. "You would move to Spain?''

"I can do my engineering anywhere.''

"I think you're getting way ahead of yourself.''

"It's called self preservation, but let's change the subject. I haven't thanked you yet for rescuing us.''

"I was happy to do it, but I must admit your phone call took me by surprise.''

"That storm sneaked up on us.''

"It made the search more difficult. The mist hung in patches out there this morning. I was beginning to get nervous when we couldn't see any sign of the boat. You'll never know my relief when we suddenly found a hole in the clouds and spotted Olivia waving to us.''

"I appreciate your coming. I can always count on you."

"You've come to my aid more times, but seriously Luc. Though Olivia got you into that mess, you have to give her credit for trying to get you out."

"Who's side are you on?"

"Yours. Always."

While they'd been talking, the limo had reached the house and driven into the courtyard. Luc felt for the door handle. "Let's get inside and eat. I want to hear about your next move to catch our jewel thief."

"I wish I knew where to start. I need your input."

Luc's hand tightened on his cane. "In a few more days I can throw this away. Then I'll be free to drive us wherever the trail leads, unhampered."

All bad things were finally coming to an end.

CHAPTER SEVEN

BY THE time the taxi had deposited Olivia at the foot of some steps leading up the steep cliff to the Varano villa, night had fallen over *Positano.* She asked the driver to wait while she found out if anyone was home.

Though cloud cover hid the sky, it seemed as if all the stars had dipped below it to light up the picturesque town with its cubed-shaped houses built into the sides of two mountain slopes.

Wherever she looked, she had an unexcelled panorama of the Mediterranean bordering the Amalfi Coast.

On the way from the train station the driver charmed her with his account of Hercules, the pagan god of strength who loved a nymph called Amalfi. But she died early, and he buried her in the most beautiful place of the world. To immortalize her, he gave it her name.

How would it feel to be immortalized like

that by Luc? The man she loved with every breath in her body...

Her heart heavy, Olivia rang the bell at the side of the door. She didn't have to wait long before a sixtyish-looking housekeeper answered.

"*Signorina?*"

"Hello. Forgive me for dropping by so late, but I just arrived on the train. My name's Olivia Duchess. I've come to see Cesar. Is he here?"

"Olivia?" a male voice called out from the interior. Suddenly the man in shorts and a T-shirt she'd traveled all this way to visit materialized behind the other woman.

Cesar's curious eyes played over her. "This is an unexpected pleasure. Come in." He bore more than a superficial resemblance to his brother. It caused Olivia's heart to bleed all over again.

"The taxi that brought me here is still waiting below."

"*Bien.* I'll take care of everything while Bianca shows you where to freshen up. Afterward you can join me on the terrace. I was eating supper. After your trip here, I'm sure you must be hungry, too." He disappeared down the steps with the agility of an athlete.

"*Signorina?*"

Olivia followed the housekeeper through the fabulous Mediterranean-styled villa to a guest bathroom. Coming directly from the train it felt good to wash her face and comb her hair.

Feeling a little more presentable, she found Bianca, who walked her out to a veranda filled with flowering plants of every color. Lavender bougainvillea overflowed the balcony. Between the fragrance and the soft night air, the scene was one of enchantment. With the right man...

When Cesar returned she looked up at him from the round glass table where she'd taken a seat. "After putting your life on the line at the track, I can see why you choose to come here to unwind. This is paradise."

He took his place across from her. "You say that with such a tragic look in your eyes, I feel the weight of the world in them. May I offer you something to eat first?" She shook her head. "A little wine perhaps?"

"Nothing, thank you. Cesar, please forgive me for bursting in on you like this unannounced. I had no way of knowing whether you were alone, or—"

"I *am* alone, as you can well see."

She bit her lip. "The thing is, you have every right to assume why I've come, but it's—"

"It's not because you've been dying of love

for me and couldn't stay away from me any longer?" he broke in with asperity. "You think I don't know that, *ma belle?*"

Olivia averted her eyes, suddenly feeling like an idiot.

"Contrary to most people's opinion, I'm not quite the shallow fool everyone believes I am, so in love with myself and my love of speed that I imagine the whole world revolves around me and no one else."

"I never said that," she murmured.

"You didn't have to. You were a fan of mine long before you met me. Believing all the hype about me goes with the territory. If I hadn't learned to live with it, I would have gotten out of racing a long time ago."

So there was a dark side to Cesar, too. Maybe it was inherent in the Falcon genes.

He finished the last of the cheese before eyeing her frankly. "There's only one person's opinion who truly matters to me besides my parents'. We used to be as close as brothers," he said with bitter irony. "These days he hates my guts."

She kneaded her hands nervously. "You're talking about Luc."

His eyes grew bleak. "Who else? I gather that's why you're here. To talk about him."

"Yes."

"Because you're in love with him."

"Yes."

"And he's being difficult."

Olivia almost choked on the word.

"I can see that he is," Cesar drawled. "Where do you want to start?"

"At the beginning."

He threw his arm over the back of his chair. "In the beginning, there was Luc. My hero. I wanted to be like him, do everything he did. But he was brilliant in math, fantastic at any sport, and could have any woman he wanted without even thinking about it.

"I on the other hand was a late bloomer who struggled in school, was only passable at most sports, and believe it or not, was scared of women."

"That's how it was with me and Greer," Olivia blurted. "She was the oldest. The smart one with all the ideas. She could do anything! She had so much confidence. Men adored her. I...worshiped her."

Cesar eyed her with compassion. "We're both victims of the youngest-child syndrome."

She nodded.

"One day Luc and our cousins took me to a Formula I race with them. Though Luc had no interest in being a competitor, it was a sport my brother loved to watch.

"When the winner of the Grand Prix walked up to the podium to collect his prize, I saw admiration in Luc's eyes. That was an electrifying moment for me. I decided I would learn to race cars so that Luc would admire *me* like that one day.

"Over the years the sport has been good to me, and with all the endorsements, I've been able to invest in several businesses."

Cesar had been leading up to something important. "But Luc didn't admire you?"

"On the contrary. He backed me, went to most of my races. Supported me when mother wanted me to quit racing before I got killed."

"Then what happened to change everything?"

His expression became a study in pain, reminding her so much of Luc she groaned.

"Her name was Genevieve Leblanc."

Olivia's heart pounded out a nonstop tattoo.

"She came to the Cote D'Azur from Toulon, looking for work. He hired her to be a secretary for the company he'd started up. One thing led to another and they got engaged."

Of course Luc had had girlfriends. But the

knowledge that he'd had a fiancée hit Olivia as if she'd been dealt a physical blow.

"How long ago was this?"

"Almost two years to the day."

She shifted in the chair. Taking her courage in her hands she asked, "Why aren't they married, Cesar?"

He unexpectedly pushed himself away from the table and stood up. "A month before their wedding, Luc had to fly to the States for a special robotics engineering conference. I was in Monza racing and came in third. To my surprise, Genevieve showed up to lend her support while Luc was away.

"It surprised me even more when she insisted on coming back here to Positano, allegedly to cheer me up and enjoy a little vacation from the frantic wedding preparations.

"I told her to make herself comfortable. Then I excused myself. You see, after a race there's a routine I always follow to restore me.

"Strapped in the car like an astronaut, you start to feel claustrophobic. To help me unwind, I get on my dirt bike and push myself physically through the mountain roads here until I've worn myself out. After a swim in the ocean, I fall into bed and sleep for ten to twelve hours without dreams.

"However this time when I got under the covers, I discovered I wasn't alone."

At this point Olivia slid off the chair and walked over to the railing, needing to cling to something.

"No one will ever know the horror I felt. Disgust drove me to the bathroom where I was literally sick. When I returned to the bedroom, she was still there with a smile on her face. She said she thought I understood she was attracted to me, and was positive I reciprocated her feelings.

"She said a lot of things, the upshot being that Luc never had to know. It would be our secret. Then she urged me to come to bed."

A moan came out of Olivia.

"I told her I loved my brother more than my own life. If she didn't tell him what she'd done, then I would. In the next breath I threw her out and told her I never wanted to see her again.

"A few days later, Luc returned from the conference. I was summoned to the family villa where he'd gathered our parents together. He informed us there wasn't going to be a wedding after all. Heartsick as I was for him, I was thankful the truth had come out.

"Later that evening I took Luc aside to talk to him about everything. To my shock he said there wasn't anything to talk about. It was over.''

Olivia swung toward him. "He never let you explain what happened?'' she cried.

"No. A wall had gone up between us. Our relationship has never been the same since.''

"But she could have told him any lie she wanted, and probably did!''

Cesar's eyes were alive with pain. "True. Still, Luc had grown up with me and knew me. He had to know I loved him too much to ever betray him like that. I would have done anything for him.''

"Then she must have painted a picture that made it impossible for him to figure out the truth without help.''

"You're right, but he never gave me the chance. In the two years since his breakup with Genevieve, the only thing he has ever asked of me was to show up on the *Piccione* to meet you after the Grand Prix. I was overjoyed because I thought it meant he'd finally worked it out and realized she'd been the one to blame.''

"So you took me behind the scenes of the racing world in order to get back in your brother's good graces?''

"Yes. But it was no penance, believe me.''

She swallowed hard. "Thank you for your honesty."

He gave her a sheepish glance. "You may not thank me when I tell you everything I did."

"What do you mean?"

"From the moment he called me and asked me to meet the two of you on the boat, I knew instinctively you'd become someone important to him."

She shook her head. "He felt an obligation to me after the horrible way he and your cousins treated us when they thought we were the jewel thieves."

"No, Olivia. Something happened aboard the *Piccione* that changed him. In one sense I was thrilled to think he could have feelings for another woman again. But in another, I was nervous because you showed such an eagerness to get to know me. Especially when you knew all my racing statistics. After the history with Genevieve, I had to proceed carefully."

"I didn't know!" she cried again in anguish. "When I couldn't get him to respond to me, I played up to you in order to make him jealous. It was the worst thing I could have done, but then I'm known for getting myself into the worst messes possible."

One corner of his mouth lifted. "I finally figured that out at the wedding. When I heard you two fighting, I decided to help nature along by inviting you to come to Monza with me.''

''You invited me on purpose? I mean, not because you were interested in me?''

''I could have been very interested if I'd met you before he did. But to answer your question, I decided to test you in the only way I knew how.''

Her eyes grew huge. ''So that business about buying me a ring—''

''Was the carrot I dangled to see if you would go for the bait. A test if you like to prove your worthiness to marry my brother.''

''Cesar—'' Her mind was reeling.

''Not only did you laugh at me, you refused to let me really kiss you. I knew then you loved him heart and soul.''

''I do!'' She clapped her hands to her cheeks. ''So *that's* what you meant on the phone when you said you hoped he would realize it.''

He nodded. ''You'll never know how happy I was to find out you'd gone straight to his house after you left Monza. I took it as a foregone conclusion that by now the two of you would be announcing your own wedding plans.'' He cocked his head. ''How come you're here instead of at the villa with him?''

"Oh, Cesar—I'm in the worst trouble imaginable. He hates me. He really hates me. After everything you've told me, now I know why. I think maybe too much damage has been done."

"Tell me what happened after our phone call."

Without stopping for breath she blurted everything. It was a relief to be able to unburden herself to someone who loved Luc as much as she did.

"When he said the thought of making love to one of his brother's pit babes sickened him, I knew his pain had to be tied up to you in some way. I was such a fool to throw myself at him like that. But nothing else seemed to be working. I thought if I could just break him down a little, then I'd propose to him.

"My greatest worry now is, even if I could get him to listen to reason, he would probably accuse me of wanting to get married on the rebound just because Greer has a husband and I'm at a loose end."

Cesar grinned. "Knowing my brother's engineering brain, that thought has probably crossed his mind already. It's even possible he believes you've picked him because he's Max's cousin and you'll do anything to keep up with your older sister."

Olivia looked stricken. "I hadn't thought of that! He's a very complicated man."

He stared at her through veiled eyes. "The best ones are. I love him. The accident he survived was a blow he didn't need after the emotional devastation of Genevieve's betrayal. He deserves all the happiness life has to give him."

She hung her head. "I don't know what to do. I know what I *should* do. Greer would tell me to go straight home and forget him."

"What do you want to do?" he asked softly.

"Find the path to his heart, but I don't think there's a way."

"After getting up at the crack of dawn to row the *Gabbiano* by yourself to find help, you're too tired to think straight. I'll ask Bianca to show you to one of the guest bedrooms.

"Sometimes when I've exhausted every idea to ace out an opponent on the track, a good night's sleep restores me and I come up with a killer strategy."

She bit her lip. "It would have to be that good to make a dent in his armor."

"The Duchess triplets have a reputation for doing the impossible under the most improbable circumstances. If you can't figure out a way to get to my brother, then it can't be done."

"I think I'm crazy about you, Cesar de Falcon."

"Now she tells me!"

While they smiled at each other with a perfect understanding, Olivia heard Cesar's cell phone go off. His gaze flicked to hers. "My bet it's big brother trying to find out where you are because he can't stand the suspense any longer. What do you want me to tell him?"

Her heart was racing. "What does your caller ID say?"

He pulled it out of his pocket to look. "It's Max."

Olivia didn't know whether to be glad or devastated. She watched Cesar click on. As soon as he'd said *ciao*, he handed her the phone. "It's Greer," he mouthed the words.

Not again—

She turned her back on Cesar. "How did you know I was here?" she demanded of her sister in a hushed tone.

"Maybe because I've lived with you for twenty-seven years and know exactly how your mind works," Greer whispered back. "Olivia Duchess—don't you know you've done the worst thing you could ever do to run straight to

Cesar? Any hope you might have had with Luc has flown straight out the window!''

Olivia couldn't stand it when her sister was right, which was ninety-nine percent of the time. ''You're supposed to be on your honeymoon instead of minding my business.''

''I'm afraid your getting involved with the Falcon brothers has made this all our business! Piper phoned Nic because she was desperate to know where you were.

''You promised to phone her and you never did! She thought you were going to fly home from Genoa, but Nic said you were taking the train to Colorno. When she called there, the maids reported that you never arrived, so she phoned Nic who phoned Max to find out if we knew anything. Piper's frantic!''

''I couldn't call her. Luc and I were marooned on Monte Cristo without a phone.''

''That's not true, Olivia! You know very well Luc had one with him, otherwise how would Nic have known to come and rescue you, let alone *where* to find you!''

Olivia's blue eyes rounded in wonder.

Luc had his cell phone with him the whole time?

Then that meant he'd hidden it...

And that meant he hadn't wanted to be rescued yet, which meant—

Excitement charged her body like a bolt of lightning. This changed everything!

"Thank you for calling me, Greer. I promise to phone Piper right away. Give my love to Max. Enjoy the rest of your honeymoon."

"Olivi—"

She clicked off.

"Is everything all right?" Cesar inquired.

She whirled around and handed him the phone. "Everything's fine! Cesar? Will you do me a favor?" Her plan *had* to work.

"*Bien sûr.* Anything."

"Walk me to the foyer and call for Bianca. When she comes so she can be a witness, tell me to get out of your house."

"*Comment?* What did you say?" he asked incredulously.

"Please just do it? Tell me to leave the premises immediately or you'll call the police and have me arrested for trespassing."

Recognition suddenly dawned in his blue-gray eyes. "Ah—you are up to one of your famous Duchess tricks."

She bit her lip. "You won't give me away?"

He crossed his heart.

Getting into his part, he grabbed hold of her

arm and dragged her into the foyer, calling out in a loud, urgent voice for Bianca as he did so. The housekeeper came running.

"Bianca? Please bring Mademoiselle Duchess's suitcase back. I want her out of this house and gone within two minutes or I am calling for the police."

When he shook Olivia off, almost causing her to stumble because he didn't know his own strength, the older woman gasped before hurrying away to do his bidding.

Taking advantage of her absence, Cesar kissed Olivia's cheek. "*Bonne chance, ma belle,* but I don't think you will need it because you have a way of making your own luck.

"When you reach the first turn in the road below the villa, wait there and a taxi will be along shortly to take you wherever you wish to go."

"Thank you, Cesar. Whether my plan works or not, I want you to know you're wonderful." She gave him a hug before he disappeared, leaving her to face the loyal housekeeper who dropped the suitcase at her feet the way she was supposed to do.

"You heard, Cesar. Go!" She made a violent gesture with her hands.

"I'm leaving, even if he misunderstood my intentions."

The older woman wagged an index finger in front of her. "He does not misunderstand why a woman comes to his house this late at night alone. The only woman he will ever have in this house will be his wife!"

"But I came to talk to him about Luc. Luc's the one I love."

"Then you find my poor Luca and tell *him*. There was trouble in this house once before," she muttered, probably revealing more than she meant to. "And stay away from my poor Cesar. They have both suffered enough!"

"I agree. Thank you for your hospitality, Bianca," she said before closing the door.

By the time she made it to the horseshoe bend in the road with her suitcase, a taxi was waiting for her.

"Thank you for coming."

The driver nodded. "*Si, signorina*. Signore di Falcone told me to take you wherever you wish to go."

"Naples airport. I have to get to Nice before morning."

"*Bene*."

No telling what Luc's plans were. Even though he was supposed to be resting his leg, he might have gone to his parents' home—or to Nic's in Spain.

She hoped not the latter. Any more travel tonight was anathema to her. Besides, she needed to be alone with Luc.

Four hours later another taxi dropped her off in the courtyard of Luc's villa. At five-fifteen in the morning, it was still dark. She paid the driver and got out with her suitcase in hand. To be certain she wasn't stranded, she asked him to wait.

Here we go again.

She walked up to the door and rang the bell. Luc had told her he employed staff during the weekdays, so she expected a maid to answer. When no one came, she pressed the button and didn't let up.

Pretty soon she heard cursing.

A smile broke out on her face. She turned to the taxi driver. ''You can go.''

By the time Luc opened the door wearing the bottom half of a pair of sweats, all she could see were two red taillights disappearing from the courtyard.

''Surprise, surprise. I'm *baaaack*.'' She stepped over his cane and walked in carrying her suitcase.

She probably looked as messy as she felt still dressed in the same skirt and blouse she'd been wearing when he'd last seen her. Everything needed laundering.

Not daring to look at him for fear his expression would terrify her she said, "Sorry to wake you, but now that I'm here you can go back to bed. I know the way to my room."

Without a second's hesitation, she trudged up the staircase to the yellow room she'd chosen for her own. It was heaven to walk in the en suite bathroom and disrobe, anticipating a hot shower.

There'd been too many boat, train and plane rides in one day. She stood under the spray and let the water wash away the grime before she worked the shampoo into a lather.

This was pure luxury. When she wandered into the bedroom a few minutes later with her hair and body wrapped in two fluffy towels, she discovered Luc standing inside the doorway watching her. He was too far away for her to see the look in his eyes. It was just as well she couldn't.

"I don't have anything clean to wear. Do you think you could lend me a T-shirt while I put in a wash?"

"There's a robe in the closet." His voice

sounded like it had come from a dark cavern, but so far he hadn't made a move to throw her out yet. A good sign.

She opened the door to the walk-in closet and found a fleece robe in pale blue hanging on a hook. After putting it on and cinching the belt around her slender waist, she emerged with both towels draped over her arm.

"It's lovely. Thank you for your hospitality. I'll wash my clothes after I've had a good six hours of sleep. Then I'll feel like a new person." She tossed the towels over the back of a chair and climbed under the covers of the bed. "Good night."

She rolled on her side so her back was facing him.

When he turned off the light, she assumed he was either too exhausted or too enraged, or maybe both, to deal with her until tomorrow. But in that regard, she turned out to be dead wrong. The side of the bed gave right behind her.

"What do I have to do to get rid of you?"

If she hadn't known he'd purposely lied to her about the phone—if he hadn't covered her mouth with a hunger equal to her own, his question would have driven her away for good.

"You still owe me a Riviera trip. All you

have to do is call someone to fit the *Gabbiano* with a new sail and repair the short in the wiring. When I wake up, I'll get us packed and we'll fly back to Vernazza. We can buy some books and groceries at the port."

"That's all I have to do," he murmured with quiet menace.

"Well, there might be some other things, but I'd rather you surprised me. Oh—there is one thing—"

She turned over and found herself wedged against his hip. "We'll need to stop by the hospital first to get your phone. We don't want to go off this time without it. You know. In case something else goes wrong and we're stranded.

"It was just plain lucky Giovanni remembered about the wiring and called Fabio. We were down to a couple of eggs and one plum. We might not be so lucky again."

He didn't move a muscle, but she saw something flicker in the silvery recesses of his eyes illuminated by the light from the hall.

"Where have you been today?" he demanded.

"Here and there."

"What in the hell does that mean?"

"Sometimes at home when I'm upset, I ride

the subway to the end of the line and back while I think."

"You were upset?"

"Well naturally. Our trip turned out to be a fiasco, and I'd had my heart set on it."

She heard a sharp intake of breath. "So you rode the train to the end of the line and back, is that it?"

"More or less."

"That must have been some ride."

"It was. I met at least fifty playboys who all wanted to show me the time of my life if I would let them."

His lips thinned to a white line. "So why didn't you take one of them up on his offer?"

"The kind of playboy I'm looking for owns the train, he doesn't ride on it."

"You wouldn't by any chance have ridden as far as Positano—" He left the sentence hanging in the air.

"Since you know I did, why don't you just be honest about it and ask me if Cesar and I went shopping for a ring? But then you already know the answer to that question because I wouldn't be here banging on your door if we were celebrating our engagement."

"What's the matter? Wasn't he home?"

Tired of the sneer in his tone she said, "Oh, he was there all right."

"And?"

"It was a sobering experience. I'd only gone there to talk to him about you because you gave me permission. He turned on me just like you did and told me to get out!"

"You're lying."

"If you don't believe me, ask Bianca. She dumped my suitcase at my feet, muttering something about how much her poor Luca and her poor Cesar had suffered.

"I ended up having to walk to town from the villa at one o'clock in the morning carrying my suitcase, which was so heavy my arm still aches." She hoped one little lie wouldn't make her a horrible person.

"I warned you those rocks might turn out to be a weight around your neck."

"At least they're not as heavy as the burden you and Cesar carry in your hearts."

Luc suddenly got up from the bed, taking away the warmth of his solid frame. "What in blazes are you talking about?"

Talking about Cesar had been a calculated risk on her part.

"Grief. I'm no stranger to it, either. What you need is a little cheering up. How about teaching me how to sail? You could lie on deck to rest your leg and bark out instructions. I'll do all the work. I'd like to take some good memories back to New York with me. They're going to have to last a long time."

He rubbed the back of his neck. "You have a sister living in Italy you can visit any time you want."

"That's the whole point. Greer needs her space with Max. He doesn't want to be married to triplets, so Piper and I aren't planning to descend on her more than once a year."

"I thought you were on the hunt for a Riviera playboy. A once a year visit's going to cut down on your window of opportunity."

"That's all right. Greer caught hers. One out of three isn't bad. Besides, I've got a new Internet business to run. But I don't want to think about work while I'm on vacation. It shouldn't take that long to repair the boat, right?

"However if the thought of being with me sickens you so much, I'll go to Vernazza and hire someone to take me sailing on the *Gabbiano*. Since you owe me, I'll put it on your bill. Now if you don't mind, I need some sleep, so I would appreciate it if you would turn out the hall light."

CHAPTER EIGHT

"Nic? Are you awake?"

Luc heard a groaning sound come over the phone line. "I am now. Another emergency must have come up for you to call at six in the morning."

"Emergency—catastrophe— You name it."

"I take it we're talking about Olivia."

He closed his eyes tightly. "She's back."

"As in—"

"As in under my roof, using my shower, sleeping in the bedroom next to mine." The sight of her in that towel would haunt him forever.

"When did this happen?"

"An hour ago."

"Where's she been?"

"I'll give you one guess."

"Then—"

"Don't ask—" Luc cut him off. "I'm not going to be able to get rid of her until she's taken her damn boat trip. Fabio will know someone who could repair the wiring and put up a new sail today. But I need you to crew for us.''

''You don't need me when you've got Olivia. She could do it if you showed her how.''

He grimaced. ''That's her plan.''

A sound of exasperation came out of Nic. ''If you really don't want to be with her, why did you let her in the door?''

''You know why. She's Greer's sister. If I offend her too deeply, it will end up affecting Max. That's the last thing I want to see happen.''

''Point taken.''

''The way I figure it, if we follow her original itinerary, let her have her fun, she'll finally go home. Then we can get back to business as usual.''

After a long silence, ''You want a fully loaded boat?''

''That's the idea. Let's not give her anything to complain about. I'll do the cooking while you play captain.''

''Just like old times.''

''Not quite,'' Luc murmured. ''This time she won't be trying to run away. If there's one good thing to come of this, a few more days rest and I won't ever need the cane again. At that point

I can leave her in your capable hands for the rest of the trip. You don't mind seeing her off on the plane in Malaga, do you?''

''You know better than to ask that question. I'll get packed and take off for Vernazza.''

Luc knew he was asking a lot of his cousin, but this was one time when he had no other choice. Being alone in this house with Olivia was bad enough. Being alone with her on the *Gabbiano* was out of the question. What he needed was the gift of forgetfulness, but there was no such animal.

I've been thinking about...us.

Us?

Yes. You and me. Since Cesar knows I turned to you, and we're probably not going to make it to Ischia after all, what do you say we take advantage of our situation for the duration of our trip.

Luc's lungs constricted because he would never know what really went on between her and his brother. Even if they hadn't made love, she'd nursed a passion for Cesar long before she'd met Luc.

Heaven help him, how long until he stopped caring?

''Nic?''

''Yes?''

Luc expelled the breath he'd been holding. "Thank you. You know what I'm trying to say."

"I do. Without you and Max, I'd never have made it this far. We'll talk later."

After they'd hung up, Luc placed a call to Fabio who told him not to worry. The repairs would be done by late afternoon.

With that settled, he went back to bed. Unfortunately his sleep was sporadic and fitful, denying him the one temporary panacea for the blackness that had descended with a vengeance since Olivia's arrival.

Another three days of torment loomed ahead of him. Three days where he couldn't hibernate in order to banish certain images from his mind.

Thank heaven for Nic who would be there to help him fight this sickness.

Like Max, Luc had caught the Duchess virus, but unlike his cousin, he'd developed serious complications for which there was no cure.

After another half hour of tossing and turning, he got up to shower and shave. He was just coming back in the bedroom to get dressed when he heard the doorbell ring.

He glanced at his watch. It was ten after ten. Whoever it was, one of the staff would get it, or so he thought. When the bell rang again and again, he suddenly remembered he'd given his help the rest of the week off.

Whoever it was didn't plan on going away any time soon.

Throwing on his robe, he started for the stairs with his cane. Halfway down he caught sight of Olivia's long, beautiful legs. She was still dressed in the blue robe and had already opened the door.

"Madame Falcon—"

Hell. That was all he needed.

"*Bonjour, mademoiselle.* Is my son here?"

"I'm here, *maman*."

She entered the house. "Don't come the rest of the way, *mon fils*. I only dropped by to see how your leg was doing."

His elegant, black-haired mother eyed him with concern, acting for all the world as if she wasn't shocked to discover one of Greer's sisters on the premises.

With those cheeks a warm pink, and her golden curls in alluring disarray, Olivia looked as if she'd just left Luc's bed. No doubt it was the same way she'd looked in the dark the night before last when he'd come close to devouring her, all rosy skin and succulent flesh.

Somehow he'd stopped short of taking the

last bite. He would have consumed a pit that would have filled his soul with bitterness.

"He's on it way too much," his nemesis spoke up before Luc could. "I'm afraid I'm to blame for that. Last night, or should I say at five this morning, I arrived on his doorstep, having just come from visiting Cesar."

Olivia had his mother's attention now.

"How is my younger son?"

"I'll tell you all about him in a minute. Why don't you go upstairs with Luc and I'll bring some tea and rolls. I discovered Luc had given his staff a few days off so I volunteered to wait on him."

"That's very kind of you."

"Not at all. It's the least I can do to reciprocate. Your sons are the greatest hosts in the world, something they learned growing up with such a wonderful mother. Between Cesar showing me the racing world, and Luc taking me sailing, I've been having the time of my life and can't bear for it to end," she added before disappearing.

Luc shouldn't have been surprised a woman with no scruples would make a comment like that to his mother.

"The Duchess triplets are so charming, aren't they?" Once they reached his room she grasped his face in her hands and kissed him on both cheeks. "I'm glad someone's here to take care of you this morning. Now lie down and put your leg up."

She took the cane from him and rested it against the end table while he got back in bed. "The first thing I want to know is, what did the doctor say about your progress?"

"My leg will never be as good as new, but in three more days I won't have to use a prop anymore."

Her eyes glistened with tears. "One of my prayers has been answered anyway."

Luc averted his eyes, aware his mother agonized over the fact that neither he nor Cesar had settled down yet. Ever since Max announced his engagement in June she'd been making maternal noises. It had only heightened the tension already existing between him and Cesar.

"Here we are."

His uninvited houseguest entered his bedroom carrying a tray with everything needed to enjoy a delicious breakfast. No surprise there, either. Olivia was a woman equally at home in the kitchen as the bedroom.

She set it down on the coffee table between the two love seats. "Please excuse me for answering the door in this guest robe, Madame

Falcon. I'm washing my clothes as we speak. The *Gabbiano* didn't have a washer or dryer.''

''The *Gabbiano*?''

Luc groaned. ''It's Giovanni's boat, *maman*. The *Piccione* wasn't available.''

''It's not a problem,'' Olivia assured his mother.

She served them a plate of rolls and tea, then poured a cup for herself and came to stand next to the bed where his mother was seated next to him.

''Right now the boat is getting a new sail and the wiring's being fixed so I can enjoy what's left of my holiday. But before Luc tells you about us being caught in a storm, you were anxious to hear how Cesar is doing.''

''I'm always anxious about him. He hasn't been home since his win.''

This was one time when Luc's mother was better off not knowing what went on behind the scenes. But it was as if Olivia could read Luc's mind because in the next breath she said, ''I don't pretend to know a great deal about your sons, but from what little I've seen, they crave their down time away from the masses.''

Shut up, Olivia.

His mother had forgotten he was in the room. ''What do you mean?''

"Cesar sits alone on his terrace high above Amalfi's resting place, while Luc contemplates the world from this eyrie. It must come from being born on a hillside."

His mother chuckled. "Their father is the same. He feels claustrophobic without a view to look down upon. You're very observant."

"So is Bianca. She fusses around Cesar like a grandmother with a beloved grandson. It was very touching the way she tried to protect him from me."

She blinked. "From you?"

Olivia smiled. "Yes. Cesar told me he always spends a week there after a race and assured me the door would be open if I wanted to visit before I left for the States. I thought with the *Gabbiano* in for repairs, I would take a train ride and drop in on him.

"But when Bianca answered the door, she had no idea I was a cousin-in-law of sorts through marriage to Luc and Cesar. She thought I was one of the women from the track who flings themselves headlong at Cesar. Apparently it's an occupational hazard."

"It's disgusting."

"I couldn't agree more. Especially since Cesar had already confided to me that a woman engaged to one of his best friends showed up at the villa a couple of years ago uninvited and caused him real grief.''

The croissant Luc had been eating fell to his plate.

"He never said anything about that to his father or me."

"I don't imagine that's something he would want anyone to know about. He's too much of a gentleman to hurt his friend. Bianca was witness to the whole thing and kept his secret. But I understand she's been his self-appointed watchdog ever since."

"Good for her!"

"I agree. That's why it didn't bother me when she practically threw my suitcase at me on my way out."

"She was that rude to you?"

"I didn't mind. In fact I admired her loyalty. Before she slammed the door, she informed me that the only woman who would ever be allowed to spend the night at the villa with Cesar would be his wife."

"His father and I live in hope he'll meet the right person one day."

"He will. Right now he's doing everything he can to be successful at what he does best. It's hard when you're the younger sibling."

Damn if that tremor in her voice didn't sound genuine to Luc.

"What do you mean, my dear?"

"Luc is like my sister Greer. You know. Perfect."

While Luc sat there in shock, his mother patted Olivia's hand. "Ah, you miss her. Of course you do being a triplet."

"No one was ever good enough for her until Max came along."

"I've never seen my nephew so happy."

"Mother and Daddy would have adored him."

"You must miss them very much, too."

"You can't imagine. Luc and Cesar are so lucky to have you."

On cue, Luc's mother turned to look at him. "Did you hear that, *mon fils*?"

Luc had already rolled out of the other side of the bed. "I heard, *maman*."

He'd heard something else, too. Until he could talk to Cesar alone, he would have no peace. But before he came face to face with his brother, he needed to be able to stand on his own two feet without help.

"If you're through eating, I'll take the tray and give you some time alone. Ask Luc to tell you about our trip to Monte Cristo."

"That dreary place?"

He shut the door to the bathroom on the rest of their conversation.

Vernazza took on a pinkish glow at sunset. Even Olivia felt bathed in it as she jumped down from the helicopter. Her gaze automatically flew to the pier. To her joy a sail not yet unfurled had been attached to the mast of the *Gabbiano*.

With the wiring fixed, she was getting a second chance for her dream trip of a lifetime with Luc. Just the two of them sailing the high seas.

The first time aboard the *Piccione* didn't count, not with her sisters and Luc's cousins around.

Olivia refused to let his vile mood dampen her spirits. Since his mother's unexpected visit, he'd been more unapproachable than usual. Instead of flinging scathing retorts at her meant to injure, he'd chosen not to talk unless absolutely necessary.

She hoped to heaven it meant the things she'd let drop about her visit to Cesar's were eating him alive. Surely at some point he would be driven to learn the truth for himself. But maybe that was wishful thinking.

Olivia had taken a terrible risk discussing

painful, private family issues with his mother. Luc might never forgive her for it, but it was that or walk away from him. Her jaw hardened. That was something she couldn't do.

As before, she carried both suitcases and paced her steps to his. When they drew closer, she spied a lot of things on deck that hadn't been there before; a sun mattress, water skis, snorkeling gear, deck chairs and a lounger.

She let out a sound of delight.

"I take it you're pleased."

"I'm delighted." She lowered the suitcases into the boat before getting in herself. Luc moved too fast for her to help him down. She assumed his medication had dulled his pain for the moment.

"Why don't you stretch out on that lounger and tell me what to do first? I'd like to sail for a while along the coast before we have to put in at the next port."

He cocked one black eyebrow. "You don't want to get settled in first?"

"We already ate an early dinner, and there'll be time to unpack later."

"Give me a minute to go below then."

"Okay. Hurry."

His mouth twisted into a strange smile before he disappeared down the stairs. She didn't know what to make of it. Maybe beneath the casement of ice beat a heart that was excited to be alone with her, too, but he would never own up to it.

Olivia hugged her arms to her waist and looked all around, soaking in the atmosphere. This was her last chance to work on him.

Earlier in the day while Luc slept, she'd gone shopping to buy some sleepwear and a few casual outfits. The white cargo pants and aqua top she'd put on were perfect for evening when the temperature turned cooler.

Just before they'd left the villa, she'd phoned Piper who was still in bed at the apartment in Kingston. Afraid her sister would try to discourage her from taking this trip, Olivia didn't give her a chance to talk.

Instead she explained she and Luc were on their way out the door, and she'd call her again in a couple of days. After telling her she loved her, Olivia hung up the phone, relieved to have touched base with Piper without letting it turn into a frustrating exchange.

A few fishermen walked past, calling out to her in Italian. Words like *bellissima*. She smiled and waved back.

It reminded her of the evening she and her sisters had run away from Luc and his cousins on their newly purchased bikes. Every male along the road had whistled and shouted at them. But she'd only wanted Luc's attention. No one else's.

Now she was alone with him. Nothing compared to the feelings alive inside of her at this very moment.

"*Señorita Olivo?* It's time to set sail for Monterosso. Are you ready for your first lesson?"

Olivia's heart did a nosedive that went straight through the floor of the boat.

She'd heard that voice before. Yesterday morning in fact. It was as familiar as Luc's. Not that she didn't like Nic. He was awesome. But his presence could only mean one thing...

Don't let him know how you feel. Don't let either of them know. She would beat Luc at his game if it killed her!

She turned around with a beatific smile on her face. Luc had come back up on deck with him.

"Nic—what a fabulous surprise! I'm so glad you're here. Can you be with us the whole trip?"

"Of course. I've cleared my calendar of business so I could come on this holiday, too. We'll sail all the way to Marbella where you will be a guest at my house for a change."

"Terrific!" She ran over and gave him an enthusiastic hug in front of Luc who by this time had stretched out on the lounger. She beamed up at his cousin. "This will be perfect. Now I have someone to enjoy the nightlife with me."

His brown eyes gleamed. "You like dancing?"

"I adore it. This is turning out much better than I'd dared hope," she replied in all honesty as visions of new possibilities to provoke Luc filled her mind. "Your presence relieves me of a worry."

"You should have no worries on vacation!"

"It's just that I promised your aunt I'd take good care of her son on this trip. With you along as captain of the *Gabbiano*, nothing can go wrong."

"You didn't always think that." He grinned.

She grinned back. "A lady is known to change her mind."

Nic chuckled. "We'll spell each other off helping Luc."

"Absolutely. But right now I want my first sailing lesson."

"Anything to please one of Max's sisters-in-law. I'd like to stay in his good graces if you know what I mean."

"That works both ways, Nic. I want to be the kind of sister-in-law he admires so he'll never wish we weren't related." *Unlike someone else she knew.*

"Max would never wish that."

"Piper's so worried about interfering, she says she won't be coming to Europe again except for the christening of their first child. Unless Max and Greer decide to adopt, that won't be happening."

A frown broke out on his face. "Señorita Piper said that?"

"Yes. I'm afraid she was born with enough angst for the three of us. It's the *artiste* in her. She has a conscience that works overtime."

Just then Olivia made the mistake of allowing her eyes to stray to Luc's. He was staring at her as if to say that explained why Olivia didn't have a trace of one.

"I believe it's the middle child syndrome," she continued to explain to Nic. "Piper's the peacemaker."

Nic's brows formed a distinct bar. "It won't please Max if she stays away from Greer with the result that his wife is upset."

"But Piper sees it as doing Max a favor. When he makes remarks about the three of us being joined in a seamless line, she doesn't think he's teasing. Frankly, neither do I.''

He eyed her with speculation. ''How is Piper handling being alone?''

Was that an idle question, or was there something more significant behind his query? Olivia decided to find out.

''Oh, she's not alone. Tom could hardly wait for her to get back from the wedding.''

The silence following her remark spoke volumes. So did his next question. ''Shall we set sail? You'll find a life jacket in the locker behind you.''

She turned to get it and put it on, aware of Luc's silvery gaze following her every movement. ''Your first mate is ready.''

Nic flashed her that stunning Castilian smile that masked many secrets. ''All right. Untie the ropes, then report to the mast.''

''Aye Aye, sir.''

They worked in harmony. He started the engine. The *Gabbiano* moved smoothly out of the harbor to open water.

''Feel that breeze?''

She nodded.

''Here comes your first lesson.''

Nic was a master teacher. Within a few minutes she'd undone the sail the way he'd told her. The wind took over the rest, filling it until it resembled a fat pillow. She almost fell as the boat listed and shot forward.

They were moving without the aid of the engine. Though Olivia was devastated to think Luc hadn't wanted to be alone with her, she couldn't help but cry out from the sheer exhilaration of knifing through the water toward the fading light in the west.

"What do you think?" Nic called to her.

She lifted her face to experience the full effect of the salt spray. "I'm in heaven!"

So was Nic. She could tell by his exultant laugh. Out of the periphery she noticed Luc glowering.

The steady breeze drove them as if by an unseen hand. It was love at the first lunge for Olivia. "I feel like a dolphin or a tuna!"

He laughed harder and she joined him. Too soon he pointed to some lights along the coast. "Monterosso!"

"Already?"

"You want to go on to the next town?"

"No! I want to see everything!"

"Then you shall!" he assured her before taking over. With the greatest of expertise he brought them around to the port. The town sparkled like a woman's diamond tiara.

Once they reached the buoys, he folded up the sail and they glided to the shore where a lot of other boats had anchored for the night.

She could hear music and voices. People were out swimming, playing on the beach.

Olivia couldn't wait to join them. She'd put on her bikini ahead of time. It only took her a minute to fling off her top and pants.

"I'll be back!" she called over her shoulder. Ignoring Luc's muttered imprecation, she got up on the side of the boat and dove in.

The cool water couldn't have been more inviting. It grew warmer nearer the sand. Olivia swam around, floating on her back so she could take in the view.

On shore a bunch of guys who looked to be in their early twenties were tossing a ball around. One of them missed it, and it flew out over the water. She caught it and tossed it back. At that point they urged her to join them.

Still in pain from Luc's latest cruel strategy to keep his distance from her, she told the guys she would love to. Why not.

They were an odd mixture of Croatians, Germans and Danes, all of whom knew a little English. For the next hour she had a great time while they teased her and laughed over her mispronunciation of words.

The one named Lars told her they were moving on to a discotheque and asked her to come. Though he seemed nice enough, she knew a guy on the make when she saw one.

Claiming fatigue, she declined with a thank you and ran into the water. Not to be daunted, Lars followed after her. By the time she'd reached the *Gabbiano,* he caught hold of one foot as she was climbing the ladder.

"Seriously." She turned to him. "It's late."

"Tomorrow you sleep. Tonight you party."

Before she could say another word, hands of steel gripped her upper arms and lifted her bodily into the boat.

"Take your party elsewhere." Luc's forbidding tone and presence had the guy doing a back flip away from the ladder. He took off like a flying fish.

Olivia had to admit she was relieved. But she refused to give Luc that satisfaction or tell him she was sorry if he'd hurt his leg helping her get away from Mr. Hands. Instead, she hurried below.

Nic was in the galley. She said hi as she rushed past him to get some things out of her suitcase.

After her shower she dried off and put on a new pair of cotton lounging pajamas that were

perfectly modest. When she opened the door to
the passageway and started for the stairs, Luc
was leaning on his cane, blocking her exit.

His eyes played over her damp curls before
wandering to her mouth. She could imagine him
kissing her like he had done the other night. Her
body turned to fire.

"You made a wrong turn. The cabin's the
other way."

"I'm going up on deck to enjoy myself."

"Not tonight, and not in that outfit. The deck
is Nic's domain after eleven at night.
Considering the long day he has put in, he's
bushed. Not that you would care about his exhaustion."

It took every bit of willpower to hold on to
her control. "Apparently you're not that worried about it, either," she struck back, deriving
pleasure from seeing the way his lips formed a
pencil-thin line. "I had no way of knowing he
would put himself at your disposal at a moment's notice without concern for his own welfare."

"Well now that you do, I suggest you climb
up in your bunk so we can all go to sleep."

"You can try," she said in a husky voice.
With great daring she raised up on tiptoe to
brush her lips against his. "There's more where

that came from. All you have to do is call out my name in the night. I promised your mother I would accommodate your every wish.''

Frozen gray shards stared back at her. ''You didn't fool her you know.''

''Of course not. She has to be an exceptional woman to have raised a son as brilliant, troubled, paranoid and dense as you, and still be alive. If Monaco gave out a prize for the best mother in the Principality, she would win hands down. Good night, my proud Falcon who flies alone. Sweet dreams.''

She went to bed and pulled the covers over her head. The routine established a pattern for the next three days; sailing lessons interspersed with water sports and good food.

It was the perfect regimen to keep from thinking about Luc who lay around on deck with his nose in a book. Except for spotting her when she went waterskiing, he pretty well ignored her. Any remarks were addressed to Nic. Mostly they discussed theories about who stole the family jewel collection.

In the evenings Nic took Olivia to the local bars and they danced or walked the streets of the little towns of Corniglia, Manarola and Riomaggiore, all part of the Cinque Terre region.

Snorkeling in and around San Remo's grottos had been an especially memorable experience for her. Luc joined them for part of a morning. Though he wasn't any friendlier to her, he seemed to enjoy the exercise and knew all the little secret spots where the tourists didn't go.

The next day they docked at Nice and spent time exploring the Chateau D'Eze positioned thirteen hundred feet above the impossibly blue water. By the time her head touched the pillow that night, she slept the sleep of the exhausted.

Unbeknownst to her, Nic had taken advantage of the wind during the night. While she was oblivious, he'd sailed them past Monaco. When she looked out the window of the cabin the next morning, the unforgettable vista of Cannes lay before her eyes.

She still had a hard time believing she'd been to places on the Riviera she'd only seen in movies and books.

Per usual Luc had gotten up early and prepared their breakfast. Since it involved no heavy lifting, that was the one job he could do using his cane without straining his leg too much.

The three of them ate on deck while the two men laid out her walking itinerary for the day with Nic. Tomorrow they'd be moving on to Marseilles, then Perpignan. In the days that followed they would sail to the famous ports along the Spanish coast.

Olivia's greatest fear was that they would reach Marbella before Luc showed any sign of wanting to be alone with her. Maybe if she bought him something he would really like, it would soften him up a bit.

When she and Nic went ashore, they spent a full morning sightseeing, but after lunch at the Carlton on the famous La Croisette seafront, she asked him to take her to a book shop that catered to science fiction buffs.

If he thought it a strange request, he didn't say so. For several hours they both poked around the huge store that sold new and used books.

Nic was big into linguistics and heraldry.

During their walks she'd discovered he was an expert on bloodlines and primogeniture. In fact he was writing a book on it in his spare time.

While he found himself some fascinating reading material, she asked the man waiting on her to look up the latest novel about robots. She risked buying Luc something he'd already read, but maybe she'd get lucky.

In the end she bought five books. The most recent one dealt with a robot named Cog. Two other books dealing with artificial intelligence had been published in the last couple of years.

The last two were some of the first books about robots ever published. They dated back to the late eighteen hundreds.

If nothing else, Luc might find them amusing to read again, if he'd read them, which he probably had. In that case he could have fun picking their research apart.

When Nic joined her at the checkout counter with three books he wanted, she insisted on paying for everything as her way of saying thank you for all his help.

Nic accepted with his usual good grace. At four-thirty they headed back to the *Gabbiano*. Once on board she called down the stairs.

"Yoohoo, Luc. We're back!"

She was excited to see his face when she gave him her gift, but there was no answer. She went below. Maybe he'd fallen asleep.

To her surprise he wasn't in bed. If he'd been swimming around the boat, she would have noticed. A little perplexed, she left the cabin and discovered Nic in the kitchen. He held a piece of paper in his hand.

Beyond his shoulder she noticed Luc's cane lying across the drop table. Olivia's eyes flew to Nic's. Their gazes met.

''He left you a note.'' The nuance in his tone alarmed her.

Olivia's mouth suddenly went dry. She knew she wasn't going to like what she heard. ''W-what does it say?'' she stammered.

''I'll let you read it.''

CHAPTER NINE

Nic left the kitchen so she could have her privacy.

She put the bag of books on the table. Her hand trembled as she picked up the paper.

My dear Duchess cousin, never let it be said that the Varano cousins didn't honor their obligations to their long lost relations from that upstart nation across the Atlantic.

You're in the best of hands with Nic. He'll make certain the rest of your ten day trip to the French and Spanish portions of the Riviera is fulfilled and memorable.

For Max and Greer's sake, let's agree to go our separate ways without bitterness. I don't want my first day of freedom from prison to be marked by rancor.

Knowing you as I do, you'll probably have success with your new Internet business.

After all, you're one of the very unexpected and astounding Duchesses of Kingston.
Luc

She stood there for a long time staring into space. Unexpected and astounding were code words for "freak of nature."

This was the end of the road. She'd gone too far. She'd stepped over an invisible line Luc had drawn long before he'd ever met her. Everyone had tried to warn her, but she hadn't played it like a Duchess.

Scalding tears ran down her cheeks.

"Olivia?" Nic whispered directly behind her.

She wiped at the tears with the back of her hand. "Did you know he was going to leave?"

"Yes. Today the doctor gave him a clean bill of health. Now that he can drive a car again, he's anxious to get on with his life. If you'd known Luc before his accident and realized how much he loved all sports, especially skiing, you would understand how hard it has been for him to be restricted in his physical activities."

"I can imagine." She sniffed. "He's very lucky to have such an understanding cousin who has been his best friend, too. Would you call me a taxi please? I'm going to fly home from Nice today."

"If you'll allow me, I'll ring for a limo and take you to the airport myself."

She loved Nic for not trying to persuade her to continue on with the trip. He would have taken her and shown her the best time in the world. That was because he was kind and honorable.

"What about the *Gabbiano*?"

"I'll arrange for someone to sail it back to Vernazza. All it requires is a phone call."

"Well then. I guess that's it. Excuse me while I pack and get things cleaned up around here." Her glance flicked to the table. "What will you do with his cane?"

"Discard it along with any refuse left on the boat."

"Do you care if I keep it?"

"Of course not."

"Thank you."

Three hours later her overseas flight was announced in the first-class waiting lounge at the Nice airport. The cane had been taken away as a security precaution and would be given to her once she landed at Kennedy airport in New York.

Nic gave her one last hug. "Have a safe flight. Give my regards to your sister."

"I will." She raised tear-filled eyes to his. "The next time you see Luc, will you make sure he gets these books? Tell him—" She bit her lip. "Tell him they're a peace offering from me."

He gave her a solemn nod before striding out of the lounge.

"Etienne? Have you seen my brother?"

The dark-blond chief mechanic who'd hit on Olivia looked up from the under-chassis he was working on.

"Luc!" He got to his feet and started wiping his greasy hands with a rag. "No one has seen you around here in a long time. Look at you— walking as if you were never in that accident. Congratulations."

"*Merci,* Etienne."

"It must feel good."

"It does, believe me. Is my brother around?"

"He's out testing the new wheels we put on his car."

"How long do you think he will be?"

"Another hour maybe, but if you need to talk to him, I'll tell him to come in."

"I'd appreciate that."

"Of course. *Un moment,*" he said before disappearing.

Luc had called the villa in Positano when he hadn't been able to reach Cesar on his cell phone. Bianca told him he'd gone back to Monaco to start training for his next race.

That explained why Luc hadn't been able to make contact. It was one of their mother's greatest concerns that when Cesar was at the track, he didn't check his voice mail until the end of the day. For once Luc could understand her frustration since it was imperative he talk to his brother. The conversation that should have taken place two years ago couldn't be put off a moment longer.

Before Luc had hung up with Bianca, he'd chatted with her for a few minutes, asking her how things were going. Never one to hold back with an opinion, she launched into a backlog of news about her family and friends, the dog next door that was such a nuisance.

And speaking of nuisances, she'd had to throw out one of Cesar's fans who was insane enough to come to the villa. When Luc commented that he thought Cesar brought women there after every race, she started raging at him for suggesting such a thing.

Luc asked her why she was so upset. She pretended not to understand and said she needed to get off the phone, but he wouldn't let her go. When he accused her of keeping a secret from him, she cried out he would have to ask Cesar.

"If you're talking about Genevieve, I already know about it, Bianca."

The older housekeeper had sounded shocked. Then she'd broken down in tears before it all came gushing out, verifying everything Olivia had alluded to.

As Luc listened, his throat swelled in pain for his silent accusations against his brother, for the two years Bianca had kept her silence.

Because Luc had believed Genevieve's lies, he'd refused to let Cesar explain. In consequence their family had suffered needlessly. With hindsight Luc could see that his intransigence had spilled over to his cousins who'd been forced to tread softly around him.

"Luc?"

At the sound of his brother's voice, he turned in his direction.

"Your cane—it's gone! You must be three inches taller!" The joy in Cesar's voice was so heartfelt, Luc felt crucified all over again for the injury he'd caused his brother.

Cesar stood in the doorway, still wearing his driver's suit. His dark hair was mussed from the helmet he'd been wearing. It took Luc back years to a time when they were young boys playing Space soldiers.

Pere Noel had brought them spacemen costumes for Christmas. Luc had immediately transformed his into a robot suit. No matter how many times Cesar begged to wear it, Luc wouldn't let him.

Olivia had accused him of always having to be in charge, like Greer. At the time he'd laughed off her comment, but he wasn't laughing now. Without Luc realizing it, Cesar had grown up to be one of the world's great Formula I drivers and a successful businessman in his own right.

But he was a lot more than that. Luc realized he was looking at the greatest brother a man could ever have. If it hadn't been for Olivia...

"How about taking a ride with *me* for a change, *mon frère?*"

There was a palpable silence while Cesar's gaze searched his. He must have seen the pleading in Luc's because he suddenly broke into a grin.

"I don't know. It's been a while since you've sat behind the wheel of a car, but I'm willing to risk it considering it's you." The last came out in a husky tone.

Luc studied his brother. He didn't deserve this second chance, but because Cesar was the better man, Luc was getting it. "If I've forgotten how, I know I've got the best there is to help me.''

''Etienne? I'm taking off with my brother!'' Cesar shouted with the kind of excitement Luc hadn't heard in years. ''Don't plan on seeing me until you see me!''

''...so what do you think? Try to picture them polished smooth.''

Piper stared at the rocks laid out on the counter in the kitchen. Then her glance shifted to Olivia. ''They're pretty.''

''No, they're not. You're just saying that to make me feel better.''

Her sister cocked her head. ''In theory I think your idea to sell them for paperweights is terrific. Tell you what. Let's get in the car and go to that lapidary shop on Decater Avenue. We'll ask whoever's in charge to give us their honest opinion.''

Olivia lowered her head. ''They won't be honest. They're out to make money and will probably tell me the end product will look like jewels.''

Piper poured them both a glass of milk to drink with their sandwiches. She brought them to the table. ''You know what I think?''

"What?" Olivia asked before biting into her bologna and cheese.

"You're beginning to sound as cynical as someone else I could mention."

"I don't want to talk about him."

"Then how come you brought home his cane?"

The last bite Olivia took tasted like sawdust. "It'll serve as a reminder of my terrible judgment. Did I tell you I'm never going to Europe again?"

"In a year's time you won't feel so awful."

"What's happening in a year?"

"Greer and Max's first wedding anniversary. I'm sure they'll throw a big party and we'll be expected to come."

"I have a better idea. We'll have one for them here. A picnic. Just the four of us. Waterskiing on the Hudson."

"In whose boat? We can't ask Fred or Tom."

"We'll rent one."

Piper finished off the second half of her sandwich. "Maybe between both our businesses, we can make enough money this year to buy our own boat."

"Yeah." Olivia would love to prove to Luc she'd made her fortune.

"Come on. Let's go see a man about a rock polisher."

Olivia drained the last of her milk, then got up from the table. "Thanks for coming with me."

"It's all for one, remember?"

When she felt her sister give her a hug, Olivia lost it. "I disgust him, Piper."

"No, you don't. It's the situation that shut him down emotionally. His fiancée committed the unpardonable betrayal by approaching his brother. When you came along and showed so much interest in Cesar, Luc thought he was being betrayed again and you received the brunt of his pain."

"But Luc was the one who introduced us! He didn't have to."

"Of course he did. Sooner or later you would have found out Cesar Villon was Luc's brother. When you were already angry with Luc and his cousins for what they did to us, how would you have felt about Luc once you found out he'd kept *that* information from you?"

Olivia looked at her sister through eyes drowning in tears. Since the answer was obvious, there was no point in responding.

"Luc was trying to make up to you for the bad time he and his cousins put us through. It was simply a ghastly coincidence that he found out your greatest wish in coming to Europe was to watch Cesar race in the Grand Prix.''

''But not all women racing fans are groupies,'' she exclaimed before burying her face in her hands.

''Of course not. You just happened to fall in love with the wrong man. Max was worried for you, so he told Greer about Luc. When Nic could see you were starting to care too much, he confided similar fears to me. Unfortunately their warnings came too late.''

''How humiliating.'' Olivia's whole body shuddered.

''Don't dwell on it anymore.''

''That's easy for you to say. Mother and Daddy were right about me. I always have to learn everything the hard way.''

''I learned a painful lesson myself this last trip.''

Olivia's head lifted. ''What do you mean?''

''When I saw you drive off with Cesar after the wedding, I thought I'd try to get a proposal out of Nic. You know, so I could laugh and tell him sorry, wrong duchess. He's such a know-it-all, I wanted to give him a hard time.''

''And?''

''It was a big mistake.''

They left the apartment and hurried out to their dad's old Pontiac. Olivia got in the driver's seat and started the car. Once they'd joined the mainstream of traffic she asked, "How big?"

"I guess you could say I made the worst faux pas of my life by getting him to try to come on to me a little bit. We'd been walking on the grounds. I asked him to show me where he used to play when he and Luc visited Max.

"He took me to a stream with an old water-wheel that had stopped working long ago. You remember how hot it was that day. I suggested we take a little nap together under the trees. No one was around."

Olivia would have been scandalized if she hadn't tried to do virtually the same thing to Luc on the *Gabbiano*. "Go on."

"Well, I lifted my arms to help him take off his tux jacket. But he grabbed my hands and pushed me away."

"He didn't physically hurt you did he?" Olivia couldn't believe they were talking about the same Nic.

Piper bit her lip. "No. He did something a lot worse. He explained he was wearing a black armband for a reason. But because I was one of the notorious Duchesses of Kingston, he would excuse me this once for not knowing how to behave in polite society.''

"You've got to be kidding me.''

"No. I thought it was a joke, too, until he made it clear that his family and the family of his deceased fiancée Nina were in official mourning until next April. If you recall, his dad was wearing an armband at the wedding, and at the party in Monaco.''

By now Olivia was so hurt for her sister, she was ready to throw rocks. "How dare he speak to you like that after the way he flirted with you on the *Piccione!* He wasn't wearing an armband then!''

"Ah—that was different. The Varano cousins were working undercover to expose us as jewel thieves.''

"So it's okay to take it off while in the line of duty. What a hypocrite!''

"I smiled and told him he'd just passed up an experience he would live to regret. Then I walked back to the villa and had a limo take me to the train. After buying a one-way ticket, I headed for Genoa. What an irony when you consider Tom would have given anything if I'd thrown myself at him like that.''

By now Olivia's tears had dried up. "I'm sorry I wasn't there for you. I was too busy

trying to make Luc jealous to think about anyone but myself.''

"We were both idiots. It was probably a reaction to losing Greer.''

"I'm sure you're right.''

Olivia spied the Arrowhead Rock Shop on
the corner and pulled into the parking area
around the back. Within twenty minutes she returned to the car carrying a tumbler that vibrated. Piper followed with some packages of
polish and three barrels to hold the rocks for
each stage of the process.

Once back at the apartment, Olivia set up her
paraphernalia in the kitchen and got started.
Every so often Piper came in from the living
room to see how things were going.

"I won't know what I've got here until we
go to bed.''

At eleven she checked her first batch. The
rocks had disappeared. They'd been pulverized.

When she thought things couldn't get any
worse, the phone rang.

Piper checked the caller ID. Her mouth tightened. "It's out of area.''

"It could be Greer.''

"No. We already spoke to her earlier today.
This late I bet it's Nic. He put you on the plane
yesterday. He knows what Luc did to you was

unconscionable. No doubt he wants to know if you got home safely.''

Olivia rolled her eyes. ''That'll be his excuse, but what he really wants is to hear *your* voice.''

''He's in mourning, remember?'' Piper snapped.

Angry for her sister's sake, Olivia reached for the receiver. ''I'll take this call with the greatest of pleasure.''

After waiting five rings, she picked up. Using a heavy Bronx accent she said, ''You want the Duchesses of Kingston? Leave yohur name and phone numbah. If yoh're lucky you might hear back from us, but it'll prwabably be next yeahr.''

As soon as she hung up the receiver they both laughed hysterically. They were still giggling out of control when they climbed into their own beds. Then the tears started, drenching Olivia's pillow.

''She's home.''

His expression grim, Luc folded his cell phone and put it back in his pocket.

On the heels of his relief that Olivia had arrived safely in New York loomed the growing fear that he'd done too much damage and she'd never be able to forgive him. Knowing she wasn't aboard the *Gabbiano* filled him with a gnawing emptiness.

A steady breeze had kept the sail filled during the night. Now he and Nic were in the waters of the Costa del Sol. The sun had been up several hours. Marbella lay off the starboard bow.

The plan he'd discussed with Nic during the night had to work, or his life really wouldn't have any meaning.

When they reached Nic's private dock, some workmen he'd alerted on the estate ahead of time were on hand to greet them.

Nic made the introductions. "Thank you for coming so quickly."

"You said you were in a hurry, Senor de Pastrana. What is it you wish to have done?"

"Luc has just purchased this boat and wants it painted flame-blue and white so it looks brand-new. Another sail has been ordered and will be delivered day after tomorrow to match the new name he'd like painted on it.

"He's in charge. While he gives you details, I'm going up to the villa to attend to some business and will talk to you later."

The men nodded.

Within a half hour Luc had instructed them on everything he wanted done. They promised to get a full crew assembled to finish the job as quickly as possible.

Since time was of the essence, Luc couldn't have asked for more than that. When he joined Nic in his study, his cousin was seated at the computer.

"Any luck tracking down Signore Tozetti?"

"His secretary said he just came in his office and would join us at any moment. I've set it up for a conference call. Go ahead and use my cell phone."

Luc sat down on one of the love seats and put the phone to his ear while he waited. Another minute passed, then they heard a voice.

"Signore Tozetti here. Good morning, gentlemen."

"Good morning."

"It's a great honor to be speaking to members of the House of Parma-Bourbon. What can I do for you?"

"The owners of Duchesse Designs, the American women whose calendars you are planning to distribute throughout the Parma region, happen to be distant cousins of ours."

"I had no idea. They never intimated—"

"That doesn't surprise us, *signore*. They believe in themselves and their product. My cousin and I believe in their product, too, and that's the reason we're calling. We want to back them. Therefore we have a proposition to make to you.''

''Wonderful! What exactly did you have in mind?''

''We'd like to see their calendars distributed in other countries besides Italy. If you are interested in being in charge of the total distribution, it would work to everyone's advantage.''

A laugh of surprised delight sounded over the wires. ''I would be very interested, *signore*. What countries besides Italy are you thinking of?''

''Monaco, France, Spain to begin with.''

''Have their calendars already been printed in French and Spanish?''

''These are points we need to talk about. Could you meet with us for a late lunch today at the restaurant of the Splendido in Portofino, say two o'clock?''

''Of course.''

''We'll talk serious business then. It's vital you present the offer you're going to make to them in such a way, they feel it's a hundred percent genuine.''

''I'll do my best.''

"You'll have to," Luc said emotionally. "Money doesn't drive them, so promising them the moon will be a turnoff. Naturally they're in the business to make a living, but the pigeon drawings of Violetta and Luigio happen to be very near and dear to their hearts.

"When you make your pitch, you'll have to convince them the words and depictions representing those lovebirds speak to your soul."

"I don't understand. You make it sound like they might turn me down!"

"That's because they're *artistes*. No matter how much they want to be a success, they have to know you believe in their work. If you can do that, then they'll agree to meet you for the signing of the contract wherever you say."

"You mean they won't be coming to Genoa?"

"No. We'll tell you more this afternoon. But there is one stipulation we must make before things go any further."

"What is that?"

"Our cousins must never know we approached you. Our names must never be mentioned or come up in future conversations. The entire project will fail and you will lose the business you already have with them if they even get a hint anyone else is involved. *Capisce?*"

After a long silence, *"Capisce."*

Piper turned to a fresh page on her drawing pad and began sketching. "How much time before we have to meet with Signore Tozetti at the hotel?"

Olivia had been looking up at the incredible wood-carved ceiling of the world famous Alhambra. Now they'd come out to the reflecting pool in the garden. "We've got about a half hour until dinner. It's already seven."

"Three days in Spain haven't given me very long to work up a decent presentation. My hand has a cramp."

"He said he didn't expect a finished product. All he wants are samples he can show the man who's willing to print our calendars here in Spain. If they prove to be as outstanding as the drawings you did of Monaco and Parma, then we'll have another outlet."

"I wish I could flesh them out more, but there isn't time."

Moving closer, Olivia looked over Piper's shoulder. "In my opinion, this grouping is the best you've ever done."

"You say that every time I start a new sketch."

"That's because you're a genius."

"No. It's because I'm seeing everything live rather than having to depend on photographs."

"Even so, Luigio and Violetta have always been products of your imagination and you've captured a new look for both of them."

"I have?"

"Yes. The one of him as a toreador, trailing his cape around Seville's corrida in front of Violetta is priceless. He has a proud, autocratic bearing about him that makes my heart race."

"You think?"

"Absolutely. Violetta's different, too. She has a crueler smile while they're dancing the flamenco in those fabulous outfits. And I love the seductive angle of his hat.

"Honestly Piper, you've caught the atmosphere of that cave we visited last night so perfectly, I can almost hear their heels clicking on the wooden floor. There's a sensual appeal that leaps out from the page."

"Thanks."

"I mean it. I also love that other drawing of him standing on the turreted rampart of the Alcazar in Segovia, staring up at Violetta who's leaning out one of the windows. They're the most romantic-looking pair I've ever seen. You can feel that tragic quality about him that melts my heart. As if he'd been pierced to the quick by love, but she's still holding out.''

Piper kept her face averted. Though Luigio was the male pigeon, Olivia knew her sister identified with his feelings.

So did Olivia...

''Mother and Daddy would be so proud to know your drawings are going to be famous all over Europe.''

''We don't know that yet,'' Piper muttered, ''so let's not count our chickens.''

''Signore Tozetti wouldn't have paid us an advance to come here if he didn't believe he was going to make a bundle off you pretty soon. When he sees what you've done in just three days, he'll be sending you everywhere... France—Switzerland—''

Piper lifted her head. ''What do you mean *me?* This was Greer's brainchild, and if you hadn't done all the East Coast marketing in the first place, we wouldn't have a calendar business period. We're in this together!

''Let's just be thankful Greer had the foresight to suggest we try to market our idea when we first arrived in Genoa. You and I may not have succeeded in getting a proposal out of a Riviera playboy, but we could end up making a very nice living for ourselves by the time we're thirty.''

"That would be an irony, wouldn't it?" Olivia laughed sadly. "Greer was the one who didn't want us to marry for fear it would get in the way of our making money."

"Yup. Now's she's got a fantastic husband and doesn't have to earn her own living."

"Yup. And my paperweight idea went down the tubes to the tune of one hundred eighty dollars."

"Hey—you didn't know those rocks were volcanic ash."

"Luc did."

"Forget him. If we make it to France, we'll go to that quarry Victor Hugo wrote about in *Les Miserables*. You know, the place where Jean Valjean was a prisoner. We'll take a bunch of rocks home from there and polish them into beads. You can sell those over the Internet. All isn't lost yet!"

"You're being very sweet, Piper, but I'm pretty sure that place doesn't exist, either. I think we'd better head for the hotel."

Piper drew a long-stemmed rose peeking out from Luigio's wing. He was hiding it from Violetta, and would give it to her later. Olivia thought it the perfect touch. Then her sister closed her sketchpad and stood up. "Let's go."

The hotel was only a five-minute walk from the entrance. "Don't be nervous," Olivia reminded her.

"I'm not nervous."

"Yes, you are. You're practically mowing all the tourists down."

Before long they entered the luxury hotel and looked around the Moorish-styled foyer for Signore Tozetti.

"I don't see him."

"Neither do I."

"Maybe he's in the bar."

"In that case he would have told someone at the front desk. Let's find out."

"Oh, yes," the man said. "We've been calling your names. Signore Tozetti has met with a minor accident and won't be able to join you until tomorrow morning at our sister hotel in Malaga."

Her eyes swerved to Piper's. Malaga wasn't that far from the Pastrana villa in Marbella, a fact both of them were agonizingly aware of. The very mention of it brought back bittersweet memories of Olivia's disastrous trips with Luc.

There'd been so many stops and starts without ever once making it all the way to the

Spanish Riviera. In her dreams he was supposed to have ended up proposing to her. The pain was almost more than she could bear.

"He's very sorry for the inconvenience and has arranged to have you driven there this evening by limousine. He hopes that will meet with your approval. Shall I send someone for your bags?"

The silence lengthened. Piper, who was as disappointed as Olivia that their meeting had been postponed, finally had the presence of mind to say yes.

Within ten minutes they walked through the arcaded entry to the portico. A uniformed chauffeur helped them into the most luxurious black limousine Olivia had ever seen. Smoked glass windows. All shiny mahogany and leather on the inside.

The closed partition between the occupants and driver guaranteed total privacy. You could lie down on the seats and still have wiggle room for your feet.

"Have you ever seen such an elegant limousine?" Piper commented after it pulled into traffic.

"No. It must be a Spanish design."

"The world's best kept secret. We could use

limos like this in New York. I wonder why we haven't seen any?''

Olivia leaned her head back against the plush seat. "I'll give you one guess."

"You're right. This thing probably costs close to a half a million dollars."

"Probably more."

"Signore Tozetti has gone all out for us. He must really want our business. Kind of makes you wonder why."

Olivia felt the hairs stand on the back of her neck. "I agree. Don't get me wrong. Your artwork is fabulous, but—"

"But not that fabulous," Piper finished the sentence for her.

"Do you remember when we first boarded the *Piccione?*"

"You're reading my mind. Greer sensed something was wrong, but we didn't believe her. Not at first."

"By the time she'd convinced us we were in trouble, it was too late to get off."

"Don't look now, but there aren't any door handles or window buttons."

Olivia felt madly for them, but nothing was there. She jerked around and tried to slide the partition so she could see to talk to the driver. It wouldn't budge.

She pounded on it with the flat of her hand.

By now Piper had joined her on the seat. "Stop the car! We want to get out!" she shouted.

Suddenly an interior light went on while the limo was still moving. Classical music began to play softly in the background. A panel lifted on one side of the car to reveal a magnum of champagne on ice and two glasses.

"Good evening, earthwomen. My name is Cog."

CHAPTER TEN

Cog?

Olivia's world reeled on its axis.

"Oh my gosh—there really are UFOs!" Piper cried out in absolute panic. "We're being abducted and taken to an alien spaceship."

"Hardly," Olivia mocked after she'd had a few seconds to recover. But her heart was beating so fast with excitement, her body was literally shaking. "Did you ever hear of an alien who spoke with a French accent? A mad scientist maybe, but not an alien.

"And this particular madman just got his driving privileges back so he has gone berserk!"

As recognition dawned, Piper's expression underwent a fundamental change. "You say his name is Cog?" she played along. "What does it stand for? Creature of Godzilla?"

"Close. Literally Cog means he's the subordinate brainchild of his deranged creator, trained to do necessary but minor tasks."

"You mean like pour us a glass of that champagne?"

"All you had to do was ask," Cog spoke again.

Like magic a cork remover appeared and they heard a pop. When it disappeared, a clamp shot out around the neck of the bottle, lifted it and poured champagne into both glasses without spilling a drop. Then it put the bottle back in the bucket and disappeared.

Delighted, Olivia reached for the glasses and handed one to Piper.

"Cog? My sister's starving because Signore Tozetti didn't show up for dinner. By the way, just how much did your mad creator pay him to lure us across the ocean?"

"I know nothing about my master's private business. What does your sister require?"

"What have you got?"

A panel on the other side of the car went up to expose a plate with half a dozen roll-ups in individual napkins. "What are they?"

"Spanish tortillas."

Piper handed her one because she was closest. It was hot. Olivia bit into it. Um. "Not bad, Cog."

After her sister took one and started munching, the panel closed.

"So where are you taking us?"

"To the mother ship."

"Why?"

"To talk of new possibilities."

At this point her heart had jumped to her throat. "It's too late for that. Your master destroyed the world I live in."

"There are other worlds."

"I'm talking about the human world. The only one I want. You know. Emotions. Hearts. Souls. Flesh. Blood. Guts. Tears. All that good stuff."

"My master made a mistake in judgment."

"I thought the masters of your universe couldn't calculate incorrectly. It just goes to show you everything I ever believed in is a myth."

"He wants another chance to restore your faith."

"Faith? Such a word isn't part of that madman's vocabulary. He's just a robot like you."

"Cog does not know what robot means. Please explain."

"Take a good look at your master and you'll have your answer."

"I only obey him. He has ordered me to bring you to him."

"That's too bad. I'm not going."

"I *must* produce you."

"What happens if you don't?"

"He will self destruct, and that will be the end of Cog."

"Don't worry about it. You're no great shakes. I know a robot that can drive two thousand miles through enemy lines delivering medicine."

"He said you would be difficult."

"Yeah, well he doesn't know the half of it!"

"Give in," Piper whispered. "Can't you see he's dying?"

Piper was such a romantic. That was because of her artistic genes. "You're just like mother."

"That's not such a bad thing you know," Piper muttered in a hurt voice. "She had Daddy eating out of her hand."

"I'd rather be eating out of Cog's hand. What do you have for dessert? I might be willing to negotiate a few terms if you've got something chocolate."

Another panel on Olivia's side flew up to reveal a plate of them. She reached for a dark chocolate truffle and bit into it.

"Hmm. That's yummy. Here, Piper. This one's milk chocolate."

"Do you wish anything else?"

"Not for now, Cog."

The panel closed.

She could feel them traveling down a slope and around several curves. Then the limo came to a full stop.

"We have arrived at the ship."

Olivia's heart was ready to burst from its cavity.

"Please step out of the car."

The door flew open on her side to reveal a glorious stretch of beach. Trembling because she knew Luc was waiting for her, she got to her feet and climbed out, expecting him to pull her into his arms. She would put up an initial struggle, then cave.

But to her surprise he was nowhere around. All she could see was a private pier and a sailboat.

Good grief. Had the car actually driven them here by itself? Her legs started to buckle.

"Piper?" she murmured.

There was no answer.

"Piper?" She cried and wheeled around.

No one. Nothing. It was as if her sister had disappeared off the face of the earth. All she could see was dense foliage interspersed with gorgeous flowering trees of all kinds.

"Luc?" She was starting to get nervous. "Luc?" she cried louder.

"I'm over here."

Cog's voice had been replaced by the real thing.

Her eyes swerved back to the pier. There he stood. Tall and rock solid. You would never know he'd had to rely on a cane for so many months.

"Come aboard the *Olivier*."

That was the name he called her in French. His compelling male voice had her walking to the pier. She stopped a few feet short of him. In well-worn denims and a white crew neck cotton sweater, his powerful male body was so appealing, she averted her hungry eyes.

"I—it kind of looks like the *Gabbiano*," she faltered.

"It *is* the *Gabbiano*. But when you sailed her, you made her your own, so I bought it from Giovanni to give to you."

Her breath caught in her throat. "I would have thought this was a brand-new sailboat. I love the blue color."

"It matches your eyes."

Luc—

"Someone did a beautiful job restoring it."

"Thank you."

"You?" she cried.

He gave an elegant shrug of his broad shoulders. "I had help. It's my peace offering to you. The first step in delicate negotiations."

"For what purpose?"

"To see if we can't find a new starting point."

Pain knifed through her once more. "That would be impossible. I'm your brother's pit babe, remember? Because if you don't, I can give you chapter and verse of every cruel thing you ever said to me."

"Don't, Olivia," he begged. Incredibly when she looked in his eyes, she saw pain and pleading.

"Don't what?" her voice shook. "Have you any idea what it's like to be compared to a piece of fruit everyone has picked over? A fruit rotten at its core?"

She could see his throat working. "You *know* I never meant any of those things, *mon amour*. You've got to hear me out." The pleading in his voice was a revelation to Olivia. "I had a long talk with Cesar."

"For his sake I'm thankful—" she blurted, unable to hold back after so much suffering. "He deserved to be let out of the prison you put him in when you wouldn't let him explain anything. If anyone understands what that feels like, I do."

"There are different kinds of prisons. I'd like the chance to tell you about mine while we take the *Olivier* out for a sail. This will be her maiden voyage under her new name and colors."

Oh, Luc.

He could make her do anything. Greer would tell her she had no spine. But like the pushover she was, she let him help her into the boat. Before jumping in after her with an agility he hadn't been able to demonstrate before now, he untied the ropes.

She put on the life jacket he handed her. Soon he revved the motor and they made their way to open water.

"Would you like to do the honors?" he asked after cutting the engine.

She walked over to the mast and released the sail. The night breeze filled it.

"Oh—" she cried softly when she saw the stylized design, against the white, of a graceful olive tree whose branches reached out in every direction.

Luc—

He came to stand by her. They guided the sail together. "While I was at that robotics seminar at M.I.T., I noticed a message from Genevieve on my voice mail that said she'd been at the hospital and wanted me to come home quick.

"I couldn't imagine what had happened, and she'd turned off her phone. I flew back to Nice and drove straight to her apartment only to learn that she'd had a miscarriage."

Olivia moaned.

"It came as a tremendous shock because I'd taken precautions and didn't have a clue she was pregnant. She admitted it wasn't mine. Then she confessed to having had a secret affair with Cesar before getting engaged to me.

"She knew it was his baby and had gone to see him since he needed to be told the truth before she broke her engagement to me. According to her story, Cesar wanted nothing to do with her and said it was her problem. His rejection brought on her miscarriage."

"And you believed her over the brother you'd known all your life?" Olivia cried.

"No. Not until the hospital did a follow-up call while I was there to make certain she had someone taking care of her. Apparently she lost a lot of blood. When I asked the attending physician the age of the fetus, he told me ten weeks.

"I'd only started having relations with her after our engagement a month earlier. That meant it couldn't be mine. I walked away from her and never looked back. But I still couldn't believe it was Cesar's child. If he'd been interested in her, I would have known about it before she came to my office looking for a job.

"Because I was so certain she'd lied about my brother's involvement with her, I sent a friend to the garage to learn what he could. Mechanics love to gossip. All it took was a few glasses of wine for Etienne to admit Cesar and Genevieve had been a hot item for a while. The date for the baby's conception fit."

Now it was Olivia who was feeling sick.

Luc's eyes grew bleak. "That began a nightmare from which I never awakened until you forced me to rethink the situation. Olivia," he whispered. His hands slid up her arms. She could hear his shallow breathing, feel it together with the wind on her lips.

"If you hadn't provoked me, I would never have gone to my brother to learn the truth. I heard some of it from Bianca, then he repeated to me exactly what he told you, and a lot more."

"A lot more?" she asked emotionally.

"Yes." His hands tightened on shoulders. "I found out he toyed with you about an engagement ring to test your love for me."

"Yes, darling." Her eyes filled. "He loves you that much. He's an amazing brother."

"He is." Olivia heard him clear his throat. "After we'd made our peace, we confronted Etienne."

"The mechanic you thought I was after," she said in a wounded voice.

"I didn't really believe it, Olivia. I swear to you I didn't, but I was in so much pain over you I became the madman you accused me of being."

She wiped her eyes. "Did Etienne admit he'd lied about Cesar's affair with your fiancée?"

Luc's body hardened. "He admitted far more. Genevieve was a fortune-hunting groupie. Unbeknownst to Cesar or me, she gave Etienne her favors to get information on the Falcon family before she entered our lives.

"Genevieve's plan was to go after me because she thought I had more money. But her plans backfired because she discovered she was pregnant with Etienne's baby."

"What?"

"It gets ugly. When she told Etienne she was carrying his child and was afraid I would find out because the dates were wrong, he told her to get rid of it. She refused and decided to play up to Cesar, hoping that if they slept together one time, she could pin it on him and he would marry her in the end.''

''That's ghastly! Now I'm beginning to understand your venom. How could a woman do that?''

His eyes glittered silver. ''It happens. But as you know, Cesar sent her packing and told her that if she didn't tell me she'd approached him, he would tell me himself.

''When nothing worked out as she'd planned, she turned on Etienne and blackmailed him into giving her money to get rid of the baby, or she'd tell his wife. There were complications from the procedure and she ended up at the hospital.''

''It's a horror story.'' Her hands slid up to his face. ''I hope they both suffer agony for what they did to you and Cesar.''

He covered her hands with his own. ''Etienne no longer has a job with Cesar of course. But my brother's the best man I know. He doesn't want Etienne's family to suffer, so he gave him a good recommendation for finding another mechanic's job.''

''I love Cesar for that.''

''So do I. As for Genevieve, what goes around, comes around. The point is, my brother and I are closer than ever. It's all because of you.''

He shook his dark, handsome head. "I loved you from the beginning, and that love grew while you fought for our love. You do love me." He shook her gently. "I know you do, *mon coeur*."

"So much it's killing me. Oh, Luc—when I returned to the boat with Nic and found you'd gone for good, I thought I was going to die."

His lips roamed over her face. "I had to leave and take care of my past. How else could I offer you a future."

"I know that now."

Unable to suppress her needs any longer, she gave him her mouth. They clung fiercely, forgetting everything in the joy of being together without strife as a constant companion.

She drowned in rapture as his mouth began devouring hers. Neither of them could get close enough. After that terrible day in Cannes when she thought her world had come to an end, she never dreamed Luc had gone off in search of the truth.

Olivia was still having a hard time believing the war was over, that she was claiming the spoils of victory and Luc was helping her with a possessive eagerness.

"Whoa—" she cried and laughed at the same

time as the boat started to list to the other side sending salt spray over them.

Luc grasped her tighter while he grabbed hold of the sail. "It's time to take the boat back to shore."

"But we just came out here!"

"There's something else we have to do first. Then we'll take off and let the wind blow us wherever it will."

"I'd love that, but what could be more important than being together right now?"

"Getting married first," he whispered against her lips before giving her a deep, salty kiss.

When he finally let her go she blurted, "You mean now? Tonight?" Her voice came out with a definite squeak.

He smiled the smile she lived for, making her heart race. "Am I to presume that was a happy 'yes' coming out of the unexpected and astounding Duchess of Kingston?"

Though he'd said it teasingly, she detected the tiniest trace of anxiety in the question. Her darling Luc was having equal trouble believing their pain was behind them.

"Yes!" She threw her arms around his neck and gave him another long, passionate kiss. "Yes, yes, yes. I want to marry you this instant, but we need a church and a priest. Mother and Daddy were very insistent on that.''

''I happen to be insistent on it myself.'' A mysterious gleam had entered his eyes. ''All we have to do is get in the limo and drive to the Pastrana family chapel where Father Torres is waiting. Then I'm taking you away with me.''

''How long a drive is it?''

''About one minute.''

''One minute? That doesn't give me time to make myself presentable. Darling—I really like your mother and I know it will hurt her horribly if she and your father don't get to see you married.''

''They'll live.''

She bit her lip. ''There's another problem.''

''What's that?'' He kissed the end of her proud Duchess nose.

''Cesar might feel left out to miss his only brother's nuptials.''

''He'll live, too.''

''Luc—I—I'm afraid Greer and Piper will never forgive me if I exclude them.''

His eyes flashed silver fire. ''So that's what your hesitation is all about. Max was right. You three really are joined at the mind, heart and hip.''

"Only for the important occasions. Weddings, births an—"

His mouth crushed hers before she could say anything else. "Do you love me?" he finally asked.

"You know I do!"

"Then trust me."

Trust.

There was something in the way he said it that told her he was going to make her every wish come true. Lucien de Falcon was that kind of man.

"I'll trust if you'll tell me one thing honestly."

"Anything for my bride-to-be."

"Were you at the wheel during the drive from Granada?"

He threw his dark head back and laughed. It was the most beautiful sound in the world.

"Was that a 'yes'?"

"When I'm your husband, then I'll tell you everything you want to know." With her clasped in his arms, he brought the boat around and they headed for shore, breathlessly awaiting their future.

HARLEQUIN®
Presents

**The world's bestselling romance series...
The series that brings you your favorite authors,
month after month:**

Helen Bianchin...Emma Darcy
Lynne Graham...Penny Jordan
Miranda Lee...Sandra Marton
Anne Mather...Carole Mortimer
Susan Napier...Michelle Reid

and many more uniquely talented authors!

Wealthy, powerful, gorgeous men...
Women who have feelings just like your own...
The stories you love, set in exotic, glamorous locations...

HARLEQUIN®
Presents

Seduction and Passion Guaranteed!

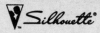

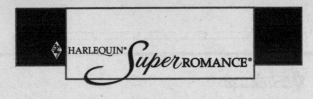
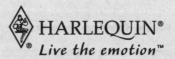

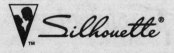